UNBRIDLED

UNBRIDLED

A NOVEL OF MURDER AND REVENGE

BY
MICHAEL SPRINGER

MILL CITY PRESS

Mill City Press
555 Winderley Pl, Suite 225
Maitland, FL 32751
407.339.4217
www.millcitypress.net

© 2024 by Michael Springer

All rights reserved solely by the author. The author guarantees all contents are original and do not infringe upon the legal rights of any other person or work. No part of this book may be reproduced in any form without the permission of the author.

Due to the changing nature of the Internet, if there are any web addresses, links, or URLs included in this manuscript, these may have been altered and may no longer be accessible. The views and opinions shared in this book belong solely to the author and do not necessarily reflect those of the publisher. The publisher therefore disclaims responsibility for the views or opinions expressed within the work.

Paperback ISBN-13: 978-1-66289-702-3
Ebook ISBN-13: 978-1-66289-703-0

This is a work of fiction. Any similarity to actual events or to persons living or dead is purely coincidental. It could also get me killed.

I do love thee so that I will shortly send thy soul to heaven and thee to the grave, I do love thee so.

William Shakespeare, *Richard III*

Table of Contents

Prologue. xi

PART 1 — HARMONY

Chapter 1 – Latonia Racetrack. 3
Chapter 2 — 'The Loneliest Road in America'. 14
Chapter 3 – Kat. 27
Chapter 4 — The Magician 41
Chapter 5 — Fireworks 51
Chapter 6 – G.B.A. 62
Chapter 7 – Live Cover 81
Chapter 8 – The Blooding 98
Chapter 9 – Deep Woods. 110

PART 2 — BAD BLOOD

Chapter 10 – Troubled Youth. 123
Chapter 11 – Commencement. 131
Chapter 12 – The Wild West 145
Chapter 13 – Night Riders. 159
Chapter 14 – Homecoming 167
Chapter 15 – Golden Boy 180
Chapter 16 – Above and Beyond 195
Chapter 17 – Crossed Swords. 203
Chapter 18 – Mister Ten Percent 210
Chapter 19 — Catch Riders. 216

PART 3 –- WAR

Chapter 20 – Warning Shots 233
Chapter 21 – The Professionals 241
Chapter 22 – Protection. 260
Chapter 23 – The Hired Gun. 277
Chapter 24 – The Hunter. 291
Chapter 25 – The Night Of 297
Chapter 26 – The Investigator 301

PART 4 – THE TRIAL

Chapter 27 – The Litigator. 321
Chapter 28 – The Witnesses. 333
Chapter 29 – Thirty Pieces. 345
Chapter 30 – The Defense 354
Chapter 31 – Lies and Damn Lies 361
Chapter 32 – The Royal 369
Chapter 33 – 'I Do Love Thee So' 372
Chapter 34 – 'That Venomous Woman' 378

PART 5 – RECKONINGS

Chapter 35 – The List 391
Chapter 36 – Settling Up. 397
Chapter 37 – The Arena. 402
Chapter 38 – Morgan's Lady 410

Prologue

THE SOUND OF HORSES SCREAMING woke him out of dead sleep.

Morgan Caine sat bolt upright in bed. His silk pajama top was soaked in sweat, and his damp hair was plastered against his brow. His breathing was heavy and irregular, and he sat stock still to give his heart a moment to slow. He glanced over at the other side of the bed, saw the rhythmic rise and fall of his wife's form beneath the blanket next to him.

This wasn't the first time the dream had come to Morgan and haunted his sleep. It was always the same, always so vivid: horses snorting and stamping their hooves in increasing panic, huge eyes scanning the stable walls, trapped and terrified. Morgan had been having this same nightmare since he was a small boy, when he and his brother were stable hands, following their horse trainer father around the racing circuit. Instead of receding over time, the dream visited him more and more, until now he could hardly escape it.

His breathing calmer now, Morgan was about to lay his head back down when he heard familiar sounds coming from the stables across the long manicured grounds. This wasn't a dream. This was real.

Morgan leaped from his bed and rushed to the heavy green velvet curtains that framed the window. He threw back the folds of fabric and stared out into the blackness, in the direction of the stables. He could hear it now, a little louder than in his dream, the horses stamping and snorting restlessly. He squinted into the darkness, then caught sight of something across the yard:

a sliver of light creeping through the cracks of the stable door. The orange light seemed to spread like daybreak, crawling slowly up the doorframe of the stable, followed by a wreath of smoke. Morgan realized what he was looking at.

"Kat!" he whispered loudly. When his wife didn't turn over, he nudged her shoulder and said more urgently, "Kat, wake up. I think the barn is on fire."

Kat rolled over and looked at him, disoriented for a moment, then pulling herself awake.

"Are you sure?"

"I'm going to go look. Call the fire department." Morgan was up now, throwing a pair of blue jeans over his pajama bottoms. He added, "Call the police too." He shoved his feet into a pair of paddock boots that sat by the bed and headed for the door.

"Morgan…" she called after him. "Be careful."

Morgan raced down the wide curved staircase, his hand tracing the oak banister to steady himself as his eyes adjusted to the darkness. The walls along the grand staircase were covered with photographs that spoke of money and accomplishment, most of it in the equestrian world: Morgan and Kat in their finery at the Mid-America Horse Show Association gala. Their daughter Meghan taking first place at the Lake Forest Horse Show when she was 14 years old. Morgan astride a polo pony scoring a goal at the Armory. His wife Kat the day she won the women's competition flying her Piper Cherokee cross country, a record she still held. A painting of their home and business, Harmony Farm and Stables, after they added the new equestrian center, their fifth major expansion.

Morgan had no time to pay attention to the photos of the past. He was locked in the present and the creeping terror that could be consuming his property outside. He hit the foyer and grabbed the front door handle. Then he stopped. His eyes shot to the left, to his home office, and he ran in there.

The room was a handsome wood-paneled den, the walls heavy with bookcases containing trophies and engraved silver trays and

Prologue

blue ribbons from countless horse competitions over the years. A massive walnut desk dominated the far wall. Morgan rushed over to it and turned on the desk lamp. He yanked the center drawer open, reached in and drew his 1911 Colt Commander. The weight of the .45 ACP was comforting in his grip. He drew back the slide and heard a round click into place in the chamber. The slide snapped shut, and he quickly checked the safety and charged for the main entrance.

Morgan threw the front door open and dashed outside. He froze at the top of the stairs, one hand resting on one of the tall columns that guarded the facade of the white plantation-style house. His eyes and ears adjusted to the night, and now he could hear even more clearly, the sounds that had shattered his sleep. The horses were stamping and circling in their stalls, their cries growing more plaintive by the minute as fear started to engulf them. Staring into the night, Morgan could see the fire clearly now as it spread along the lines of the massive doorway in the stable entrance a hundred feet away. A broad smooth swath of lawn stood between the house and the stable, with a copse of shade trees off to the side.

Morgan rushed down the front steps and started to cross the yard, then he stopped. A shadow seemed to be moving at the edge of the tree line. It was fall, the trees nearly naked, glimmers of red and yellow amid the silver of the night. For just a second he thought he detected a shape – a man's shape – lurking in the trees. He peered harder into the darkness, and at that moment the flames from the barn door flared and part of the door gave way. That's when he saw the man standing just behind a maple tree with a rifle in his hands, sighting in a scope, aiming straight at him.

The bullet hit him a little high, in the left upper quadrant of his chest just below his shoulder and spun him around but didn't knock him off his feet. Morgan opened his mouth to shout, but the gunshot covered his cry.

Morgan tried to lift his .45 but found that his arm wouldn't respond. Blood – his own blood, hot and wet and pulsing – was streaming down his arm, and his hand and the gun quickly became slippery. He tried to shift the weapon to his right hand, and just as he did, he heard his wife's voice behind him.

"Morgan!" she cried, in a terrified gasp that pierced the night sky. He saw Kat out of the corner of his eye, charging out the front door and down the stairs. He turned to her and waved his one good arm at her, pushing her away, willing her back, out of the line of fire.

"Get in the house!" Morgan hissed at her, his arm flailing again. He felt frozen in place, unable to charge forward or to go backward to protect his wife. In that moment, he heard the bolt of the rifle across the courtyard, as if in slow motion, the cartridge being ejected from the chamber as another one slid into place. The shooter took his time now, sighting in a little more carefully, and squeezed the trigger.

The second shot caught Morgan squarely in the chest as he twisted toward the house. This time he went down, practically thrown off his feet by the high-caliber burst as his chest exploded. He heard his wife scream his name again and sensed her running toward him, mindless of the danger. Kat reached him at almost the same moment he hit the ground, catching him in her arms, rolled him over. Her hand swept his damp hair off his forehead. She rocked him, keening into the night as the life flowed out of him.

Morgan stared up at the sky, at his wife's hand wiping his face and crushing the tears from her own cheeks. He tried to look toward the cluster of trees, but his eyes wouldn't focus, and anyway, the silhouette had vanished, deep into the woods leading to the road. Morgan could feel the blood spurting out of him with every beat of his dying heart. The gun lay useless in his hand, his arm limp at his side. He tried to sit up, tried to speak, but the blood was rushing from his lungs, filling his mouth with its wet metallic taste.

Prologue

"Don't try to talk," his wife whispered to him. "Just rest, darling. Stay calm, help is on the way…."

But Morgan knew there would be no help for him. The fire was spreading now, the flames leaping higher, the horses screaming to him for help just as they had for years in the dreams. In the distance he could hear the far wail of the sirens as the fire engines sped toward the farm.

Morgan leaned back in his wife's arms, clawed the blood-splattered sleeve of her nightgown. He seemed desperate to tell her something, to speak to her. He choked on his own blood, but he had to get it out, one word, maybe his last word. He looked at her wildly, deep into her eyes, and whispered a single name before his own eyes closed:

"Cyrus…."

Part 1
HARMONY
God and the Devil Were Brothers Once

Chapter 1

Latonia Racetrack Florence, Kentucky 1933

"COME ON, CYRUS! COME ON, LUCKY!" The 10-year-old boy hung on to the railing with one hand and waved his oversized cap with the other as the field of horses thundered past. Out on the dirt track, the young jockey didn't hear him or see him. His black eyes were totally focused on the blur of track ahead of him, every muscle in his body in sync with the powerful horse beneath him, a single thought cycling through his brain:

I'm going to win this race.

Cyrus Caine tightened his grip on the reins, holding the charging animal back just a bit, not opening him up too soon. He felt the muscular stallion surging between his legs, straining to move up and close on the other horses, but not yet. The cluster of thoroughbreds was rounding the far turn, with a half mile to go to the finish. Cyrus was right where he wanted to be: in fourth position, the leading horses tightly bunched, the rest of the field starting to fall away behind them.

Cyrus was not yet 14, but he had been around horses his whole life and running in high stakes and match races since he was eight. Latonia was different. These horses were the best of breed, from all over Kentucky and beyond, and he had studied them all diligently, watched them in training, looked them over in the stalls or just out being exercised. The three leaders were strong, but none of them could sprint the way his horse, Lucky Day, could do when he put the whip to him in the home stretch. Lucky was the most expensive horse he'd ever ridden, the best horse his father had ever worked in his itinerant and eclectic career as a trainer, breeder and drunk. This race would make them all – his father, Old Cyrus; the jockey who was his namesake; and the future champion, Lucky Day.

This was the 51st running of the Latonia Derby, one of the biggest races in the country. This was where Kentucky Derby winners ran, where the sport of horseracing had played out since the 1880s. Cyrus's family had been working with this horse since he was a colt, and now, as a 3-year-old, Lucky Day was poised to join the winner's circle and a $10,000 purse.

Even now, with the country deep in a depression, the stands were filled with 10,000 rowdy patrons cheering the thoroughbreds on, wagering money they could ill afford, hoping for a breakout winner, a horse they could cheer about. Up ahead, comfortably in the lead, was the crowd's favorite, Gold Basis, out of New York.

As they came around the last turn Cyrus allowed himself a quick glimpse at a man standing at the railing. Tall, heavily muscled and glowering – his father. Old Cyrus leaned hard against the top rail, a cigar clenched tensely in his jaw, his gimlet eyes focused on every move, every step the magnificent horse took. The older man looked at the stopwatch in his meaty hand, and Cyrus thought he detected a glint of satisfaction. It was going well.

Next to the old man, Cyrus's kid brother Morgan was half hidden in the big man's shadow. Morgan's face was grimy with the dirt and sweat of the racetrack where they all spent their lives, but his face lit up as his brother came into view again. His bright blue eyes were shining, and he watched adoringly as Cyrus steered his sleek animal around the throng of horses.

Latonia Racetrack Florence, Kentucky 1933

"You can do it, Lucky!" the boy shouted as horse and rider thundered past. Cyrus almost smiled. Good kid.

The racers were panting and sweating as they entered the last quarter mile. Just a few seconds more, Cyrus thought. Lucky was fighting him more than usual, eager to break away, and it took all the strength in Cyrus's muscular arms to keep him in check.

"Wait for it," Cyrus whispered into the wind, as though the horse could actually hear him. "Not yet." They flew into the straightaway, and Cyrus raised his whip. "Now!" he shouted, so loud it looked like the other jockeys heard him.

Lucky took off in a spurt and moved up into third place, long slender legs stretched out for miles, chest heaving. Cyrus crouched lower in the saddle and whipped the horse for all he was worth.

"Go! Go!" he screamed with every stroke. The second-place horse was just a half a length ahead, and Lucky soon pulled past him. Now for the leader, Gold Basis.

Cyrus worked Lucky toward the inside rail, hoping to get the lead horse pinned between the fence and his own horse and giving Lucky some room to run on the outside. The lead jockey glanced over his shoulder and saw Cyrus closing on him and spurred his own horse for a last burst of speed. The two animals were so close now the riders could have touched. Cyrus used the whip with a frenzy, his face twisted in angry determination. It took all his self-control not to reach over and beat the other jockey over the back or strike him in the face, but Cyrus kept his control. He urged his horse forward, driving the animal to the length of his limits.

Then it happened.

Cyrus could feel his horse slowing down, still running but only on three legs. Lucky Day's right foreleg seemed to give out even though the horse kept charging forward. It took all of Cyrus's strength to stay in the saddle, trying to urge the horse forward but knowing something was seriously wrong. Out of the corner of his eye Cyrus saw Gold Basis rock his massive head and pull away, all alone toward the finish line. Cyrus fought to get Lucky under control as the other horses galloped past him. Lucky slowed, then stopped.

The people in the stands gasped. Cyrus's father, so confident a moment before, looked on in horror as the prize horse stood frozen on the track, head hanging down, trying to keep his weight off his obviously injured limb. The finish line was still 30 feet away. Old Cyrus threw his cigar in the dirt as he charged down the stairs and ran out onto the track.

"God damn it! What the bleeding hell!" He lunged forward, his face purple with anger. He moved so fast he didn't realize his younger son could barely keep up with him. And he didn't care. All that mattered now was that victory had been snatched away from him, for reasons he couldn't fathom.

Lathered in sweat and still breathing heavily from exertion, Lucky Day held his injured foreleg slightly off the ground, the pain clearly written on his face. Cyrus, still stunned by events, started to slide off the horse's back, but he felt his father's powerful hand grab him by the back of his shirt and yank him out of the saddle.

"You sonofabitch!" Old Cyrus yelled at his son. "What did you do? What did you do to this horse?"

"I didn't do nothin'," Cyrus shouted back, bracing himself for the blow he knew would come. "He was running fine."

Old Cyrus ignored the jockey, his son. He was busy now inspecting the horse's leg, running his rough experienced hand along the horse's limb. He quickly found the problem.

"'Didn't do nothin,'" he mocked his son. "This god-damned nag mighta snapped a tendon!"

"That ain't my fault. She just pulled up short," Cyrus protested, but knew if would do no good. Someone always needed to be at fault with his father, and it wouldn't be the horse. The old man spun on him and clipped him across the face with the back of his hand. Cyrus's head jerked back, stinging with the inevitability of it more than actual pain. His younger brother tried to

Latonia Racetrack Florence, Kentucky 1933

jump in and keep his father from launching another assault. He grabbed Lucky's reins, which were dangling to the ground.

"Pa, let's get him to the barn. Maybe if I walk him real slow …."

The father's eyes were still boring in on his elder son. He turned away and spat at Morgan, "Take him." He turned away and walked off, a black cloud of anger and frustration swirling around him. A hundred feet away, the jubilant mob pressed in around the day's champion in the winner's circle, the horse of the hour, Gold Basis. The horse's owner, Mr. M.L. Schwartz, was pumping hands and accepting backslaps, mentally counting his winnings and the huge stud fees he'd be taking back to New York. Now Cyrus Senior would have to find his boss and tell him that his champion racehorse was dog meat.

Morgan ran a hand gently along Lucky's injured limb, then stroked his neck and his muzzle, murmuring to him. "It's all right, boy. It's all right, Lucky."

Cyrus wiped his face with his cap, staring at the receding figure of his father for a moment. Then he looked at his brother and patted the horse's neck.

"Come on. Let's get out of here," he said to Morgan, and the three of them limped off toward the barn.

It was growing dark in the stable, and Morgan found it hard to see what he was doing by the light of a kerosene lantern. For such a fabled racetrack, the management didn't waste a lot of money on electricity for the barns. Morgan was in Lucky's stall currying the horse's coat. His strokes were smooth, methodical, and he hummed quietly to himself and to the injured horse. Lucky's three good legs were wrapped, to have him ready for transport once Pa got back with the vet and they decided what to do. Morgan had run a cold hose on his right foreleg for an hour. Then he applied a poultice to draw out the heat and finally wrapped the leg in a wet gauze bandage. He hoped his father would bring the vet soon so they could get Lucky fixed up and get out on the road. It wasn't unusual for his father to disappear for hours or even days at a time, but Morgan was more worried than usual tonight, especially for the horse.

Cyrus had changed out of his riding silks and was wearing an old undershirt, jeans that were too short for him and a pair of Western style boots. He mucked out Lucky's stall, keeping his back to his brother and to the horse, thinking to himself, his face dark and scowling. Usually mucking out the stall was Morgan's job as the youngest, but today Cyrus wanted to do it himself. It helped him think. Cyrus was almost always in a black humor, but this night his mood was even darker than usual. The waning light in the stable, the wounded horse in his stall, the two brothers working in dark silence made the barn feel more like a ramshackle church just before a funeral service.

Morgan kept glancing over at his older brother, wondering what he was thinking, wishing he'd say something. Three years older than Morgan, Cyrus was broad-shouldered, lean but well-muscled. His forearms, which Morgan could see below the rolled-up sleeves of his shirt, were covered with ropy veins, and his hands looked like they belonged to a grown man. Cyrus had been handling horses since he could walk, and the power showed in his arms. He began riding early too, and when he was eight convinced his father to let him compete as a jockey. In truth, Cyrus was too tall to be a jockey now; he'd sprung up over the summer, at least half a head, and just barely made the weight restriction for the Derby by starving himself for two weeks, then burying himself in a manure pile behind the barn to sweat off the last couple of pounds. Morgan wondered if Cyrus's increased size had anything to do with Lucky's injury. Maybe the horse was carrying too much weight, even though they had loaded fewer lead weights in the saddle pad at the weigh-in. Cyrus might have been thinking that himself. Their father almost certainly was.

Morgan wondered when their father would get back with the vet. It was getting late. Most of the other trainers and owners

Latonia Racetrack Florence, Kentucky 1933

had loaded up their horses and left the track hours ago, with only a few horses now bedded down for the night, awaiting freight haulers in the morning. In the stable next to Lucky was a broken-down quarter horse they called Old Brownie, which Old Cyrus kept as a companion horse to his prize stallion. Brownie munched languidly on some hay, breaking the tomblike silence of the stable.

The barn door swung open and Old Cyrus staggered in. He stood in the doorway a moment, trying to focus his eyes, whether from the dim light or the copious amount of bourbon he had recently ingested. A pint bottle, nearly empty, was in one hand. In the other he held his "doctor bag," a worn leather satchel that Old Cyrus said held "all my secrets – and all I'll ever need."

Young Cyrus stopped pushing the straw and stepped out into the aisle, in the light of the lantern. He leaned on his pitchfork and regarded his father. Morgan stopped working down Lucky and held his breath, watching the father and son glaring at each other.

Their father stepped into the barn. He took a swig from the brown bottle in his hand, licking off the last drop of the cheap bourbon, and waved the bottle in the direction of his elder son.

"Well, there he is. The champion. The man of the hour," he said with a snarl. "Cleaning up horseshit while the other fella's out celebrating." He tossed the empty bottle in an open stall and stepped forward. "You know what that little Jew jockey is probably doing right now?" He meant Max Hersch, the winning rider from New York. "Probably eating a steak as big as his saddle and fixing to get laid."

Cyrus didn't reply. His black eyes avoided the older man. Old Cyrus wasn't through.

"And here we are – father and son. Cleaning up the shit. Cleaning up the mess you made." He took two steps toward his elder son. Cyrus stood his ground. "A ten-thousand-dollar purse. That's what you cost my boss today. My ex-boss, I should say. He fired my ass, and yours too. And yours," he added, swinging toward Morgan. He smirked. "I'da been better off letting the Little Bastard ride that horse than give the reins to you." Morgan was "the Little Bastard" more often than not, but always when his father went into one of his drunken rages.

"There's other races," Cyrus murmured. His father snorted at him.

"Really? You're the expert now, are you? The track in Lexington is shutting down. Latonia's on its last legs. Just where do you think we can go without a horse?"

"He's still a good horse," Cyrus protested. "You just need to rest him a bit."

"Bullshit. He's not fit to pull a plow now, after the way you rode him into the ground."

"You know why he was pulling so hard," Cyrus muttered under his breath, but the old man heard him. Old Cyrus closed the gap between them until he was right up into the boy's face, his breath reeking of whisky fumes.

"Do I now? Why don't you tell me?"

"Because you doped him up."

Old Cyrus's arm shot out so fast his son didn't have a chance to deflect it. He found himself pushed back into the pile of straw he'd just gathered up. He sprang to his feet again, just out of the old man's reach.

"You know it's true," the boy said through clenched teeth. "He was off his mark the whole ride. It was all I could do to hold him back the first mile. He'd a run himself to death if his leg hadn't a given out."

"It's your fault you don't know how to handle your own animal," his father snarled.

"Maybe the vet can fix him up," Morgan offered tentatively, but his father's black look made him shrink away.

"There ain't goin' to be a vet. Waste o' money," said the old man. He set his "doctor's bag" down on the saddle table and started rummaging through it, cursing the poor light, until he

Latonia Racetrack Florence, Kentucky 1933

found what he was looking for. He picked up a vial of clear liquid, then inserted a long needle and started drawing the liquid into it.

"What are you gonna do, Pa?" Morgan asked tremulously. He already knew. He placed himself between his father and the injured horse. Old Cyrus flung him aside.

"Get the hell out of my way," he snapped. "At least the boss can claim the insurance. This horse is worth more dead than alive."

"That's not true," Cyrus shouted at him. "It might be his tendon or a ligament is all. A few months' rest, it'll heal...."

"I don't have a few months," his father hissed. "And neither do you. We're getting out of here tonight. Now bring that lantern over here so I can see what I'm doing."

Old Cyrus advanced toward the horse, but his elder son jumped in his path. Old Cyrus struck the boy with his free hand and he landed in the dirt. Young Cyrus came down hard but scrambled up again. Then he stamped his foot on the upturned tangs of the pitchfork he'd been using, grabbed the handle and held it in front of him like a staff.

Furious, his father swung at him again, but Cyrus parried the blow with the handle of the pitchfork. He turned it around and pointed the tangs toward his father's eyes.

"You little shit," the old man cursed. "You think you're ready to fight me?"

"Morgan," Young Cyrus said calmly, "go wait for me outside." His eyes never left his father's. The younger boy froze, not knowing who to obey.

His father sneered. "Now you're going to defy me too, you little bastard?"

"Do it," Cyrus said.

Morgan eased away from the horse, keeping a cautious distance from his father. Cyrus circled, the pitchfork raised to defend his brother.

"You're making the biggest mistake of your life, boy," his father said. He set the loaded syringe down on the table and rolled up his sleeves, relishing the beating he was about to administer.

"Get back, old man, or I'll stick you," Cyrus said evenly. He was calm, never raising his voice. But his black eyes were filled with a lifetime of hate. Morgan reached the barn door and slipped out with a quick backward glance at his father and brother. He closed the door quickly, and as he did he heard a flurry of commotion, feet scuffling in the dirt, the grunts of two male bodies thudding against each other. Morgan ran to the pickup truck parked outside. The lot was empty, there was no one else in sight, no one to run to for help even if he'd wanted to.

The minutes crawled painfully. Morgan kept glancing at the barn, waiting for his father and his brother – or maybe just one of them – to emerge.

Finally, he saw a flicker of orange at the edge of the barn door, then a curl of smoke rising from the ground. Morgan held his breath. He saw the barn door swing open, and in the light of the rising fire behind him, his brother Cyrus walked out with Lucky Day behind him on a lead. The horse was limping. So was Cyrus. They moved at a slow steady pace, and Cyrus kept whispering encouragement to the horse. Morgan strained to look for his father but saw no sign of him.

As he ran to meet his brother Morgan could see the large red mark on the side of Cyrus's face. The older boy's shirt was filthy, and his hair was disheveled. There was blood on his left arm. In Cyrus's free hand he held their father's doctor bag.

"Cyrus, are you all right?" he called. "Where's Pa? What hap...."

"No time for that now," Cyrus replied through gritted teeth. "Get Lucky into the trailer. We gotta get out of here."

"But Cyrus, the stable's on fire. Where's Brownie?"

"I moved him into Lucky's stall. Keep moving."

"But where's Pa?" His brother cut him off.

"Don't ask so many goddamn questions. Just get this horse loaded." Morgan took the lead rope from his brother and guided the injured horse the rest of the way to the trailer. As the boy secured him and closed the trailer door, Cyrus jumped behind the wheel of the beat-up truck his father drove. It was gassed up

Latonia Racetrack Florence, Kentucky 1933

and ready for a quick departure – his father was always ready to get out of town fast. Cyrus scrambled around in the dark looking for the keys, realized with relief they were in the ignition. He started the engine. He threw open the passenger door and yelled to his brother, "Get in."

Morgan did as he was told. He closed the door tightly and stared at his brother, his lip starting to tremble. Cyrus was calm, but his arms shook a little as he grabbed the steering wheel. Morgan glanced back through the rear window. The fire in the barn was spreading now, the flames catching and consuming the old timber. Morgan could hear the horses, kicking at the sides of its stall and shrieking in fear as the flames leaped around them.

"Cyrus, there's horses in there. We got to get them out."

"No time. We gotta move."

Morgan tried to keep his voice steady but he was on the verge of tears. "Where's Pa?"

Cyrus stared straight ahead into the black night and put the old truck into gear.

"He ain't coming," was all he said as they drove off.

Chapter 2

'The Loneliest Road in America'

CYRUS POINTED THE TRUCK NORTH and kept driving into the darkness. There were no streetlights or reflective signs to show him the way, so he kept one eye on the road in front of him and the other on the outside mirror. His brother knelt backwards on the cracked leather seat, mouth open, tears rolling down his cheeks, gaping at the burning stable. The flames of the old barn were spreading now, licking higher and higher in the night sky, and from a distance he could see flashing red lights starting to rush to the racetrack. Cyrus knew he needed to put as much distance between himself and the track as fast as possible – as fast as a broken-down truck hauling a half-ton horse could go.

Cyrus's heart rate had slowed a little, but it was still painful every time he drew a breath. He wondered if the old man had managed to break his ribs this time, or if they were just bruised like all the other times. His left arm ached from deflecting his father's repeated blows, but he was pretty sure it wasn't broken. He moved his hand up the steering wheel and saw that there was blood from a long cut, but it didn't look too deep, and the bleeding seemed to have stopped. He tucked the arm against his side so his brother couldn't see the wound. The boy felt battered and worn out, but at least he had walked away from the fight. More than he could say for the old man.

Out of the corner of his eye Cyrus could see his little brother pressed up against the passenger door, staring at him, his face

'The Loneliest Road in America'

white with apprehension. Morgan clutched the doctor's bag against his chest for all he was worth; Cyrus had given him a job, to hang on to that bag. Morgan looked like someone might burst into the truck cab and try to wrestle it away from him at any moment. Finally, his younger brother spoke.

"Cyrus, where we going?"

Cyrus didn't answer right away, for a good reason. "I don't know yet," he replied finally. "North. Chicago maybe."

"Chicago," his brother said, as if Cyrus had suggested the moon. "What's in Chicago?"

"Racetracks," Cyrus replied. "There's nothing for us in Kentucky."

"What about Pa? How will he know where we gone?"

"He don't need to know."

"But won't he come after us? Won't he want his truck back?"

Cyrus almost smiled, or maybe it was a grimace as the pain in his ribs pierced him again. Typical, that they both knew their father valued the old truck more than either one of them.

"Don't worry about it," the older brother said. "Right now, we just need to get across the river."

It was only a few miles to the Ohio border, and even driving at a steady pace the trip seemed to take forever. As they drove over the bridge into the neighboring state, they could see the last lights of Cincinnati in the distance as the city started to wind down from its Saturday night reverie. Cyrus drove on a bit farther, and when he found an isolated stretch of road he pulled over and shut down the engine.

"We've got a long drive ahead," he told his brother. "Give me the bag."

"Why?" Morgan asked suspiciously, drawing the bag away from his brother.

"Lucky will feel better if we give him a little something for the drive." Cyrus held out his hand and waited. Morgan considered it for a moment, realized his brother was right. He handed the bag over handle first. Cyrus opened it, peered inside, held it up to try to get a little light so he could see what he was doing. But he knew the contents of the bag very well. He found the correct vial with the sedative, drew out a needle and prepared it. Then the boys got out of the truck, went back to the trailer and dropped the tailgate.

"Easy, Lucky. Easy, boy," Cyrus cooed as he stepped up into the trailer, one hand running softly along the horse's flanks to reassure him. Cyrus could sense the tension in Lucky's body. The horse's breathing was shallow and his nostrils were dilated, but he was quiet. Morgan moved to the front of the trailer to check the bandage on Lucky's foreleg while Cyrus expertly administered the sedative. After some stroking and murmuring from Morgan the horse seemed to settle down. The boys withdrew, raised up the tailgate, climbed into the truck cabin and drove on.

Before too long they saw a sign for US 50. Cyrus turned and headed west, just because he remembered the route number. He recalled a teamster in some greasy spoon diner remark to his father one time, "US 50 – the loneliest road in America. Starts nowhere, goes nowhere, and nothing to see in between." Cyrus thought it sounded perfect for two boys who wanted to get themselves lost in a hurry.

He rubbed his hand across his face, wiped his eyes trying to keep them open. The fatigue was starting to hit him, the lactic acid fading from his arms and legs. He shifted his hands on the steering wheel, grasping it tighter, and sat up straight against the stiff bench seat back. Driving the truck was the least of his problems, and the fact was, any other time he'd be enjoying the practice, and the freedom. Like most country boys, Cyrus had been driving from the time his feet could reach the pedals. He was an expert at backing up the truck with the horse trailer attached and maneuvering into tight spaces. He liked night driving best, something he rarely got to do unless his father was too drunk to

'The Loneliest Road in America'

drive himself. Now that problem was gone at least, but a whole slew of new problems had taken their place.

Cyrus did a quick inventory of his assets: He had one dollar and 31 cents, rifled from his father's coat pocket. He had a truck that needed engine work, a trailer and hitch, and a racehorse that might never run again. And he had a little brother who was now his charge.

He looked down at the bench seat where Morgan had spread out, his knees bent and his feet nearly touching Cyrus's leg. He was sleeping, and even his brother had to admit there was something angelic about him. The old man never had any use for Morgan – "the Little Bastard," he called him, behind his back and to his face. Cyrus reflected on some of the bitter fights between his mother and father before his mother disappeared, and he had come to understand why. Because according to his father, Morgan wasn't really his brother, not really a Caine. But for Cyrus, he was now the only family he had left.

Cyrus's memory of his mother grew dimmer with each passing year. He recalled a pinch-faced woman with auburn hair, prone to headaches and sleeping in darkened rooms whenever she could, especially after a brutal round of fighting with the old man. "She enjoys poor health," his father used to sneer, and though it was meant to be cruel it also looked to be true. Esther Caine's primary mission in life was to stay away from her husband as much as she could, and that meant retreating to her room and from her children as well. Old Cyrus accommodated her by staying on the road whenever he could and staying drunk the rest of the time.

One day while Old Cyrus was on one of his frequent horse-buying trips, the man from National Life and Accident Insurance Company of Nashville, Tennessee appeared at the door. He was good-looking, smooth-talking, well dressed – precisely the type a man wouldn't want to leave at home alone with his wife. "He could sell ice to Eskimos," his mother said once, smiling in soft approval and something more her young son couldn't read. They seemed to have a lot of insurance issues to discuss, because the

Man from National Life became a regular visitor whenever Old Cyrus was out of town. Not long after that friendship started, Mother announced that Old Cyrus was going to be a father again.

When the baby came, Mother insisted on naming him Morgan – which by great coincidence happened to be the National Man's first name. Father didn't care, never put two and two together – he told people they had named the kid after a breed of horse. But the day came when Old Cyrus returned home to find that his wife was gone; people said it was with a nice-looking man from National Life and Accident Insurance. Old Cyrus was furious, but mostly because he'd been left with two kids to tend to and decorated with horns. Morgan became "the Little Bastard." The Old Man forbade them to listen to the Grand Ole Opry on Saturday nights because National Life and Accident was the sponsor.

The truck and trailer rolled on, mile after mile. The hills of southern Ohio turned to broad flat stretches of Indiana farmland, with corn starting to fill in and green up. Names of towns flew by but offered no sense of direction or place. One farm looked pretty much like another, and except for the occasional silo or crossroad there was nothing to break the monotony. Over the horizon, Cyrus could see slivers of lightning from the heat. It wasn't dawn yet, but Cyrus knew the day would be hot again, in the 90s, and he could feel the sweat starting to creep down his back. He rolled down his window and hung his injured arm out to try to catch a breeze.

Morgan stirred after a while. He sat up, looked out the windshield and saw a world that looked just the same as when he dosed off – dark, flat and unfamiliar.

"Where are we?" he asked, rubbing his eyes.

"No idea," Cyrus replied.

"What time is it?"

"You ask a lot of questions." Behind them, the sky was starting to lighten, a thin sliver of pink above the gray flatlands.

Morgan sat up, yawned and stretched a bit to take the stiffness out of his back.

"I'm hungry," Morgan said. Cyrus's stomach was rumbling too. It occurred to him he had not eaten since the morning of the race, which felt like a year ago. "Maybe we should stop."

"You see anyplace to stop around here?" his brother asked. At that moment the truck seemed to have heard them, because it balked and slowed. Cyrus pressed the pedal further to the floorboard, but the truck didn't respond.

"I think we got a problem," he said as he downshifted and eased the truck over to the side of the road. He stared at the dashboard, as though the problem would reveal itself, and then he saw the gas gauge in the growing light – frozen but hovering just above the E. He slapped it hard with the palm of his hand and yelled, "Shit!" Then again, "Shit-shit-shit." He pounded angrily on the steering wheel, grabbed it so hard Morgan thought his brother might pull it off the stalk. The two brothers exchanged looks.

"We're fucked," Cyrus said.

The red sun crawled slowly into the morning sky and the heat rose with it. By 9 a.m. the temperature was already past 80. The two boys leaned forlornly against their disabled truck, staring up and down the endless stretch of road and wondering what to do next. Finally, Cyrus decided they might be stuck there a while, so he ordered Morgan to get Lucky out of the trailer and walk him a bit. He could see a stream not too far from the road, no fencing to bar their path, so the two of them walked the horse down to the stream. While Lucky grazed on the rich grass along the bank, Morgan took his bucket down to the stream and filled it with water for the horse to drink.

When Lucky had been watered Morgan went to work on his bandages. He exposed the injured foreleg, which was still swollen but didn't seem to be giving off as much heat. Morgan cheerfully went to work wiping down the leg, adding cool water to clean it. He walked down to the bank of the river and scooped some of the soft mud into his bucket. He carried the bucket back to the horse, crouched down and began to smooth the wet mud on Lucky's leg to sooth the injury. When he was done, he wiped his hands in the grass then on his jeans, then carefully wrapped the injury with a fresh bandage.

While Morgan worked his older brother went down to the stream and knelt at the water's edge. He pulled his shirt off over his head with difficulty, the sharp pain in his ribs stabbing him with every movement. He felt the skin over his ribs, testing them to see if any felt broken. The color of the skin over his ribcage was turning from blue to a deep purple. Cyrus submerged his head in the stream, raised it and shook the excess water from his hair. For the moment at least he felt a little cooler.

He looked at his left arm. The bleeding had stopped, and it didn't look like the cut was too deep. He washed down the wound as best he could. He shot a quick look at his brother, who was still occupied with Lucky. Then he reached into his boot and drew out the knife – his father's knife. The old man always carried – used to carry — a *sgian dubh,* a Scottish single-edged knife. It could be easily concealed in a boot or a sock and came in awfully handy in a barfight. Carefully, Cyrus drew the knife from its scabbard and washed the blade in the stream. He watched the blood swirl in a slow circle and disappear down the stream, his own blood and his father's, comingled forever and now washed away. He shook away the thought of their last struggle and went back to his business. He wiped down the blade with his shirttail and slipped the skene back into the scabbard, then tucked it back in his boot so his brother wouldn't see it. He shook his shirt out and pulled it back over his head.

An hour passed. Morgan decided to stay in the field nearby and tend to Lucky while Cyrus caught a quick nap in the shade of the truck. He had been driving all night, didn't realize how exhausted he was until he stepped down from the cab. He fell asleep immediately and didn't wake until he felt the toe of a boot nudge his leg.

"You OK, son?"

Cyrus opened one eye and regarded the man standing over him. He was good sized, or at least looked big from Cyrus's prone position. A straw hat sat atop a round ruddy head. He wore steel-rimmed spectacles and a florid moustache that had turned from red to white a long time ago. He had a barrel chest that had bloomed into a formidable belly, which hung over his dungarees and was set off by a tired pair of red suspenders. He might have been in his 60s, but Cyrus had no sense of age except in horses. The stranger just looked old.

His eyes now fully open, Cyrus realized that the man had pulled his own truck up in front of theirs and parked it along the side of the road. Cyrus has been so tired he hadn't even heard the other vehicle approach.

"I'm fine," Cyrus mumbled as he started to get to his feet. The man extended a meaty hand to help him up, but Cyrus ignored it. He brushed himself off.

"Got some mechanical trouble?" the man asked him.

"Out of gas," Cyrus replied. The man nodded, acknowledging that that was indeed a problem. "You know any gas stations around here?" The man's mouth crinkled a bit.

"A gas station open on Sunday morning around here? Not likely," he said. "You picked a bad place to run dry." The man's gaze swept past Cyrus's shoulder. "That's a fine-looking animal."

Cyrus turned his head quickly and saw Morgan slowly walking Lucky up to the road. He had seen the strange truck pull up and thought this might be good news. Cyrus's reaction was just the opposite. He was wary of the stranger's interest.

"Yeah he is," was all the boy said.

"He yourn?"

"Yeah." The man nodded again.

"He looks to be a little tender on that front leg," the old man observed. Cyrus did not reply. The older man said, "Mind if I take a look?" Cyrus shrugged.

The old man walked toward Morgan and the horse, trying to spare the animal from having to cover too much ground. He called cheerfully to Morgan, "Morning, young fella. Mighty fine animal you got there. Mind if I take a look at his leg?" Morgan shook his head shyly.

The old man eased up to Lucky, murmuring to him, letting the horse get to know him, gently stroking Lucky's powerful neck. From somewhere in the pocket of his dungarees the man produced a carrot and held it to the horse's mouth. Lucky chomped into it gratefully. The man rubbed his large, calloused hands along the horse's chest, then his withers, and finally ran his hands along the injured leg. He started to unwind the bandage as he said, "Let's take a look, see what we got here." The man was kneeling now and glanced up at Morgan. "Someone did a mighty fine job with this bandage. This your work, young fella?"

Morgan nodded, pleased with the compliment. The old man concentrated on Lucky's tendons and ligaments, gently probing to check the injury.

"Strange thing about horses," the man said as he worked. "Most beautiful creature God ever put on this earth. But he took a half ton of bone and sinew and muscle and set it on the shakiest set of sticks you'd ever want to see."

Morgan asked, "You a vet?"

"No. Not a school-learnt one. But I've cared for a lot of big animals on my farm. They call me Doc. Doc Reese."

The old man rose slowly to his feet. He produced a red bandanna from his pocket and wiped the sweat from his eyes and dabbed at his forehead. Cyrus had joined them by now.

"What do you think?" Cyrus asked at last. The old man regarded him.

"Hard to say. Bowed tendon maybe, or a torn ligament. He might do all right if he stays off it for a while."

"How long?" Cyrus wanted to know, trying not to sound too anxious.

"Hard to say. Six months. A year maybe." He nodded in the direction of the truck. "Standing up in a trailer ain't helping him much." The stranger looked at the two boys for a moment, then nodded his head in Morgan's direction. "Who's the chatterbox?"

"That's my brother," Cyrus answered. The old man nodded as if to say he could have figured that out on his own. Clearly he wasn't going to get much from the dark sullen one. He turned to the younger boy. "What's your name, son?"

"Morgan. Like the horse." That was his typical reply. It usually brought a smile, as it did this time.

"Where you boys from?" the man asked casually. Before Morgan could reply, Cyrus stepped between him and the stranger.

"Indiana," Cyrus said. The old man nodded. His gaze wandered to the old truck and trailer up ahead, took in the Kentucky license plate.

"Indiana," the man repeated. "Whereabouts?"

When Cyrus didn't answer, Morgan jumped in helpfully, pulling up one of the names he'd noticed on a road sign as they'd rolled along in the darkness. He remembered it from a book he'd read.

"Versailles," the younger boy said matter-of-factly. The old man suppressed a smile beneath the heavy moustache.

"Really?" the old man said. "You two must be French royalty. Hoosiers like to call it '*Ver-sales.*'" Cyrus realized they'd been caught out.

"We didn't live there long," he offered.

"No, I suppose not." The old man took out his kerchief again, wiped down his neck and his moustache. "How about if you tell me what you two young fellas from *Versailles*" – he used the French pronunciation – "are doing out here in the middle of nowhere on a Sunday morning?"

"What do you mean?" Cyrus shot back, stalling for time.

"I mean here you are, two kids with a beat-up truck but a Westphalia trailer, driving around with what looks to be a pretty expensive piece of horseflesh."

"We're taking him to Chicago," Cyrus answered. "We're going to sell him."

"Uh-huh. I suppose you have papers on him?" That gave Cyrus pause. He'd seen his father and various owners shuffling paperwork a thousand times but never thought he'd need it himself.

"Sure. In the truck."

The old man nodded again but looked skeptical. Cyrus became angry.

"You don't believe me?"

"I got no reason to believe or disbelieve you," the man said. He regarded Cyrus closely. "How old are you, son?"

"Eighteen," Cyrus shot back.

"What year were you born?"

"Nineteen tw…." He caught himself. "Nineteen fifteen."

The old man's eyebrow arched upward. "You're fast at math, I'll give you that." He looked down at Morgan. "How about you, your highness? What are you? Thirty?"

"I'm ten," Morgan said, puzzled that the old man should be so far off.

"What's it to you anyway?" Cyrus challenged him. "You the law or something?"

"No," the old man said slowly. "I'm not the law. Just another pilgrim along the road." The old man stood for a moment, considering the situation. Then he turned and started walking toward his pickup truck. Cyrus followed him a couple of steps, craning his neck to see what the man had on the truck bed. He spotted the shotgun on the rack in the rear window. Cyrus slowly eased his hand along his pant leg and kept it poised in case he had to grab his knife.

The old man reached into the truck bed. He looked back at the two boys, focused on the older one, the coal eyes blazing with aggression, the hand creeping slowly down his leg, maybe moving toward a weapon of some sort. Slowly, Doc drew something from the truck bed, but it wasn't a gun; it was a large gas can, heavy judging from the grunt the old man let out. He walked the canister around to the other side of the boys' truck and set it down on the ground.

"Here's what I propose. I got enough gas to get you to a town where they can sell you some gas. Won't get you all the way to Chicago though." He looked Cyrus in the eye. "You do have money for gas and what not?"

Cyrus didn't answer. The man continued:

"Or, if you want to, you can follow me up the road apiece. My place isn't too far. That horse of yours needs looking after." He nodded at Cyrus's arm, which was bleeding again, and mentioned it for the first time. "Looks like you could do with a little patching up yourself." Cyrus turned away so that his arm was partially hidden behind his back.

"Why would you help us?" Cyrus asked. The old man looked genuinely surprised.

"Because it's the Christian thing to do," he said. "Don't look like you boys have a whole lot of options. Besides, it grieves me to see an animal suffer." He looked down at Morgan and added, "My wife is making fried chicken for Sunday dinner, if that factors into your thinking at all."

The old man quietly lifted the cowl of the truck, unscrewed the gas cap and began transferring the gas from his container into the tank. While he worked the boys looked at each other, trying to decide what to do. The old man finished up, tightened the cap on his cannister and said, "That ought to do 'er. Give her a crank why don't you."

Cyrus got behind the wheel, paused a moment, then tried the ignition. The old truck balked and sputtered a time or two as the fuel started to circulate, then the engine caught. Blue smoke belched from the tailpipe, but the engine was running. Cyrus made sure the brake was on, then ran back and helped Morgan load Lucky into the trailer. Both boys jumped into the cab. The old man climbed into his own vehicle, started it up, then with a casual wave out the window he slipped the transmission into gear and started rolling up the road.

Cyrus and Morgan followed at a distance, still leery of the stranger. But he was right: there weren't a whole lot of choices open to them. They saw the old man's truck slow at an intersection and his taillight flashing to the right as he made the turn. The boys exchanged glances, then resolutely pulled into the turn and followed the other truck home.

Chapter 3

Kat
Harmony Farms 1933

THE GIRL HEARD HER GRANDFATHER'S TRUCK pulling into the yard and called, "Grandma! He's home."

"It's' about time," her grandmother said from the kitchen. "Why don't you set the table so we can eat as soon's he gets cleaned up? Kat?" But the girl was gone, dashing outside with the squeak of the screen door in her wake.

Kat ran across the yard, past the massive cottonwood tree that shaded the entire farmhouse. It was a wide two-story white frame house with asphalt shingle roofs. A broad porch ran the length of the house, and there was a glider loveseat with patchwork cushions on it – Kat's favorite place to sit when the evenings cooled off. Sometimes her grandfather would sit with her and slowly rock. Kat would curl up next to him, her head resting on his shoulder, and more often than not started to fall asleep right there.

She ran across the lawn and waved happily at her grandfather's truck. Then she noticed a second truck pulling into their lane – a tired-looking machine with a red horse trailer attached to it. She stopped waving, turned and ran to her grandfather's truck just as the old man was engaging the brake. He swung the door open, slid out of the cab, and held out his arm as Kat crashed into him.

"Hello there, nixnuts," he said to her and kissed the top of her head. She hugged him around his ample waist.

"What took you so long?" the girl said. "We thought you'd be here an hour ago."

"Had a little engine trouble," her grandfather replied. He looked at the girl sharply.

"Is grandma mad?"

Kat nodded her head gravely. Then she caught her grandfather's eye and shook her head with a big smile. She had a beautiful smile, with most of her adult teeth coming in after a couple of years of the jack o' lantern stage every child goes through. Her eyes were bright, piercing blue that missed nothing. All framed by a wondrous head of red hair – not orange, but a coppery red that set off her pale white skin. Her legs were long and seemed to have a mind of their own. She was only 10, but it wouldn't be too many years before she would be what her grandfather called "a looker."

By this time the other truck had pulled up behind Doc's. A man got out from behind the wheel. Only when Kat looked closer she realized it wasn't a man, it was a boy. An older boy, but he looked strong like a man. His hair was dark and curly and matted with sweat, and his clothes needed a good washing. The boy/man scowled at her, and Kat was arrested by his eyes, dark as coal, fierce looking, but with beautiful long lashes. Kat didn't know what to make of him or the way he stared back at her. She pressed closer to her grandfather.

"Who's that?" she asked.

"Couple o' friends of mine," the old man replied. "I asked them to dinner."

"Why?"

"Because it's Sunday, and it seemed like a nice thing to do. Why don't you run inside and tell Grandma to set two more plates while I get these boys settled." Kat nodded her head, threw one more wary look at the dark-haired stranger and ran back into the house.

Kat

Cyrus stood next to the door of his truck and looked around the yard. He had spent a lot of time around horse farms and stables in his young life, and he knew a nice property when he saw one. The white house with the wide porch looked cool and inviting despite the heat, and there was a nice breeze that whispered through the grove of fruit trees behind the house. A lush green lawn set the house off from the rest of the place, which was a working farm. There was a massive truck patch on the other side of the house, with lettuce and tomatoes and every other variety of vegetable growing in neat rows. Fifty yards further down the lane, amid some other outbuildings, was a huge white barn, recently painted and in solid condition. There was a sign on the front of it that said, 'Harmony Farm & Stables – Croydon Co. Ill. – 1922'.

Cyrus noticed that the old man was standing next to him now, looking at him.

"Why don't you boys drive on around the barn and park your rig there?" Doc said. "I'll show you where the stables are. We can put your horse up, then take a look at him after dinner. Sound all right to you?"

"Sure," Cyrus replied. He climbed back into the truck and started it up again. Doc ambled down to the barn behind the truck. Cyrus noticed the red-haired girl standing at the screen door of the house, watching the whole scene with something between curiosity and suspicion.

What had been planned as a Sunday dinner for three, just family, was now dinner for five, with two strangers. Kat wasn't sure she approved. But her grandmother had been very welcoming. She was a short but formidable woman with curly white hair that once may have been the same shade of red as Kat's, but that was long ago. She had the sturdy torso and forearms of a woman used to working on a farm. Still, she had an easy smile and a hospitable manner. She greeted the newcomers warmly and showed them where they might get cleaned up – a gentle suggestion but really a command if they expected to be fed at Maggie Reese's table. On Sundays she brought out the white lace tablecloth and napkins that had belonged to her grandmother, just because she liked them and used them every chance she got.

Doc had taken the two boys into his study once their horse was unloaded and settled in the stable. He brought out a medical kit and began tending to Cyrus's injuries, starting with his arm. He cleaned the wound with antiseptic, then carefully bandaged it. Thankfully the cut was long but not too deep. Next he turned to the bruises and scrapes on the boy's cheek and above his left eye. The antiseptic stung, and Cyrus kept flicking his head away like a horse refusing the bit, but eventually he surrendered and let Doc do what he needed to do. When Doc had finished cleaning up his face he said,

"Now. You going to let me take a look at your ribs?"

"Why? Nothing wrong with them," Cyrus snapped back, but even as he said it a sharp pain stabbed him, and he caught his breath. Reluctantly, he lifted his shirt and let the old man look at him. Doc didn't say anything at first but let out a low whistle. Before he could ask, Cyrus offered,

"I fell off the horse."

"That'd do it," the older man replied. He reached into his bag. "Let' tape 'em up for now. But if you're not feeling better in a day or two you may need an x-ray."

"I'll be fine," Cyrus said as the old man started winding the tape around him.

Now the strange boys were sitting at the dinner table, and Kat was studying the younger one. He looked about her age, with chestnut hair that needed cutting and large blue eyes that seemed alternately curious and fearful. Both of the boys were dressed poorly, but there were a lot of children at school who lacked nice clothes during these hard times, and Kat knew it was impolite to comment.

Kat

The younger boy kept staring at the fried chicken once her grandmother set the platter down on the table. Kat was afraid he'd leap at it before anyone could take it away. She saw the boy pick up his fork, but her grandmother gently pressed his hand down. She looked at the other end of the table to her husband.

"Father, will you say grace?" she asked. To Morgan's surprise, Maggie Reese took his hand, and took Kat's with the other. The two boys exchanged glances, wondering what they were supposed to do next. Doc Reese held out a powerful mitt and took hold of Cyrus's hand, and soon they were all joined. Kat saw the two brothers start, and for a moment she thought they might jump up and flee through the door. But they settled after a moment. The three Reeses bowed their heads. Morgan, in imitation, dug his chin into his chest.

"Heavenly Father," Doc began quietly, "bless this food to our use and us to Thy service, through Christ Our Lord. We thank you for bringing these two young pilgrims to help us share in Your bounty. Amen."

"Amen," Kat and her grandmother added.

Morgan leaned over to his brother with a worried look. "What's that he said about a bounty?" His brother shushed him.

"Kat," Mrs. Reese began, "why don't you start the green beans around? I'll serve our guests." Mrs. Reese built a plate for Morgan – a large leg and thigh, mashed potatoes, green beans from the garden – and set it down in front of him.

"Would you like some bread and butter to go with that?" she asked. Morgan nodded eagerly.

Kat glanced over at the older boy. He was watching her grandmother pile the food on to the plate with a wolf-like gaze, but he was very still. Quietly he picked up his own plate, speared a wing and added it. Then he took a spoonful of the green beans, set his plate down again and began to eat.

"Is that all you're having?" Kat wanted to know. The boy looked at her self-consciously.

"I have to be mindful of my weight," he told her.

The younger boy didn't seem to have that problem. As soon as her grandmother set the plate down in front of him he tucked into the meal as if he'd never eaten before. Kat stared at him outright until she heard her grandmother clear her throat and caught the gentle reprimand in her grandmother's eye.

"Father, why don't you tell us how you come to meet our guests?" she said to Doc. Doc nodded while he finished chewing, took a swallow of buttermilk.

"They had a little misfortune with their truck," he explained. "I thought they might stay with us a day or two while they sort things out."

"That would be very nice," his wife said. She was used to her husband bringing home strays, be they animals or people. She turned to the boys. "If you're going to be staying with us I should really know your names."

Doc nodded to the younger boy. "This one's Morgan-like-the-horse."

Morgan nodded acknowledgment but was too busy with his drumstick to say more.

"And what about you?" Mrs. Reese said to the older boy. For a moment it looked like he wouldn't say anything.

"That's my brother Cyrus," Morgan said, his mouth half full. Kat looked at him skeptically.

"You don't look like brothers," she said.

"Katherine," her grandmother said disapprovingly. "That's not polite. A lot of siblings look different from one another."

But it was true. Seeing them seated side by side at her dinner table, the boys didn't bear much resemblance to one another, the older one tall and lean and threatening as a storm cloud in summer, the younger one quiet but with an open and sunny disposition. One was dark, the other fair. But it was more their manner that set them apart. She was frankly intrigued by the older boy but thought she could be friends with the younger one.

The grandmother tried to set the conversation back on the right tone by asking them,

Kat

"Do you boys have family around here?"

"No, ma'am," Cyrus replied. He didn't offer more than that.

"They're from Versailles," Doc added without looking up. Morgan looked up the table at him and realized the older man was yanking their chain. Doc winked at him.

"Well, I'm sure that's very nice," Mrs. Reese concluded and let the subject drop. She turned to her granddaughter, "Kat, maybe you can show the boys around after dinner and help them get settled?"

"Yes'm."

When the dinner dishes were washed and returned to their place in the china cabinet Kat led her guests outside. Her grandfather had taken up his customary Sunday afternoon spot on the glider on the front porch. He had a thick copy of the Sunday *Chicago Tribune* in his hands and was settling in to read it. Kat knew he would be asleep in ten minutes.

"Let's go down to the paddock," she said, and ran off with the boys struggling to keep up with her.

Cyrus and Morgan got their first real look at Harmony Farm. It wasn't at all what they had expected meeting the old man on the side of the road. The main house was substantial, almost stately compared to all the other farmhouses they had passed since they left Kentucky. The fields that surrounded the house weren't the flat dry plains of Indiana. The ground was covered with grass, not corn, and seemed to undulate gently for miles, though the green shoots were stressed in the early July heat. The fields around the property were divided into multiple paddocks set off by white-washed rail fences. Down a long riding path there was a patch of forest at the edge of the property, which the boys assumed marked a demarcation of Reese land from someone else's. Across the road was a small red house and a crop of corn stalks with numerous bare patches of sandy-looking soil thirsty for water in the harsh mid-summer glare. The property reminded the brothers of the horse farms they had worked with their father down in Lexington, Kentucky, although the green of the Midwest couldn't compare with the blue grass there. Nevertheless, Morgan thought this was one of the prettiest farms he'd ever seen. Cyrus admired it too, but for a different reason: Harmony Farm looked like a perfect place to hide out.

Kat ran to the edge of the paddock and leaped onto the fence, lacing her slender arms over the top rail. In the field beyond her several horses were grazing languidly. She paused and watched them for a while until Morgan and Cyrus caught up with her. Morgan jumped up on the fence too and looked out at the animals lolling in the sun.

"You ride?" he asked the girl. Kat seemed a little put out with the question.

"Course I do. It'd be kind of silly if I didn't," she replied. "I have my own horse."

"Really? Which one?"

She pointed out into the pasture, but her vague gesture didn't convey much information.

"Which one?" Morgan asked again. Kat wrinkled her nose in annoyance – boys could be so obtuse sometimes. She tucked two fingers at the corners of her mouth and let out a sharp whistle, as if she were hailing a taxi in Midtown. One of the ponies, solid black with patches of white, pricked up its ears and ambled over to the fence. Kat stroked the horse's muzzle and cooed affectionately at it, and the horse nuzzled her back.

"This is Calico," she told the boys. Morgan stroked the pony's neck and patted it.

"Hey there, boy. Hello there," he murmured. Kat watched him closely. He was good with horses. More than that – more important to her – he seemed kind. Cyrus leaned against the fence, facing away from the two of them, untouched by the precious moment.

"Do *you* ride?" Kat asked Morgan, now that she had established her credentials as an equestrienne.

Kat

"Kinda," Morgan answered. "I'm OK I guess." He nodded to his older brother. "Cyrus here is a great rider. About the best I've ever seen."

"Really?" the girl replied, looking at Cyrus with newfound interest. She asked him, "Do you ride English?"

"I can ride any style there is," Cyrus replied, yawning. He was a little bored with these kids, but glad the conversation had at least turned to something that interested him. His gaze swept across the pasture, the grassland that ran all the way to the tree line, seemingly for miles. "Your grandfather own all of this?"

Kat nodded. "This side of the road," she said, then with a twitch of her head took in the farm next door. "Other side of the road too. Over there, see that red house? That's where grandpa was born. That's the Old Farm. He said he got tired of raising crops one day and decided he liked raising horses better. So he bought this one."

"Nice," Cyrus acknowledged. He plucked a piece of long grass from beside the fence and put it between his teeth. Having exhausted conversation with the older brother, Kat turned to Morgan.

"Where are your parents?" she asked him. Morgan stiffened a little. He glanced at Cyrus, who gave his head a slight shake that the girl couldn't see.

"They're gone," Morgan said, as short an explanation as he could offer without an outright lie. Kat seemed to accept it though.

"Mine too. That's why I live here with Grandma and Grandpa."

"They good to you?" Morgan asked impulsively. Kat stared at him as if it were the oddest question she'd ever heard.

"Course they are. They're my grandparents."

Morgan nodded as if he understood what she meant. But he and Cyrus had no frame of reference, no scale along which to measure "good" grandparents or any other kind. Morgan didn't even know if they *had* grandparents, let alone whether they were good or bad. Their mother had never spoken of her family, if she had any. And their father . . . if he had parents, Morgan thought to himself, they'd likely have been just like him. He looked up at his older brother and wondered if Cyrus would ever get around to telling him what had happened at the Latonia stable the night before, which now seemed like a thousand years in the past.

At that moment Cyrus stifled a yawn, tossed the blade of grass at the corner of his mouth away and said, "I'm going to go check on our horse."

Morgan climbed down from the fence. He said to the girl, "Want to come?"

"Sure," she answered, and the two of them chased off after Cyrus, struggling to keep up with his longer strides.

The three of them rolled back the large square door and entered the stable. Lucky had been quartered in the first available stall off to their left. When the boys approached him he raised his head in acknowledgment and let out a low nicker. Cyrus ran his hand along the horse's sleek back and murmured to him, "It's OK, boy. You're going to be OK. It's just us."

"And a friend," Morgan added, by way of introduction. He patted the horse's muzzle gently. Lucky didn't seem to mind. Morgan nodded to Kat, who made the same gesture. She was careful around horses – not afraid, but attentive. She knew you had to approach the animal carefully, let them get to know you and to trust you.

"He's beautiful," she said in quiet admiration. Even Cyrus smiled.

"Yeah he is."

Kat noticed the bandage on the horse's foreleg for the first time and wrinkled her nose. "What happened to his leg?" she asked. The brothers exchanged glances, then opted for the truth.

"We were racing," said Cyrus. "He was running real good, moving up fast. Then suddenly he pulled up lame." He patted the horse's leg gently, still feeling a bit of heat in the limb.

Kat

"I'll bet my grandpa can fix him up," Kat said; not a boast, just a flat statement of fact. "He knows everything about animals." She stroked Lucky's neck. The horse seemed to like the girl.

"Where are you going to go now?" the girl asked. Cyrus shrugged.

"Don't know yet. Haven't thought much about it."

"Well, you can't run all over the country with an injured horse. He needs to rest." Miss Kat Reese was a girl of firm opinions. She looked up at the two boys. "Maybe you can stay here a while. If Grandma says it's all right."

"That'd be nice," Morgan said, smiling at her.

"We don't want to put anybody out," Cyrus affirmed. "We want to get to Chicago."

"Chicago?" Kat asked. "Why? What's in Chicago?"

"I hear they have a big market for horses. Horse tracks, stables, that kind of thing."

"That's true." She gave Lucky an affectionate pat on the muzzle. "I wouldn't want to sell a beautiful horse like this though."

Cyrus's eyes, which had seemed almost engaged a moment before, now narrowed into a less friendly look. "I wouldn't either, lessn I had to."

Kat gave Lucky one more pat, then stepped back and straightened her dress.

"You should talk to Grandpa," she said. She turned and left the stall.

Finally some cooler air moved in as the evening sun began to wane. In the softer light the farm seemed to run on for miles, like a painting by some old Master. The grass turned a deeper green and seemed to shimmer and wave as a light breeze swept away the heat of the day. Doc's hired hands had let the horses in for feeding time. Cyrus and Morgan were happy to help with the familiar chores. Doc introduced the boys to his top hands.

"This fella here is Texas Slim," Doc said, nodding to a stocky man who didn't look like he was from Texas and wasn't too slim. "We used to have another fella, Oklahoma Slim, but he left. And this here's Pasquale." He nodded to a Mexican man with a thin moustache and a copper-hued face below a beat-up straw hat; he was sturdy looking with a belly that spread over a silver belt buckle. The two men nodded to the boys but didn't seem too interested, just went about their business.

Doc nodded to a white-washed one-story bungalow adjacent to the main barn.

"Come on along with me," he said to the brothers. "I'll show you where you can bed down."

"We can sleep in the truck," Cyrus answered. "Or in one of the stalls."

"Now why would you want to do that?" Doc asked. "Get your stuff from the truck and come along with me." The brothers did as they were told.

The bungalow was nothing fancy but more comfortable than the stable. It was used for itinerant workers during harvest season. Doc led them to an empty room with two twin beds. Bedrolls had been spread out on top of the beds. There was a plain pine dresser and a nightstand between the beds. A mirror and a wash basin sat on top of the dresser. The room was functional, but nicer than what the boys were used to.

Doc had the front section of the newspaper with him, rolled up in his hand. He tapped it quietly against his thigh as the boys chose their beds and put their meager possessions away. Morgan was close to asleep on his feet. He pulled off his shoes, tucked them under the bed and stretched out on top of the bedroll. His lids were heavy.

While Morgan was getting settled, Cyrus withdrew the knife from his belt and slipped it under his pillow where he could get to it quickly in the night if he needed to.

Doc said to them, "You boys have had a long day. Get some rest now. We'll talk in the morning about what you fellas are gonna do next." He looked over at Morgan. "Good night, Your Highness." Morgan smiled sleepily, then he was out.

Doc turned his gaze on Cyrus. He took the newspaper, which he still had in his hand, and tossed it on Cyrus's bed.

"You might want to do a little reading before you go to sleep," the old man said. "Helps to settle the mind." He nodded to the boy and left the room, closing the door quietly behind him.

Cyrus sat down on the edge of the bed. He pulled off his boots, then tugged his shirt over his head. His ribs still hurt, but not as bad as they had earlier in the day. The tape Doc had applied kept him from breathing too deeply, and he could almost feel himself starting to heal.

He picked up the newspaper Doc had left him and held it closer to the small lamp on the nightstand. He didn't see anything in the headline or the top of the paper that looked to be of particular interest. He turned the paper over, and he froze.

In the lower righthand section, below the fold, he saw the headline:

'Fire at Ky Racetrack
1 Man Dead; Arson Suspected'

Cyrus's dark eyes quickly scanned the story. He knew what he would find. In fact, he knew more about it than anyone else – anyone alive. But he needed to know what others knew. The dead man had not been identified according to the report, his body charred beyond recognition; it would require dental records to do a positive identification, and authorities had no idea where to start. The burnt carcass of a horse was found in the stall with him and was thought to be Lucky Day, a promising three-year-old that had run well in the Latonia Derby that afternoon before pulling up lame.

There was no mention of missing boys or a missing trailer and truck. Why should anyone miss them, or care? It was unlikely anyone was looking for them.

There was just one problem, Cyrus thought as he placed the paper under his pillow next to his knife. Now Doc might have some suspicions about what they were running from. What would happen in the morning? Would the old man kick them off his farm? Or worse, call the police and have them dragged away to some juvenile home? Cyrus put out the lamp and stretched out on the bed. His eyes were still open wide, his breathing shallow. He looked over at his brother, who was in a deep sleep. He reached under the pillow and wrapped his fingers reassuringly around the handle of the knife.

Chapter 4

The Magician

THAT WAS THE FIRST NIGHT Morgan had The Dream. It started in darkness; all he could see was an inky blackness. The blackness turned to gray, and he realized it wasn't light that was spreading around him, it was smoke. Out of the swirling wreaths of smoke he heard a muffled sound that steadily grew louder until he recognized it: the snorting and whinnying of horses. As the equine noises became more intense he could tell that the animals were frightened. The sound of hooves stamping the ground and crashing against the walls of the stable in a crescendo of animal terror. Then the light started to break through, and he saw that it was fire. A door swung open, and in the light he could see the black shapes of horses thrashing about, fighting and flailing as the flames swirled around them. Finally, coming toward him from the darkness, he saw his brother's face, dark and serious and terrifying. The boy thrashed around in his bed and started to cry out:

"Cyrus . . . Cyrus no…."

He felt someone grab his shoulders and shake him hard. He sat up in bed, crying and trembling, and saw that it was his brother shaking him.

"Morgan. Morgan, wake up," Cyrus said. "You're having a dream."

The boy started, looked around the unfamiliar room. He had no idea where he was or how he got here. The only thing he recognized was the scowling face of his older brother, hanging on to his shirt front and shaking him. He wiped his eyes, shook his head slightly, ran fingers through the damp mop of hair on his forehead.

"I'm all right," he told Cyrus. "I'm all right."

"Go back to sleep now," Cyrus said, guiding his shoulders back down, firmly but not roughly. Morgan's head sank back into the pillow. But it would take a while before he could fall asleep again. And years before he could sleep peacefully.

First light was always one of the most beautiful times of day on the farm, and Kat was often up before the sun. Today was no exception. Sunlight steamed through the pink-and-white checked curtains that framed her window. The curtains matched the homemade quilt on her bed and the tablecloth on the stand next to her. Not a color scheme Kat would have picked for herself – she never considered herself a girly-girl – but Grandma Reese was in charge of decorating, and this was the theme she had picked for her granddaughter. Doc liked to tease Maggie about her decorating flourish.

"Pretty hoity-toity for a farm wife," he'd say. Maggie would wrinkle her nose at him.

"I am a *countrywoman,* not a 'farm wife,'" she would sniff at him, and it was true. Although she had been raised on Harmony Farm, her family had always seemed to be better off than the other neighbors. Certainly better off than the ragtag Reeses, who owned the farm with the red clapboard house across the road from them. Doc would shake his head at her and sigh.

"Don't know how you ended up with a Croydon County plowboy," he would say, then go back to whatever he was doing. Doc had married well when he lassoed Maggie–"the prettiest gal in the county." She was a doubly good catch, because she had no brothers, and when her parents died Harmony Farm passed to her and her husband. She had come with land, but it took

The Magician

Doc Reese to make something special of it, something unique. Within a few years the farm was flourishing, driven in no small part by a thriving business in livestock trading, augmented by the income they made from growing crops on the adjacent property. Even now, when times were hard, Harmony Farm seemed stable and prosperous, even if Doc was a little more careful with his spending than he might normally be.

Although it was still early, Kat heard voices outside and ran to her window. In the main paddock she could see a boy about her own age slowly walking a sleek brown stallion in wide circles. She remembered now: the two boys who had suddenly appeared with her grandfather the day before. Where was the other one, the taller boy with the black eyes and curly hair? Then she saw him, his ropy arms draped over the top rail of the fence around the arena next to the paddock. He was watching the head wrangler, Slim, trying to settle a new mare her grandfather had purchased recently, a distress sale from a local breeder. Curious, Kat threw on her clothes and ran down to the arena.

As she dashed outside Morgan was just headed back to the stable with his horse. He greeted her with a shy smile.

"Morning," he called to her. She smiled and gave him a small wave.

"You're up early," she said.

"Used to it," the boy replied. "Besides, I wanted to see how Lucky was doing." He pointed to the horse's foreleg. Indeed, the horse did seem to be moving a little better today, although Morgan was still being careful walking him.

"What's your brother doing?" she asked, glancing over at Cyrus. Morgan followed her gaze.

"Dunno. Fixing to tell somebody how to do their job I expect."

Cyrus was leaning harder into the fence, studying Slim and the recalcitrant horse. The wrangler had a long lead line on the mare and every now and then would tighten his hold, which only seemed to make the horse more anxious. When he tried to draw closer the horse would zig and zag and move in any direction that was away from the man. Slim was not having a good morning.

Cyrus unfolded himself from the railing and swung over the fence in a fluid motion. Kat watched him in fascination as he walked into the center of the arena, strong and athletic and confident despite his youth.

Cyrus said to Slim matter-of-factly, "Looks like it's not going so good."

"She wants no part of being saddled," Slim replied. "We've been doin' this little dance for better'n a week."

"Can I try?" Cyrus asked. Slim looked over at the youth and smirked at his cockiness.

"Be my guest, kid," Slim replied. He handed the long rein to Cyrus and stepped back to observe.

As Kat watched, Cyrus produced a pair of worn leather gloves from his back pocket and slipped them on. He took the long line in one hand and held it loosely. He stood stock still in the center of the arena, studying the horse. The mare snorted and pawed the sawdust-covered ground a few times. Cyrus didn't move. Eventually, the horse looked in his direction. Cyrus tightened the rope slowly, making no sudden moves, drawing it a little tighter but not pulling, never taking his eyes off the horse's. Keeping his body language relaxed, he approached the horse quietly, angling along the side, reaching out his hand, murmuring to her and lightly stroking her neck. With his free hand he deftly unsnapped the lead.

"What's he doing?" Kat asked Morgan, who had joined her at the railing. He shushed her.

In the center ring, the boy walked around until he was facing the horse head-on again. The mare took a few tentative steps to the left to try to get around Cyrus, but he quickly stepped in to cut her off. Then the horse cut right, and Cyrus again blocked her path, his arms still spread out at his sides. The boy made some soft sounds meant only for the horse, and slowly lowered his hands as if to quiet her. Cautiously, he closed the distance between them.

The horse would twitch and think about bolting one way or the other, but Cyrus was always there to cut off her escape.

Doc Reese had come out of the house by this time. He joined Kat, Morgan, Slim and a couple of other hands who were all watching the show in the center ring with puzzlement. Everyone took their cue from Cyrus and was quiet.

Cyrus closed the distance between himself and the horse until he was able to touch her again. He gently placed a hand on her neck, and when she twisted her head away he kept his voice and his hands steady as he made soothing sounds. Eventually the horse relented and allowed herself to be petted. Cyrus ran his strong hands over her neck, then her withers, then stroked her back. The horse stood still, receiving the boy's affections. One hand on the horse's shoulder, Cyrus quietly reached in front and snapped on the lead again. He played it out a few feet and turned, so that he was even with the horse's head. He started to walk, more of a stroll really, and the horse walked with him. The two of them circled the arena once, then again. Then Cyrus turned and took them in the other direction.

Kat and her grandfather looked at each other in quiet amazement. Doc raised an eyebrow at Morgan.

"That's quite a sight," the old man said. Kat turned her eyes back on Cyrus. There was a new look on her face. Interest, fascination, curiosity – she couldn't look away from the boy in the ring.

"He's a magician," she said to no one in particular. Morgan, who had always known that about his brother, just nodded in agreement.

Doc studied the boy in the ring, who now literally had the horse eating out of the palm if his hand, with some oats he scooped out of a bag near the fence. His look wasn't quite as admiring as his granddaughter's, but it was thoughtful, as if he were taking his measure of the lad. He turned and started back toward the house.

As he passed Slim the wrangler said, "Kid has a way with horses." Doc nodded.

"Best keep an eye on that one. Give him something to do."

The day spun by. The Caine brothers were kept busy helping Slim and Pasquale tend to the horses. This was work they were used to: grooming, feeding, exercising, mucking out stalls, laying fresh straw. They spent time tending their own horse, making sure that Lucky was properly fed and watered and continuing the treatment with cold hoses and poultices. Cyrus noted that they had enough feed to maintain the horse for a couple more days. After that they would need to either strike a deal with Doc or be on their way. But where? He had no idea.

That night, the brothers ate in the kitchen with the rest of the family, after Kat came and found them and said, "Grandma says you're to eat with us. And get cleaned up first." Turned out, the family only used the dining room for Sunday dinner and holidays. Other days they ate at a round oak table in the kitchen with ladderback chairs set around it. Mrs. Reese did the cooking for the whole place, and it was Kat's job to deliver the meals for the hands to the bungalow at supper time. Cyrus made a note that maybe he and Morgan could eat there the next night – if they were still here.

After supper, Doc took his usual place on the glider on the front porch and picked up his copy of the *Tribune*. Cyrus froze when he saw Doc open the paper. He grabbed his brother by the arm.

"Hey!" Morgan protested. He and Kat were just about to sit down to a game of checkers. She was very competitive, as it turned out. In fact, Morgan suspected she cheated. But he enjoyed her company so much that he didn't care.

"Come on. We've got work to do." Kat looked disappointed. Doc didn't look up from his paper.

Cyrus withdrew, and he and his brother went down to the paddock and busied themselves. Morgan noticed that Cyrus kept glancing back to the porch.

"What are you looking at?" he wanted to know.

"None of your business," Cyrus told him, and that was that. Then he saw Doc stand up and stretch. The old man held up the folded newspaper, opened the screen door and made a sweeping gesture to his granddaughter, who scurried inside ahead of him. Then Doc set the paper down on the glider and went inside the house.

When he was sure the Reeses were securely inside, Cyrus crept to the porch. Morgan tried to follow him, but Cyrus shooed him away. Cyrus climbed the wooden stairs slowly, careful not to make the panels creak. He picked up the newspaper, tucked it under one arm and quick-walked toward the bungalow.

Once in their room Cyrus closed the door and started flipping through the pages. Nothing on page one. Or two, or three. Nothing in the front section. He tossed it on the floor. On the first page of the second section he saw the story:

'Racetrack Fire Still a Mystery
Dead Man Unidentified

(FLORENCE, Ky.) State investigators continue to look for clues as to the identity of the man found dead in a stable at legendary Latonia Racetrack following a fire Saturday night. The victim appeared to have a stab wound in his chest, but a medical examiner said smoke inhalation was the likely cause of death. The man may have set the fire himself, one investigator theorized, adding that evidence pointed to arson as the cause of the blaze. One horse was found in the stall with the dead man. Several other horses also died in the blaze and were . . .'

"What are you reading?" Morgan had come into the room and was standing at the foot of the bed. Cyrus started. He put down the paper, folded it a couple of times and put it aside.

"Nothing interesting," he answered.

"Is there something about Pa?" Morgan demanded. "About the fire?"

"Why would they write about Pa in the newspaper? Stop being an a-hole and get ready for bed."

Morgan was cowed but unconvinced, but his brother was done talking. He gathered up the sections of the newspaper, folded them over a couple of times and smoothed them, then stepped toward the door.

"Where ya going?" Morgan wanted to know.

"Be back in a minute. Brush your teeth while I'm gone why don't you?" Cyrus closed the door behind him and stepped out into the mild summer night.

He walked behind the bungalow to the trash pile behind the big barn. There were two large, rusted steel drums that were used as incinerators. One of them was half full. Cyrus stuffed the newspaper down as far as he could and scattered some other trash on top of it. Anyone would have to dig to find it. He hoped no one at Harmony Farm would be interested enough to go digging.

Cyrus barely slept that night. The continuing interest in the Latonia fire troubled him deeply. Had Doc Reese noticed those stories too? Did he suspect the boys somehow were connected to the fire and the death of the 'unidentified man?' Was he going to turn them in in the morning? Cyrus wasn't sure he could stick around to find out. He sat up in bed, grabbed the rucksack from the corner and began stuffing his possessions into it. He could be gone before anyone else woke up.

First he had to figure out what to do about their horse. Could he get into the stable, get Lucky ready to travel and load her into the trailer without anyone hearing him? Not likely. And what would he do on the road with an injured horse anyway? How would he care for the animal? Maybe the best thing to do was to travel light, just move on his own. With luck, he could make it up to the main road and hitch a ride into Chicago before the sun was even up. That made more sense. Travel light.

A soft moan rose from the other bed. Morgan was tossing and turning. Looked like he was having that same dream he'd had the night before. Cyrus grimaced. How did he get stuck taking care of this kid? Of course it wasn't just any kid; this was his brother, the only family he had left. He couldn't leave him behind. Cursing under his breath, Cyrus dropped the rucksack and stretched out on his own bed to try to get a little rest.

The sun was barely up when Cyrus rousted his brother from his bed.

"Get up and get your stuff. We're getting out of here."

"Wha…? Why're we …."

"Just get dressed. Come on."

The brothers threw their meager possessions into their rucksack, Morgan jumped into his clothes. He started to smooth out his bedding.

"Leave it," Cyrus hissed at him. "Come on."

Morgan followed his brother out of the bungalow, imitating Cyrus's stealthy stride. They slid along the side of the building and rounded the corner, to where their truck was parked behind the horse barn. There was a 50-gallon steel tank on an elevated platform at the edge of the building. Cyrus threw the satchel into the bed of the truck and dug into his pockets for the keys to the truck.

"See that tank up there?" Cyrus whispered to his brother. "I saw Doc fill his truck with gas yesterday. We can fill up our tank and get out of here…."

"You fellas goin' somewhere?"

The boys whipped around to see Doc Reese standing casually at the corner of the barn, arms folded. The old man pulled his pipe out of the pocket of his coveralls and hunted around for a match. When he found it he lit the pipe and ambled toward the truck.

Cyrus replied, "You been real nice to us, mister. But we figured it was time for us to leave."

"Why?" Doc asked, shaking out the match and tossing it aside. He saw Morgan look up at his brother, his expression echoing the question.

"We don't want to take advantage," Cyrus said.

"No problem," Doc replied. "I'd tell you if it was. Besides," he said, "today's a holiday. Nothing open."

The boys looked at each other as they realized the date: the Fourth of July. Cyrus cursed under his breath. Doc continued,

"Even if you do leave, you likely won't get far."

"You can't let them leave, Grandpa," came another voice, higher pitched. It was Kat, rubbing the sleep from her eyes, coming down from the house. The expression on her face was determined. She looked at Morgan.

"You've got to stay and see the fireworks," she told him. "It'll be lots of fun. There's rides at the fairgrounds, and food, and …"

Morgan looked at his brother pleadingly. "Please, Cyrus? Can't we at least stay for the fireworks?"

Cyrus looked at his brother, then at the girl. Finally, he looked at the old man, who waited with raised eyebrows. Cyrus replied with a wintry smile, but there was no merriment in his black eyes.

"I guess the lady has spoken," he said coolly, and reached into the truck bed for their satchel. Morgan let out a yip, and he ran to Kat as she started to chatter excitedly about the night's festivities.

Doc's expression was neutral. It was driving Cyrus crazy. What did the old man know? And if he knew, why would he let them stay? But this wasn't the time to figure it out. He brushed past the old man and headed back into the bungalow.

Chapter 5

Fireworks

WHAT MORGAN CAINE REMEMBERED from that Fourth of July evening – what he would remember until his dying breath – was the light in Katherine Reese's eyes.

They rode in Doc Reese's pickup truck, the four of them: Doc driving, Kat and Morgan squeezed in next to him. Morgan could feel the girl's shoulder pressed up against his. Sometimes she turned and looked at him sweetly, but most of the time her gaze was focused on the fairgrounds up ahead and the excitement to come. Cyrus was in the bed of the truck, sulking, in no mood for holiday merriment, but there he was anyway. What choice did he have?

Doc joined the line of cars and trucks pulling up on the open field adjacent to the fairgrounds. It was a warm night but pleasant. They had come in time to get a good parking spot. Doc pulled the hand brake, then turned the door handle.

"Everybody out," he said, and the boy and girl tumbled out on the passenger side.

A few hundred people were already milling about the fairgrounds, admiring the rides and the food stands while they waited for the fireworks to start. A Ferris wheel lurched above the crowd, flanked by a merry-go-round and a couple of worn-out whirligigs left over from a carnival that had gone bust. It all looked glorious to Kat, whose blue eyes radiated excitement and anticipation. Morgan couldn't keep the smile off his face, the goofy grin boys get when they are close to a girl they like. He followed her eyes to the top of the Ferris wheel. Doc saw the two of them gazing upwards. He snorted a bit, then dug into his pocket and came up with a quarter. He pressed it into Morgan's palm.

"Why don't you two go get a closer look?" he said. Morgan squeezed the money eagerly.

"Yes, sir!" he said, and looked at Kat. "Want to go for a ride?"

"Sure," she answered eagerly, and the two of them ran off to join the line for the Ferris wheel. Cyrus watched them go then turned away in disgust to find more interesting diversions. Doc soon found himself in a crowd of good old boys talking fertilizer and the weather.

Kat and Morgan shuffled along the line until it was their time to climb into a seat. The chain was fastened across their laps, presumably to keep them from tumbling out. A bored-looking attendant threw a lever, the wheel lurched. Kat squealed and found herself gripping Morgan's arm as the Ferris wheel started its balky ascent. Around they went, their own cries of delight mixing with the voices of other kids, other couples on the ride, and after three revolutions the wheel suddenly shuddered and they found themselves frozen at the very top.

They stared out across the fairgrounds.

"Look how small they all look," Kat breathed, pointing to the people on the ground below them. "They look like ants." She scanned the horizon and pointed. "Look, Morgan! I can see our farm from here." Morgan followed her gaze and could make out the white barn and outbuildings of Harmony Farm.

"It's beautiful up here," he murmured, and realized that he wasn't talking just about the scenery. Not that he liked girls, or knew anything about them. There wasn't much opportunity to talk to girls traveling from racetrack to racetrack. But Kat was different from the girls he had known. She knew her own mind, and she was fun to be around. Maybe he liked girls after all, Morgan concluded.

Fireworks

Kat caught him looking at her and punched his arm lightly. Before she could say anything the Ferris wheel started up again with a jerk and they continued their revolution.

Laughing and breathless, the two of them exited the ride. Morgan asked, "What do you want to do next? Want to try that teacup thing?"

"No," she said. "Let's get some cotton candy."

As they were walking away Kat recognized someone in the crowd and waved to her frantically.

"Nancy! Over here!"

An attractive girl with a blond ponytail in a red, white and blue outfit waved back to her and made her way through the crowd. She was pretty, Morgan thought, but in a different way from Kat. Too flashy. Too obvious.

"That's Nancy," Kat explained. "She's my best friend from school. Nancy, how are you?" The girl had joined them now and the two of them hugged as if they had not seen each other for years, although it was only since the end of school a few weeks before.

"I thought that was you on the Ferris wheel," Nancy said, then cast a sly look at Morgan. "Who's your friend?"

"This is Morgan," Kat said. Nancy held out her hand and shook Morgan's, her touch lasting a little too long.

"Pleased to meet you, Morgan," she said. "I don't think I've seen you before. Kat, where have you been keeping him?"

"He's not from around here," Kat said, but that was the only explanation she was prepared to give. "We were just going to get something to eat. Want to come with?"

"Sure," her friend replied. Arm in arm, the three of them headed to the concession stand. The line was long but moving quickly. They edged their way up while the two girls chatted about classmates and plans for the rest of the summer.

As Morgan was about to step up to the counter, two teenaged boys bumped in front of him and cut him off. One was tall with curly blond hair and a smirk on his face. The other boy was taller and more muscular, with a butch haircut.

The girls protested. Morgan said, "Hey, no cuts!"

"Oh really?" the blond boy answered. "It looks like our turn."

"Get out of here, Robbie," Nancy said to the blond boy. She explained to Morgan, "This is my idiot brother."

"Don't forget me," the crewcut companion said with a sneer.

"Either way," Morgan said evenly, "it's our turn."

The two teenagers turned their full attention to Morgan now, forming a solid wall between him and the counter. They were each a half a head taller, solid and athletic looking. Robbie looked down at him and pushed his face closer.

"And just who the hell are you, punk? Giving us orders."

"He's my brother," came a cold voice over Robbie's shoulder. There stood Cyrus, his black eyes focused on the two teenagers. They were larger than he was, maybe a year or two older. But Cyrus had a look that discouraged messing with him.

"You should mind your own business," the crewcut guy said to Cyrus, trying to sound tough. The two of them turned to face Cyrus, but he quickly cut them off and blocked the way for Morgan and the two girls to move ahead in the line. The teenagers took a step forward and bumped Cyrus with their chests. Cyrus held his ground. Quietly, his hand crept toward his boot, where his knife rested in its sheath.

A large, calloused hand landed on Cyrus's shoulder and turned him away before he could draw his weapon.

"You kids having a good time?" said Doc Reese. Doc turned his gaze on the two teenagers. "Robbie, Brad.... I thought I saw your parents over there."

The teenagers took a step backward. They exchanged looks and decided to withdraw. As he walked away Brad let out a loud greasy burp in Cyrus's face, a souvenir of an earlier hotdog or three. He bumped Cyrus with his shoulder and said, "This isn't over."

Fireworks

Doc watched the boys as they walked away, glancing back at Cyrus and muttering to each other what they would have done if old Doc hadn't shown up.

Doc turned to Nancy and smiled. He knew her well from the stables. Her father made sure Nancy had whatever Nancy wanted, and since she had turned 10 what Nancy wanted was to ride horses. Fortunately, Doc had horses and Nancy's father had money.

"Nice to see you, Nancy," he said. He turned to the other three. "We should probably go stake out a space. The fireworks are about to commence. You want to come with us, Nancy?"

"No thanks," the blond girl replied. "I better go find my parents before they get worried. I'll see you, Kat."

"See you, Nance."

The blond girl looked at the two brothers. Her eyes lingered on Cyrus, and she smiled demurely, a ten-year-old temptress practicing her wiles.

"Nice to meet you, whoever you are." She turned and walked away, hoping that his eyes would follow her. They did. Nancy looked back over her shoulder and gave him a friendly wave.

Doc and his three charges made their way toward the crowd standing in the open field beside the fairgrounds. Kat fell back so that she could walk alongside Cyrus, while her grandfather and Morgan charged ahead to find a good spot. Without looking up at him, Kat said,

"I'm glad you showed up when you did." It took Cyrus a second to register what she was talking about. He snorted a laugh.

"What, because of those two dipshits? Morgan could have handled them."

Kat smiled at the idea. "I don't think so. Brad is the captain of the upper school wrestling team." Cyrus was unimpressed.

"Still a dipshit," he said, and they hurried up to catch the others.

Just as the four of them settled into an open spot in the crowd, the sky exploded with rockets and missiles and explosions of every color. The four of them gazed upward and watched in wonder as the night sky lit up.

Kat tilted her head down and stole a look at Cyrus. He was a strange one, she concluded. So chilly most of the time, but he had come to their defense so quickly. What would have happened if her grandfather hadn't materialized, she wondered. She had no doubt Cyrus could have held his own against the two bigger boys. He looked like someone who could take care of himself. Or his brother if he had to.

Cyrus turned at that moment and caught her looking at him. Kat looked away quickly, happy that the fireworks disguised how red her face was.

That night when they got back to farm, even though it was very late, Cyrus went up to the farmhouse porch and looked for the newspaper. There it was, neatly folded on the glider, just as Doc had left it the night before. Cyrus snatched the paper and ran back to the bungalow to read it. There was a follow-up story, this one smaller, on the third page of the paper's second section.

"Racetrack Victim May Have Met With Foul Play

(FLORENCE, Ky.) The investigation continued into a mysterious fire that took the life of one man and several horses at fabled Latonia Racetrack last Saturday night. An autopsy of the victim confirmed that he had received a stab wound prior to his death. The condition of the body, which had been burned beyond recognition in the fire, meant that the knife wound was not immediately apparent to investigators.

According to Dr. Larry Fields, coroner of Boone County, Ky, the wound could have been inflicted prior to the fire or suffered as the man attempted to flee the scene. An empty kerosene can was found next to the body, which leads sheriff's deputies to believe the fire may have been set deliberately. Deputy Jim King of the …"

Cyrus took the paper with him and stuffed it into the metal drum with the other editions.

Doc walked into the kitchen and found his wife sitting at the round oak table, doing some sewing. His eyebrow arched in surprise.

"You're up late," he greeted her. Maggie Reese rarely stayed up this late. "Should've come to the fairgrounds with us and seen the fireworks."

"I don't want to talk about the fireworks, George. I want to talk about these two boys."

"What about them?"

"For starters, what are you going to do with them?"

"'Do?' I haven't really figured yet. Do I have to do anything?"

"Shouldn't you notify the authorities? They're awfully vague about where they came from, whether they have family or not. And what are they doing with an expensive horse like that? It doesn't make sense."

Doc sat down heavily on a kitchen chair and sighed. "Lot of families broken up in this depression, Maggie. Parents can't afford to feed their children. Sometimes they just desert them. I get a feeling these lads are strictly on their own, whatever the circumstances. I'm not inclined to push it if they don't want to discuss it."

"Maybe you should have a talk with Rob Ward," she offered. Doc cocked an eyebrow at her.

"The sheriff? Now why would I bring Rob Ward into this?"

"I don't know. Maybe the horse is stolen. Maybe they're on the run."

Doc chuckled at her imagination. "Oh yes. A couple of real *banditos*."

"I'm serious, George. The older one, Cyrus, looks like he's no stranger to trouble." She softened. "Although Morgan seems to be a sweet child. Don't forget," she cautioned, "we have our granddaughter living under our roof. I want to be sure she's safe."

Doc became exasperated. "I'm not going to do anything that would put Kat in danger, woman. Don't you know that?" He checked himself. "Anyway, suppose I do turn them in to the authorities. What do you think happens to abandoned children these days? They'd throw the younger one into some county home. As for Cyrus, he's too old for the orphanage. He'd be out on the street and on his own with no one to keep an eye on him. Then he'd get into real trouble."

Maggie Reese's mouth was a tight line. She hated when her husband was right.

Doc continued, "Both those boys have a real talent around horses. We've got the room, and I can use the help. Might work out for all of us." He moved his head around until Maggie had to look at him. "Assuming it was all right with you."

Maggie bit off the end of her thread and put her sewing away. "All right, George Reese. But if anything happens it's on your head." She stood and smoothed her apron. "But if they're going to be living here I want both of them to go to school." She turned out the light and went upstairs to bed.

For the next several nights the ritual between Doc and Cyrus continued. Every evening Doc read his *Chicago Tribune* while he smoked his briar pipe. When he was done he would fold the paper neatly, set it on the glider and walk into the house. Cyrus would then pounce on the paper like a cat with twine and run back to the bungalow to search for more news on the Latonia fire. Nothing appeared in the paper the third night, or the next night, or the one after that, or the rest of the week. The world seemed to have tired of the story. Or at least The World's Greatest Newspaper (as the masthead proclaimed) had moved on to other news.

Cyrus was troubled by Doc's silence on the matter. During the day the Caine brothers worked hard, tending to the horses, mucking out the stables and doing whatever else needed to be done on a busy and productive farm. They worked alongside the other hands, who came to ignore them just as they would any other itinerant laborers. Sometimes during the day, and always in the evening, they would see Kat, who had taken a keen interest in both of the brothers, each in his own way. Morgan was a peer, someone her own age to hang out with. He was funny and sweet and excellent company. Cyrus generally ignored her, as older boys did, but she found him interesting to watch and very mysterious, with his dark curls and smoldering eyes.

"He looks like Lord Byron," Kat confided to Nancy when the two girls got together for a shopping trip in downtown Croydon. They were sitting at the counter of Kresge's having chocolate malts. Nancy looked at her quizzically; she had no idea who Lord Byron was but was pretty certain he wasn't from Croydon. She was more interested in the news that Doug Fairbanks and Mary Pickford had broken up.

After they had been on the farm about a week, Cyrus went looking for Doc. Maybe, he thought, it was time to face the music and figure out a plan of action. He found the old man in Lucky's stall, inspecting the horse's foreleg.

"He's coming along all right," Doc said approvingly as he rose to his feet. "I seen your brother walking him out in the paddock. No pressure, no dipping his head. A few more months and he'll be right as rain." He paused. "Never going to race again though."

Cyrus froze. He felt the hairs on his neck stand up. His face didn't betray him though.

"That's what I wanted to talk to you about."

"Oh?" said Doc. He produced his trusty briar from his overalls, filled it with tobacco from a pouch, struck a match and lit the bowl thoughtfully – all the while giving Cyrus a bit of time to squirm. Finally, he drew in a mouthful of smoke, exhaled it and looked up at the boy, ready for an explanation.

"I know he won't race," Cyrus said. "But he's a fine horse, good lineage. And fast, before . . . well, just before. I think he'd be a good stud horse."

"Stud horse, eh?" Doc answered. "That's an interesting thought. You have any particular brides in mind?"

"You have a couple of good mares out in the paddock, seem to be the right age. There's got to be others around here too. We can breed our own, or we can offer his services for a fee."

"'We' can, huh?" The old man peered over the top of his glasses. "Did I take on a partner and not know it?"

"That's what I been thinking about. I could run the servicing, take care of Lucky, plus me and Morgan will do whatever other work you can give us. In exchange, you put up room and board for us and feed for the horse. We split any profits."

"Fifty-fifty I assume?"

Cyrus paused. "Whatever you think is fair. I also want to sell our truck and trailer rig. The truck ain't much, but the trailer is a Westphalian. Cost a lot of money new. I could offer that as my part of the startup costs."

Doc hid a smile. He was amused by the young man's brass, but not surprised.

"You have a pair on you, I'll give you that," he said, inhaling a taste of pipe smoke again. "But you handle yourself pretty good for a young fella. And you sure as hell know your way around horses. So happens I'm in need of a trainer."

Cyrus couldn't hide his excitement. "A trainer? Really?"

"I expect you'd do a fine job. After the other Slim took off, I been one hand short. The job comes with room and board and pocket money at the end of the month. Course, come September we'd have to work around your school schedule."

"School?" Cyrus protested. "I'm finished with school."

"Maybe you are, maybe you aren't. But your brother certainly isn't. Seems like a pretty bright lad."

"He is," Cyrus admitted. "He was always better at book learning than me." He thought for a minute and said, "I guess we could make that work."

Fireworks

"Good," said the old man. "I'll give some thought to the rest of your proposal. In the meantime, you and your brother are welcome to stay. Long as you stay on your good behavior."

"We will," Cyrus assured him. The old man nodded and stuck out his hand to shake. Cyrus looked at the outstretched hand for a minute, then shook it. Doc clenched the pipe between his teeth and walked out of the stable.

Cyrus stood there a minute, unsure how to process what had just happened. He had half expected the old man to call the sheriff on them as a pair of horse thieves, maybe even murderers. Instead, he offered them a job, shelter, and maybe, just maybe, a future training horses. Cyrus's stroked the side of Lucky's sleek head and smiled.

"You here that, Lucky boy? Looks like we got a place to stay." The horse shook his mane as if in approval. Cyrus patted his neck and turned to go. "I better go tell Morgan."

Just then he heard a noise from the tack room, like someone may have knocked over some tools. He looked up. Kat stepped meekly out of the shadows. Cyrus frowned at her.

"Looks like we got us a barn cat roaming around," he said to her. Kat shrugged.

"I didn't mean to eavesdrop," she said.

"Bullshit."

"All right, maybe I did. Anyway," she added shyly, "I'm glad you're staying."

Cyrus appraised her a moment. Then he said quietly, "Yeah, me too." He started toward the barn door. Without looking back at her he added, "You coming?" She followed him out into the yard, neither of them realizing that the course of their lives had just been set.

Chapter 6

G.B.A.

THE CAINE BROTHERS TOOK UP RESIDENCE at Harmony Farm from the moment they arrived that steamy day in July 1933. Once Doc Reese had taken their measure and kept them under observation for a while, he realized he was getting a couple of good hands who didn't cost much, since they seemed not to have anyplace they needed to go or anyone who needed them urgently. The Depression was biting hard, and it was not that uncommon to find children forced to survive on their own. The younger brother, Morgan, was a cheerful and hard-working lad with a ready smile and a quick wit. Best of all, he seemed to have taken a shine to their granddaughter Kat and made a pleasant companion for her. Doc felt sorry for Kat sometimes; she had no parents, no siblings, stuck out there in the country with a couple of old people and some field hands. It was nice having some fresh young blood on the property.

Then there was Cyrus. He was a brooding sort of fellow, but by god he knew horses. Doc watched as the teenager quietly assumed the lead role in training the new horses at Harmony while the experienced hands like Slim and Pasquale came to defer to him. They didn't seem to resent the young man because, simply, he was a better horse handler than they were. Every morning Doc would come out to the main paddock and watch Cyrus putting one of the horses through their paces. He stood in the center like a ringmaster, sometimes holding a long lead and trotting them around the circumference of the field, sometimes unsnapping the lead and commanding them by voice and with his hands.

"Like being at the circus," Doc murmured more than once as he watched the boy take an unbroken animal and bend them to his will.

Doc wished he had that same ability to bend Cyrus. It was clear from the first day that Cyrus wasn't one to break. He knew his own mind, he stuck to it, and he had the physical strength to impose his will on others when he needed to. Doc had noticed that the boy was very careful with his weight when he first arrived; probably a habit from his days as a jockey, Doc guessed, although neither of the boys talked much about their past. The way Cyrus sat a horse, especially after their stallion Lucky had recovered enough to bear the weight of a rider, suggested that he knew how to ride competitively. When Cyrus would mount Lucky the horse seemed to perk up, as if it were about to be led into the starting gate. It would take all of Cyrus's considerable skill to get him to relax into a gentle canter.

In time Cyrus developed a heartier appetite, and as he did he started to add weight and muscle to his wiry frame. He shot up three inches by the end of the summer. His shoulders grew broad from working the horses, and his powerful arms were even stronger. Doc knew he would have to keep an eye on a boy that hard, physically and temperamentally. He could also tell from the way his granddaughter sometimes stared at Cyrus with a moony gaze that he would bear watching.

In September it came time for school. Doc drove the three youngsters into town in his truck. The Croydon Public School was a single square red-brick building that held all 12 grades and about 200 students. Cyrus took one look and wanted to jump out of the moving truck.

"Do we really have to do this?" he complained to Doc. "I have a lot of work back at the stables. How is this going to help me?" Doc pulled the truck to a stop in the parking lot. There was only one other car there, a well-worn Model A.

"Go," Doc commanded. Cyrus glared but swung the door open. The four of them walked into the building, and Doc herded them through the linoleum-covered corridors. Kat skipped ahead, thrilled to be back in her old school. Soon they reached the principal's office. It was a place Cyrus would come to know well in a very short time.

The principal, Walter Frazier, was a nervous-looking man in a tweed vest and bow tie. He was standing in his office, pulling on a pipe and flipping through a sheath of papers. He looked up when Doc walked in and smiled in greeting. Then he saw the two boys Doc had in tow and frowned at them as if they were urchins from a Dickens novel.

"Doc, good to see you," the principal said. Doc was one of the town's leading citizens. Mr. Frazier gazed down over his glasses at the two boys. "What have we here?"

"Walter," Doc began, nudging the boys forward, "I want you to meet my new wards. This is Morgan and Cyrus Caine." Morgan stepped forward and offered his hand to the principal to shake. The man looked at it like it might be a loaded gun, then shook it reluctantly. Cyrus hung back, a sullen look on his face, offering nothing.

"Nice to meet you, boys," Mr. Frazier said.

"I'm thinking they need to get enrolled in school," Doc said, cutting to the chase. The principal's eyebrows shot up, as if this were some extraordinary situation.

"Really? Well, now . . . The term is just about to start, it's pretty late in the …"

Doc held up his hand. That was all he needed to do to signal the principal to cut the nonsense.

"But of course we can always make accommodations if we need to. Tell me, boys, what grades were you in at your last school?"

Cyrus and Morgan exchanged glances. Schooling had been a hit-or-miss kind of thing, traveling the racing circuit.

"We moved around a lot," Cyrus answered. "We went wherever they put us."

G.B.A.

"I see," said the principal, regarding the boys with something between suspicion and disapproval. He said to Morgan, "You look to me to be about Katherine Reese's age, young fellow. Maybe we'll start you out in the fifth-grade class with her and see how it goes."

Morgan seemed delighted at the prospect of being in Kat's class. She was standing in the doorway behind them, listening in as usual. Morgan looked back at her, and she nodded affirmatively. He smiled.

"That'd be great," the younger boy said. Mr. Frazier looked Cyrus over, like a piece of furniture he wasn't sure he wanted to buy.

"As for you, young man, maybe we'll do some testing with you, see if you're ready for the upper school. You're certainly tall enough."

"Whatever," Cyrus replied. The principal raised his thick eyebrows at the young man's curt response. But then, he was used to teenage moods.

"Come see me first thing tomorrow morning, and we'll do an evaluation. It won't hurt a bit, I promise." He smiled at his own witticism. Doc nodded to him.

"Obliged, Walt," he said. "I'll have him here in the morning."

After Labor Day the brothers joined Kat Reese as students at Croydon Public School. Cyrus was placed in the upper school, so he and Morgan didn't see much of each other during the school day. Morgan didn't mind though; he had been placed in Kat's class. She sat toward the front of the room where she seemed to always be waving to get their teacher, Mrs. Boesch's, attention. Morgan sat two rows behind and was pleased with the view. He loved watching the way Kat's hand shot up whenever Mrs. Boesch asked a question, her red hair bouncing on her shoulders. Morgan wasn't so distracted that he couldn't do the work; in fact, schoolwork came easily to him. Too easily it seemed. A month after the term had started Mr. Frazier appeared and summoned him out into the hallway. Morgan exchanged looks with Kat, wondering what he might have done wrong. He thought about making a run for it. Instead, he listened as the principal said,

"I've been talking to your teacher, Mrs. Boesch. She says you're doing very well."

"Thanks," the boy replied, wondering why the principal would come by to tell him that.

"In fact," Mr. Frazier continued, "we think you may not be challenged enough in this class. We've decided to move you up to sixth grade."

Morgan's face fell. "I'm not all that smart," he protested. "I'm just good at tests." The thought of not being in Kat's class anymore upset him more than he knew or understood. The principal was unsympathetic. He placed a hand on the boy's shoulder, turned him around and pointed him to the sixth-grade room down the hall. As he walked away Morgan looked through the glass of the fifth-grade classroom door. He saw Kat peering back at him through the glass, wondering what was going on. He gave her a weak smile and a wave and marched off to meet his fate.

Cyrus was having a very different kind of academic experience. He sat in the back of the classroom, bored and indifferent, as far from the blackboard as he could possibly get. His grades reflected it. He was sharp with numbers and had a quick tongue but no interest in formal studies.

One day in October Doc Reese got a call from the school and a request to come down to the principal's office at his earliest convenience. Doc put his work aside with a mutter, climbed in his truck and drove to town.

When he reached the principal's office he saw Cyrus slumped on a bench out in the hallway. He raised his eyebrows and started to ask for an explanation, but Cyrus just glared back at him with those black eyes. There seemed to be a bruise developing on the side of his face, and he turned away so the old man couldn't see it. Mr. Frazier opened the office door and ushered the older man inside. The principal was dabbing his forehead with a handkerchief that seemed rather damp already.

G.B.A.

"Thanks for coming in, Doc," the principal began.

"What's the matter, Walt? You look like you've been sucking on a lemon," Doc said irritably. The principal dabbed his forehead again.

"There's been some trouble with Cyrus," he began. Doc reached into his overalls and produced his pipe.

"What sort of trouble?"

"Well, if you've been reading the notes I've sent home, Cyrus appears to have what we call G.B.A. – general bad attitude."

"Notes? I haven't seen any notes. Anyway, he's kind of a restless sort. Has a lot on his mind."

"Yes, well today it all came to a head. He got into a fight."

"You called me down here in the middle of the day for that?" Doc protested. "Boys his age fight all the time. Lets 'em work off the hormones."

"This is no small thing, Doc. The other two boys were hurt pretty badly."

"Two boys? That sounds like a problem right there. Who were these other hoodlums?"

"Robbie Randall was one of them."

"No surprise there," Doc said, remembering the blond teenager from the 4th of July at the fairgrounds.

"Cyrus broke his nose," the principal explained. Doc frowned.

"Well, that's not good. But it could have been worse."

"It was," the principal said ominously. "Brad Henshaw also got into it."

"Brad the wrestling captain Brad? That boy's built like a brick outhouse."

"Brad got behind him, put him in some kind of choke hold. That's when Cyrus pulled a knife."

Now he had Doc's full attention. "Go on," he said to the principal.

"Sliced his arm pretty bad. Lots of blood everywhere. He'll be out the rest of the season."

Doc rubbed his chin. "Don't get me wrong, Walt. I don't condone fighting. But those two fellas are older and must have 20 pounds apiece on Cyrus. Can't blame him for fighting back."

"No, no," the principal said, but he still looked squeamish. "But I can't condone carrying a weapon on school property."

"No," Doc said slowly. "I suppose not. Anyone else see this little set-to?"

"Nobody's saying. It all happened pretty fast. But Doc, pulling a knife . . . . Who knows what could happen the next time?" He pushed his glasses up on his nose. "How much do you know about this boy?"

"Not a whole lot," Doc admitted. "All I know is, he's a hard worker. Takes good care of his brother." A thought occurred to him. "Was his brother there? Was Cyrus defending him?"

"No," Walt replied. "He was defending Kat." The principal tugged at his collar, which suddenly seemed a little snug. "Apparently the boys were . . . I'm not sure what they were doing exactly. Cyrus told them to knock it off, and that's when the fight broke out."

Doc nodded. "What do you intend to do now, Walt? Are you going to punish those two?"

"I think they've had their punishment," the principal said. "As for Cyrus, well…." He took a breath and looked up at Doc sheepishly. "I'm afraid I have no choice but to expel him."

"Don't you think that's kind of harsh? Sounds like he was sticking up for a younger person." He looked at the principal evenly. "A member of my family."

"I know that, Doc. But carrying a weapon on school property, well, that's no small offense. I've already heard from Brad's parents. They mentioned getting the police involved."

Doc cocked an eyebrow. "The police, huh? No cause for that, I'd say." Doc rubbed his chin and took a draw on his pipe. "What about Morgan? Do I have to pull him out too?"

"Oh no," said the principal. "Morgan is doing fine. Bright boy, seems to get along with everyone. He's settled in nicely."

Walter sampled his own pipe. "You know, maybe the best thing to do is give these boys a little space from each other. You could be doing them a favor."

Doc wasn't so sure. He studied the tops of his work boots for a moment, then said, "All right if I take Cyrus home?"

The principal nodded in relief. Doc shook his head and left the office without another word. In the hallway he stopped and looked at Cyrus, still slumped on the oak bench. Neither of them spoke for a moment. Finally Doc said, "Come on. There's work to do at the farm."

At fourteen, Cyrus Caine's academic career was over.

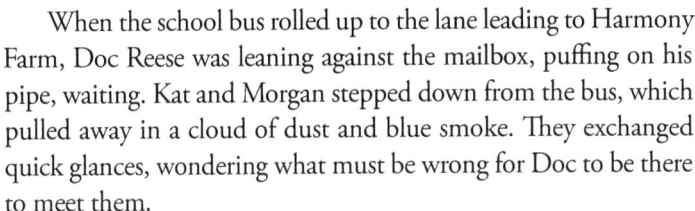

When the school bus rolled up to the lane leading to Harmony Farm, Doc Reese was leaning against the mailbox, puffing on his pipe, waiting. Kat and Morgan stepped down from the bus, which pulled away in a cloud of dust and blue smoke. They exchanged quick glances, wondering what must be wrong for Doc to be there to meet them.

"Morgan, why don't you go on ahead and get busy with the horses?" Doc said without preamble. "I want to talk to my granddaughter."

"Okay, sure, Doc," Morgan replied amiably. But his parting look to Kat was concerned. When he was out of sight, the old man turned toward the house and motioned for Kat to walk beside him.

"Heard there was a little trouble at school," the grandfather said finally. He didn't look at Kat, but he could tell her neck had reddened where usually it was a pale white.

"I suppose everybody's heard about it by now," she replied.

"Want to tell me what happened?"

"It was all so stupid. Robbie and Brad were just being their usual jerky selves. Then they got into it with Cyrus, and before I knew it both of them were on the ground. Robbie was bleeding from his nose. And Brad…" She paused.

"…And Brad?" her grandfather continued.

"He was screaming like a baby." She dropped her eyes, studying the gravel road at her feet. "I guess Cyrus hurt him pretty bad."

The old man nodded slowly. "Did he pull a knife?"

Kat didn't answer. She felt like she'd said too much already. When Doc saw he wasn't going to get a straight answer he took another tack.

"What started this all anyway?"

Kat hesitated. Finally she said, "They pushed me."

"Pushed you?"

"Well, not really pushed me. They were . . .I don't know. Touching me. They pinned me up against a locker. Cyrus saw them and told them to cut it out."

"And they didn't."

"No." She looked up at her grandfather. "I heard Cyrus got in trouble."

"They kicked him out."

Kat let out a little moan. "That's not right. He didn't do anything wrong. He was trying to . . ." She searched for her next word. "He was trying to protect me." The girl placed her pale hand in her grandfather's large rough mitt. "You're not mad at him, are you? I hate to see him get in trouble."

The old man stopped and turned to her. He pulled a worn kidskin pouch from his overalls pocket, tamped some more tobacco in the briar pipe and lit it. Kat knew this motion well. It always meant he was considering his answer. Finally, he spoke.

"I don't hold it against Cyrus for trying to do the right thing," he said. "In fact, I'm obliged to him for looking out after somebody I love." He looked closely at the girl. "But you need to understand: boys like Cyrus, well, trouble looks for them, even if they're not looking for it. You need to be careful around him."

"But he was on my side."

"I know. But you still need to be careful. He's like a wild horse. Not easy to tame. And if you don't approach him just right he's likely to kick you in the head."

"I'm not worried about that," the girl said confidently.

"I'm sure you're not. That's why I'm telling you: Watch out."

They resumed their walk up the lane. At last Kat said, "You are going to let him stay, aren't you? Both of them, I mean."

A wreath of smoke drifted from the old man's mouth. "They can stay. But I'm keeping Cyrus here on the farm. Maybe he can work out some of that anger he's got. And I can keep an eye on him."

Kat rose up on her toes and kissed the old man's cheek. "Thank you, Grandpa." She turned with a flip of her red hair and ran up the porch steps into the house. Doc watched after her, puffing thoughtfully on his pipe, contemplating whether he was making the right choice.

That day began the next phase – what he would come to think of years later as the happiest phase – of Cyrus's life. First, though, he knew he would have to get through the inevitable hard talk with Doc Reese.

The old man sat him down after supper. They were in Doc's office off the main stable. The old man sat at his rolltop desk, with Cyrus seated on a straight back chair next to the oaken desk. Cyrus tried to listen while the old man went on about the dangers of starting fights – "Particularly when the odds are two to one." Cyrus nodded his head at what seemed like appropriate moments, waiting to see when the ax would fall. Except it didn't. Cyrus had no experience with fatherly talks; his own father had done most of his talking with the back of his hand or a leather strap, usually after a pint or two of rye. Cyrus was remembering those times when he realized that Doc had stopped talking. The boy looked up at him, his eyes unfocused.

"I'm sorry, what?"

"The knife," Doc repeated and held out his hand.

Cyrus looked at the hand for a moment, then into Doc's warm but unyielding eyes. Reluctantly, Cyrus reached into his boot produced the skene. He hefted it in his hand but didn't release it.

"I need this for work," he said. Doc was unmoved, and so was the hand.

"My father gave me this knife," Cyrus said. *Blade first*, he added in his head.

"You cut that boy pretty bad today. He'll be lucky if he gets to wrestle at all this year."

"He's lucky I didn't cut his balls off."

The old man studied him a moment. "A weapon is only as dangerous as the man who holds it. Learn to harness that temper of yours and maybe you won't need one as much. In the meantime, I can't have you carrying it around town."

Cyrus hesitated a moment, then rested the knife handle first in Doc's hand, as if he were parting with an old friend. The older man nodded in satisfaction. He put it in the bottom drawer of the desk, then produced a ring of keys. He locked the drawer, then patted it. "It will be right here, nice and safe."

The next morning, as Morgan and Kat hurried up the lane to catch the school bus, they saw that Cyrus was already out in the main paddock working one of the horses. Unlike other mornings, when he had approached the day with a black look and a lot of grumbling, Cyrus seemed to be in his element, his shoulders square, his curly black hair catching the wind, his strong hands guiding the animal before him. This was the work he was meant to do, the way he wanted to spend his life. The boy and girl waved to him, but he wasn't looking. He had work to do.

Cyrus's first order of business was starting the stud service he had discussed with Doc weeks ago. Lucky Day was much stronger now. The foreleg had healed well, although once Cyrus saddled him and took him for a gentle canter he knew Doc was right: the horse would not race again. Chances were he'd never be able to breed racehorses either – too many questions, too much documentation. Still, the stallion had a lot to recommend him: a handsome head, good size and strong bones, athletic – he might be perfect for siring show hunters and jumpers. What the horse needed first was a new identity – just like Cyrus himself, he mused.

Cyrus had noticed that Kat had a fine hand. Her penmanship was excellent, unlike Cyrus's, which tended to look like a spidery scrawl. Late one afternoon, when Doc wasn't around and Morgan was busy feeding the horses, Kat was currying her pony when she heard Cyrus call to her.

"Barn Cat, come here. I need a favor," he said. Kat followed his voice to her grandfather's office. Cyrus was standing at the desk, bent over some papers.

"What do you need?"

Cyrus waved a hand over the papers in front of him. "I messed up," he confessed. Kat was surprised. It wasn't like Cyrus to admit error ever in her experience. "When I was registering my horse they accidentally wrote down the wrong name."

"Really? Let me see." She studied the paper on top and found the line where the name had been written in. "'Lucky Day,'" she read. "Isn't that your horse's name?"

"No. It was supposed to be 'Lucky Daylights.' The idiot at the Jockey Club got it wrong. I didn't notice until I left the registration office. Then it was too late."

"What do you want me to do about it?"

"You've got good handwriting. Fill in the rest of the name."

Kat considered this a moment. Something didn't feel right. But if she was just correcting the name, what could be the harm in that? She picked up the fountain pen that lay on the blotter and made a couple of preliminary sweeps on a piece of scratch paper.

"Hand it over," she said. Her pink tongue stuck out of the corner of her mouth as she concentrated on getting the writing to match. After a few painstaking minutes she lifted her pen, blew on the ink to dry it, and held it up to Cyrus. "How's that?"

Cyrus admired her work and smiled. "Thanks, Barn Cat," he said. He added quietly, "Don't tell anybody." Then he winked at her. She waived him off impatiently, but inside she felt a little thrill she couldn't explain. To be in Cyrus's confidence, to see him smile at her – those were rare things. And exciting in a strange way.

Under Cyrus's management, Lucky Daylights became one of the most popular stud horses in Croydon County. They started with two mares Doc had bought at a distress sale the year before. Doc took a close interest in the horses as they came to foal, measuring their girth, checking their feed, keeping them in good shape. But Cyrus was way ahead of him on the care of the animals, assisted by Morgan. When it came time to foal, Doc let Cyrus do the honors while he, Morgan and Kat all huddled around like expectant parents.

The colt was beautiful. Doc could see as the young animal stood up on its wobbly legs and took its first steps in the barn that it was going to be a fine horse, perhaps a valuable one. He had Lucky's smooth sable brown coat, and a white blaze on its forehead inherited from the dam. Cyrus was eager to sell the colt as soon as he could to start making the operation pay off, but Doc deterred him.

"You need to advertise. Let people see what old Lucky can produce." Cyrus demurred, and the new colt, named Blazing Daylights, or Blaze, by Kat and Morgan, became a walking billboard for Cyrus's nascent stud service.

As it turned out, the best advertising Cyrus could ask for was Doc Reese himself. Every Saturday morning Doc took himself to town and had breakfast with a circle of good old boys at Mary Ida's Café. The group was known to the locals as the BBIT Club, short for 'Best Breakfast in Town,' the sign in Mary Ida's front window. No one could remember who originally came up with the name, but it stuck. Some of the founding members had retired to town when they got too old to work their farms, and the group gradually expanded over the years. Doc was one of the younger members. While they looked like just a bunch of aging coots, the BBIT Club represented some of the shrewdest and most successful men in the county.

"Honestly," Maggie would say as he headed out the door on Saturday morning. "It's not like I won't make you breakfast here at home."

"Not the same," Doc would reply.

"That bunch of yours sits around and gossips like a bunch of old hens in a sewing circle." At this Doc would quietly pick up his straw hat from the rack, tip it to Maggie and head to his truck.

The regulars all greeted Doc as he walked in the door. It always took a few minutes to get to his usual table in the back. He'd have to work his way down the counter, talking with this neighbor, joshing with another, asking about their families. When he finally sat down Mary Ida would have a cup of coffee waiting at his place – half cream, half coffee, no sugar. Without asking, she would go to the kitchen window and shout out Doc's usual to the cook: "Adam and Eve on a raft – wreck 'em." Minutes later the cook would slide out a plate of eggs scrambled and bacon crisp with a pile of toasted bread – the BBIT special. At the table, the conversation turned immediately to the weather, the price of corn and soybeans, and whatever local gossip the members had picked up in the last 24 hours.

"Hey Doc," one of the old boys said one day, "I saw that new colt of yours out in the paddock yesterday. Fine-looking animal."

"He is that," Doc replied and proceeded to give them all the details about Cyrus's new business. The BBIT Club members were all experts on breeding horses – you just had to ask them. In fact, they were experts on most things to hear them tell it. But they were impressed that Doc had found a young man with such talent and initiative.

"Might be I could use that big stud," his friend replied. "My mare's in season. Just about time to breed her."

"I'll mention it to Cyrus if you like," Doc replied. "We can bring Lucky on by."

"Lucky's the word all right," one of the other boys offered, to the general amusement of the group. "That's a business I wouldn't mind being in."

"Charlie," one of his companions countered, "if you had to live on your stud fees you'd starve to death."

With Doc as matchmaker, Lucky was soon servicing some of the choicest mares in the county. His reputation grew with the quality of his stock. Doc held on to the stud fees for the boys and kept the books for the business; he was a partner in the enterprise, after all. Morgan was doing well at school, and according to Walt Frazier might even be college material, so building a nest egg seemed like the sensible thing.

While the money was good and Cyrus was building a solid reputation among the horse owners in the area, he had other business ideas that he thought might have even more promise. The Depression was still being felt by most people in the country, and some of the farms and other businesses in Croydon had gone bust. But Cyrus noticed that some people were recovering faster than others financially. Monied people from downtown Chicago were taking notice of the lush landscapes and depressed prices in Croydon County, which was an easy drive from the city. Weekend estates and "farmettes" were springing up at such a rapid rate that the county board decided they needed to put some restrictions in place. Now you needed a minimum of five acres for any residence in Croydon township. The new buyers didn't seem to mind; they had come out to the country for the space and to get away from the grit of the city. The lot requirements also made Croydon just that much more exclusive. Some of Chicago's well-heeled businessmen sent their families out to the country home for the summer while they continued their pursuits (often of their secretaries) in town free of supervision.

That summer, Cyrus proposed that Harmony Farm offer horse boarding services and a riding program to the daughters of these wealthy and leisured families. He started with the Pony League for children aged 8 to 12. Nearly all the regulars were girls. Kat was a little miffed when Cyrus drafted her pony Calico into the operation, but she was pleased to have other girls to hang around with over the summer break, and she quickly became a part of the team, sharing her expertise and giving the other girls tips. Cyrus drafted his younger brother to help him build an arena and to serve as one of the instructors. The girls were thrilled to have these two good-looking boys as their riding coaches, and Cyrus especially played to this new and susceptible audience.

"They may be young," he told Morgan about their junior clientele, "but they're going to grow up someday."

"Yeah? And then what?" Morgan replied. Cyrus smiled at him crookedly.

"Then I sell them a better horse."

Next, Cyrus and Morgan got Doc's permission to lay out a bridle path through the Harmony Farm property. The dirt path ran along the edge of the paddock, then meandered into the woods at the north edge of the property, across the lane to the original farm, then back again to an open field for a brisk canter home and return to the stable. Kat was the guinea pig for the new trail, and she couldn't hide her excitement. At Cyrus's suggestion, she had graduated to a standard-size horse, a thoroughbred that Doc took in trade for some of Lucky's amorous services. She named her chestnut mare Summer Breeze – Summer for short. Kat's biggest thrill was when the two Caine brothers would mount their own horses and the three of them would go riding at dusk. There was no greater delight than feeling the wind in her hair and the powerful animal surging beneath her as the three of them raced back to the stable before supper. Cyrus was the best rider of the three, and Kat 's heart leapt in her chest the first time she beat him in a race. The riding was exciting, and as she grew more mature, the company of the two Caine boys was pleasing as well.

Kat wasn't the only one who thought so. Her friend Nancy Randall spent more and more time out at "the barn," as she and her other fashionable friends began to call it. Nancy's father didn't hold a grudge that Cyrus had broken his son's nose. It wouldn't have mattered. Nancy was horse crazy, and whatever Nancy wanted she got. It was just easier to throw money at the situation than to deal with Nancy's moods.

Kat was a little dismayed that Nancy was developing faster than most of the other girls – certainly faster than Kat. At 13, Nancy had almost achieved her adult height of 5 feet 5, but it was her figure that got all the boys' attention. Her breasts seemed to grow over a single summer – one day she was boyishly flat, the next she developed a pleasing fullness complete with cleavage. Her mother bought her a bra because she needed the support. She was stunning in her tailored riding blouses, and the snug fit of her jodhpurs showed the rounded contours of her hips and thighs. She looked womanly and she knew it. Kat remained her friend, even if it was hard standing next to her. Kat felt like a farm hand next to the curvaceous Nancy. As if the long blond hair didn't get attention enough.

One day Nancy was out in the ring getting a jumping lesson from Cyrus. He had set up a line of easy hurdles around the ring, and Nancy was pleased that she hit all her distances and rode each line correctly. She was even more pleased that she had Cyrus's undivided attention as he called commands to her from the center of the ring.

"Heels down. Shoulders back. Eyes up. Give him his head over the fence. Look ahead to the next jump."

The course completed, Nancy circled her horse around and stopped next to Cyrus. She patted her forehead with the back of one hand. With the other she fanned the open collar of her blouse with languid motions.

"That was good," Cyrus said to her. "You're getting better."

"Do you think so?" she said, practically batting her eyelashes at him. "I'm not sure. Buttermilk was thinking about stopping at that last fence." She gave her horse a gentle pat.

Cyrus held the reins to her horse. Nancy slid one leg over the saddle and started to slide down. Cyrus reached out to help her, his large strong hands encircling her slim waist. Nancy took her time dismounting, letting herself enjoy the sensation of her soft trim body sliding along Cyrus's muscular frame. Her feet finally touched the ground, and she looked up at him demurely.

"Of course," Cyrus said, his eyes locked with hers, "you could do a lot better if you had a better horse."

"Do you think so?" she replied. "What do you suggest?"

"It so happens I just saw a horse that would be perfect for you. Good jumper, brave and careful with his feet." He ran his arm across his brow, wiping the sweat away. "I think you two would be perfect together."

"Whatever you think, Cyrus. I'm in your hands," she said, smiling suggestively. She still had not moved away from him. "I'll talk to Daddy about it tonight."

The next day, Doc was down at the ring doing some work with Slim and Pasquale. Cyrus emerged from the barn leading a gray warmblood. The horse had recently been groomed, and someone had thought to tie small blue ribbons in its mane.

"What's this?" Doc asked as Cyrus passed by.

"New horse for Nancy Randall," Cyrus answered.

Doc's eyebrows lifted in surprise. He happened to know the provenance of this horse. Although its health was reasonably sound, the horse was older than it looked. It was a decent jumper, but in a year or two its legs would likely give out.

"You really think this is the horse for her?" Doc asked him.

"What does she know?" Cyrus answered. "She buys horses for the color."

"How much?"

"A thousand."

Nancy and her mother pulled up in the family's Lincoln and the two women got out. The daughter was a junior version of her mother: blond, shiny and expensive. Mrs. Randall waved to Cyrus. Nancy caught sight of the new mount and her hand went to her heart. She let out a squeal of approval and ran toward the horse. As she did, Cyrus glanced over at Doc and raised an eyebrow as if to say, 'What did I tell you?'

While the girl fussed over her new plaything and Mrs. Randall rummaged through her purse for the check her husband had written, Doc walked back to his hands, shaking his head slightly.

"That boy's a magician," he said, once the three of them were out of earshot. "He can take a hundred-dollar horse and turn him into a thousand-dollar profit." The hired hands nodded their heads. They had seen this drama play out many times since Cyrus started taking charge of the riding academy. Even after a year or two, when the horse he had sold the girls gave out or developed health problems, Cyrus was there to help them with a pharmacopeia of expensive balms and tonics from his magic bag to treat their lameness, their digestive systems or whatever. If that didn't work, there was always the ultimate solution: a new horse. The system worked brilliantly for everyone, but especially for Cyrus Caine.

He had found his calling.

Chapter 7

Live Cover
Harmony Stables 1938

KAT REESE WALKED HER HORSE into the arena. This was her newest thoroughbred mare and her new favorite, Pego – short for Peg o' My Heart, from the two unusual little heart-shaped marks on the horse's forehead. Kat's best friend Nancy Randall walked her latest horse Silverblade alongside her. Both horses were saddled and ready for the day's lesson. Kat was careful to close the gate behind them when both horses had cleared it. This was the third horse Cyrus Caine had sold Nancy's father in the last four years – each one more expensive, each one guaranteed to make her an even better rider. The horses did seem to perform better, or perhaps at 15 Nancy was getting to be a more skilled horsewoman. She should be, Kat thought to herself. She practically lives here during the summer. Kat also knew that horses weren't the only reason Nancy spent so much "barn time," as she liked to call it.

Kat glanced over to the end of the arena, where Cyrus was unloading bales of hay from the back of a truck. His shirt was off, and his broad shoulders and powerful chest glistened with sweat. "Perspiration," she could hear her grandmother correcting her. In the years since they had come to Harmony Farm, both brothers had grown tall and strong. But Cyrus, nearly 19, was a full-grown man, over six feet tall, lean and muscular. Sometimes Kat caught herself staring at him while he was working out in the paddock, fixated by the ridged muscles across his stomach, his powerful forearms grown stronger from working the horses all day. She blushed thinking about it. Morgan was very good-looking too, but in a different way. She and Morgan were about the same age – 15, although he was a few months older and a full year ahead of her in school. His straight brown hair tended to flop over his forehead, unlike Cyrus's tight black curls. His eyes were a bright and welcoming blue and had little lines at the edges from his tendency to smile easily and often. Morgan was sweet and attentive toward her – the very opposite of his brother. Cyrus was sardonic and tended to torment her, when he bothered to pay any attention to her at all. Cyrus was dangerously handsome, she decided. Most of the girls at the stable agreed.

Kat woke from her reverie when she realized Nancy was looking at her, watching her watching Cyrus. There was an amused smile on Nancy's bright red lips.

"I don't know how you do it."

"Do what?" Kat asked her.

"Live on a farm with two handsome studs so close. It's like living in a candy store."

Nancy had matured seemingly faster than any of the other girls at Croydon. This summer she had really "blossomed," as Grandmother Reese discreetly put it. Blossomed indeed. Kat couldn't help but notice the full round breasts beneath Nancy's starched riding blouse – and neither could any of the boys at school. The jodhpur pants she wore to the stable every day fit tightly at her slim waist and highlighted the womanly curves of her hips. She had a firm round behind that looked wonderful walking away or sitting a saddle. Her makeup was always perfect, even when she had been riding all afternoon, and her honey blonde hair made her look a little like Carole Lombard, the film star.

Kat glanced down at her own developing shape and winced at the comparison. Kat had shot up in height since last year – she was nearly 5 feet 7, one of the tallest girls in her class – but the rest of her body seemed slow to follow. She was still very trim, almost boyish (riding horseback every day of her life contributed to that, she supposed), and though her breasts had started to fill out they were smaller than Nancy's by an order of magnitude. Kat had a slim athletic build that was meant for the outdoors. Sometimes Nancy teased her and called her Jordan Baker, from the Fitzgerald novel they had read in English class the year before. Kat didn't really care what she looked like; she was fit and healthy, and that was enough for her, having lost both her parents so young. But she realized with a sigh that boys like Cyrus — probably Morgan too, if he were honest — were attracted to more obvious types like Nancy.

Cyrus happened by at that moment.

"Afternoon, ladies," Cyrus greeted them. "Mind if I get through here?" Kat thought, Even when he's being friendly he sounded like he's mocking us. Nancy didn't seem to mind.

"Hey, Cyrus," she purred at him. "Are you giving us our jumping lesson today?" How did Nancy make everything sound like a double entendre? Cyrus shook his head.

"No time today. I've got real work to do."

"Too bad," said Nancy. "Maybe some other time?"

Cyrus didn't reply, but Kat noticed how he brushed the back of Nancy's blouse as he passed her. Kat could almost feel the shiver of excitement that ran up her friend's spine. Nancy's gaze followed Cyrus unabashedly.

"I would be in so much trouble," she said, admiring his walk. "But it would be so worth it."

"Put your tongue back in your mouth before you trip on it," Kat told her coolly, but she had to admit to having the same thoughts herself sometimes.

Morgan came into the arena at that moment, leading his horse Blaze. He latched the gate behind him and joined the two girls.

"Ready for a lesson?" Morgan greeted them.

"Ready," Kat replied. Morgan swung into his saddle and reined his horse around.

"OK then. Nancy, how about you go first?" He cantered down to the far end of the arena. Kat admired his perfect posture, the elegant way he rode. Cyrus wasn't a finesse rider. "He could ride a horse through a brick wall," her grandfather had once observed. But Morgan was different. He rode like a gentleman.

"He likes you," Nancy said, nodding in Morgan's direction. Kat cocked an eyebrow in surprise.

"Morgan? No. We're good friends, that's all. We ride together. We go to school together. He's – you know, fun to hang out with."

"I don't think he sees it that way," Nancy replied. She knew about these things. The girls swung up onto their horses and followed Morgan down to the starting position.

Maybe Nancy was right, Kat thought. Morgan was always nice to her. He was sweet and steady and kind, the type of boyfriend girls dreamed about. He had overcome some of his boyhood shyness and now was one of the leaders in his class, a member of the Student Council and a star athlete. The other girls at school seemed to have taken notice of him too. She saw the way they looked at him as he walked down the halls at Croydon Upper School. Many of them had taken up riding lessons at Harmony Stables just to get a chance to be near him.

She had to admit, business at Harmony Stables was thriving since the brothers Caine started running it. They seemed to know the secret ingredient: teenage girls. After a long hard slog through a Depression, the rich were back to their main occupation of getting richer, even if most other people weren't catching up to them. More and more wealthy Chicago residents were buying up land in bucolic ex-urban areas like Croydon, either as country homes or, for some, their primary residences. The new train line into the city made it even easier to commute, so people of means could enjoy the best of both worlds. Cyrus was an expert at tapping into the needs and yearnings of horse-crazy young girls like Nancy Randall and persuading their rich daddies to open their wallets. Nancy, Kat suspected, wanted to open more than that when she was around Cyrus. She pushed the image out of her mind and realized Morgan was calling to them.

"Come on, Nancy."

Nancy nodded. Her first instinct was to make sure her riding outfit looked good. She adjusted her helmet, tightened her grip on the reins and cantered forward. The first jump was good – not perfect, but she cleared it easily. The second looked better, and by the third she and Silverblade looked comfortable together.

Nancy finished her round and rode on a little further, to where Cyrus had resumed unloading the truck but took a minute to watch her jumps.

"Nice form," he said to her as she drew close to him. Nancy practically batted her lashes at him.

"You're not so bad yourself," she replied with a smile. Cyrus paused a moment, studying her.

"What are you doing tomorrow morning?"

"Same as every morning. Coming out here."

Cyrus nodded to her. "Come by early. There's something you might like to see."

"I'll be here," she promised.

Cyrus glanced down the arena in Kat's direction and fixed his eyes on her. "Bring your friend too," he added, then turned back to his work.

Kat looked away from her flirtatious friend and concentrated on the hurdles in front of her. She lined Pego up for the approach, leaned over to pat her neck and seemed to whisper something in her ear. Then with a nudge from her heels she set the horse cantering toward the fences at a perfect pace, neither fast nor slow. They cleared the first obstacle with ease and aimed for the second set with a steady stride. Up and over easily, gracefully. Then the third. When she had cleared the last hurdle she heard applause coming from behind her. She turned and saw Morgan astride his stallion Blaze, waving encouragement to her.

"Nice, Kat, good!" he shouted to her. "Keep a straight line from elbow to bit over the jump."

"Why don't you show me?" Kat called back playfully.

Cyrus turned around at that moment, running his arm across his forehead to wipe the sweat away. As Morgan approached the fences, Cyrus held out a hand and waved his brother off.

"Hold up a second," Cyrus called. He marched out to the first fence and raised the pole to the next cup, then took it up another one. He walked down the line and did the same for the second obstacle, then the third. He looked back at his brother and smiled crookedly.

"Let' make this interesting," he said, then stepped back to watch.

Morgan studied the fences. Blaze was a good jumper with plenty of scope, but they had never tried the fences at this height before. "No time like the present," he said, half to himself, half to the horse. He reined Blaze around and gave him a measured jab with his heels.

Blaze cantered forward and took the first fence – just.

"Come on, boy. Settle down," Morgan murmured to him.

They cleared the second hurdle cleanly and charged toward the third. At the last minute Morgan realized they had misjudged the jump, and as horse and rider sailed over the top pole Blaze's rear hooves just grazed it, making it wobble but not knocking it off.

Cyrus, watching the whole display, looked a little disappointed.

"Not bad, little brother," he said. "A little more practice and you might be a horseman." He laughed darkly to himself, turned and walked back toward the truck.

Kat woke up early the next morning and dressed quickly. She threw on a pair of dungarees and a print blouse, her standard uniform on days when she wasn't riding or taking lessons. She ran downstairs and saw that her grandmother was already at the stove. Grandma Reese spooned some oatmeal into a bowl and set in down on the kitchen table at Kat's usual place. Doc had already been up for hours of course, had finished a cup of coffee and gone into town. Kat poured some milk and some maple syrup over the oatmeal, picked up her spoon and started to shovel it into her mouth. Her grandmother looked around with mild disapproval.

"Good morning to you too, Katherine," her grandmother said. "Why the big hurry?"

"Nothing special," Kat replied, once she had swallowed a mouthful of oatmeal. No point in compounding her felony by talking with her mouth full. What she said wasn't true, of course. She thought she knew what the morning's event was going to be, and she was excited. Not enough to talk about with her grandmother though.

The bowl was empty with a few quick shovels full. Kat dabbed the corners of her mouth with her napkin, downed a glass of orange juice her grandmother had set down in front of her, and stood up.

"May I be excused?"

Her grandmother sighed. "Go ahead, whatever's so important…." But Kat was already through the screen door.

Out at the stable, Kat went about her chores with studied impatience, replenishing the hay in each of the stalls, checking to see that the horses had enough feed and the right mix. She could see that Cyrus was already at his work at the far end of the stable, quietly whistling to himself as he curried the coat of a sleek mahogany bay mare. She was a beautiful horse with a reddish brown coat and black points. Cyrus had picked her out personally at an auction the year before.

"I have special plans for this one," he had said after he loaded her into the trailer. When Kat pestered him for specifics, he just smiled at her and said, "You'll see, Barn Cat. Don't be so impatient."

Today was the day. Kat had noticed Cyrus over the course of the last few weeks spending extra time with the mare, taking her temperature, checking her vital signs and then writing things down in a black moleskin notebook he kept in his room.

Now Cyrus slipped a halter over the mare's head and led her down the rows of stalls on a lead rope. Halfway he stopped in front of the stall where Blazing Daylights, Morgan's favorite jumper, was kept. The stallion reared its head and stuck its muzzle out of the jealousy gate, which Cyrus had opened. Blaze nodded his head a few times and edged closer to the door of the stall.

"Morning, Blaze," Cyrus greeted him. "Big day for you today."

Cyrus led the mare forward and stopped when her tail was just inches from Blaze's muzzle. The stallion sniffed her and the mare started to kick, but Cyrus quieted her.

"Now now," he said. "No wedding day jitters."

He turned the mare around and walked her back to Blaze again. The two horses brought their heads and necks toward one another and seemed almost to be hugging, rubbing up against each other.

"That's more like it," Cyrus said. "No need to be unfriendly." The two horses continued to nuzzle each other. Cyrus kept his eyes on them, his hand still on the rope attached to the mare's halter in case she acted up again. Without looking up he said, "Morning, Barn Cat."

Kat realized she had been standing in the center of the aisle, gawping at the horses. She must look like such a ninny.

"Morning," she answered.

"Your friend Nancy here yet?"

"Nancy? No, it's kind of early for her. Why would she be out here now?"

"I invited her," Cyrus said. Kat's brow wrinkled at him but she let it go.

"Where's Morgan?" Kat wanted to know.

"Went to Valparaiso with the old man to pick up that new gelding," Cyrus replied. "Won't be back til tonight."

Live Cover

They heard a car driving up on the gravel outside. Kat knew the sound of Nancy's mother's Lincoln. Even the tires sounded expensive. Kat turned to the door.

"I'll go see if she's here," she said, and walked quickly out of the barn.

Nancy was closing the passenger door of her mother's car and waving her off. Nancy got irritated when her mother lingered at the stable. "It's embarrassing," she explained once. "I don't need you spying on me. I'm not a kid." Now her mother had been trained to just drop her and run.

Nancy waved cheerfully as she saw Kat walking toward her across the yard. Unlike the dungaree-clad Kat, Nancy was in full regalia: starched pleated blouse in the palest shade of pink, tan riding breeches, and a pair of black half-boots that would have taken Kat six months to save for. Nancy seemed to have a different pair for every day.

"Hey Kat," Nancy called to her as they met in the middle of the lane. "Where's that dishy riding instructor you keep out here?"

"Which one do you mean?"

Nancy laughed. "Fair point. I'd take either one of them."

At that moment, Cyrus emerged from the stables leading the mahogany bay alongside him, murmuring to her. Nancy especially admired her.

"Oh, she's beautiful," she sighed. Cyrus gave the girls a wave and turned the mare out into the paddock. He closed the gate and went back into the stable.

"What now?" Nancy wanted to know. "I thought Cyrus had something special to show us."

Kat took her arm and led her to the rail fence. "Best get a seat," she said, hopping up on the top rail. "Show's about to start." Nancy gave her a puzzled look but followed suit. She jabbed her elbow into her friend's ribs.

"Come on, give," she pleaded. "What's on the program?"

Kat looked at her evenly. "Do you know what a live cover is?" Nancy shook her head. Even though there was no one else around,

Kat had a little trouble talking about it out loud. She whispered in her friend's ear. As she did, Nancy's cheeks reddened, and her eyes grew wide with excitement.

A few minutes later Cyrus emerged from the barn again, this time leading the stallion, Blaze. Cyrus escorted him into the paddock and removed the lead from the horse's halter.

"Have fun, sport," he said to the horse. He exited the paddock, closing the gate behind him, then joined the girls at the fence.

"What are we supposed to be looking for?" Nancy asked him.

"Just wait," Cyrus replied. "And watch what happens." The three of them turned toward the paddock to watch the two horses.

The mare was at the far end of the yard, grazing peacefully on a pile of hay. She hardly seemed to notice when Blaze entered the yard. The stallion caught her scent and cantered toward her, but she continued to ignore him. When he had nearly reached her the mare raised her head briefly, whinnied in recognition, acknowledging that they had been nose-to-tail only a short time earlier. Blaze brushed up next to her, nuzzling her until they were only inches apart but facing in opposite directions. The stallion extended his powerful neck, and his muzzle found the underside of the mare's tail. She squealed at him in protest and ran to the other side of the yard.

"What are they doing?" Nancy asked Cyrus. "Dancing?"

"It's called The Tease," Cyrus explained. "He wants to see if she's interested in him."

"Of course she is. Anyone can see that."

"We'll find out," Cyrus murmured, eyes fixed on the ballet going on in the paddock.

The girls were spellbound. At this age, Cyrus knew, girls were happy just watching horses eat grass. He also knew what was coming.

Blaze circled the yard again, and the mare ran in the opposite direction. The stallion stopped, seemed to be listening for something. The mare, curious, ventured closer to him.

Live Cover

"That old boy knows what he's doing," Cyrus explained to the girls. "He's letting her come to him."

"Does that work?" Kat wanted to know.

"Most of the time,' Cyrus answered.

The two horses were nose-to-tail again. The mare started to bolt away, but Blaze had tired of the game. He muzzled the mare beneath her tail with greater insistence, and when she squealed and tried to run again, the stallion cut her off.

Blaze leaped up onto the mare, bared his teeth and clamped down hard on her neck to hold her still. What had begun as a courtship quickly turned violent. The horses circled as one, each jockeying for a position of dominance, but Blaze was clearly in charge now. The mare tried to buck him off, but the stallion's teeth sank deeper into her neck, then his front legs found her back and he mounted her. Now Blaze was behind and on top of her. He lifted his forelegs and tried to settle them on the mare's back. As he did, his penis began to extend itself, growing and growing until it seemed about a yard long.

Nancy put her hands over her eyes, but only for a moment, and let out a squeal.

"Oh my god, would you look at him! He's huge!"

Cyrus shrugged. "I've seen bigger. But it'll do the job."

The girls watched, fascinated, as Blaze mounted the mare. This time she stopped struggling and held still while he thrust his giant member into her, his forelegs firmly in place on her back. He pushed deep into her, held for what seemed like a full minute, and when he was done withdrew himself. As he dropped his forelegs back to the ground he gave the mare a final nuzzle on the flanks–his way of saying thanks – then dropped his head and returned to grazing.

The girls were speechless. To Kat, growing up on a horse farm, this ritual was nothing new. But Nancy had never seen the spectacle close up, and she seemed riveted by it. Her eyes were still fixed on Blaze's organ, which had shrunk back to its normal proportions but was still impressive. Cyrus's eyes burned into the girl, watching how her cheeks flushed and for once she didn't have a wisecrack.

"I've never . . ." Nancy started to say. But she didn't know how to finish the thought.

Cyrus smirked at her. His dark eyes looked straight into hers.

"Maybe you should," he said. Kat shot him a dirty look. She had seen animals mating many times on the farm; it was perfectly natural. Only Cyrus could make it seem dirty.

"Come on," Cyrus said. "Show's over. Let's let these lovebirds have a little privacy."

"Are they going to do it *again*?" Nancy exclaimed in astonishment.

"Oh yeah. They may go at it a few times today. Until the old boy gets wore out."

Nancy looked intrigued by the idea and started to settle in for the second show. But this time her eyes were on Cyrus, who returned her gaze. Kat took her friend by the arm.

"Come on, Nancy. Let's go for a ride. I think you need to cool off." The two of them hopped down from the railing, leaving Cyrus to himself. He drew a pack of cigarettes from his pocket, lit one, and watched as the two horses circled each other once more.

Kat walked Pego back to the stable after a good long ride. She and Nancy had parted when they reached the woods; she had no idea where her friend was now, and didn't really care. The morning's activities had left her disquieted – not because of the sight of the horses coupling, but at Nancy's reaction and Cyrus's wolfish attention toward her. Nancy had been a tease since middle school, and it had only left Kat feeling exasperated, sometimes amused, sometimes annoyed. But one of these days, she thought, Nancy would go a little too far. You couldn't tease someone like Cyrus, who was practically a grown man. And a dangerous man at that.

Live Cover

Kat walked her horse around the yard to let her cool down, then took her into the stable to unsaddle her and brush her down. She led Pego into her usual stall and uncinched the saddle and draped it over the railing. She removed the blanket, picked up her grooming brush and began to stroke the horse's coat methodically. When she was done she fed the horse an extra ration of oats, then she picked up her saddle to take it back to the tack room.

She was a few feet away when she heard noises coming from the room. There was someone in there, or more than one person. Curious, she set the saddle down and approached the door, peering through the opening into the darkened room.

What she saw there shocked her.

Cyrus had Nancy locked in a powerful embrace. Her head was tilted up toward his like an ingenue, blue eyes wide and innocent, her lips moist and welcoming. Cyrus kissed her deeply, his tongue finding hers as he pulled her soft warm body up against his. Nancy locked her arms around his neck and returned his kisses greedily, seemed to be enjoying it at first. She pressed her groin hard against Cyrus, and Kat blushed to notice how hard he became as he returned the pressure. Nancy squirmed a bit, but Cyrus grabbed a handful of her hair and pulled her head back. His rough hands explored her body and finally found her breasts. She tried to guide his hand away, but he wouldn't be refused. Before she knew what was happening his fingers found the buttons of her blouse. He pulled it open, stripped it from her and tossed it to the floor. He found her breasts again, and now she was wrestling and trying to push him away, but it was like pushing a rock. Cyrus had her arms pinned and was reaching around behind her. Then magician that he was, he unhooked her brassiere with one hand and deftly slid it from her shoulders with the other, revealing her soft full breasts. His hands and his mouth found her nipples greedily. She tried to push his head away, her fingers digging into the black curls on top of his head.

"No, Cyrus…" Nancy said. She was naked from the waist up, tried to cover herself with one hand. She turned her head away, but Cyrus continued kissing her. His hands were all over her, squeezing her breasts, finding the pink nipples and devouring them with his tongue. Then his hand slid between her legs.

"Cyrus, I can't do this . . ." Kat heard her say. Now she was hearing something else in Nancy's voice: Fear.

Cyrus's powerful arms enveloped her. "It's a little late for that, don't you think?" he said, and he whirled her around roughly. His hand found the snap of her riding breeches, and with a firm motion he pulled down her pants. Then he slid his hand into her underpants and pulled them down too. Now Nancy was panicked.

"Cyrus no…." she said. But she couldn't stop him. Cyrus undid his silver belt buckle and unzipped his jeans and let them drop to his knees. Kat stared at the hard firm cock as he maneuvered it into place behind Nancy's pale round buttocks. She couldn't help staring. Seeing animals was one thing, but she had never seen a man's erect penis before. She heard her own sharp intake of breath. She knew she should turn away, maybe call for help. But she couldn't move, couldn't look away. She watched as Cyrus reached one arm around Nancy's breasts and lifted her off the ground, while with the other he angled himself upward and bent her over. He thrust himself into her. Kat could hear her cry in pain. Cyrus grabbed her round white buttocks so hard Kat could see the blood rushing to the newly forming welts. He kept thrusting, harder and deeper until he looked like he would tear her in two. Nancy stopped struggling and leaned forward, hot tears rolling down her pale pink cheeks.

Then a strange thing happened. In the midst of penetrating Nancy, Cyrus turned his head to the doorway and his eyes locked on Kat's. He smiled at her and kept on thrusting.

Kat gasped and took a small step back into the shadows, shocked at having been discovered. Cyrus saw her reaction and laughed. Then he turned back to the business at hand, ramming himself into Nancy again and again. He squeezed her buttocks, hard, and with a sudden shiver he froze, took one more deep thrust and held it. After what seemed like an eternity, he released her backside and pulled out of her. Nancy crumpled to the ground, shaking and crying. Cyrus smacked her on the buttocks. It was meant to be playful, Kat thought. But this wasn't play. This was sadistic.

Nancy sagged to the floor sobbing, her clothes in a sorry pile beside her. Cyrus grabbed a rag from the nearby table and threw it to her.

"Here, wipe yourself," he said as he pulled up his jeans, zipped them up and fastened his silver buckle. Nancy was too shocked to speak. She took the rag and wiped her eyes and her nose, then applied the cloth to the sticky dampness between her legs. Kat saw that the rag had blood on it.

"Hurry up. Your mother will be here soon to pick you up."

Cyrus turned toward the door. Kat, who had been frozen motionless, suddenly woke up. She backed away, turned and ran out of the stable, nearly tripping over her discarded saddle.

It was after dark when Morgan arrived home with Doc Reese. Doc was tired after the long drive, so Morgan offered to get the new gelding settled and park the truck. Doc went into the kitchen, where his wife had supper waiting for him.

When he was done bedding down the gelding, Morgan walked around behind the stable to get some feed. He heard a soft whimper coming from behind the building and realized that someone was crying. He peered into the fading light and saw the form of Kat sitting on the ground, her back against the wall, her head and shoulders jiggling up and down. She didn't hear him as he approached her.

"Kat? Are you all right?"

She looked up at him with a start. Even in the dim light, Morgan could see how red her eyes were. She started to say something, but her voice caught.

"Go away, Morgan," she managed finally, waving him away.

"Kat, what is it? What happened?" He knelt down in the grass next to her. He pulled a handkerchief out of his back pocket and held it out to her. She took it, dabbed at her swollen eyes and wiped her dripping nose. "Why don't you tell me what's wrong?" Morgan said.

She blew her nose again and looked hard into Morgan's eyes. They were so soft, so kind, and filled with concern. She said,

"Can you explain to me how you and your brother could be so very different?" Morgan looked at her quizzically.

"Why? Did something happen with Cyrus?" Then there was a note of concern. "Did he hurt you?"

"I'm fine," she insisted. Morgan didn't look convinced. "He's just … I've never known anyone like him. He's so ∴. I mean, he's a brute …."

"He's always been a hard guy," Morgan said evenly. "From the time he was a little kid. I remember hearing my mom one time – I was too young to understand what she was saying, she was talking to some man – there was a time when Cyrus got bitten by a goose."

"A goose? So what?" Kat said, not seeing the point. Morgan paused.

"Cyrus went into the barn, got a hatchet, and killed six geese before my pa came out and stopped him." Morgan shuddered as he related the story. "He was five years old."

Kat's mouth gaped in horror. She thought bitterly, Nancy was lucky Cyrus didn't have a hatchet with him. She shook her head.

"I don't understand it. He's so . . .cruel? Is that the word? Cruel and mean. While you …." She looked into his soft blue eyes. "You're so nice and considerate."

Morgan hesitated a moment. He decided this was the moment to share something he'd never told another soul, and this was the person he wanted to tell.

"Kat, there's something you should know about Cyrus and me. It might explain things a little."

Kat could see that he was trying to build his courage. She touched his arm. "Why? What is it?"

Morgan drew a breath and said, "Cyrus and I aren't really brothers. I mean, not full-blooded brothers. We're half-brothers."

"What does that mean?"

"We had the same mother but different fathers. Our pa used to say, 'Same brood mare, different stallions.'"

"How do you know? I mean, when did you find out?"

"I guess I've always known. Our pa always treated me way different from Cy. He used to call me 'the runt' or 'the monkey' or 'that little bastard.' That was a dead giveaway." He smiled ruefully.

"So who was your father?"

"I don't know. I mean, I don't think I ever met him. He and our ma ran off when I was little. She couldn't take living with Pa anymore I guess." He paused. "He was a lot like Cyrus. Especially when he was drunk, which was most of the time." Morgan sat down next to her and leaned back against the stable wall, stretching his legs out on front of him. "I've seen it the last few years. The older Cyrus gets, the more he's like Pa. Bad tempered, impatient. Mean sometimes. He was always good to me when we were little. We only had each other. But I don't know. Now, even I'm a little bit afraid to be around him."

His hand found Kat's in the closing darkness. She realized she didn't want to draw it away. She held it firmly in her own and closed her other hand over it.

"You don't need to be afraid of him or anyone else," she said quietly.

"Oh, I don't worry for myself. I can handle Cy. But if he ever hurt you . . ."

Kat put a finger up to his lips.

"He won't hurt me. Not now, not ever," she said with quiet firmness. "We won't let him. We'll take care of each other."

They settled back against the wall of the barn, holding hands, staring up as the last rays of the sun vanished, aware that they had made a new alliance, and perhaps something more.

Chapter 8

The Blooding

THE AUTUMN MORNING WAS CRISP AND GOLDEN as Kat looked out her window over the shorn fields. The forest on the far side of the farm was exploding in harvest colors of red and yellow, and in places she could see bare branches already starting to appear. This was her favorite time of year, and this was an exciting day. Today she would be riding in her first fox hunt.

More than a year before Cyrus had had another of his entrepreneurial ideas. Horseback riding was becoming a big sport in Croydon County, and there were enough moneyed people with enough pretensions that Cyrus thought the area was ready for a hunt club. He had seen this idea taking off in neighboring counties, but Croydon had the expansive fields and fences and forests that made it ideal to the new/old sport. There was nothing the exurban gentry enjoyed quite as much as imitating their wealthy English cousins, and Cyrus was there to provide them with the right horses and livery and equipage to give the pageantry full effect. Naturally, Cyrus became the Huntsman of the newly formed Croydon County Hunt Club. Harmony Farm and Stables also took to breeding hounds to add to the festivities. Cyrus could even provide the fox if nature didn't cooperate.

Cyrus refused to let Kat join the hunt at first, even though she was an expert horsewoman, and one of the best jumper riders in Croydon County. He kept telling her she wasn't ready, but Kat wondered if that was the real reason he didn't want her too close to his new enterprise. Since the incident with Nancy Randall, Cyrus had been standoffish, regarding her with a wary eye. Kat gave Cyrus a wide berth as well. She tended to make sure Morgan was around so that she didn't have to deal one-on-one with his elder brother.

Nancy had not come out to the stable the weekend after Cyrus had ravaged her in the tack room. That was Kat's polite word for it. What she had seen through the crack in the door was not some genteel bodice-ripper, and Cyrus was no Heathcliff. What she had seen was an act of violence, not passion. Kat was wise to keep her distance from him.

Three days later, Nancy's mother dropped her off at the barn as usual, lit a quick cigarette and took off in the Lincoln. Nancy walked across the yard stiffly. She nodded to Kat but didn't stop to talk. She walked into the stable and started to ready her horse for a ride. Kat saddled her own mount and waited for her friend outside.

Nancy walked the horse out of the barn and joined Kat. As she swung up into the saddle she winced and seemed to have trouble getting a comfortable seat.

"Are you okay, Nancy?" Kat asked her. "Sure you feel like riding today?"

"I'm okay," Nancy replied. Her face was paler than usual, with blue shadows beneath her eyes from some uncomfortable nights with little sleep. "Maybe a ride is just what I need."

"If you're not feeling well, maybe you should talk to someone," Kat offered.

"No," Nancy shot back quickly, cutting off the conversation. "I'd rather ride." She turned her horse around and with a cluck of her tongue guided her out toward the trail. Kat looked after her for a moment. The conversation was over. She gripped her own reins and followed along at a distance.

Nancy returned to her regular schedule soon after. Kat often observed her returning her horse to the barn when no one else was around, looking around as she went inside. Cyrus would follow her in a few minutes later, flipping his cigarette aside nonchalantly, trying to suppress the wolfish grin on his face. Kat knew what they were doing, but she kept her counsel to herself. Her friendship with Nancy was strained after that, and though she tried to bring up the subject of Cyrus a time or two, Nancy clearly didn't want to have that conversation with her.

Nancy had been one of the first junior riders that Cyrus initiated into his secret club. But Kat knew something that Nancy didn't: the membership was much wider than Nancy could have known. Cyrus made himself available to any number of young girls out at the stable, always careful to make sure they didn't run into each other or have the same schedule for their lessons. In fact, the only teenage girl at Harmony Stables that Cyrus wasn't having relations with was Kat, or so it seemed to her. She was fine with that. The girls certainly seemed willing, most of them anyway. Kat didn't think it was her business how Cyrus spent his time, although the initial scene with Nancy made her wonder just how willing these young girls were. Until one of them complained, it wasn't her business. And the stable was certainly thriving.

Once Cyrus started the Hunt Club, every girl in the county with a horse seemed to want to be a part of it. There was more to it than just the excitement of the hunt: There were the clothes and the pageantry of it, galloping across the open fields in pursuit of the fox, the hounds baying and charging, the horses taking the fences out in the wild rather than in a sterile arena. It was a great event, and Kat had to admit she longed to be a part of it.

Today was the day. Cyrus had finally relented. He said to her offhandedly one day, "All right, Barn Cat. Be ready Sunday morning. You're riding with the hunt."

Her heart almost exploded with excitement. She ran inside right away to have her grandmother help her put her costume together. As usual, Maggie Reese was way ahead of her and had already secured the necessary wardrobe for the event.

Now it hung on the open door of the armoire in Kat's room. Kat slipped the white blouse on, then pulled up the buff breeches.

They fit her perfectly, and as she looked at her reflection in the mirror Kat had to admit that they set off her figure quite well. She would never have the curves that Nancy and some of the other girls had, but she was born to wear riding clothes. She fixed her stock tie carefully, then put on the canary yellow vest. She sat down on her bench at the dressing table and pulled on the new pair of high black riding boots her grandparents had given her for her birthday. She had vowed not to wear them until she could wear them on her first hunt. She stood up and slipped on the black Melton wool riding coat, buttoning it carefully. As a new rider and a female, she was required to wear black; only the Huntmaster and the hunt officials wore the scarlet coat. The other women riders were allowed to sew the hunt colors to the collars of their black coats once they had "earned their colors." Kat carefully tucked her hair up into a bun and added the crowning touch: her black velvet riding cap. She picked up her chamois leather gloves, studied the overall effect in the mirror one last time, nodded in approval and went downstairs.

Kat swung through the front door and came to a halt on the porch. What she saw out in the yard astonished her, although she had seen it before. The scene in front of her looked like an 18th century English tableau: men in scarlet riding habits and white breeches mingled with friends and other members of the squirarchy of suburban Chicago. Women in black tunics clustered together, smoking and gossiping and assessing one another, whispering about any newcomers, and looking generally like they were posing for *Town & Country*. Kat noticed them turning their gaze toward her and she tilted her head down, trying to become invisible. Boys in green tunics (she recognized some of them from school, hired for the day) circulated among the crowd passing out silver cups with bourbon and warm apple cider (actually silver plate; her grandmother refused to use actual silver on what she called "this crowd"). Men from the stable were bringing the horses forward, ready to be mounted by milord and milady, while the participants enjoyed their "stirrup cups."

The only element that charred the pastoral picture was that Kat knew these people. They weren't English gentry, but the closest the western suburbs could produce. One man she knew was the top plastic surgeon in Chicago with offices on Michigan Avenue. Another man, short, extremely round and red faced, was a banker at the Northern Trust; Kat felt sorry for his horse. Merchants and lawyers and real estate brokers rounded out the Croydon County gentry. Cyrus was standing next to Nancy Randall's father, a tall silver-haired man with a perpetual suntan, who cut quite a figure in his hunt livery. Mr. Randall was Master of Foxhounds ("MFH" for short), in his case a largely ceremonial title granted because Randall money had underwritten most of the expense of getting the hunt club started. He was busy appraising his latest acquisition, an Irish hunter that Cyrus had sold him for ten times what it had cost, while Cyrus nodded earnestly and sold him (again) on the fine features of the horse. Mrs. Randall was on the other side of the yard, looking bored, casting a skeptical eye on her husband and surveying the rest of the men in the pack for likely conquests. She didn't ride herself, but she did enjoy the cocktails at seven o'clock in the morning.

In the center of the tableau was Cyrus Caine. Tall, dark and brutally handsome, Kat had to admit he cut a dashing figure in his scarlet coat and white breeches. His black calfskin boots had a trim of brown leather at the top, signifying him as staff, but he was unquestionably the Hunt Master, the man actually in charge. He moved among the gentry with ease, making a joke to one, complimenting another's horse, nodding to all the men, one eye always open for the women. Nancy Randall hovered in his orbit, and Cyrus seemed to tolerate her presence, but he had business to conduct this morning and shooed Nancy off to tend to her horse. Cyrus's riding cap was in his hand as he circulated among the riders in a custom called "capping," literally collecting money from each of them for the day's ride.

On the other side of the yard she saw Morgan, also in hunting pinks and black boots with russet leather trim, talking to Grady, a local farmer who managed the pack of American foxhounds for the day's event. More than a few Randall dollars had gone into breeding this handsome pack of hounds. Cyrus and Morgan had argued endlessly about which breed of hound they should use, American or English. Finally they had landed on the American Foxhound because they were lighter, taller, and faster than their English cousins and better suited to gallops through the wide-open soybean and hay fields that were the local hunting grounds. The goal of the Caine brothers was to make the Croydon County Hunt the best in the Midwest through attention to details like these.

Morgan was one of the whipper-ins, responsible for the foxhounds. Kat caught her breath when he turned from Grady and looked straight at her, smiled warmly and started walking toward her.

"Ready for the big day?" he called to her when he was within hailing range.

"Ready as I'll ever be," she replied, trying to conceal her nervousness. "You?"

"The hounds do all the work," Morgan grinned. "I just have to make sure they do their job."

Slim was walking out of the barn leading Peg o' My Heart. Kat's face lit up as it always did when she saw her horse – more than for any boy she had ever met or ever would, she thought. She noticed Cyrus stepping away from a circle of laughing men and cutting across the yard to intercept Slim. A quick exchange, then Cyrus took the reins and led the horse to where Kat was standing. He looked her up and down and smiled his sardonic smile.

"Well, Barn Cat. You clean up pretty good. Ready to ride with the grownups?"

"You know I am," she replied. Morgan didn't seem to appreciate his brother's intrusion but didn't say anything.

"Time to head out," Cyrus said, turning to Morgan. "Are the hounds ready?"

"They're ready. I've got the whips assembling the pack."

With mock gallantry, Cyrus stood next to Pego and cupped his hands. "Can I give you a leg up, milady?"

Kat shook her head and fastened her chin strap. "I can do it myself." With one swift and graceful motion she swung herself into the saddle and took the reins.

Cyrus shrugged. He said to his brother, "Keep an eye on the bitch." He looked up at Kat and added, "Take care of the hounds too."

Cyrus turned and walked toward his own mount which Slim was holding for him nearby. Cyrus's horse was a handsome black gelding with a white star named, appropriately, Brutus. The Huntsman swung up into his saddle and donned his black hunt cap. Even Kat had to admit he looked damned handsome at the head of the hunt.

Cyrus's black eyes landed on Kat one last time, and he murmured to her, "Remember, Barn Cat – new riders in the second flight." He smirked and turned his horse away. He spurred Brutus in the flanks and rode out into the field, the other riders falling into formation behind him. Morgan and the other whipper-ins guided the pack of hounds into the lane, and the hound pack took off as the riders got into formation: the MFH and the hunt members up front in their scarlet livery, other riders in black tunics just behind. Kat rode with the newcomers in the second flight, but she didn't care. The hunt was on!

Cyrus and the hunt staff trotted their horses out of the main yard and through the large gate at the end of the lane. The foxhounds ran ahead of them, sniffing and babbling and bumping into one another with excitement, trying to pick up a scent. The sun was up now, and the woods beyond were blazing with the colors of autumn. Kat had never felt so alive.

Ahead of her she could see Morgan on his handsome gelding trotting along beside the hounds, making sure the riders didn't get too close and trample them. He glanced back, caught her eye and winked. Kat had to admit, he looked quite fetching in his scarlet coat. She turned her mind away from those thoughts and forced herself to concentrate on her riding.

She saw Morgan's head turn toward the end of the field at the same moment the hounds at the front of the pack sent up a baleful howl. Morgan sat straight up in his saddle and peered down the field to the path at the far end.

A hunting horn sounded, and Morgan pointed to the left. The riders turned as one to see where he was pointing. From her place at the rear of the parade, Kat caught a distant streak of red sprinting across the bridle path. She heard a murmur among the riders: "There he is! Headed for the woods. I see him!" The fox disappeared into the forest at the end of the field.

Cyrus and the hunt staff were keeping pace behind the hounds, and as they broke into the open field they picked up speed. The hunting horn sounded again, and a shiver of excitement ran through the riders. The hounds were gone away, baying and snuffling as they ran after their quarry.

Kat was too far back to actually see the fox's movements, so she just kept her eyes on Cyrus and followed him. He leaned slightly forward in his saddle as the riders closed on the edge of the forest, made the corner and charged into the woods. Kat knew there was a brush fence just up ahead – she had spent the last two weeks helping Morgan and his crew lay out the course, clearing trails, smoothing out some of the fences and trees to make them easier to jump. She rounded the corner just in time to see Cyrus and his horse clear the first log effortlessly and ride on. Most of the other hunters took the jump, pleased with themselves when they cleared the obstacle. A few, like the fat bank manager, opted to ride around it. The front runners were keeping a steady pace, staying in close formation and cutting the distance between them and their prey. Some of the riders in the second flight started to veer off, either intimidated by the jumps or looking for an easier trail, but most of the riders managed to stay with the Huntsman.

Through the branches of the trees Kat could see a blur of black and scarlet coats, could hear the horses' hooves thumping on the damp ground and the hounds baying at their prey. The foxhounds barged into a grassy clearing and, where they had been gathered in a tight formation before, suddenly started to split and to sniff around in all directions. Cyrus charged into the clearing followed by the other huntsmen and suddenly pulled his horse up short, his hand upraised to the other riders.

"Hold hard," he commanded, looking around at the hounds on the ground below, but they seemed to be checked. "Damn it," Kat could hear him curse to himself. "She's gone to ground."

Morgan leaped from his horse and plunged into the pack of hounds, trying to read their signals. Most of the hounds just seemed confused, as if the fox had vanished into thin air. Morgan could see that his strike hound–usually the first to find a scent — was casting about, trying to pick up the trail again. The other hounds rummaged through the damp leaves of the forest floor, picking up the occasional scent of scat. The riders looked from one to the other, mopping brows, blowing noses, and watching the hunt staff to see what they should do next.

Kat and the other riders had caught up with the field by now. She took in the jumble of hounds and snorting horses and impatient riders milling about in the covert. As she reined in her horse, she caught a flash of red fur and white tail darting under a fence on the other side of the clearing. In her excitement, she blurted out "Tally-ho!" and pointed.

Morgan perked his head up and saw where she was pointing. He turned his strike hound in that direction and sent him off. The other hounds fell in obediently around the leader, and soon they had reclaimed the scent and dashed off after their quarry.

Cyrus shot a black look at Kat. As the junior-most rider on her first hunt, she had no business calling out. He would deal with her later. Now he spun his horse around and led the riders off after the reinvigorated hounds.

Morgan looked up at her as he swung onto his horse and gave her an "OK" sign before he dashed off with the other riders.

The Blooding

Horses and riders came charging out of the forest following behind the hounds. The fox scampering several lengths ahead of the lead dogs. The wily animal came upon a low stone wall that ran along the field and managed to slip through a crack in the masonry.

The hounds scrambled over the wall and carried on as the riders, led by Cyrus, charged over the jump. It was an elegant sight to behold and fun for everyone save perhaps the fox. Hounds and hunters reunited on the other side and continued their hunt.

The fox led them a merry chase for the better part of the morning. As the riders cantered along the edge of the field, littered with flattened corn sheathes from the recent harvest, Cyrus or Morgan could be heard to call, "Headland, please!" reminding the riders to stay to the edges of the field, as much to protect the horses' hooves and legs from the sheathes as to prevent further trampling.

The bright blue sky that had started the morning diminished as a cover of thick clouds rolled in from the west. By midmorning the clouds looked heavy, the riders were looking tired and Cyrus was ready to finish up this little bit of mounted theater. Finally the fox seemed to have outrun its hunters, bolted back into the woods and made a final sprint toward the covert. The hounds coursed after their quarry.

Up ahead Kat could see the exhausted fox dashing into a clearing with the hounds close on its tail. The strike hound surged forward, snapped and caught the fox by its hind leg and locked its jaws.

The terrified fox fought to pull away, tumbled and hit the ground as the rest of the pack clambered into the covert. With nowhere to retreat, the hounds descended on their prey.

A moment later, as the riders cantered into the clearing and circled the animals, they were greeted by the grisly sight of the hounds tearing the fox to pieces. Blood and fur spurted up into the air as the dogs pulled the hapless animal apart. Some of the riders looked away from the gruesome spectacle, and one of the women riders looked like she might faint.

Morgan leaped down from his horse as he waded into the pack of hounds. When they were done worrying the carcass Morgan stepped forward and retrieved the remains.

Cyrus and Mr. Randall pulled up together and dismounted. The other riders circled around, wondering what to do next. Cyrus stepped forward and looked down at the mutilated carcass, a thin smile of satisfaction on his face.

"A good run," he said to the approving murmurs of the group. The fat banker said, "Hear hear." Cyrus looked up at Kat. She was seated at a discreet distance, her face flushed a bit from the run but looking exhilarated. A stray lock of red hair escaped from her riding cap.

"Step forward, Katherine Reese," Cyrus called out. Kat hesitated, then slipped off Pego's back and handed her reins to Nancy, who was riding alongside her. She walked into the center of the covert.

"There's a custom," Cyrus explained to the crowd of riders, "when a new rider has participated in their first kill. He or she has been blooded."

Kat was now standing next to him. Cyrus bent down and grabbed the fox's tail, still dripping blood. He placed a hand on Kat's shoulder, turned her toward him and smeared a streak of blood on her forehead. The other riders looked on, smiling or calling encouragement. Kat started to turn away, but Cyrus grabbed her arm in a vise-like grip and pulled her toward him. He plunged his hand into what was left of the fox's bloody carcass and smeared more blood on her face. Kat saw the cruel glint in his eye.

"Don't pull away," he said under his breath. "That's not nearly enough. You need to be initiated."

Cyrus seized her neck now and pressed her down until she was on her knees. He swirled his hand in the fox's blood again and smeared it on both sides of her face, on her nose, her cheeks. Kat fought back the tears but couldn't break Cyrus's grip.

The Blooding

"That's enough, Cyrus." It was Morgan's voice, cold as ice.

"Not yet," Cyrus answered, clearly enjoying his sport. The crowd started to murmur and squirmed in their saddles. The blood was running down Kat's face, and she felt it in her eye. She bit her lip, determined not to cry in front of this crowd as Cyrus continued to humiliate her.

Morgan charged forward and with a powerful shove sent his brother sprawling on the ground.

"I said enough!" he yelled. Breathing hard, he raised his hands to meet his brother's charge.

Cyrus did no such thing. He glared up at his younger brother, gave him a thin smile. Without a word he climbed to his feet, flicked a bit of dust from his tunic and walked back to his horse.

Morgan wrapped his arms around Kat's shoulder and gently lifted her to her feet. He pulled out a handkerchief and wiped the blood out of her eyes and began to clean her face. The other riders looked at each other in silent shock.

His breathing slower now, Cyrus swung up into his saddle and turned his horse toward home as though nothing had happened.

Chapter 9

Deep Woods

KAT PUT HER HORSE PEGO into a canter as soon as she reached the open field. It was early spring, and the path along the cornfield was still soggy. Sprays of mud and rainwater sprung up from the horse's hooves as they rode down the trail. It was a fine afternoon, and Kat was happy to be out on her own, her work behind her, able to enjoy the company of her favorite horse and no one else.

She heard a sound coming from the woods up ahead, a sound like popping. A parliament of crows took flight from the branches up ahead, cackling and complaining. Curious, she turned her horse in that direction. As she approached the opening to the forest she pulled up, listening for the sound again but heard nothing. She waited. There it was again: two quick pops. It sounded like gunfire, but softer. It might be hunters in the woods, although it wasn't the season, and she knew her grandfather was busy back at the house. As quietly as she could, she and Pego edged toward the forest.

Kat drew her horse to a halt at the edge of the woods and looped her reins on a nearby branch. Carefully, she moved deeper into the forest on foot, listening for the sound again. The trees parted, and in a clearing up ahead she spotted Cyrus.

He was standing with his back to her. There was a pistol tucked into the back of his belt. About 50 feet beyond him there were bottles and cans lined up on top of a fallen log.

Deep Woods

Cyrus pulled the gun from his belt smoothly and fired off two shots – pop pop! Two cans flew up in the air. Cyrus nodded in satisfaction, then tucked the revolver into his belt again. Quietly, he turned and looked straight at her.

"Hello, Barn Cat," he greeted her. "Out for a stroll in the woods, are you?" There was always an edge of mockery or menace when he talked to her these days. They had not spoken much since the blooding incident the first day of the hunt last fall, just passing conversation when they absolutely had to. She was determined that he not know she was frightened of him. She stepped forward into the light filtering through the trees.

"I heard gunshots. Thought there might be hunters out here."

"No, no hunters. Just practicing."

Kat couldn't help but be curious. "Where'd you get the gun?"

Cyrus drew the revolver, a Smith & Wesson .38, from his belt and looked at it as though just realizing he had it on him. "This? I have a buddy who's a deputy sheriff. He loaned it to me." He flicked open the cylinder and spun it a couple of times. Kat watched him, the way a cat stares at a cobra.

"What do you need a gun for?"

Cyrus shrugged. "Never know when you're going to need to defend yourself. Besides," he added with a bit of a sneer, "the old man still has my knife."

Kat's jaw dropped a little.

"You sure carry a grudge a long time." Cyrus stared at her.

"Little lady, you have no idea." He produced a box of cartridges from his jacket pocket and methodically slipped the bullets into the chambers.

"You know how to handle a gun?" he asked her. Kat looked at him defiantly.

"Of course," she answered. "Grandpa taught me how to shoot when I was seven."

Cyrus shook his head and stepped toward her. "I'm not talking about plunking at squirrels with a .22. I mean a real handgun. Something you'd use when you have to look a man in the eye and be ready to shoot him."

"Not when you put it that way."

He flicked the cylinder closed and stepped closer to her, the pistol held out in front of him.

"Come here. I'll give you a lesson."

"No thanks. It's late, I have to get back …."

"Come on. You'll pick it up in no time." He smiled at her, a taunting smile, daring her. She stared at the gun in his hand, then reached for it. He drew it away from her.

"Ah-ah. First lesson: Treat every gun like it was loaded."

"It is loaded. I saw you do it."

"OK then, you got that right. Second lesson: Never put your finger on the trigger unless you're fixing to shoot it."

Gingerly, she took the gun from his outstretched hand, careful to keep her index finger outside the trigger guard. The revolver was heavier than she expected. She hefted it in her hand, feeling the weight and balance of it.

"Good. That's good." He put his arm around her and gently guided her to where he had been standing, facing the targets he'd set up.

"Now, lesson number three: Never point the gun unless you're ready to fire. 'Cause anything you point at you might very well kill."

Cyrus was standing directly behind her now. He slid his arms around her and guided her into a firing position – slowly, seductively. He adjusted her hands, placed one under the butt of the pistol, supporting the hand with the gun in it. He drew her closer to him, and Kat could feel his muscular body molded against hers, the cold hardness of his silver belt buckle pressing into her lower back. His head was next to hers, and she could feel the stubble of his beard against her cheek.

"Now sight down the barrel, fix the target on top of that little blade, right between the V of the rear sight. Got it? Good. Now take a breath, and as you let it out, squeeze the trigger."

Deep Woods

She did as he said. The gun went off and jumped in her hand. She saw a piece of bark splinter below the targets.

"Not bad," he said. "But squeeze it this time, don't jerk it. Keep your breathing nice and steady. Like this."

He pulled her closer to him and slowly pressed his open hand against her abdomen. She could sense the rhythm of his own breathing in sync with hers, felt his closeness. She tried to concentrate, sighted the target, released a breath and fired. This time one of the bottles shattered.

"There you go," he said. "Nice shot." He took the pistol from her hand. His other arm was still firmly wrapped around her. She wriggled a bit and tried to shrug him off, but he squeezed her tightly, like an anaconda with its prey. His face was close to hers, and he pulled her toward him. They were face to face now, close enough to kiss. Kat found herself staring into his eyes, her stomach churning with curiosity and fear. The crack of a tree branch snapped her out of her reverie.

"Kat? Are you all right?" It was Morgan's voice. He was standing at the edge of the clearing.

Cyrus whipped around fast, the gun out in front of him. Morgan saw that it was pointed straight at his chest. He held both hands out in front of him, the way he would quiet a horse. When Cyrus recognized his brother standing there he smiled, turned the gun to the side and released the hammer slowly.

"Well well, a family reunion," he said. "You shouldn't sneak up on people, little brother."

Morgan stepped toward them. Kat could see the wary look on his face as he appraised his brother.

"I was just giving Kat a little shooting lesson," Cyrus continued easily. "Care to join us?"

"No thanks." Morgan turned to Kat. She slipped out of Cyrus's grip and eased away from him. "I saw Pego tied up at the edge of the woods. Then I heard shots."

"So you thought you'd come rescue her, is that it?" Cyrus said sardonically. "Don't worry, little brother. Your girlfriend is safe."

He took a step toward Morgan and held the Smith & Wesson out to him butt first. "Come on. Take a try."

"I don't have to prove anything to you, Cyrus."

"Not to me maybe." He held out the gun again. "Come on. Show us what you got."

Morgan hesitated. The three of them stood frozen in the lengthening afternoon shadows of the forest. Morgan took the gun from his brother's outstretched hand and stepped forward, squaring himself opposite the targets. He let his gun arm hang loosely at his side. Then in a rapid move he drew himself into a shooting stance and fired off two quick shots, shattering two targets.

Cyrus and Kat gaped at him in surprise. Morgan took his finger off the trigger and handed the gun back to his brother.

"I got to say, I'm impressed," Cyrus said. He almost sounded like he meant it. "Where'd you learn to shoot like that? I know I didn't teach you."

"Scouts," Morgan replied. "Come on, Kat, it's getting late." He guided the girl out of Cyrus's grasp and the two of them walked back to their horses.

They rode back toward the farmhouse in silence. Kat looked over at Morgan. His face was hard set, his brow furrowed. When she couldn't take it anymore she said to him, "Exactly when were you in the Scouts?"

After a beat he replied, "Never."

"Then why did you say it?"

"Why were you out in the woods with Cyrus?" Kat was taken aback.

"Is that what's bothering you? I was out there for the same reason you were: I heard someone shooting in the woods."

"Well, you need to be more careful."

Deep Woods

It was Kat's turn to retreat into silence. They rode on a bit further, the bad feelings hanging between them. After a moment Morgan spoke again.

"Listen. When I was little there was only one person who ever took care of me. That was Cyrus. I'm older now, and I've learned some hard lessons the last few years."

"Like what?"

"Like there are bad people in the world. Sometimes I'm afraid my brother is one of them." Kat was thoughtful for a moment.

"So that's why you learned to shoot?"

Morgan didn't answer at first. He said, "I don't want Cyrus thinking he's the only one who knows how to take care of himself. Besides," he added, eyes straight ahead, "I don't want to see anything happen to you."

When Kat was angry her copper hair seemed to blaze bright red, as if someone had struck a match head. She was angry now.

"I don't need a knight in shining armor," she snapped at him.

"Never said you did."

Kat realized she sounded harsh. She knew he meant her no disrespect. His protectiveness came from a good place, a place of genuine affection. Maybe even love. She softened a bit when she spoke next.

"There is one thing you could do. You could teach me to shoot like that."

She smiled at him, and she noticed the worry lines in his forehead melt away and his face relaxed. She nudged her horse's flanks and cantered out ahead of him, and the two of them rode home.

A week later, Morgan and Kat found themselves immersed in a scene that would change their lives forever.

They were driving along the access road that led to Harmony Stables. Morgan had his driver's license now, which made it easier getting back and forth to school and sports events and meetings. Doc Reese had given him free use of his old pickup, which Morgan tinkered with and kept in good running order.

Kat sat beside him, chattering brightly about the baseball game she had just watched. Morgan was captain of the high school team. His face was streaked with sweat from the afternoon's exertions, but his face was bright since they had won the game.

As they turned into their lane Kat stopped talking abruptly and pointed at the house. She let out a small cry of alarm.

"Morgan, what's that?"

"Where?"

"In the driveway. Is that an ambulance?" She grabbed his arm. "Did something happen to Grandpa? Hurry, Morgan!"

The wheels of the truck spit gravel as Morgan punched the gas. As they pulled to a stop in front of the house they realized with relief that the vehicle parked out front was not an ambulance. It was a police car. 'Croydon County Sheriffs Dept' was written clearly on the side.

"The police?" Morgan said. "What . . . "

They ran into the house just in time to watch the sheriff turning Cyrus around and slapping a pair of handcuffs on his wrists.

"Cyrus Caine, I'm placing you under arrest," the sheriff announced. Rob Ward had been sheriff of Croydon County for as long as anyone could remember. He was a lean man with hawk-like features that looked even sharper when he was doing his job, as he was now.

Next to him was a nervous-looking young deputy. He had a long thin nose that made his eyes seem too close together. He appeared to be in his early 20s, but the uniform made him look older. The deputy's hands rested on his gun belt, and he was watching the drama in front of him as if he were just a spectator. A river of perspiration flowed down the side of his face under the broad-brimmed campaign hat, and he seemed more anxious than anyone in the room. Kat looked at him hard, then finally recognized him. He had attended the high school just a few years ahead of her class.

"Ned? Ned Paulson?" she said, then she froze.

She recalled what Cyrus had told her just the week before about where he got the Smith & Wesson. "I have a buddy who's a deputy sheriff …." Is that why the police were here? Because of the gun?

Ned stared back at her, looking a little frightened.

"Oh, hi, Kat," he said, but that was all. He turned his full focus back to the sheriff and his prisoner. Cyrus was leaning forward, the cuffs behind his back, his face expressionless. The sheriff turned him around and handed him off to his deputy.

"Ned, why don't you go on and take Cyrus out to the car?" the sheriff said. Ned took Cyrus's arm and led him toward the door. As the two of them walked out of the room Cyrus kept his eyes focused straight ahead, never glancing at Morgan or Kat. As they brushed past, Kat heard Ned say something to his prisoner in a low voice, so the sheriff couldn't hear him.

"Sorry about this, Cyrus."

The sheriff was talking to Doc and Maggie Reese. Doc wanted to know, "What happens now?"

"I'll take him down to the station and book him. There'll be a bail hearing, probably tomorrow morning. If you want to get him out." The emphasis was on the "if," Kat noticed. Doc pulled at his moustache. Kat hadn't noticed how much whiter it had become the last few years.

"OK, Rob. Appreciate your coming out yourself," Doc said. They had known each other for years.

"I had to,' the sheriff replied. "Mr. Randall would have my head if I didn't take care of this personally." He straightened his hat and nodded to Doc and Maggie. "I'll see myself out."

When the sheriff had gone Morgan turned to Doc and asked, "What was that about? What's he done?"

"Maybe we should talk about this later," Doc murmured.

"Is it about the gun?" Kat blurted. Doc looked at her quizzically.

"I don't know anything about a gun," Doc said slowly. "Is there something else I should know?"

"I deserve to know why my brother's been led out in handcuffs," Morgan protested. Mrs. Reese tsked at her husband.

"George, go ahead and tell them," she said. "Everyone in town will know before Rob gets him to the station."

Doc squirmed a bit, obviously uncomfortable with the conversation. Finally he said,

"He's been arrested for rape." Morgan looked stunned, Kat less so.

"Rape?" Morgan repeated. "Who? When?"

"Nancy Randall," Doc replied.

"Nancy Randall? That's ridiculous," Morgan said. "She's out here practically every day. There was never any trouble between her and Cyrus." He noticed that Kat was silent. He tried to meet her eyes, but she wouldn't look at him. "Kat? Am I missing something?"

"Nancy's pregnant," Doc said stiffly. They were farm people. They didn't use gentler terms like "with child" or "in a family way." Doc continued, "Tom Randall had a fit and fell in it. He made Nancy tell him who the father was, and she pointed to Cyrus. Randall called the sheriff and made sure he got arrested."

Kat was studying a spot in the carpet. Morgan looked at her.

"Did you know about this?" She didn't answer.

"Even if he did . . ." Morgan started. He glanced at Mrs. Reese awkwardly. "Even if he is responsible, knowing Nancy, she most likely went along with it."

"Doesn't matter," Doc said. "Nancy's a minor. The charge is statutory rape, whether she was willing or not."

Morgan peeled off his baseball jacket with the large varsity letter sewn on it. "I'm going down there. Didn't the sheriff say something about bailing him out? We have to get him out." He paced the room, growing more frantic by the moment. Doc put a steadying hand on his shoulder.

"Let's all calm down. The best thing to do right now might be to let this all play out. I'll go down there in the morning and talk to Rob, see what can be done. You can come along if you want to."

"I want to," Morgan insisted. He looked at Kat, who still had not said anything. There was nothing to be said. She had known for months that this moment could come. It could have been Nancy, or any one of a dozen different girls at the stable. It might even have happened to her. She touched Morgan's arm, found no words, then turned and ran to her room.

Part 2
BAD BLOOD
'I love competition. It's losing I can't abide.'

Chapter 10

Troubled Youth

THE LAW OFFICES OF J.C. BUSEY were located in a tired-looking three-story brownstone building in the heart of downtown Croydon. A walk up the worn marble stairs to the second floor led to the attorney's offices. A mottled panel of frosted glass in the door at the end of the hall proclaimed 'J.C. Busey, Attorney-at-Law' as it had for more than 40 years.

The counselor sat behind his highly polished mahogany desk. He was a tall man with snow-white hair, thinning a bit on top and combed over, the sides curling at his ears for want of a haircut. His moustache was white as well, and thick enough to rival that of his visitor. Doc Reese's gaze wandered upward to the fan spinning languidly from the ceiling, moving the dust around, waiting for the attorney to address him. Busey adjusted his gold-rimmed glasses as he studied the contents of the thin manila folder open on his desk. In time he looked up, as if just realizing that he had a client. He cleared his throat.

"Let me be frank with you, Doc," Busey began. "It doesn't look good."

Doc nodded. He already knew this. He reached for his pipe without asking permission. Busey's office carried the permanent scent of Turkish tobacco from his own pipe, which smoldered quietly in the ashtray on his desk. Busey continued.

"Cyrus seems to have a history of getting himself into trouble. Strange, a young man with as many talents as he has just can't seem to walk the straight and narrow. I had a talk with Walt Frazier over at the high school."

"Oh?" Doc replied, exhaling some smoke.

"He said Cyrus dropped out after less than a month. Kicked out is more like it. For fighting."

"I am aware. What does that have to do with the matter at hand?"

"On the face of it, nothing. To a jury, it suggests a boy with a history as a troubled youth."

"The problem in this case isn't with boys," Doc pointed out.

"True," the lawyer replied, clearing his throat again. "Let's talk about girls then, shall we?" He picked up a sheet of paper and studied it. "According to Nancy Randall's statement, Cyrus first assaulted her in the tack room of your stable when she was 15."

Doc's jaw muscles stiffened. "I don't like the idea of besmirching the girl's reputation, J.C. But between us, now that I'm putting things together, Cyrus seemed to have 'assaulted' her just about every weekend for the past year. I never heard a complaint from her. Or her father."

"No. Not until she found herself in a family way." The counselor picked up his own pipe and relit it. "The problem is, this isn't a matter of consent. Nancy is underage. That's it and that's all."

"Oh hell, J.C. If every boy who diddled a teenage girl in the barn was brought up on charges, the high school would be empty."

"Perhaps. But not all of those girls have Tom Randall for a father." He paused. "The DA plans to charge Cyrus as an adult."

"How can he? Cyrus isn't 21 yet." He paused. "Not really sure how old he is, come to that."

"He's over 18. Legally that makes him an adult." The two men puffed in silence for a moment, letting the weight of this news swirl around the room like the smoke. The facts didn't make any difference when your father was rich and powerful.

Doc said, "Can you talk to the district attorney again? Cyrus doesn't have a record. Maybe he could reduce the charges?"

"Not a chance. The DA and Randall go way back. Randall is furious. This is personal with him, after all the money he's spent on horses and hunt clubs and what have you. All the while Cyrus is having his way with his little girl? He wants to see the boy punished. Severely." Busey put his pipe aside. He folded his hands in front of him, his two long forefingers forming a steeple. He was on to another topic.

"Any chance Cyrus could just marry the girl? That's the way these things often get resolved. Many a happy family in Croydon County started that way."

Doc shook his head. "I tried to bring that up to him."

"And? What did he say?"

"He didn't 'say' anything. He just kind of sneered." Doc sighed. "Even if Cyrus had a mind to marry Nancy – and he doesn't – Tom Randall would never allow it. Not in the frame of mind he's in."

"I see." The lawyer's face puckered. This was his last best hope. "What about Nancy? Maybe she could see her way to dropping the charges? She obviously likes the boy."

The attorney said drily, "Nancy is enjoying an extended visit out of state until after the baby is born. Maybe longer. It's not up to her, in any event."

Doc rubbed his chin. He was out of options. "So it looks like we're back to the district attorney. Maybe you can talk him around?"

Busey shook his snowy head. "I tried to sound him out on some sort of plea agreement. A lesser charge. Perhaps counseling for the boy, something along those lines. Anything that would keep him from going to jail. I don't see how that would serve anybody."

"And?"

"He was immovable. He intends to prosecute."

"That's too bad."

"Wait, it gets worse. If the DA adds multiple counts to the rape charge, that increases the possible prison sentence." Doc was startled.

"Prison? What kind of time are we talking?"

The attorney replied, "If he's convicted, he could be looking at 3 to 7 years."

"So what do we do?"

The lawyer steeled himself. Giving hard advice to clients was the worst part of his job.

"It may be in Cyrus's best interests – long term, of course – to enter a guilty plea and hope Judge Finfrock is in a lenient mood. If he seems remorseful."

The two men looked at each other in silence. They knew there was a big 'if' hanging in the room. They would just need to wait it out and see how Cyrus behaved.

"All rise."

The sound of chairs scraping on the plank floors filled the courtroom. Judge Finfrock, a sour-looking man in his sixties with a shiny pate and round rimless glasses, mounted the steps behind his bench, black robe flapping like a crow, and took his seat.

Cyrus stood at the defense table with the lawyer, J.C. Busey, next to him. Cyrus looked presentable if not exactly chastened. The light gray suit he was wearing was too tight – something Doc had bought for him a couple of years earlier to wear to weddings and such. Morgan had bought him a new white shirt and a dark tie, so at least that part of the wardrobe fit him properly.

Morgan sat in the spectator seats directly behind the defense table, behind the polished mahogany bar. Kat sat next to him, with her grandfather on her other side. Cyrus did not look at them.

"Be seated," the bailiff instructed the spectators. On the other side of the aisle, where the district attorney sat with one of his associates, Tom Randall sat alone, watching over the proceedings with hooded interest. Nancy was in Michigan, at an expensive home for wayward girls, enjoying the late summer weather of Petoskey. Mrs. Randall was indisposed.

Doc cast a quick glance over at Tom Randall, who did not meet his eye.

Judge Finfrock took his time perusing the case file in front of him, pausing to clear his throat and to take a sip of water from a glass that had been thoughtfully placed at his side.

"The defendant will please rise," he said at last. Cyrus stood up, tried to button his suitcoat, found it too snug and gave up the effort. Mr. Busey stood next to him and lifted his chin to the bench, looking dignified.

"Mister Caine," the judge began, "you have entered a plea of guilty to the crime of statutory rape. Is that still your intention?"

Busey looked at his client and nodded to him.

"Yes, Your Honor," Cyrus murmured.

The judge looked at a document in front of him, then put the papers down. He turned to the prosecuting attorney.

"Does the State wish to add further comment in this case?"

Doc noticed Tom Randall lean across the railing and whisper something to the district attorney. The DA shook his head, murmured a reply, then turned to the bench and rose.

"No, Your Honor, no further comment."

"Very well. Then we will proceed to sentencing." Cyrus and his attorney simultaneously squared their shoulders. Kat slipped her hand into Morgan's and squeezed so hard her knuckles turned white.

"Young man, this is a very serious charge," Judge Finfrock began solemnly. "And a grievous offense to this community. The district attorney has seen fit to try you as an adult in this matter, which he is within the law to do. It is my duty to see that you are punished as befits an adult, within the guidelines of the law of the state of Illinois."

Cyrus's eyes drifted to the ceiling. He wished the old man would just get on with it.

"I hereby sentence you to four years in Stateville Penitentiary." A murmur rippled through the courtroom. Mr. Busey's mouth gaped open like a trout pulled out of the river and laid on a flat rock.

"Your Honor, I must protest. Stateville is for the confinement of the most hardened criminals…."

"Perhaps your client should have thought of that before he violated one of our young girls," the judge replied drily. Tom Randall and the DA exchanged satisfied looks. Randall shot a scornful glance over in Doc Reese's direction.

"Sentence to commence immediately. You are remanded to the custody of the county sheriff for transport. This court is adjourned." The judge rapped his gavel once, and they were done.

Kat's eyes swelled with tears, and she buried her face on Morgan's shoulder. He put his arm around her. Cyrus turned around at that moment, saw the touching scene and gave them a thin-lipped smile.

Mr. Busey placed his hand on Cyrus's shoulder and muttered false encouragement, which Cyrus didn't hear and didn't care about. The sheriff's deputy, Ned Paulson, stepped forward, his expression glum, took the handcuffs from his belt and held them out.

"Sorry, Cyrus. Got to cuff you." Cyrus stretched his hands out in front of him, his eyes still fixed on his brother and Kat.

Doc Reese wrapped a thick arm around Kat's shoulder and pulled her to him.

"Don't worry about Cyrus," he murmured to her. "He's a tough kid. Besides, maybe some time in prison will settle him down a bit."

Cyrus heard that. He and Doc locked eyes. Then the deputy gave Cyrus a tug and left him out of the courtroom.

That was the end of Cyrus Caine's first trial. It would not be his last.

Troubled Youth

Cyrus slumped against the rear door of the squad car, staring out at the flat fields as they rolled past the window. The windshield wipers beat out a steady rhythm as they slapped back and forth in the gray rain. Cyrus wasn't afraid of where he was going, nor was he surprised. This was the way he somehow figured it would always turn out: him doing the heavy lifting, getting the business started, doing the deals, while his brother, the Golden Boy, played baseball and led the student government. And of course, got the girl. Cyrus figured he could do the time. But the picture of Morgan and Kat, huddled together in the courtroom, looking so goddamn cozy together, made him angry. This wasn't happening to them, goddamn it. It was happening to him. It was his life that was getting blown up.

He turned away to the window and looked at the back of the deputy's head.

"Hey Ned," he called. "You still awake up there?"

"Yeah Cyrus, I'm awake."

"Got a cigarette?"

"I'm really not supposed to," the deputy said as he pulled a pack of Camels from his shirt pocket, tapped one out, took it between his lips and lit it. He handed it over his shoulder to the prisoner. Cyrus was still in manacles laced through an eyebolt welded to the floor of the cruiser. There was just enough slack for him to take the cigarette and smoke it by leaning forward.

"I'm really sorry about this, Cyrus," the deputy said. "You know I volunteered to be the one to drive you out to Stateville, if it came to that."

"I'm obliged."

"I think you got a bum rap, if you don't mind my saying. I mean, Stateville – Jesus. What kind of plea deal is that? There's easier places to do time. It's not like you killed somebody or something."

Cyrus took a deep drag, took his time exhaling. "I think I'm right where they want me to be."

They drove on in silence for a while. When he'd finished his cigarette Cyrus reached for the window crank to roll it down, then he remembered: he was in the back of a police car. He crushed out the butt in the ashtray in the seat arm and left it smoldering there.

"Mind if I give you some advice?" Ned asked him.

"Shoot."

"They've got some tough customers in here. You know this is where they transferred Leopold and Loeb."

"Historic then."

"Yeah. Loeb got shanked by some other prisoner."

"Is there a point to this happy story?"

"That's what I'm trying to tell you. You got to watch out in there. My advice? First day, look for the meanest sonofabitch you think you can take. Give him a head butt, make sure he goes down. Then they'll leave you alone."

Cyrus nodded. "Thanks for the advice," he said quietly. He turned his gaze to the window again, watching two raindrops racing slowly to the bottom and disappearing.

Chapter 11

Commencement

STATEVILLE PENITENTIARY WAS BUILT in 1925 on more than 2,200 acres outside the town of Joliet, Illinois. The place was a fortress: sixty-four acres surrounded by a 33-foot concrete perimeter marked off with 10 watch towers. The hulking gray center of the complex was a prison house built in a "panopticon" design, one of the first prisons of its kind in the country. Created by an English philosopher named Jeremy Bentham, he believed the layout would be a tool for better reformation in prison. An armed tower in the center of the floor was surrounded by several tiers of cells. By having the "eye" in the middle, prisoners never knew when they were being watched or not. If they thought they were under observation, prisoners would be more likely to modify their behavior, or so the theory went. The state of Illinois's first executions by electrocution took place on December 15, 1928, when three convicted murderers were put to death. It was a serious place.

Morgan drove his pickup truck down Route 53 on the last leg of his trip. He had left after lunch, telling Doc he had some supplies to pick up in Naperville. He doubted that Doc was fooled, but the old man didn't say anything. Certainly Kat had been suspicious from the first. He found it hard to hide anything from her.

"Where are you really going? I want you to tell me."

"Nowhere. Just picking up supplies."

"Then why is your face so red? Are you going to visit Cyrus?"

"Of course not. I thought we agreed."

"I didn't agree. If you're going, why don't you take me with you?"

Morgan shook his head. "I'm just sure. Why don't I take you to a men's prison? You figure it out."

Kat flushed but was undeterred. "I'm sure they get women visitors all the time."

"Yeah, gangsters' molls maybe. Not sweet little high school girls like you."

That seemed to settle the argument, at least this round. Morgan climbed in the truck and closed the door. Although she was still miffed, Kat leaned on the mirror and tucked her head inside the lowered window. He gave her a quick kiss.

"I'll come see you as soon as I get back."

"Be careful," she said. She didn't just mean the driving.

An hour and a half later he wheeled the truck down the long snow-covered macadam road that led to the main gate of the prison. Stateville was a desolate place, and it was meant to be. Sitting in the middle of endless flat, frozen acres of snow and mud, twisted black trees with no leaves off in the distance, nothing but stone walls and barbed wire and misery. Morgan looked up at the watch towers as they rolled past, saw the guards staring down at him, Tommy guns ready. And he was trying to get in. Imagine if he was trying to get out, he thought to himself. He parked his truck in the lot marked for visitors and followed the signs to the entrance.

Twenty minutes later he was sitting at a long table separated from the other side by wired partitions. It reminded Morgan of a line of confessional boxes, if they were hearing confessions in hell. A few minutes later a heavy steel door on the other side of the partition creaked open to the jangle of keys, a gray uniformed guard stepped into the room, followed by Cyrus.

He was thinner than the last time Morgan had seen him, in the courtroom the day of the sentencing. He looked strong, but his face had already taken on the gray pallor common to men behind bars. He wore the standard issue jumpsuit, also gray and buttoned at the throat. His eyes were black and suspicious as he looked for his visitor. They softened only a little when he saw it was Morgan. He moved slowly to the stool across from Morgan, swung his leg over and sat down. Neither brother spoke right away.

"Merry Christmas," Morgan said finally. It was only Tuesday. Christmas was the next day. Cyrus smirked.

"Same to you, little brother. Out making the holiday rounds? Did you drop off a turkey and some cranberry bread?"

"I didn't know they'd let me bring anything," Morgan started to say, before he realized his brother was just busting on him, like in the old days, the "before prison" days. He smiled. At least they were on some familiar footing.

"How are you?"

"I'm in fucking prison," Cyrus replied. "That about says it all."

The brothers fell into an awkward silence. Morgan listened to the dull hum and sizzle of the fluorescent lights overhead and studied his brother's face more closely. Cyrus had changed. He was still good-looking, except for the prison haircut, but the lines etched in his face were deeper, making him look older than his years. His eyes, which had always been dark and impenetrable, now had a dead stare, seeing everything, revealing nothing. The brassy neon overhead lights gave everything a yellowish cast, but he noticed marks of different colors, yellows and browns and purples, along the side of Cyrus's face. Morgan's gaze drifted down to his brother's forearm, peeking out of the sleeve of his jumpsuit.

"What's that on your arm?" he asked, pointing. Cyrus smiled, seemed almost pleased, and rolled up his sleeve. Rendered in blue and black ink – painfully, no doubt — there was a tattoo that ran almost the full length of the inside of his forearm. It pictured a knife — a *sgian dubh* — slicing through two interlocking horseshoes that looked like the letters 'CC'–Cyrus's initials. A single red droplet of blood dangled from the knife point. Morgan studied the prison art, something gnawing at his memory.

"How do you like it?" Cyrus asked.

"I've seen that knife before." Then it struck him. "Didn't Pa have a knife like that?"

"Maybe," Cyrus replied. He rolled down his sleeve. He dug into a pocket, pulled out a pack of cigarettes and lit one. "So. How are things with you?"

"OK. Almost finished with school. That's a good thing."

"I suppose it is. Nice to have someone in the family with a high school diploma."

"Yeah, well. That's one of the things I wanted to talk to you about."

Cyrus drew in some smoke, exhaled slowly, waited. He had become good at waiting.

Morgan said, "You remember Mr. Frazier from school."

"How could I forget? He kicked me out my first month."

"Yeah, well, I get along with him OK. Anyway, he looked into it, and he thinks I'd have a chance at a scholarship at U of I in the fall."

"College, huh?" A drag, an exhale. Waiting.

"So what do you think?"

"About college? I'm sure it would suit you fine. What do you plan to do with all this education? The horses sure don't care."

"I'm not sure yet. Study business. Ways to make the farm more profitable."

"That's a good thing." He paused. "What does the Barn Cat think?"

"She's for it. It would be hard at first, just her and Doc running the place, with me at school and you . . . well, with both of us away."

"I'm surprised you didn't bring her. It being Christmas and all."

"She wanted to come. I didn't think it was a good idea."

Cyrus smirked. "Definitely not a good idea." He took another drag. "Little brother, if you're asking my advice, here it is: Do what you want. I'm sure the stables will survive either way. As for me . . ." He crushed out his cigarette on the concrete floor. ". . . I am a non-factor."

'Meaning what?"

"Meaning I don't give a shit. I have commitments elsewhere, as you can see." He made a lazy wave to take in the gray walls, the neon lights, the steel doors. He stood up and called over his shoulder, "Guard!"

The uniformed officer appeared again and stood at the open doorway. Cyrus headed for the door, then turned back to look at his brother.

"One more thing. Don't come back here. This ain't a place for college boys."

Cyrus's cell was not in maximum security, a small mercy for which he was grateful. Instead of having to fight his way every day through the worst murderers in Illinois, he was housed with the merely bad: men incarcerated for assault, armed robbery, extortion, and other less horrible crimes. His cellmates may not have been the most evil criminals in the state, but they were bad enough. He got to know a lot of them well during his time inside. "This is my college," he thought to himself as he walked back to his cell after his brother's visit.

The full impact of how his life had changed hit Cyrus full force the moment he walked through the prison gates. Once Ned Paulson remanded him to his new keepers, they made it clear: Cyrus's life belonged to them. They stripped him, photographed him, searched every orifice, hosed him down, handed him his new gray uniform and some sheets and threw him in a cell. As the steel door slammed shut behind him Cyrus experienced something he had not felt in a long time: fear. His youthful bravado abandoned him, and his focus shifted to one thing: staying alive.

Sitting alone on his steel bunk, Cyrus found his leg shaking violently. His chest was tight, and his throat swelled with what could have been a sob if he had only released it. He fought to get his body and his thoughts under control, knew that if he did not conquer his emotions he would not survive this place. He tried to shut out the malevolent thrum of activity outside his cell – the shouts, the curses, the slamming doors, the sudden fights — and did a sober assessment of his situation.

First he did an inventory of his assets. He was young and good-looking – but that was a plus and a minus in prison. He might be a predator, but he was more likely to be prey. He was strong physically and knew how to handle himself in a fight. But this wasn't a schoolyard; a lot of these men did violence with their hands for a living. How would he survive an attack by one, let alone a gang of criminals? Maybe Ned Paulson had a point. Maybe the only way to save himself was to bring someone else down, fast.

Cyrus was mindful of a piece of advice one of his cop buddies back in Croydon County had given him; "When you get inside, keep your eyes open and your mouth shut." Cyrus was good at that. Keeping to himself came naturally to him. That was the way he decided to play it, at least at first.

Those first couple of days as he got to know his new surroundings – the dining hall, the exercise yard, the walkway of his cell tier — Cyrus kept a watch out, sizing up potential opponents. There were other sex offenders in the block with him, but there was no victory in taking one of them on. They were at the lowest end of the prison food chain, held in contempt and abused by the tougher inmates. The white-collar criminals, those in for check kiting or embezzlement, tended to huddle in small groups of their own, talking about appeals and praying no one would notice them.

It didn't take long for Cyrus to identify a possible prospect, a holdup man a few years older than himself, doing his second stretch for robbery and assault. Cole Harmon was from the west side of Chicago and was said to have done some leg-breaking for the Irish gangs, but only as a foot soldier, nothing big. He was bigger than Cyrus, a solid block of human flesh with a square head and a wary disposition. He was always in the middle of a circle of other no-goods, mostly from his old neighborhood. But Cyrus was certain of one thing: he was an alpha male. He might be a good person to know, or to stay away from.

Cyrus knew he probably couldn't take Harmon in a fair fight. But whoever heard of a fair fight in prison? The secret to a quick win was to take him by surprise.

They were standing in the lunch line the next afternoon, Harmon and his bunch circling one way to return their empty trays, Cyrus on his own circling the other. As they passed one another Harmon happened to throw a sideways glance in Cyrus's direction.

"What are you staring at?" Cyrus called out at almost the same moment he gave Harmon a wicked headbutt. The other convict went down hard as planned. But then something happened that was not part of the plan: He got back up.

Cyrus knew he was in for it now. He threw up his hands, ready to fight for his life. Harmon shook his head, wondering what had just happened to him. He glared at the newbie and charged. Cyrus sidestepped and used the man's own weight against him – experience from years of wrangling horses. On the way to the floor again Cyrus laid in two well-placed punches to the side of Harmon's head. He pivoted and put his hands up again, showing he wasn't afraid to continue the fight. Harmon's friends jumped in and picked him up, keeping the two men separated.

"Later," one of them hissed to Cyrus as they pushed out of the lunchroom. The guards paid no attention.

Cyrus stayed away from the showers for the next day or two – he'd heard that was the most dangerous place in a prison – and he kept to himself in the dining hall. Wherever he went he felt the eyes of one of Harmon's cronies burning into the back of his head, watching his movements, waiting for an opening.

It came on the third day.

The men from Cyrus's block were taking their turn in the exercise yard. Harmon and his gang were in their usual corner, smoking and griping, the most popular pastimes. Cyrus stayed close to the wall, within the view of the guard at the door. Cyrus realized something was different: the guard wasn't in his usual position.

He felt a powerful arm grab him from behind and half-carry him to the corner of the yard, where Harmon was waiting. The man who had grabbed his arm spun Cyrus around and nearly knocked him into the dirt. Cyrus sprang up, but he was only halfway to his feet when Harmon cold-cocked him with a powerful fist to the head, then a couple of jabs. Cyrus leaped up from his crouched position and plowed back into his assailant, fists hammering away at Harmon's torso. The big man brushed him off like a flea and hit him again, two lefts and a hard right cross.

This time Cyrus went down. He wiped the back of his hand across his lip, tasted blood. He jumped up and charged again. Harmon flung him back, then knocked him to the ground again. The other cons circled around, blocking the view from the door in case the guard stepped out again.

The third time Cyrus rose to his feet, one of the convicts whispered to him, "Stay down, kid." But Cyrus wasn't one to listen. He circled around Harmon as he would an unruly horse, and when the big man looked to the side Cyrus charged him. Harmon went down, but quickly pulled himself to his feet and slammed Cyrus with a wicked right to the head, sending him sprawling in the dirt.

After several minutes of this, both men were getting winded. Cyrus was on his back but still ready to fight. Breathing hard, Harmon stepped toward him, grunted and reached out his hand. Cyrus was suspicious at first, then he took the hand and let the man pull him upright.

"Let me ask you something, kid," Harmon said, wiping blood from the corner of his mouth.

"What?"

"Why'd you hit me in the cafeteria?"

"Friend of mine who's a cop, told me to look for a big guy and bring him down," Cyrus explained. "Then the others would leave me alone."

Harmon stared at him. "That's the dumbest thing I ever heard. You could get yourself killed that way." He brushed off his trousers. "Where'd you learn to move like that? You a fighter?"

"Horse trainer," Cyrus replied. "I train horses."

Harmon was looking at him with curiosity bordering on admiration. Finally the big con said,

"I like horses."

From that day forward, Cyrus was part of Harmon's circle. By the time of his release, they would be known as the Caine Gang.

The surest way to turn an honest man into a criminal," Cyrus Caine opined much later, "is to put him in prison for a few years."

Cyrus's lack of formal education had not been an impediment to him so far. The trouble he had found in life didn't stem from a lack of formal schooling. Rather, it was a question of temperament: Cyrus was an angry young man, hot-tempered and impetuous, not to mention good with his fists. He found a lot of companions with similar profiles at Stateville, and they had technical expertise that Cyrus so far lacked: Picking locks. Extortion. Knife fighting. And one that was to become his favorite: Arson. When it came to committing crime, this was his master class. Of course it did not dawn on him that the men who were teaching him these skills were all serving time along with him.

After their set-to in the prison yard, Cyrus and Harmon became, if not exactly friends, then close colleagues. "Thick as thieves" was the expression that came to mind. Although he looked 10 years older, Harmon was only a few years' Cyrus's senior. Life on the mean streets of Chicago's west side put a lot of mileage on a young man, and Harmon had been on his own since he was 12.

"Just me and my younger brother," Harmon said once. "Except he's more like a little sister these days."

"What does that mean?" Cyrus asked.

"Kind of a poofter. He'd have a tough time in here."

Cyrus nodded. Of course he was aware of the men inside who did sexual favors in order to get by. For some it was voluntary, but for most it was that or take a shiv in the yard or get raped by a gang some night after lights out. Things happened in prison, and Cyrus wasn't one to judge what a person did in order to survive. He was relieved that his alliance with Harmon's gang spared him those kinds of assaults, since he was "pretty" by prison standards. But he couldn't see a man on the outside wanting to follow that kind of life if he didn't have to.

The older Harmon brother had nothing soft about him, and two stretches in prison had hardened him even more. Sometimes he and Cyrus would smoke during a break, and Harmon talked about his days growing up rough in Chicago.

"There was one place I really liked," he said once. "When I was hard up or on the run or something, there was this old man run a stable on Western Avenue. Been there since they used to haul milk and deliver beer with horse-drawn wagons. They still kept horses, even though the beer wagons went away with Prohibition. Anyway, this old guy would let me sleep there if I'd muck out the stalls for him. I didn't mind. I liked being around the horses."

"Me too," Cyrus said. "I never met a man I'd trust more than I would a good horse."

After a time, Cyrus and Harmon began to develop a plan for what they'd do after "graduation." Cyrus had never spent any time in Chicago except to make occasional supply runs with Doc or take some of their cattle to the Union Stockyard. Cyrus warmed to the idea of running a stable of his own. Maybe he and

Harmon could acquire the place together and run their operations from there.

"What if the owner doesn't want to sell?" Cyrus asked one day.

Harmon just raised one eyebrow and took a drag on his cigarette.

"You have a lot to learn about life in the big city," he said.

Cyrus enjoyed the dream of owning his own place. Dreams kept you alive, kept you from going crazy inside. Realistically though, he thought it probably wouldn't happen. He had a brother to look out for. He'd probably go back to Croydon County, back to Harmony Stables, maybe help the college boy build up the business again.

Or so he thought.

———⟫•●•⟪———

Cyrus stood impatiently in front of the large steel door, shifting his weight from one foot to the other, waiting for the guards to complete their paperwork. His civilian suit – the one he had been wearing the day Ned Paulson drove him to Stateville in his squad car – seemed smaller than when he went in. Cyrus had grown even more muscular, the product of endless workouts with little else to do in prison. His waist was thinner though, and he kept tugging his pants up; they had confiscated his belt when he first checked in. It was good to be wearing civilian threads again.

After 32 months in prison, Cyrus Caine was waiting to be released.

Finally one of the guards finished scribbling on the form attached to his clip board.

"All right, Cyrus, paperwork's done," he said affably. Cyrus had made it a point to get along with the guards. One never knew when a favor would be needed. The guard put down the clipboard and approached the heavy metal door, keys jingling. As he unlocked it he asked, "Anybody meeting you?"

Cyrus looked at him quizzically.

"Hadn't thought about it," he replied. The door swung open and the guard held it for him.

"Keep your nose clean," he said.

Cyrus walked out into the open yard for the first time in months. He held his hand up to shield his eyes from the sun, squinting as he looked at the end of the lane. Standing there was a solitary figure. He was older, heavier, but the solid stance and the pipe clamped in his jaw were as familiar as ever. Cyrus approached him slowly.

"Hello, Doc."

"Cyrus." The old man hadn't dressed for the occasion. He was in his usual overalls, the same straw hat fixed squarely on his head. "You look all right, considering."

"Considering," Cyrus repeated, his lips twisted in a cynical smile.

"Glad they let you out early."

"'Good behavior,' they said. Guess they needed the space." The two men regarded one another for a moment. Doc was taking his measure. Nearly three years ago, they had sent a wild young stallion away. But the man standing here was different – older, yes; harder too, and even more dangerous looking. Prison had not mellowed Cyrus, Doc thought. If anything, it had toughened him and darkened his outlook. Standing toe to toe with him, Doc was even more convinced of what he needed to do.

"What are you doing here, Doc?" Cyrus asked. "You come to pick me up? I thought Morgan might do that."

"I didn't tell Morgan you were out," Doc replied flatly. "I wanted to be the one to see you first. And to give you this."

For the first time, Cyrus noticed the cigar box Doc Reese held under his arm. Doc held it out to him.

"What's this?"

"Open it."

Cyrus took the box and lifted the lid slowly. His hooded eyes widened just a bit. Inside there were banded stacks of 20-dollar bills.

"That's a lot of money," he said.

"It's your share from the business. I've been saving it up for you all these years. Now it's yours. You earned it."

Cyrus rummaged through the box, trying to quickly calculate how much he might be holding, when he found another object at the bottom of the box. He wrapped his fingers around the handle and lifted out his father's *sgian dubh,* the knife Doc had made him surrender years before.

"Been holding that for you too," Doc said. "Now we're square."

Cyrus hefted the skene in his hand, admiring the blade, remembering the weight of it the night he took it from his father, the way he had waved it to hold off Robbie Randall and that bone-headed wrestler when they jumped him. He slid the knife into his pocket.

"You came all this way to give me presents, Doc? Could have waited til I got home."

"I came to wish you luck, and to give you what's rightly yours," the old man said. "It's up to you to make something of yourself now."

"Meaning?"

"Meaning, you're the best damn horseman I've ever seen. And you are a mean judge of horse flesh. You'll do well." He added, "But you're not to come back to Harmony Farm."

Cyrus's black eyes grew cold. This was no surprise really. Many times in prison he had wondered if he would be welcome back in his old world, with his brother, with Doc and Mrs. Reese. With Nancy Randall and her sweet little bottom. And with Kat. Now he had his answer.

"Life has dealt you some bad hands," Doc continued. "But the way you chose to deal with them . . . well, it just doesn't give me a lot of confidence. Especially around the people I love."

"Meaning Kat?"

"Her. Your brother too. The two of you . . . well, let's just say I think you'd both be better off if you kept your distance. Besides, he's off in the army."

Cyrus looked surprised. He knew a war had been declared, although being behind bars made it a distant abstraction. He didn't know it affected his family – the only family he had.

"When did that happen? I thought he was at college."

"He was, until the Japs bombed us. He signed up right away. Army Air Corps."

"Where is he now?"

Doc started to answer, thought better of it. "He's serving his country." He tamped out his pipe and turned toward his truck, parked a few yards away in the lot. "I best be getting back. Long drive. Can I drop you someplace?"

Cyrus shook his head. "There's a bus stop over there."

Doc nodded. "Well then." The old man shuffled to the truck, opened the door and slid behind the wheel. He rolled down the window and looked back at the young man standing at the prison gates. "You've got a lot of talent, Cyrus, and a big enough stake to get you started. Just decide to make something of yourself. Don't end up back in here."

"I'm never going back inside," Cyrus said firmly. Doc nodded, not quite believing him but wanting to. He started the engine and slowly drove away.

Cyrus watched the truck for a while, followed it down the long entrance lane until it turned at the corner and pulled onto the main road. He watched the cloud of dust until he couldn't see it anymore. Then he walked up to the bus stop, squinted in the other direction, where he saw the outline of a bus lumbering toward him. He couldn't make out the sign at the front of the bus, had no idea where it was going. Then he realized, it really didn't matter. When the bus pulled up Cyrus stepped aboard. He peeled a twenty-dollar bill from the cigar box and handed it to the driver with a flourish.

"Home, James."

Chapter 12

The Wild West

Texas A&M University
April 5, 1942

Dear Kat,

It's Sunday, so I finally have a few minutes to write to you. They sure keep us busy, although it feels a lot more like being at U of I than it does being in the Army. I think they sent us to a college campus until they figure out what to do with us, or until they build more airplanes they can actually train us in. I haven't seen the inside of a plane yet, but I sure know what the inside of a classroom looks like. We're up before dawn every morning doing drills, calisthenics, running, etc. etc. Then breakfast followed by inspection. Then we're in classes until evening. Hard ones too, not like what I was taking in Champaign. Calculus, trigonometry, electrical engineering, navigation – at least that will come in handy if I ever actually get to fly.

Last night was my first real night off. One of my buddies, Jim Martin, is from San Antonio, and he took a bunch of us out to the river and showed us how to gig for frogs. At least it passes the time. Then we went to a Mexican restaurant. I've really come to like Mexican food. Not that your grandmother isn't a good cook, but she always stays away from the seasoning. I like it really spicy. Goes perfect with a cold beer, and there's lots of that here too.

As we were riding out to the river we passed a herd of mustangs grazing in a field. When they heard our Jeep they scattered and took off running. It was a beautiful sight. It made me so homesick, thinking of the farm, but mostly missing you. Being so far away makes me appreciate how much you mean to me, and how lucky I was that we got to spend nearly every day together. I just hope that we get this war over soon so I can get home to you and we can start a life together.

Write to me when you can. It doesn't matter what you say. I just want to hear from you and know that you're thinking of me.

*Love,
Morgan*

Kat read the letter for the third time, smiled and folded it carefully. She hated that she was acting like such a girl – a girl with a fiancé away in the service. Like so many other girls in town, and around the country. She knew that what she was feeling – the loneliness of separation, the ache, the worry – would only get worse once Morgan and all the other servicemen got their wish, got their training, and got shipped off overseas. Then the real worrying would start.

She was happy for Morgan that he had gotten his wish and been accepted into the pilot training program. He had always had an interest in flying, ever since they had first seen a barnstorming pilot at the county fair years before. Now, thanks to the army, it looked like he would be able to learn to fly. Kat's mouth curled into a small moue of dissatisfaction. Do they take women pilots too? she wondered. Or are we still confined to rolling bandages and passing out donuts at the USO?

It didn't matter at the moment, not really. With Morgan away, Cyrus in jail, and her grandmother ill, her choices were limited. Her role, for better or worse, was to guard the home front and help her grandfather take care of the farm.

She creased the letter again, then placed it carefully with the other letters she had accumulated since Morgan enlisted. She retied the satin ribbon that held them together, placed the bundle in the top drawer of the dresser and closed it slowly.

"Just come home safe," she said silently. "That's all I want."

The Wild West

This really is the Wild West, Cyrus thought to himself as he looked around the stable. The Wild West Side of Chicago.

Cyrus leaned back in the wooden armchair and kicked his booted feet up on the old scarred desk. He pulled a pack of Pall Malls out of his shirt pocket, flicked open his lighter and fired it up. Probably not smart to smoke in a stable – all that dry hay and animals everywhere. But what the hell, he was the owner. He could do what he wanted, whenever he wanted.

The place was redolent with all of Cyrus's favorite, or at least most familiar, smells. Hay and horse feed, piss and manure, and the earthy aroma of sweaty horses with mud caked on their hooves. Cyrus had seen the inside of dozens of stables in his short life, and they were all pretty much the same. The biggest difference with this one was, when he stepped outside he wasn't in some country field but just off Western Avenue in the second biggest city in the country. The stable had been there longer than the neighborhood. High Time Stables was more than 50 years old, built originally to house draft horses that pulled the beer trucks and milk wagons that serviced the thirsty city. Most of that work was now relegated to gas-driven vehicles, but with shortages of gas because of the war some of the horse-drawn conveyances were back in demand. High Time sheltered them and had enough business to pay the utility bills as well as the stable hands.

Cole Harmon had been right about the property. The former owner had balked at first at the idea of selling out. But once Cyrus flashed him some cash from the cigar box, while Cole Harmon and a couple of members of the Caine Gang lowered in the background, the old owner was quick to seize his good fortune and move on.

Cyrus quickly found another good use for the stables. The location was close enough to the moneyed set on Chicago's Gold Coast that Cyrus was now catering to that crowd with rentals and riding lessons. He was building a small but steady flow of bored wealthy matrons with husbands busy with the war effort and time on their hands. Cyrus's patented formula of good looks and thorough lack of scruples was proving successful on an even bigger stage. Chicago offered a couple of racetracks where Cyrus was a regular attendee, and he was an expert at converting former racehorses into show horses for gullible patrons. The war was starting to cut into his business though. Lincoln Fields had shut down in 1941. Now there was talk that Arlington might shift their races to Washington Park, in southern Cook County. He needed to keep looking for more horses to support his growing enterprise.

There was another line of business that was proving most lucrative of all. With access to most of the horse flesh in the city, Cyrus had discovered another byproduct of the war: there were shortages of meat. Cyrus and his team were building a thriving enterprise selling horsemeat to restaurants. Diners in some of Chicago's top eateries would be shocked to learn that they were eating horse, not beef. But Cyrus and his gang kept the kitchens full, and in Chicago, feeding the city's appetites was all that mattered.

War time was pretty good for a young man with no scruples to start making his fortune.

Less than a half mile away from High Time Stables, La Fontanella restaurant had its usual crowd of midweek patrons – not a full house, but enough tables to keep the waiters busy and the kitchen humming. The restaurant was housed in an unassuming brownstone with the inevitable red awning over the entrance, facing out onto the street. The food, while good, wasn't exceptional, but the dishes were authentic in keeping with the manager's hometown in Abruzzo, Italy.

At La Fontanella, the real action was at the private table in the back room. A heavy maroon curtain shielded a small dark hallway that led to the office of the restaurant's real owner, John

"The Beak" Panazzo. Panazzo controlled the numbers game for the West Side of the city as well as doing a brisk trade in the protection racket. Ever since the conviction of Al Capone a decade before, the various families of The Outfit (the name they preferred over Mafia or The Mob) went about their business without as much of the violence and notoriety of the Capone era. Panazzo had earned his nickname, "The Beak," because he was known to have a little piece of every business that was worth having in his territory. Not enough to break the owners – everyone needed to make a living, after all – but "just enough to wet my beak."

The Beak was sitting at his dinner table surrounded by some of his business associates. A red and white checked cloth was wrapped around his neck to protect his shirt front from the red tomato sauce ladled onto the "macaroni," accompanied by a rather tough *bistecca* but washed down with a very pleasant Montepulciano old vine red. Panazzo chewed thoughtfully while his *capo* briefed him on the day's receipts and other pressing business.

"The steak's not too bad," he said between mouthfuls. "Could be a little more tender." His crew nodded in agreement.

"Hard to get good meat these days," one of them said. "Damn rationing. Shortages everywhere." He smiled, a strand of pasta dangling from the corner of his mouth. "Not bad for business though."

"Tell me about this kid, the new one with the stables," Panazzo said with another slurp of wine. "I hear he's into all kinds of things."

"He is," the *capo* affirmed. "I see him out at the track all the time."

The boss's eyebrows sank into a glare of disapproval. "He got some gambling action going?"

"Nah, he's not making book or nothing. There's rumors he might juice the horses now and then. He's a trader, buys and sells horses. Buys mostly. Then he fancies them up and sells them to the *medegones* on the Gold Coast."

"That's a business?"

"Seems to be doing all right. His big business is selling meat on the side."

"Meat? What kind of meat?"

The *capo* let out a whinny and stamped his hands on the table like a pair of hooves. The other gangsters laughed until the boss glared at them.

"You're shitting me," Panazzo said. "People eat that?"

"How do they know what they're eating?" the *capo* said with a shrug.

Panazzo's jaw muscles stopped moving as he stared down at his own plate. He stuck his fork into the piece of steak and held it up. "Bring me the chef," he snapped to one of his henchmen.

A moment later the cook, a nervous-looking man named Guardini, was dragged out to see the boss. Panazzo held up his steak and gestured at the frightened man.

"Don't lie to me: Where'd you get this meat?"

"I got a new supplier," the chef murmured. "Nice young guy, give me a good price."

"'Give me a good price,'" the boss mimicked. "Am I eating Seabiscuit?"

The chef broke out into a sweat. After a moment, he shook his head yes. Panazzo dropped his fork, pulled the napkin off his neck and threw it down on the table. He grabbed the chef by his kerchief, spun him around and kicked him back toward the kitchen.

"Get outa here. Next time you bring me a steak it better be a cow." He whirled on the rest of his gang and growled. "Who are these punks?"

"Bunch of young guys, street punks mostly, hang out at the stable. I know one of the guys, Harmon. He's tough. Does some muscle for one of the Mick gangs."

"We're the muscle in this part of town," Panazzo said. "He needs to learn that. Are they paying the *pizzo* at least?" He meant protection money. The heads around the table sank, finding a sudden interest in the tablecloth.

"Damn punks need to show a little respect." He muttered under his breath, "Selling horsemeat to my own restaurant. The kid's got balls, I'll give him that."

Panazzo turned to a hulking man sitting at the far end of the table.

"Frankie," said the boss. "Go pay them a visit."

The big man looked up under the brim of his pork pie hat, as if he were hearing the conversation for the first time. He nodded once, then went back to eating his pasta.

Cyrus heard a ruckus coming from around the corner of the stable – the whinnying of a horse, hooves pounding on the hard dirt, men sweating and cursing and shouting at each other. He let out a curse himself, jumped up from his desk and went to see what the trouble was.

Two of his hired hands were struggling to get a large gray gelding under control. The horse had come out of the trailer easily enough, but now it was fighting them every step of the way as the men heaved and tugged, trying to get the horse to walk up the ramp toward the stalls. The great beast kicked and writhed, trying to throw off the ropes and knock its captors senseless. The hands were new, a couple of street kids without a lot of horse savvy.

Cyrus cursed again and jumped in to help them.

"Settle down there, you!" he shouted as he grabbed one of the lunge lines. He gave the horse's line a sharp tug, but the horse threw back its head and charged at him. Cyrus yelled at one of the hapless young men, "Stay along side of him! You don't want to get anywhere near those hooves if he kicks you."

Cyrus charged ahead of the horse and threw open the Dutch door to the last stall in the row. The thrashing horse broke away from one of its handlers, knocked a second one to the ground and charged into the stall, in search of a safe space. Cyrus slammed the door of the stall shut behind the animal and slipped the bolt closed. The horse kicked wildly at the door, sending shudders through the old timbers of the stable. Cyrus wiped his arm across his brow.

"He'll wear himself out after a while," he said to the two hands, who looked pale and shaken. "Where'd you pick this one up?"

"Some Wild West show down by Kankakee," one of the boys said. "They were glad to be rid of him."

"I'm not surprised." Cyrus regarded the young man. He didn't know him very well. He had only been working at the stable a couple of weeks. "You're Cole's brother, right?"

"Yes, sir," the young man said. "My name's Cary."

"Cary, huh? I thought Cole said your name was Carlton."

"I changed it," the young man replied and offered a winning smile. He was in his mid-teens, and though Cyrus's thoughts never turned this way, he had to admit this was one of the best-looking young fellows he had ever come across – "matinee good looks," one of the ladies at the stable had observed. His hair was black and wavy, and his brown eyes were set off by the longest lashes Cyrus had ever seen on a man. His nose was chiseled like a Greek statue, not something you saw very often in kids from the streets. He had a dimple in the middle of his chin, and Cyrus then recalled that the other hands called him Cary, after Cary Grant the movie star. He could see why.

"Well, Cary," Cyrus said, "just be careful not to get too close to a horse like that or sneak up on him from the rear. You'll get a bad surprise." He wiped the grime from his hands. "We'll want to move this one over to the meat plant first chance we get. Bad tempered beast."

Cary nodded, then he and his companion went back outside to park the trailer. Cyrus went back to his desk, ignoring the clash of the horse's angry hooves pounding against the stall door.

The Wild West

———⟫••⟪———

By six p.m. it was dark in the stable. Cyrus had turned on the green-shaded lamp he used when he was going over the company's accounts. He was so engrossed in the numbers that at first he didn't notice a figure standing in the doorway.

Filling the doorway was more like it. The hulking form took up almost all the space in the opening and blocked out what little light shown in from the street. The new arrival was six foot three at least, taller than Cyrus, and must have weighed three hundred pounds, most of it neck and shoulders. He wore a black pork pie hat, a fashion accessory Cyrus had always thought was silly looking on a grown man, but he wasn't about to share that opinion with a stranger this big.

"Help you?" Cyrus asked, looking up.

The man didn't answer at first. He stepped toward the desk, into a circle of light from the lamp so that Cyrus could see him better. Cyrus was right about the man's physique: under the tight wool suit he appeared to be solid muscle.

"If you're looking for riding lessons I don't know we have a horse big enough to carry you," Cyrus said lightly. The stranger didn't crack a smile. He sniffed the air.

"Place smells like shit," he answered.

"Well, it's a stable."

"I'm here on business."

"Oh? Buying or selling?"

"I sell insurance."

Cyrus rose slowly from the desk. The big man took a step closer. Cyrus said, "Why don't you start by telling me your name?"

The other man smiled menacingly. Cary and the other stable hand had seen the stranger arrive and now stood in the entrance to the stalls, leaning on their brooms.

"I know who he is," Cary said, surprised by his own boldness. "My brother told me about you. You're Frankie the Hat."

Frankie "The Hat" Capello was John Panazzo's number one enforcer, a stone cold killer, a legend on the West Side. His business was collections, and people beyond the neighborhood knew that he had a deadly talent for his work. Cole Harmon's advice to his younger brother was to stay the hell away if he ever saw this man. But there was no time to give Cyrus Caine the background.

"Smart kid," Frankie replied.

"Well, Mister . . . Hat," Cyrus said slowly, shifting his weight. He rested his fingertips on the top of the desk, within reach of the drawer where he kept a revolver. "What kind of insurance do we have to discuss? You interested in horses?"

"I come to welcome you to the neighborhood," Frankie said in a tone that was anything but welcoming.

"Well, that's nice of you. A fruit basket would have been enough."

Frankie's lips curled into a threatening line. "That's funny. You're a funny guy." He took another step forward. Cyrus could feel himself tense. The two boys shrank back.

"You're new around here, so let me explain something," Frankie said slowly. "You're not out in the country with a bunch of shitkickers now. This is the city. When you operate in the city, you want to protect your business."

"Protect it how, exactly?"

"Things happen." He looked around the stable, took in the beams, the ceiling. "Old place like this, all this wood and straw lying around. Bet it could catch fire real easy."

"And you, you're an insurance agent?"

"You might say that." Frankie put a meaty fist on his hip, so that Cyrus could see the .45 stuck in his belt.

"You see, the thing is," Cyrus said, stalling for time, "we're just getting started here. We don't have a lot of extra cash."

"That's not my problem. You wanna work in this neighborhood, my boss expects you to be under his protection. That way, nobody gets hurt. None of these pretty animals. Or you neither."

Cyrus nodded. "So that's how it is. Tell you what, Frankie. Would you take a down payment right now?"

Frankie nodded. Cyrus came out from behind his desk. He saw the big man brace. But Cyrus smiled his most engaging smile. "Come this way. I do have a little stashed away for a rainy day. Looks like it's raining right now."

Frankie smirked. This *medagone* wasn't a complete idiot after all. Too bad. It would have been fun smashing his insolent face in. Cyrus led him into the alleyway and started walking past the stalls.

"Where we going?" Frankie demanded, hand resting on his pistol.

"To get the money," Cyrus said. "That's what you came for, right? To get the money?" He and the enforcer brushed past the two stable boys, who looked at their boss quizzically. Cyrus led the big man all the way down the row of stalls to the last one.

"In here," Cyrus said, nodding to the last door.

"You keep the money in with the animals?" Frankie said skeptically.

"Sure. No one would think to look for it there. Smells like shit," Cyrus said easily. His hand reached for the bolt on the stable door. On the other side he could hear a horse shifting its weight, snorting, pawing the ground. Cyrus swung the door open so he was standing behind it.

"Go on in," he said.

Frankie the Hat stepped forward, and just as he did the gray gelding let out a savage squeal and delivered a double-barreled kick. The animal's rear hooves caught the gunman in the head and chest and sent him flying against the far wall of the stable. The heavy body slammed into the timber and slumped to the ground. Cary and his friend ran to see the spectacle.

"Get that door latched," Cyrus yelled to them, and they slammed the door shut before the mad horse could do more damage.

Cyrus rushed to the motionless form of Frankie the Hat. He tilted the pork pie back on the man's forehead and looked into his vacant eyes. He felt the thick neck for a pulse, found none.

The front of the man's skull was caved in where the horse had kicked him.

Cyrus heard footsteps running through the stable toward them. He snatched Frankie's gun from his belt and swung it around, in case the man had come with backup. But in the dim light he recognized Cole Harmon.

Cole took in the scene: his boss standing over a body, a gun in his hand, his brother and some other kid looking down with their mouths hanging open. He took a closer look at the man on the floor.

"Holy shit. What happened here? Is he dead?"

"Looks to be," Cyrus drawled. Cole looked harder at the body, then his hand went to his mouth.

"Sweet Jesus, do you know who that is? You killed Frankie the Hat!"

"I didn't kill him. The horse did."

"Oh my God … Frankie the Hat," Cole murmured. He wasn't one to show fear, but he knew this was big. "Do you know what the Panazzos will do to us?"

"Not if we keep our heads," Cyrus said.

"What'll we do with him?" Cary asked. Cyrus looked around the stable, trying to sort out his thoughts. He turned the gun around and handed it to Cole.

"First, get rid of the gun. You two," he said to the stable hands, "grab his hands and feet."

They reached down and groaned as they tried to lift the body, three hundred pounds of dead weight. This would be more dragging than carrying. Cary spied a wheelbarrow nearby, and with great effort the three men managed to heave the body into it. Cary grasped the handles and looked to his boss.

"Where are we taking him?"

"You know that pile of manure out behind the barn?" Cyrus asked. The two boys nodded. "Take him back there."

"Then what?"

"Then bury him in it," Cyrus said. He leaned over, picked up Frankie's hat from the floor and brushed it off.

Two nights later, John Panazzo and his crew were gathered for dinner at La Fontanella again. One waiter was filling their glasses with wine, while another brought in a tray with their entrees and set it down in the corner to serve.

The *capo* of the Panazzo family entered the room carrying a package. Panazzo looked at him in annoyance.

"What do you got there? We're just about to eat."

The *capo* shrugged. "Some kid dropped it off in the bar. It's addressed to you." He set the package down on the table. It was a ladies hat box from Marshall Field's, the finest department store in the Loop. The Beak wrinkled his sizeable schnozz.

"Smells like shit. Who'd send me something like this?"

The *capo* shrugged. He lifted the lid of the box carefully and set it aside. The Panazzo crew peered inside cautiously, then reeled back.

"It really does smell like shit," Panazzo growled. He covered his nose with his napkin.

The *capo* reached into the box carefully and removed something, held it up for the gang to see. They all recognized it right away. It was Frankie Capello's pork pie hat, sitting atop a fresh pile of horse manure. There was no note.

The various factions of The Outfit gave Cyrus Caine and his gang a wide berth after that. The ex-con was too unpredictable to be dealt with, and that made him dangerous. Not worth the risk, Panazzo and the other family heads decided. Besides, he wasn't in their business.

Word of the disappearance of Frankie the Hat spread quickly, and the stable on the West Side, with its ragtag crew of young thugs and ex-cons, took on a certain cache. Anyone who could make Frankie the Hat disappear had to be crazy. More than that, they were to be feared.

"What'll we do with the horse?" Cary wanted to know after he and his buddy had buried Frankie's body deep in the manure. The young men learned another valuable lesson that night, one they would apply at other times in their careers: horse manure is a very effective agent for composting large animal carcasses – including humans. High Time Stables always had an active compost pile going, and not because they were avid gardeners. "Should we get rid of it?"

"Hell no," Cyrus replied. "I'm appointing that horse chief of security. He's a made man, after all."

From that night on, the Caine Gang had another moniker to go with their new-found reputation for nerve as well as viciousness. Around this city of Capone, they were known as The Horse Mafia.

Chapter 13

Night Riders

FRIDAY NIGHTS WERE USUALLY QUIET in Croydon. Not usually, Kat thought to herself. Always.

Most of the Croydon men – the young and eligible ones – were away in the service. Except for the occasional herd of gangly recruits enjoying a night off from the naval base on Lake Michigan, there weren't any young men in town to speak of. That made for clusters of bored and listless young women hanging together in lonely solidarity on the weekends, looking for distraction and sometimes trouble, anything to make the time pass until the war was over and husbands and boyfriends came home.

The mood was often tense as these women gathered. News was starting to filter back from the front lines, and it wasn't good. The war in the Pacific was not going well, and the Allies were struggling to gain traction in North Africa. Now it wasn't just the British fighting and dying at the hands of the Axis, but American soldiers too. Women clutched their hearts when they saw the Western Union delivery man making his rounds, praying that he would not stop at their door, then feeling awful because they were wishing for some other woman's heartbreak. Gold stars indicating a lost serviceman started to appear in windows of homes all around town, whether wealthy or poor. People who had rarely read a newspaper before started pouring over reports from faraway locations like North Africa and Sicily and the Pacific islands.

Kat was one of those people. She didn't know much about Morgan's assignment now that he was overseas. He had completed his pilot's training and was assigned to a bomber group somewhere in England. His letters, which came less frequently, were filled with cheerful but empty stories about army life, with any details about his missions carefully excised, usually by Morgan but sometimes by the censors. Still, she lived for his letters, adding them to the growing stack bound with a ribbon in her top dresser drawer.

This Friday night Kat sat at a booth with three other girls at The Roundabout, the local bar and grill where most young people in town either started or ended their weekend evenings. The place looked like what it was: a typical midwestern tavern that did more business in beer than in cuisine. Burgers and cheese curds were the most popular menu items, owing to the Roundabout's proximity to the Wisconsin border. A long well-polished mahogany bar ran the length of the room. Red leatherette booths and chairs were scattered around scarred oak tables. The floor was always sticky, but the prices were right.

Nursing her first beer of the night, Kat still didn't know why she had agreed to come out other than the fact that her girlfriends kept insisting. She felt guilty leaving her grandfather home alone, but then he went to bed by 8 o'clock every night, so why feel guilty? Maybe a night out would get her mind off her troubles, the farm, and a certain Air Corps lieutenant. A circle of sailors on leave from Great Lakes hovered at the end of the bar, eyeing the table of girls, but they were of no interest to Kat.

She glanced up and saw a figure step into the bar and knew her night was about to change.

Kat had not laid eyes on Cyrus Caine in more than three years, the day a judge pronounced him guilty and a deputy led him away in handcuffs. Time had changed him, but she had to admit, not necessarily in a bad way. Cyrus still had that full head of curly black hair that made her think of Heathcliff on the moors. The lines in his face were deeper, especially around the eyes, but in a sunburnt movie serial cowboy kind of way. He was wearing a checked shirt that showed off his broad shoulders and trim waist to good effect. A pair of blue jeans tucked into cowboy boots finished off the look. Here was a rugged son of the Old West, living in northern Illinois.

Kat tried to turn away from the door and seek cover among her girlfriends, but it was too late: Cyrus had spotted her. He was crossing the room and stood at the edge of their table. The other girls, who had never met Cyrus, looked up and swooned, the silly geese. Didn't they know who he was?

"Hello, Barn Cat," he greeted her.

"Hello, Cyrus."

"Never expected to find you in a place like this."

"Neither did I."

One of her friends scooted over and created an open space. "Would you like to join us?" she asked with a bat of her eyes. Kat tried to kick her under the table.

"Thanks," Cyrus replied, then slid into the booth right next to Kat, close. Too close.

"What brings you here, Cyrus?" Kat asked him, making conversation.

"Just doing a little business. Sully over there is a customer of mine." He nodded to the owner, standing behind the bar, who nodded back.

"A customer? What are you selling?"

"I provide his burgers," he said evenly. Same old Cyrus. Never gave anything away.

One of the girls, the flirtiest one who asked him to sit down, said "Are you from around here, Mr...?"

"Caine," Kat told her. "This is Cyrus Caine. Morgan's brother."

"Really?" said the girl, whose name was Betty. "I didn't know Morgan had a brother."

"We try to keep it quiet," Cyrus said, and turned his full attention to Kat, as if the other three were not there. "How is my little brother? What's he up to?"

"Serving his country," Kat said. "I can't say the same for you."

"I'm not eligible," Cyrus replied.

"Oh? Why not?" Betty asked, trying to move his attention back to her. Kat started to offer some excuse, but Cyrus cut her off.

"I was in prison," he said. Betty jumped back in her seat, as if John Dillinger had just introduced himself. Flustered, she rummaged through her purse for a moment and turned to her friends.

"Girls, why don't we go powder our noses and let these two get caught up? I'm sure they have a lot to talk about."

Kat started to protest, but the three friends deserted her. Alone with him now, she and Cyrus regarded each other for a moment.

"I thought they'd never leave," Cyrus said finally. Kat gave a small smile despite herself.

"I was sorry to hear about your grandmother," Cyrus went on. Kat's eyes dropped to her hands, folded on top of the table.

"Thanks. We miss her."

"How's the old man holding up?"

"He's all right. He doesn't have the spark he used to have when she was around. But he manages."

"Must be hard, just the two of you, trying to run that big place."

"It's all right. Slim and Pasquale are still around, although they're not getting any younger either." She took a sip of her beer. "The biggest thing we have to worry about right now are horse thieves."

"Horse thieves, really," Cyrus said without interest. Sully came by and set a bottle of beer in front of him. Cyrus nodded his thanks.

"Horse thieves," Kat repeated. "There's been a slew of robberies in this area. The Eyestones lost half a dozen head a couple of weeks ago."

"That a fact?"

"Then Herbie Walton's place got hit, right across the road from us. They haven't touched our place yet though." She took another sip of her beer, peered at Cyrus over her bottle. His eyes were flat and noncommittal. Maybe now she understood what he was doing in town. Cyrus caught her look.

"You think I had something to do with it?"

Night Riders

"I never said that," Kat replied. Now she was sure. In her experience, Cyrus always had something to do with it, whatever 'it' was. He just continued to nurse his beer. Then he edged a little closer to her. Kat felt his thigh pressed against hers, as if they were conjoined.

"It can't be easy, you taking care of things all on your own. Maybe I can help."

She laughed. "What, do you want to come work for me now?"

Cyrus shook his head. His hand brushed across hers on the table with unnerving gentleness.

"Not to work…." he said. He started to say something else, when he felt a hand on his shoulder.

Cyrus turned around to see a circle of young sailors standing around their booth. They looked to have been overserved.

"Hey mister," one of them, the one with his hand on Cyrus's shoulder, said to him. "How come you ain't in uniform?"

Cyrus took the man's wrist and removed his hand from his shoulder. "I don't see how that's any of your business."

"Maybe it is our business. All of us went out and signed up." He gestured to his friends, who were just as red-faced and unsteady. One of the other swabbies pushed Cyrus's shoulder. "Why aren't you fighting?"

"I may start fighting if one of you boys lays a hand on me again," Cyrus said coldly. Kat knew the look in his eye, knew that he meant it. She put an arm between the sailors and Cyrus.

"Fellas, why don't you go sit down and have a beer on us?" she said lightly. "Anchors away and all that."

Now the drunken focus turned to Kat. One of the sailors reached out and grabbed her arm.

"What are you doing with this bum, honey? Come sit with us." He tried to pull her out of the booth, but he didn't get very far.

Cyrus was on his feet in a shot. He grabbed the first sailor's tunic and smashed his face on the table before hurling him into the bar. He spun around and took down the next sailor with a quick sucker punch before he had a chance to react. Another swabbie, a big brawny kid from Iowa, tried to throw a haymaker but missed. Cyrus leveraged the big boy's weight and sent him crashing to the floor. Kat jumped back as if her dinner plate had just exploded.

By now the sailor from the bar had found his feet and came after Cyrus waving the business end of a beer bottle. He swung, Cyrus blocked his arm and took him down with a quick punch. Two more sailors were charging him now, and Cyrus picked up a chair and broke it over their heads. Five-on-one sailors was equal to three-on-one in a prison yard, and he was handling them.

The sound of breaking furniture prompted Sully into action. He waded into the fray with an ax handle in hand and started to break things up, deflecting a few drunken swings in the process.

"Come on, you fellas. Nobody came to fight. You want to fight, take it outside…."

By now there was no one left to fight. Cyrus's fists were still up, but the sailors were either on the floor or nursing their wounds. One by one they crawled away and regrouped at the other end of the bar, as far from Cyrus as they could get. Whatever the man's reasons for not being in the service, it wasn't because he didn't know how to fight.

Breathless, Cyrus turned back to the table and looked for Kat. She was gone.

A moonless night, the empty fields stretching endless and black with only the dim outline of an occasional barn to break the gloom. A tractor trailer rig idled slowly at the edge of the country road, its lights turned off, only the occasional cough of the engine giving it away. The driver of the truck engaged the emergency brake and shut down the engine.

"Growing up on the West Side, I always figured I was in for a life of crime. I never figured I'd be a horse thief," Cole Harmon said.

Cyrus Caine grunted. "Just shows what a man can become if he dreams big enough." He nodded to the third man in the truck cabin, Cole's kid brother Cary. "Come on, let's get started."

The three men slid down from the truck. The night air was chilly even though it was early summer. They wore dark clothes to conceal their presence. Motioning for quiet, Cyrus led them from the gravel road through the grass embankment. They reached a woven wire fence. Cole dug into his pocket and pulled out a pair of wire cutters. Cyrus knew just where to cut – he had strung every foot of this fence years before. That fast they were on the other side of the fence, approaching a resting cluster of horses.

The men each carried halters with lead ropes already attached. They readied the first one and played out a length of rope as they crept toward the herd. The plan was to halter the horses and guide them back to the rig. They approached softly, not wanting to spook the animals or alert the house down the lane.

The sound of a rifle lever being cocked brought them up sharply. A figure on horseback rode out from a nearby stand of trees.

"Hold it right there," said Kat. She was mounted on her favorite mare Pego, who snorted gray bursts of fog as she emerged from the woods. The three men froze. Cyrus raised his hands in a conciliatory gesture, a grin on his face even though Kat couldn't make out his features clearly. She didn't have to. She knew it was him.

"Hey hey now, Barn Cat. Take it easy," Cyrus cautioned her, taking a step toward her. As he got closer he could see the business-like Winchester pointed his way. "I thought I taught you, never have your finger on the trigger unless you're meaning to shoot."

She fired into the dirt next to his feet. That stopped him in his tracks.

"I do."

"Okay okay, no need to get hostile."

Kat raised the rifle to her shoulder.

"I knew it was just a matter of time before you showed up."

"So, what, you've been camping out in the trees every night? By yourself?" While Cyrus talked the other two men circled about slowly, spacing themselves out so they wouldn't be such an easy target. They started to close in on Kat's horse. Cole Harmon slipped his hand into his jacket and wrapped it around his pistol, but Cyrus stayed him with a hand signal.

The sound of two more rifles being cocked brought the thieves up short. Slim and Pasquale stepped out from the woods, guns shouldered and ready.

"Not by myself," Kat said. Cyrus raised his hands.

"OK, Barn Cat, you win. Tell you what let's do: The boys and I are going to back away, real easy like, and go back where we came from."

"You do that. And if I catch you on this farm again, I won't bother with a warning."

The Harmon brothers were already walking backwards across the pasture. Cyrus joined them, after a small salute to Kat, then they crossed through the hole in the fence and headed for the rig.

The three of them slipped into the cabin of the truck and caught their breath. Cole drew his pistol and held it in his lap.

"Want me to go back and finish them?"

Cyrus shook his head.

"Think they'll call the cops?" Cary asked.

"No. She made her point." Cyrus shook his head and gazed out the window. He could just make out the silhouette of the mounted girl, still watching across the field, rifle resting across one arm. He let out a small sigh.

"Hell of a woman." He snapped out of his reverie and tapped Cole's arm. "Let's get out of here."

Chapter 14

Homecoming

THE PLATFORM AT THE DOWNTOWN Croydon train station was packed. Red, white and blue bunting festooned the red brick station house, and a raised wooden platform had been erected to host a small military band and a speaker's podium. As the train from Chicago lurched into the station, belching smoke and steam, Kat and her grandfather pushed their way through the crowd, smiling and excusing themselves as they went. No one minded. Everyone was happy today. The war was over. The boys were coming home.

Kat searched the open windows of the train, where young soldiers in khaki and green were hanging out, searching back. She recognized classmates and old friends, waved to them, but she began to get nervous when she didn't see the one face she was looking for. Then from the end of the platform she heard a familiar voice, and her heart melted.

"Kat! Kat! Over here!"

She followed the sound to the first car just as Morgan stepped off the train. He was more handsome than ever – older, but intact, and that was all she cared about. He was wearing his officer's uniform, the double silver bars on his shoulders reflecting the midday sun. Rows of campaign ribbons glinted over his left breast. When he saw Kat running toward him he gave a big wave and dropped his duffel bag on the platform. She flew into his arms and hugged him tightly around the neck, then released him just long enough to deliver a deep hard kiss. They stood frozen that way for what seemed like forever, until Morgan felt a heavy paw thump him on the back.

"Welcome home, my boy," he heard Doc Reese say. "Plenty of time for that. You're home now."

"Yes. You're home," Kat added, taking his face in her hands. Morgan studied her face as though he hadn't seen her in years, as though he might devour her whole right there on the platform.

Suddenly he felt a body trying to invade the space between them. A man in a fedora hat with a press card sticking out the grosgrain band worked his way in between the couple.

"Captain Caine, Bob Edsall of the *Croydon Courier*," he said in a rush. "How does it feel to be home?"

"Feels great," Morgan said brusquely. "Now if you'll excuse me...."

"You were part of the big air raid over Berlin, right? What was that like?"

Morgan's discomfiture was becoming obvious. "Why don't you go talk to some of these other fellows? They've all got stories to tell."

"Yeah, but they're not wearing the Distinguished Flying Cross. Now about Berlin..."

Doc cut in at this moment and pried Morgan away from the reporter. He wrapped his burly arms around Morgan and Kat and steered them toward the platform.

"Excuse me, friend. The captain's wanted on the podium." The three of them pushed away, leaving the reporter with an open mouth and an empty note pad.

"I don't really have to get up on the podium, do I?" Morgan whispered to Doc.

"'Fraid so," the old man replied. "The mayor asked for you personally." Morgan wrinkled his brow in irritation, but he was used to taking orders. He gave Kat a quick kiss.

"Hold my place," he said, and mounted the steps up to the impromptu speaker's platform.

Homecoming

Mayor Dave McCarty pumped the captain's hand heartily, muttered a few words of welcome which Morgan didn't hear, then turned to the band and the crowd and motioned both of them to silence. Morgan fell in with a group of other veterans standing behind the mayor.

"Ladies and gentlemen," Mayor McCarty began. He was a tall fellow, gray at the temples, born to the role of politician. "This is a proud day, and a happy one for Croydon, as our husbands and sons" – he looked in Kat's direction and gave her a knowing wink " – and boyfriends are starting to come home. This is a day to celebrate a great victory. With that, I want to introduce one of the many heroes of the late war, our own hometown hero, Captain Morgan Caine."

Applause and whistles greeted the introduction. Morgan squirmed and offered a brief wave.

"Captain Caine, as you can tell from that chestful of medals, was one of the brave pilots who led the bombing raids in France and Germany that brought the Nazis to their knees. He earned the Distinguished Flying Cross for his bravery when he managed to fly his aircraft home on one wing, saving the lives of every one of his crew. Maybe we can get him to tell us about that. Captain Caine, step up here."

The crowd cheered as Morgan took his place beside the mayor. He looked out over the assembled group, glanced back at his fellow soldiers, and spoke in a subdued voice.

"Thank you, Mayor. I'm not here to talk about me. Every one of the men and women standing with me could tell you stories. But really, we don't want to talk about it. We just want to be home." Some of the men standing behind him nodded agreement.

"Instead, let me speak for all of us when I say it's great to be back home with the people we love." Applause rose behind him and in front of him. "It was an honor to serve, to do our part to protect the greatest people, the greatest country on the face of the earth, the United States of America."

The crowd roared. The band struck up a tune. The mayor thumped him on the back and made a joke about a future in politics. Morgan smiled briefly, waved to the crowd and got off the stage as quickly as he could. Kat met him at the bottom of the stairs.

"Let's get out of here," he said, taking her hand.

They started to thread their way through the assembly, shaking hands and accepting accolades from friends and neighbors, when they heard a low rumble rise from the far end of the street. The mayor and the other people on the dais peered down the street, and the crowd turned and craned to see what was causing the noise. The rumble grew louder and closer, the ground seemed to shake, and at the corner a cloud of dust started to rise. The noise rose like thunder and pressed in on them, and charging out of the dust Morgan could make out a herd of horses.

Riding at the head of the herd was his brother Cyrus. Looking like a cavalry officer from another war, he carried a large American flag that flapped in the breeze.

The herd bore down on the station as Cyrus drove the horses through the main street of Croydon. Fortunately, the train station was one street over from the main drag, otherwise Cyrus and his wild herd might have trampled the bystanders. Several other men rode with Cyrus, whistling and whooping and waving their hats at the horses to keep them moving. Morgan didn't recognize any of the men with Cyrus.

Kat did. As they drew closer, she spotted two of the men flanking Cyrus as the bandits who had accompanied him to Harmony Farm, the night Cyrus tried to steal her horses. One of the outlaws was thick set and rough looking. The other man, who could have been a whittled-down version of his brother, was slight, not yet out of his teens, with a face that was unmarked and could almost be called beautiful. She wouldn't be likely to forget these two, even if she only saw them in the dark and at the end of a Winchester.

Homecoming

Cyrus and his gang rode through the streets like they owned them. It was a scene out of an old Western movie, with horses stampeding through the streets of town and scattering the townspeople, shattering windows, while the cowboy gang whooped and hollered. People coughed and rubbed their eyes and waved the dust away. Some of them smiled, thinking perhaps this was part of the welcome ceremony. In a sense it was. Cyrus turned to the hard-looking fellow on his right and handed off the flag.

"Take this for me," he said. "Keep 'em moving." Cole Harmon nodded and whistled, and he and the rest of the herd kept trotting down the street, the flag fluttering in the wind. Cyrus steered his horse over to the edge of the bandstand and pulled up right in front of Morgan, Kat and Doc.

"Welcome home, little brother," Cyrus called out. "How'd you like the show?"

"This for my benefit, Cyrus?" Morgan replied. "You could have just sent a note."

"Naw. I like to send a message to the whole town." Cyrus tipped his cowboy hat in Kat's direction. "Good day, Katherine. Doc. It's a grand day, don't you think? Fit for a hero." His voice, as usual, had a mocking twist to it, Kat thought.

"What are you doing here, Cyrus?" Kat challenged him, clearly displeased. Cyrus smiled at her.

"Didn't you hear? I'm opening a stable this week."

"A stable?" she said, her blue eyes flashing at him. "Where? What stable?"

"I bought Cold Creek Farm."

Morgan's brow furrowed. "Cold Creek Farm? Isn't that Judge Finfrock's old place?"

"Yeah. Poor old fella had a run of bad luck."

Doc interjected, "Place burned to the ground. The judge died the next day of a heart attack. Broken heart, they say. That place had been in his family near a hundred years." Doc's eyes leveled on Cyrus, who looked away innocently.

"Like I said, bad luck. Anyway, it's mine now." Morgan and Kat exchanged uneasy glances.

"You don't look happy," Cyrus observed. "I thought you'd be thrilled. Now we'll be neighbors." He shot a glance at Morgan. "What do you think of that, brother?"

"Congratulations," Morgan said tersely. Cyrus leaned across his saddle.

"Maybe now that you're done flying around all over the place you'll be looking to do something closer to home. What would you think about joining me in the business?"

"You and me? Partners?"

"Something like that. Course, you've been gone a long time. But I'd let you work your way up."

"What about your place in the city?" Kat asked.

"Oh, I'll keep that. My associates will look after my interests there." He nodded in the direction of Cole and Cary Harmon. Kat glowered at them. "I plan to put all my focus on growing this new enterprise."

Morgan cast a hard look up at his brother's grinning face.

"I wish you luck, Cyrus. But I have plans of my own."

"Really? What plans are those?"

"I'm going to be working at Harmony Farm." He wrapped a possessive arm around Kat's waist. "Kat and I are getting married."

The news had the desired effect. The smile died on Cyrus's face, and any pretense of friendliness drained from his dark eyes. He studied the couple hard for a moment, caught a look of defiance from Kat that was aimed straight at him.

"My my," Cyrus said at last. "This *is* a big day. A brass band, a hero's welcome, and now wedding bells." He tipped his hat again and took the reins up in one hand. "Be sure to send me an invitation."

Cyrus pulled his horse around hard, nudged its flanks and charged off down the street to catch up with his herd.

Homecoming

———))•●•((———

The First Congregational Church of Croydon was just what one would expect to find in a town this size in this day and age: a simple whitewashed brick building with a tall thin spire, red curved doors, leaded glass windows that let the afternoon light pour through in soft diffusion. Simple arrangements of white lilies and baby's breath stood on either side of the altar, and the well-worn red carpet had been covered by a white cotton runner, awaiting the bride's steps.

The bride, Katherine Reese, had just arrived at the back of the church and stood with her grandfather. Kat regarded the old man with joy and sadness. He looked thin in his dark charcoal suit, the garment hanging loosely from his shrinking frame. His sparse white hair had been plastered across the top of his head. But two things were still the same: his florid moustache, white with a bit of yellow at the corner where he usually kept his pipe; and his blue eyes, pale and watery now, but still full of reassurance and love.

Kat looked at the altar as Morgan stepped out to take his place next to the minister, Reverend Nagy. Her soon-to-be husband seemed poised and confident, not at all the gangly young man who had gone off to college and then to war just a few short years before. Morgan wore a blue worsted suit that fit his lean frame beautifully. A white carnation was pinned in his lapel. There had been some talk of his wearing his Army Air Corps dress uniform, but Morgan had quickly vetoed the idea. "I'm done with that," he said, and headed into town to buy a suit of civilian clothes.

"You've kept that young man waiting a long time," she heard her grandfather saying.

"I hope he'll recognize me with all this makeup," Kat said. "I feel like a kewpie doll."

"You look beautiful," her grandfather said, adjusting her veil. Kat looked down at the floor-length wedding dress and admired the beads and pearls, the long straight lines that suited her tall slim figure.

"It's the dress," she said. "I can't believe Grandma actually made it. I never even saw her working on it."

"She did most of her best work before anybody else got up." A tear started to well in the old man's eye, remembering his love, his life partner, gone now on this day of all days. He added wistfully, "That woman could do just about anything. Especially with a needle."

"Where did she even find the fabric? You can't find silk in any of the stores."

"Funny story there," the old man said, straightening himself. "Friend of Morgan's was in jump school over at Fort Sheridan. Morgan persuaded him to borrow some supplies and deliver them to your grandma."

"Supplies? What kind of supplies?"

"A parachute."

Kat's jaw dropped slightly. "You mean this is black market?"

"No no. More like government issue."

Kat started to shake her head, then broke into a laugh, and in a moment the two of them were laughing at the back of the church. "Making a spectacle of themselves," as her grandmother would have said. When Kat caught her breath she said, "And where did your suit come from? Horse blankets?"

"Not at all," the old man huffed. "This is the best suit they had at Alden's Men's Wear. You don't mind spending money on a suit if you get some wear out of it. I figure when this is done you can bury me in it." He smiled at her, that reassuring twinkly smile that always made her feel like things were all right. She placed a steadying hand on his arm.

"Are you sure you're up to this, Grandpa?"

"I promised your grandmother I'd see you to the altar, and that's what I plan to do," the old man said. He heard the organist, Mrs. Feeney, working her fat fingers through the last few bars of

Homecoming

"Oh Promise Me." He took Kat's arm and winked at her. "If I start to swoon, just hold me up."

The best man, a young officer from Morgan's unit whom she had not met until the night before, stepped up next to the groom and whispered something to him, and the two young men bantered nervously. The crowd in the church was not large, mostly old friends and classmates and the usual cohort of Doc's cronies from town.

"At least Cyrus isn't here," Kat said.

"Did you invite him?"

"No. But when has that ever stopped Cyrus?"

The old man shook his head. "You know, your grandmother used to worry about you and him."

"About me and Cyrus?" She was astonished. "Why would Grandma worry about him?"

"He was – is I guess – a good-looking devil."

"Devil being the operative word. I don't think we should be talking about him in church."

"She was always afraid you might pick the wrong brother."

Kat looked resolutely down the aisle. Morgan caught her eye and winked at her. She smiled back.

"I picked the right brother," she said confidently. The old man patted her hand. Mrs. Feeney, on cue from the minister, launched into a vigorous version of the Wedding March. Morgan looked at his bride and gave her a wide smile as the rest of the congregation turned around and craned their necks.

"Guess we better get this show on the road," Doc Reese said, and they started down the aisle.

The service was mercifully short. Mr. and Mrs. Morgan Caine were introduced to the congregation, exchanged a long passionate kiss and walked back down the aisle and out the double doors, where they lined up next to Doc to greet the guests. Kat ran her arm through Morgan's and kissed him on the cheek.

"That wasn't so bad, now was it, Captain?"

"Are you kidding? I'm the happiest man in Croydon County."

Kat looked past her new husband and saw her grandfather, shaking hands and laughing with the crowd like he was the mayor of the town.

"You may have to settle for second happiest," she said.

The newlyweds smiled and nodded and accepted kisses and best wishes from friends and neighbors. Morgan was in the middle of saying something to Mr. Frazier, his old principal, when he looked out at the street and froze.

"We've got more company," he murmured to Kat.

Rolling down the street was a striking black phaeton coach drawn by a pair of white horses. The lacquered wood was polished to a high gloss and festooned with a bright array of flowers. The wheels and the trim were finished in gold leaf. The horses's manes had been braided and their harnesses decorated with flowers and bells. Crepe paper streamers and tin cans tied to string dangled from the back of the coach and jangled as the vehicle pulled up to the sidewalk in front of the church. In the driver's seat, reins held loosely in one hand, sat Cyrus Caine. He wore a black cutaway coat, an open collar white shirt and a pair of jeans. A tall silk hat finished the effect. The ever-present Pall Mall dangled from his lower lip.

Cyrus pulled the coach to a halt in front of the church. He set the brake, tied off the reins and rested one of his shiny black cowboy boots on the coachman's step. He gave the couple an insouciant wave. Morgan and Kat hesitated, then walked to the end of the sidewalk to meet him.

"Congratulations, kids," Cyrus greeted them, with a mocking tip of his silk hat. "Need a lift?"

Homecoming

"Hello, Cyrus," Morgan greeted him awkwardly. As he drew closer to the coach Morgan thought he smelled whiskey. He immediately thought of his father.

"I figured my invitation got lost in the mail," Cyrus was saying. "So many details to take care of and all. But I didn't want to let such a happy occasion go by without some expression of my joy." He waved his hand to take in the horses and carriage. "What do you think? It's a beauty, isn't it? Brought it all the way out from Chicago. Used to belong to Marshall Field I think. Or the Kaiser, one of the two."

Cyrus jumped down from the rig and flicked his cigarette away.

"It's beautiful, Cyrus," Kat admitted, looking for something to say to her new brother-in-law.

"It is, isn't it? Seems fitting for such a beautiful bride." He looked at her with a leer. For a moment Kat was afraid he would kiss her. Instead he smiled and reached around behind him for the reins. He held them out to Morgan. "Here you go."

"You expect me to drive this thing?"

"Doesn't come with a driver." He doffed his hat to Kat. "I'm off duty as of now."

He held the reins out to his brother again. The look on his face was hard and mocking. "Think you can handle her?"

The brothers locked eyes. Morgan took the reins, and Cyrus took a long step backwards. "Make way for the bride," he said with a sweep of his hat. Morgan helped Kat up into the carriage, arranged the folds of her silk dress around her legs, then climbed up next to her. He released the brake and prepared to pull away.

"Wait. I almost forgot." Cyrus reached onto the floorboard of the carriage and came up with a small paper sack. He thrust his hand into it, pulled out a fistful of rice and threw it above the newlyweds' heads. Morgan clicked his tongue and flicked the reins. The carriage pulled away, leaving Cyrus laughing on the street and flinging rice after them.

"Your brother is a psychopath. I hope you know that."

"A psychopath?" Morgan repeated, his expression somewhere between shock and amusement. "Did you go to medical school while I was away?"

"I'm serious," Kat replied. "It's bad enough he shows up at the wedding uninvited. Now we're going to have him as a neighbor. And a competitor." The two of them were alone, finally, in a quiet suite at the Deer Path Inn in Lake Forest. After a pleasant reception at Harmony Farm, they had finally been able to pry themselves away from Doc and the neighbors, climb into Morgan's Ford truck and drove to their honeymoon destination. Now he was throwing off his suit coat and taking off his tie, which had been choking him all day.

"I don't think offering us a carriage ride makes him a psychopath," Morgan said mildly. "He just wanted to be part of the celebration."

"Cyrus is always the center of everything. At least in his mind."

Morgan crossed the room and stood in front of her. His hands began to stroke the soft swirls of her dress along her sides, down her hips.

"Not everything," he said, continuing his exploration. "Did I mention how beautiful you look in this dress, Mrs. Caine?"

"You can thank your paratrooper friend for that," Kat replied. Morgan pulled her closer, running his strong hands gently along her back, as if memorizing each of her vertebrae. He found her tailbone, then finally, both hands came to rest on her buttocks. He nuzzled her neck.

"Are you looking for something, Captain?" she said playfully.

"The ripcord," he answered. Kat smiled, moved his hands away and took a step backward. She reached behind her, and with the unfastening of a few strategic buttons the dress came open and slid to the floor, billowing at her feet. She stepped out of it and laid on top of the bed. Morgan stretched out next to her. With one hand he found the snap of one of her garters and released it. Then very slowly he rolled the silk stocking down her leg, pausing now and then to kiss the exposed flesh of her inner thigh. Kat watched him with fascination.

"You seem awfully experienced at this, Captain Caine," she teased him. "Learn this from lots of mam'selles over in France, did you?"

"It was a long war," he murmured as he started to work on the second stocking. When he was done he drew her close to him and kissed her deeply, finding the curve of her long white neck, smiling as he heard a soft purr come from her throat. He reached behind her and found the snaps of the longline bra she had worn under the silk dress, and in a moment it was open. He took it in one hand and threw it over his shoulder.

Morgan took one of her pale breasts in each hand. He paused just long enough to say,

"The last thing I want to talk about tonight is my brother…."

Chapter 15

Golden Boy
1950

MORGAN CAINE TURNED UP the collar of his topcoat and shifted his body away from the sharp October wind. The last leaves had fallen from the trees that surrounded the Croydon cemetery, the black branches snaking out against the swift-moving clouds. Morgan pulled Kat closer to him and felt her shivering beneath her wool coat. He reached out and took their two-year-old daughter in his arms. The little girl snuggled into her father's shoulder, partly from cold but more from sleepiness. Morgan kissed the top of her head and smiled. They had named her after her great-grandmother – Meghan, a variation of Margaret. Like her mother, she was a redhead, and the wayward locks falling over her pale forehead always made his heart leap. He held his little family close, noticed Kat placing her hand on her growing belly, their next child she was carrying, and felt incredible joy in the midst of their sadness.

Reverend Nagy — the same minister who had married them just a few years before — stood at the head of the gravesite, reciting verse. The minister had done this service so many times, Morgan wondered if he actually read the words or if he knew them all from memory at this point.

"Let not your hearts be troubled; believe in God, believe also in me. In my Father's house are many rooms; if it were not so, would I have told you that I go to prepare a place for you? And when I go and prepare a place for you, I will come again and will take you to myself, that where I am you may be also. And you know the way where I am going…."

Morgan stared at the polished oak coffin that bore the remains of the only father he could remember, Doc Reese. The old man had fought hard at the end, determined to see his great-grandchildren come into the world. At least he lived to see Meg, Morgan thought to himself. Too bad he had not been able to hang on for the new one, but by the end the pain was just too much. Now he would be laid to rest next to his dear wife Maggie, who had been so kind to Morgan and his ungrateful brother when they were young and had nowhere in the world to go. Doc and Maggie had reared them, given them shelter and an education and a life. For Morgan, they had also provided their grand-daughter, now his wife, whom he adored.

Then there was the farm, the only real home he had ever known, and now his life's work. He and Kat had been managing the property for years, but now Kat owned it outright. They worked together in the horse breeding and trading business, which had thrived since Morgan's return from the war.

"I owe you a lot, Doc," Morgan whispered. "I'll try to be worthy of it."

Morgan saw Kat's eyes looking beyond her grandfather's service to another pair of graves in the next row. When the service was done and the casket lowered into the ground, the minister and the neighbors thanked for their attendance and their sympathies, Kat picked up an armful of flowers from the graveside, and the three of them went to lay the flowers on her parents' graves.

"It seems so long ago," Kat said, as much to herself as to Morgan. "It's so sad. I never really knew them."

Morgan nodded. Kat's parents were dead before he even arrived at Harmony Farm.

"I don't think you ever told me how they died," Morgan said.

"Car accident. Daddy was teaching Mama how to drive and she took a turn too fast. She was a daredevil."

"Imagine that," Morgan said. Kat nudged him gently in the ribs.

Meg rubbed her eyes and reached out to her mother. "Mommy, cold. Home?"

"Sure, honey," Kat replied, taking the little girl in her arms. The three Caines made their way back to the car. Kat paused for a moment and blew a final kiss to her grandparents.

"Sleep well, Grandpa. We'll miss you."

The drive home from the cemetery took them straight out of town and onto the main road leading to Harmony Farm. Kat leaned back on the headrest and stroked the head of her daughter, resting on her lap. Meg had been asleep before Morgan could put the car in gear. Morgan had bought this car used the year before — a 1947 Lincoln Zephyr 4-door sedan with a big V-12 engine. He said it was for Kat, but she knew how much he loved driving it. They needed a second car now that the family was growing and the truck was tied up most of the day.

A sense of wistfulness crept over Kat as she watched the fields rolling by outside the window. It had been hard losing her parents as such a young girl, but now it seemed so long ago that she had to try hard to remember her mother and father. Then her grandparents had taken her in and loved her as much as any child could be loved. Now they were gone too, first Grandma, then Doc. She had been orphaned twice. Kat brushed a stray lock of copper hair from Meg's forehead and pulled up the velvet collar of her coat against her alabaster cheek to keep her warm. She looked at her husband, driving in silence, and felt an overwhelming sense of love, of safety and security. This was her family now. She and Morgan and their daughter would take Harmony Farm into the future.

Kat's reverie ended as the big car turned left at the intersection and the massive gate of Cyrus Caine's property loomed ahead of them. There was no way to avoid going past Cold Creek Farm without a long detour. Kat was sure her brother-in-law had bought the place for exactly that reason.

Morgan glanced over at her at exactly that moment.

"Looks grander every time I see it," he said. "Like San Simeon."

The horse farm wasn't quite as grand as the Hearst estate, but Kat knew what he meant. Cyrus had expanded the place considerably in the few years since he had bought it. The first thing he did was to bulldoze the remnants of the Finfrock family homestead, grinding it into powder. Then he built his own home over the remains, a two-story limestone structure that looked like a fortress. The most striking feature was the whitewashed brick entryway that stood in front of the property. At the top was a wrought-iron sign announcing the place – 'Cold Creek Farm — Riding Academy and Stables' – with a pair of interlocking Cs fashioned from a pair of horseshoes that formed a crest of sorts. Most locals assumed the 'CC' was for Cold Creek, but Morgan knew differently. He had seen that same design tattooed on his brother's arm the day he visited him in prison, before the war. The dagger was gone though; "Might scare the youngsters," Cyrus explained when asked why he had deleted that part of his crest.

A few miles further brought them to their own home. Morgan had to admit, Harmony Farm had changed a lot since he and Kat had taken over as the main proprietors. Doc had insisted on moving out of the main house and giving it to them. He took up in one of the smaller buildings behind the main residence and fixing up what he called "the outlaw apartment." It consisted of a small living room that opened onto the kitchen, with a high counter separating the two. A bedroom, a bathroom, and an office were all Doc required. In the last year the apartment had been turned into a nursing facility, with a hospital bed moved into the main room and an assortment of oxygen tanks, IV stands and other equipment. An attendant was on duty around the clock in the last days. Morgan missed the old man, but he knew that the past year had been agony for him. Doc had been glad to see it done.

Kat had thrown herself into a remodeling project of the main residence. They had pushed out the front walls of the house and added a new livingroom, a dining room, a library and the main foyer connecting to the older part of the house. The new façade was done in red brick with green shutters setting off the full-length front windows. A broad porch wrapped around the front of the house and was braced by wide white pillars. It reminded Morgan of the elegant horse farms he had seen around Lexington Kentucky on his many buying trips to the state. "We're bringing a bit of bluegrass horse country to the northwest suburbs," he joked, but he was right. The rest of the property, from fencing to outbuildings, all matched the same motif, with white paint and green trim as the dominant palette. Set against the rolling pastures and paddocks, Harmony Farm was a lovely place to see from the road or to spend time at if riding happened to be your passion.

The business had continued to thrive, and the farm made an inviting haven for the pre-teen girls who were the heart and soul of the business. (Most boys didn't seem terribly interested in learning to ride hunters and jumpers. Those who did come out to ride horses preferred Western saddles, like Gene Autrey, the Lone Ranger and other celluloid cowboys.) Kat supervised the riding lesson program, and she had trained up a couple of young women as her junior instructors. These young ladies knew how to ride but also how to relate to their younger charges, to make it fun while instilling discipline and good habits. Harmony Stables had become the place to go for anyone seriously interested in riding or jumping competitively, and the married Caines had made quite a success of it.

Horse shows were becoming a big part of the business model. Not only was there a lot of money to be made selling jumpers and other showhorses to new and improving riders. There were fat fees for boarding, coaching, and trailering to horse shows around the country. Business was good.

Morgan remembered hearing two dads talking, leaning against a fence as they waited for their darlings to finish a lesson.

Golden Boy 1950

One of the men was a prominent eye ear nose and throat doctor from Kankakee. Drawing on his pipe, he said to the other man, "I've taken out nearly every tonsil in Kankakee County to pay for all this. What it costs to keep this operation going – the horses, the lessons, the new riding habits. English boots and saddles. The entry fees. The boarding, the feed, the vet's bills. Getting up at 4 a.m. to drive halfway across the state for a hunt or a horse show."

The other man nodded mournfully. "Having a horse is like having a kid who never graduates from college."

"You're right. And for what? A ten-cent ribbon. A plastic loving cup. But you know what?" He took another draw on his pipe, his eyes fixed on his daughter in the ring. "It's worth every damn penny. Because she loves it. We're at the stage now, her mother and I, where we are the dumbest two people on the planet. But it gives her something to talk to us about. Something to be happy about. I wouldn't trade it for the world."

Morgan walked away, realizing that the doctor had just described his entire business plan. The next month he sold the doctor a new horse for his daughter.

It was a different world over at the Cold Creek Riding Academy. Cyrus was still one of the best traders in horse flesh in the country and was widely known for his expertise. It was also known that he was a sharp trader, slippery on the ethical curve, willing to do business just once if he could make a quick killing on a sale. "There are always more suckers," he would say. Cyrus ran a thriving business importing horses from California, which were then either dressed up and sold to unsuspecting customers looking for show horses, or sold to the slaughterhouse in Chicago for dog food. "Every horse has a price," Cyrus was fond of saying. "It might be two hundred thousand for a prime jumper, or it might be 29 cents a pound for prime dog chow."

The brothers crossed paths frequently; in the horse world, running into Cyrus Caine was inevitable. They attended the same horse shows, the same races, still took part in the Croydon hunts on weekends in the fall. Sometimes they bought and sold horses from each other, once in a while even bought livestock together. And if the two branches of the Caine family were never exactly close, at least they made it look as if the relationship was amicable.

That was mostly Morgan's doing. Morgan was known as a gentleman. He had the polished air of the sophisticated horseman. He was well spoken and looked the part in his tailored riding apparel. It also didn't hurt that he was an educated man and a decorated war veteran. People warmed to Morgan, they trusted him.

Cyrus was cut from coarser cloth. He was handsome too, although the older they got the less the brothers looked alike. While Morgan's hair was brown and straight, Cyrus's was wiry and black, starting to gray at the temples although he was barely thirty. He was tall and hard, like a piece of timber that had been through a fire. He was a man's man, always quick with a joke or a lewd aside, which made him seem companionable even though he detested people. Morgan was a man you respected; Cyrus was a man you feared. "Can't believe you two are brothers," was the comment they each heard most often.

The biggest difference was their approach to business. If you wanted a straight deal, you went to Morgan Caine. If you weren't too particular about bending the rules, talk to Cyrus. Morgan was known for trying to treat the other guy fairly, the way he'd want to be treated. "A chump, in other words," Cyrus would say. Cyrus was always in for the kill, sometimes literally. The whispers in the horse community every time a horse met a mysterious death, or a barn burned down, or the words "arson" or "extortion" were murmured, the name Cyrus Caine was mentioned too. Morgan had heard the whispers on the horse circuit about the 'Horse Mafia,' and knew that his brother was said to be the ringleader. He shut his eyes and ears to the rumors in the early days, figuring these were just the rumblings of jealous competitors. Whenever Cyrus's name came up in conversation, Morgan walked away. He had learned that it did no good to ask Cyrus about his dealings or to share what other people in the horse world were saying.

"None of their goddamn business," Cyrus would growl. "Or yours."

Another major difference was the way they ran their operations. Morgan's riding academy was open and inviting and almost had the atmosphere of an expensive summer camp — all thanks to Kat's influence, Morgan was quick to acknowledge. Cold Creek Stables was another story. While Morgan and Kat favored hiring young women as instructors, Cyrus's "faculty" tended to be muscular young men. That attracted a fair number of young girls, but often for the wrong reasons. Young riders came to Harmony Stables as children because they loved horses. They stayed because it was a fun and safe environment, where kids were kids, and Mrs. Caine was really nice. When they got to their pre-teen years, a lot of the girls were more interested in gossiping and sneaking a drink or a smoke behind the barn and flirting with the handsome stable hands. Cold Creek Stables was the party place. If the parents had known what their little darlings were doing when they "needed to stay late at the barn," they would have been horrified.

Cyrus wasn't immune to the pleasures of the stable himself, although he seemed too busy for that sort of thing most of the time. One day Morgan stopped by to drop off a saddle he had borrowed from his brother's tack room. As he carried it inside Cyrus walked out of the room, hitching up his pants, followed by a girl who could not have been more than fifteen. Her cheeks were flushed, and she was hurriedly buttoning the front of her blouse. When she recognized Morgan she let out a little yelp, glanced down and realized her shirt was still gaping open. She clutched the front of her blouse and whipped around in the other direction, walking away as fast as she could.

"What was that all about?" Morgan said to Cyrus as he slung the saddle over the railing. "Didn't you learn anything in Stateville?"

"Oh, I just like funning with them," Cyrus said dismissively and spat in the sawdust.

UNBRIDLED

While the Caine brothers could find ways to make room for each other in the business world much of the time, they were fierce competitors in the arena. Morgan seemed more genteel about riding; he was mindful of his horse, careful in his own posture and performance. Cyrus was out to win at any cost. As Doc had once said, Cyrus could ride a horse through a brick wall if it meant winning.

The Onwentsia Hunt Club Horse Show in Lake Forest was one of the fanciest events of the season for hunter and jumper riders in Illinois. Morgan and Kat pulled into the parking area on the grounds early the first morning. Meghan was with them. Although she was barely three years old at the time, they wanted to introduce her to the world of horse shows as early as they could. The little girl loved being around horses and had no fear of the big animals. Horses seemed to sense that this tiny person was no threat, and most of them were affectionate or at least indifferent to her. Kat kept a close watch on her at all times though, since one enormous hoof making a misstep could be dangerous.

Morgan walked around to the rear of the trailer and undid the latch to start backing his horses out. He was competing in the open jumper classes later that day. Sometimes he came to events just to watch, to cheer on his students and mingle with the customers. But he was a competitor, and modesty aside, one of the best riders in the state. He liked to keep his edge and keep his name out in front of the market.

Morgan looked across the parking lot and saw a white Cadillac, Cyrus's trademark vehicle, hitched to a large trailer. His brother was unloading a mount of his own with the help of the young good-looking stable hand Morgan recognized from Cold Creek.

"Looks like Cyrus is riding today too," Morgan commented to Kat. She looked over at her brother-in-law, then looked away. "Guess I'll go say hi to him."

"Do that," Kat replied, and busied herself with the horse.

"Hello, Cyrus," Morgan called as he came within range. Cyrus glanced up, neither friendly nor hostile – a good day for him.

"You riding or watching?" Cyrus asked.

"Riding. Open jumper classes this afternoon."

Cyrus looked at his brother more closely now. "Really? Me too." He busied himself tying off a rope on his mount.

"Beautiful horse," Morgan commented, admiring the sleek chestnut animal next to Cyrus's trailer. "Dutch warmblood?"

"Yep. Class A. Hell of a jumper. I plan to take him around the circuit this year. You'll have to go some to beat this one, little brother."

"You know what they say – You're only as good as your horse." Morgan looked around at the other riders arriving in their trucks and trailers, getting their horses ready for the day's events. "Have you seen Bob Bentz around here yet today?"

"Bob who?"

"Bob Bentz. I heard he was going to be here. He won the Open Jumper Division last year."

"Nope, haven't seen him."

Another rider, a tall suntanned commodities trader named Mark Bauer, happened by at that moment and overheard them.

"You talking about Bob Bentz? Hell of a thing, isn't it?"

"What is?" Morgan asked.

"His horse died night before last. Some intestinal thing they think, came on suddenly. Too bad. Bob would have been the man to beat."

Morgan looked at Cyrus, who avoided his eye and busied himself tying off his horse.

"Wasn't that the horse you sold him, Cy?"

"What of it? The vet gave it a clean bill of health."

"Your vet, you mean."

Cyrus's eyes narrowed. "They don't come with a warranty, you know."

"Hell of a thing," Morgan murmured and turned to go. Then he remembered something and turned to his brother again. "Hey, by the way – Heard you got married a while back."

"I did," Cyrus said curtly. "Didn't last long."

"Oh? Sorry to hear that. What was her name?"

Cyrus looked at him long and hard, then finally said, "To tell you the truth, I don't remember."

Cyrus's eyes followed his brother as he walked back to his own trailer. Cary Harmon was standing close by, adjusting the halter on the Dutch warmblood. Cary was the same good-looking guy he had been when he started at High Time Stables. At the moment he looked worried.

"Why was he asking about Bentz's horse?" Cary asked Cyrus quietly. "Think he knows something?"

"He doesn't know shit," Cyrus growled. "Wouldn't even occur to him."

What Cary knew, and Morgan didn't, was that the night before last Cary, on orders from Cyrus, had snuck into the Bentz stable and administered a shot to Bentz's prize jumper. The next day the horse was found dead, the supposed victim of a torsion colic common to horses.

"That's one less horse we have to worry about," Cyrus had said when Cary returned from his errand. He looked sharply at the young man.

"Take this horse on in and get him ready," Cyrus ordered. He added, "And keep away from the other stable boys."

The jumper classes began that afternoon. Several riders went clean in the first two rounds, resulting in a timed jump-off to pick the winner. Each rider would take a turn around a set of barriers at varying heights and widths, trying to beat each other's time. If all the riders cleared the obstacles, the winner was the one with the fastest time. Points were deducted for knocking down a rail or for a horse refusing a jump.

As the jump-off was about to begin, Morgan and Cyrus ended up next to each other, awaiting their turn in the ring.

Golden Boy 1950

Cyrus looked majestic on the sleek chestnut horse named, appropriately, Devil May Care. The Dutch warmblood snorted and pranced, eager to get the jumping started.

Morgan rode a new horse that he had bought on a trip out west. He had been quietly working with the animal ever since, developing his jumping skills, practicing turns and cuts, and getting ready to show. Today was his debut. He was a cavalry-bred horse, a palomino, with a coat the color of gold and a mane and tail that were nearly white. The previous owner in the military had named him Golden Sun.

As Cyrus rode up alongside his brother he looked the horse up and down and smirked.

"What the hell are you supposed to be? Roy Rogers?" Morgan ignored the jibe.

"Palomino's just a color, Cy," Morgan said quietly, stroking the beautiful horse's neck. "Wait'll you see what he can do on a course."

"I'm quaking in my boots."

Through the succeeding rounds the horses were eliminated one by one. Morgan had to admit, Devil May Care was born to jump, and Cyrus was a very skilled rider. Both horse and man took the fences aggressively, launching cleanly with a great extension of the horse's long legs. When it was his turn Golden Sun held his own, to Cyrus's displeasure. Morgan was also a talented rider, more cautious, taking chances only when he needed to. The horse went through its paces like a veteran, clearing each hurdle with room to spare. To Cyrus's annoyance, his brother's horse quickly became the crowd's favorite, with cheers and whistles every time the big golden horse took a jump, with cheering and applause when he finished his round. Morgan's wife and daughter seemed to lead the cheering section, and once the little girl pointed to the arena and exclaimed "Daddy! My daddy!" to the delight of the crowd.

After several rounds, Cyrus on his dark beast held the best time at 35.73. Cyrus rode up next to Morgan as he exited the arena and pointed up at the clock.

"Beat that, Golden Boy."

"Ladies and gentlemen, if you'll take your places, it's time for the final round. Devil May Care of Cold Creek Stables, ridden by Mister Cyrus Caine, is in the lead at 35.73." Polite applause greeted the announcement.

"We're down to the final six," the announcer continued. "Riders seem to be having trouble with that single red rail this afternoon. Let's see how they adjust their approaches as they try to clear it."

Only the best riders were left. Having had the chance to make it around the course a few times, they knew how each fence should be ridden. Only one of the riders made a fault in that round, but in the end they fell off one by one as they failed to beat Cyrus Caine's time.

"Now Number 37, Golden Sun, owned by Harmony Stables and ridden by Mister Morgan Caine, trying to beat the best time of the afternoon," the loudspeaker declared, to enthusiastic applause from the spectators. Morgan made his courtesy circle, surveilling the hurdles one last time, then lined his horse up for the first jump. Golden Sun wasn't the fastest horse in the field – that would be Devil May Care – so Morgan decided to make his turns tighter to close the time. He took the first hurdle perfectly in eight strides and rode on through the course – a vertical, a spread leading to an in-and-out, another vertical. He sailed over the troublesome red rail with ease. The crowd cheered.

"He's keeping a good pace," the announcer said. "Closing in on the winning time . . . ."

The last two hurdles – a double rail followed by a two-stride combination – lay ahead. Morgan angled his run at the inside turn and took it wide. Golden Sun launched over the double bar and seemed to hang there, suspended in the air. The crowd caught its breath at the sheer beauty and mastery of the ride. The horse's rear hooves cleared the fences with ease. Then Morgan picked up speed and took the last fence in an easy jump.

Golden Boy 1950

"That's it, ladies and gentlemen! Time is 34.71! A faultless ride by Mister Morgan Caine on Golden Sun."

Morgan and his golden horse cantered toward the gate amid the applause. As he rode past his wife and daughter he blew a kiss to them. Meghan caught the kiss and slapped it on her chubby cheek. Morgan smiled and rode on.

"Our last rider of the afternoon, Mister Cyrus Caine on Devil May Care. He's got his work cut out for him to try to beat the new winning time. But this may be the horse that can do it."

Cyrus scowled as his brother cantered off the field. The Golden Boy was pretty damn good, he had to admit. And that dressed-up pony had made a respectable showing. Now it was his turn. He jerked his reins a little too hard, the bit digging into the horse's mouth, and rode out to begin his course.

Cyrus pushed the horse hard, taking the first set of hurdles easily. Devil May Care threw his head up, ready to take the next one. Horse and rider were fast and focused. They sailed over the first set of doubles gracefully. On the second set, the big horse's hoof just grazed the first railing. The crowd gasped, but the top rail stayed in place. Cyrus cut the horse at an angle, trying to make up time, and charged at the next fence, taking it in stride.

The last two hurdles lay ahead. Two things happened then that stunned the crowd.

Still pushing for speed, Cyrus cursed his horse on toward the final combination. The big horse took off a little too fast, and as it flew across the top its rear hoof hooked the railing. The crowd held its breath as the railing wobbled, then seemed to tumble to the ground in slow motion. A collective gasp went up in the arena.

Cyrus, face clouded in fury, pushed his horse toward the last hurdle at a gallop. A leap, a grand extension, and the two of them seemed to hang in the air. They landed cleanly to applause. The big warmblood kept running, carried away by the momentum. Near the out gate the high-strung jumper spooked at an umbrella in the grandstands and began running backward. Furious, Cy tried to drive the horse forward with his legs. Panicked by the rough handling, Devil May Care reared high in the air. Realizing his mistake, Cy leaned forward in the saddle and gave the horse its head but was a second too late. Off-balance, the jumper toppled over backward, sending horse and rider careening into the dirt. Cyrus managed to scramble away in time to avoid the 1,200-pound animal landing on top of him. The crowd gaped in astonishment. Cyrus's team and some of the other handlers charged out onto the field and tried to help Cyrus up.

"Get away from me!" Cyrus yelled at them. "I'm all right. Get ahold of that horse." Someone caught Devil May Care's reins and led the shaken animal off the field, luckily unhurt.

"That's it, ladies and gentlemen," said the announcer, trying to refocus the crowd. "A new winning time of 34.71, Mister Morgan Caine on Golden Sun." At that moment, Morgan and his winning horse cantered into the arena. The crowd settled and raised a cheer as the champion took his victory lap. Morgan glanced at his brother to see if he was hurt, but Cyrus's expression was so full of hate that he looked away and focused on his riding. Cyrus brushed himself off and exited the field.

When the awards were presented, it was Morgan Caine in first place, with Cyrus Caine in second and Mark Bauer riding French Twist in third. The judges crowded around the winning horse to pose with the silver trophy and present him with his blue ribbon. The judges attached ribbons to the bridles of the second and third place finishers as well.

As Cyrus walked out of the arena, his groom was tending to Devil May Care and getting ready to brush him down.

"Mister Caine, don't forget this…." He removed the ribbon from the horse's bridle and proudly handed it to Cyrus. Cyrus snorted and tossed the ribbon in a trash barrel.

"I've got no interest in second place," he growled. The next week, he sold the Dutch warmblood to an optometrist from Glencoe.

Chapter 16

Above and Beyond

A LIGHT BREEZE WAS COMING THROUGH the kitchen window, rustling the sheers, as Kat started to get supper ready. Her two-year-old, Morgan Junior, was sitting quietly on the kitchen floor, playing with some toy trucks. Her four-year-old, Meghan, sat at the kitchen table, drawing tablet in front of her, pink tongue sticking out of the corner of her mouth while she drew her latest masterpiece in crayon – a horse, naturally. Kat smiled. Why wouldn't the girl draw horses, when she saw them every day, unlike most children? Some days Kat had to pinch herself, so grateful for the life she and Morgan were making at Harmony Farm.

After Doc Reese died, Kat and Morgan had thrown themselves into building the business and renovating the house and the stables. Morgan spent a lot of time trading and breeding horses, and his diligence was paying off. He ran the operation himself, now that his two right-hand men were no longer there. Texas Slim had died shortly after Doc did; they found him out in the woods one day, leaning up against a tree as if asleep, his horse tethered to a nearby tree limb – a cowboy's death. Pasquale retired soon after, saying he was getting too old for the strenuous work of wrangling horses. He went back to his little village in Mexico where, unbeknownst to the Caines or anyone else, he had a wife and six children. He was the richest man in the village, having never spent a dime of his earnings from Harmony Farm. As a gesture of continuity he had dispatched his youngest daughter,

Consuela, to help Mrs. Caine with the housework and child care, and her very capable husband Alberto to help Morgan with the horses. They were a wonderful couple, hardworking and dependable, and Kat was grateful they were there. Kat glanced over at Consuela, who was working on some *verde enchiladas* for dinner. Since his days in the Air Cadet Corps in Texas, Morgan loved Mexican food and could not get enough of Consuela's cooking.

Kat heard the Lincoln Zephyr spinning down the lane, too fast as usual. Her nose wrinkled in disapproval; she had admonished Morgan many times not to drive down the lane so fast since the children might be outside playing. He had been gone most of the day, and she was happy he was home. She heard the horn honking outside as the Zephyr came to a halt in front of the house. When the honking continued Kat dried her hands with a dishtowel and went out to the front porch to see what the commotion was about.

Morgan was standing by the car with the V12 engine still running. There was a broad smile on his face.

"Come take a ride with me," he said when he saw her. Kat wrinkled her nose in annoyance.

"I'm just getting supper started…."

"Never mind supper. Come on!"

"What about the children?"

"Consuela can watch them for a little while. Come on, get in."

Exasperated, Kat knew it would do no good to argue when Morgan got like this. She ran back into the house, grabbed her purse from the front hall table and called out, "Consuela, *voy a volver en un rato.*" They were exchanging English for Spanish lessons. Then she ran outside and slid into the front seat next to Morgan.

"What's so important?"

"You'll see." He turned the car around and sped down the driveway again.

They drove through the rolling fields and farmland for several miles. Morgan still would not give a hint where they were going or what he was so excited about. Kat suspected it was a new horse he wanted to buy – that was usually the cause for this kind of enthusiasm. He took a turn onto a long access road that led to an open space with a couple of hangars, a concrete runway and a sign that read "Greater Croydon Airport."

"You're taking me to the airport? Why? Are we going someplace?"

"You'll find out."

Morgan wheeled the car toward the hangars, pulled into a parking space outside the big doors and stopped. He opened his door and climbed out of the car, looking like a kid on his way to a birthday party.

"Come on," he called to her, and Kat followed.

Outside the hangar there was a trim yellow single-engine plane with a black lightning bolt painted on the side. The long wings gleamed in the afternoon sun, and it looked like someone had just given it a thorough washing. Morgan stopped next to the plane and pointed to it proudly.

"How do you like it?"

Kat still wasn't following. "It's …fine, I guess. Why do I care?"

"Because it's ours. We own it."

"You bought this plane?"

"I traded it. You know that Army buddy of mine down in Manteno? He bought this right after the war. Piper made a lot of J-3s for training, reconnaissance and stuff like that. This one's a J-4, so it has a little more oomph to it. My buddy did the restoration himself, suped up the engine, and here it is."

"Yes, but why do you own it?"

"He was looking for a horse. I traded him for that roan gelding we bought a couple of years ago."

"An airplane costs the same as a horse?"

"The right plane, and the right horse." Morgan dangled a key on a chain. "Come on, it's all fueled up and ready. Let's take her for a ride."

"Morgan, I can't just…"

"Sure you can. Come on."

Over Kat's protests, Morgan helped her into the cockpit. There was a stick and a throttle for each of the pilots — or in Kat's case, for a reluctant passenger. Morgan walked around the plane, checking struts and lines and flaps although he had done it just an hour before.

"Do me a favor, honey. Put your foot on the brake and stand on it." Kat did as instructed.

Morgan stood behind the prop of the plane, with one foot in front of the tire (he said he was "chocking it"). With his left hand holding the front of the door for balance, he placed the other hand on the prop. He bounced the prop once, let it spring back, then completed the swing. The engine fired, then he reached inside the plane and pushed the throttle back to idle. He disappeared for a moment, and Kat looked back to see him untie the mooring line. He swung easily into the cockpit, pulled in the rope holding the chock blocks and threw them behind him, then took his seat at the right-hand controls.

"Okay, ease off the brake." As quick as that, they were taxiing down the runway.

Morgan settled into his seat and admired the console in front of him. As the little plane scooted down the runway, Morgan talked with enthusiasm, pointing occasionally.

"I trained on one of these babies. It's the perfect plane to learn in: All you have is a wet compass, an altimeter, air speed indicator, a couple of gauges for oil pressure and temperature. Simple to fly, but it doesn't hide your mistakes."

"Aren't you going to close the door?" Kat shouted over the noise of the engine.

"Are you kidding? It's summer." He looked over at her and smiled. "Don't worry. I'll catch you if you fall out." She didn't look amused. She wrapped her hand around the doorframe, knuckles white, hanging on for dear life, as Morgan eased the throttle forward.

As the end of the runway came upon them – too soon in Kat's judgment – Morgan eased the stick back. Then something amazing happened: Kat felt the little plane's wheels float away from the tarmac, the air caught the wings and the plane lifted off. So did her heart. What she thought was a lurch in her stomach was something different, a feeling of lightness and freedom she had never experienced before, to be actually flying. She gasped a little. Morgan put his hand on hers briefly and squeezed it.

"That's what I feel every time I take off," he said. Now she understood.

They rose slowly, approaching 60 mph, eventually leveling off at 400 feet. Morgan swung the plane around the airport, mostly to get out of the way in case there were other planes that wanted to use the runway. Kat looked down, awestruck by the view. She looked out the door on her side and pointed excitedly.

"Look! There's our farm."

"You bet. Let's get a closer look."

He added a bit of power and pointed the nose eastward. Harmony Farm lay below them, the familiar stretches of field and farmland rich and green in the lengthening shadows of the late June afternoon. The fences and the outbuildings, all freshened and restored through many hours of hard work, glistened white in the waning sun. The fields ran on like a checkerboard in every shade of green, with ribbons of gravel and concrete slicing the countryside in straight angles. She saw her horses grazing in the pasture, so far below yet so close she could almost touch them. In the outdoor arena, two girls were just cooling down their horses after a ride.

"This is heaven," Kat sighed. Morgan smiled.

He eased the stick over and did a gentle circle, heading the plane in the other direction. In no time Kat looked out and recognized Cyrus's property, Cold Creek Farm, looming beneath them. A lot of new construction had gone on there too, but at this time of day most of the action was indoors.

"If those buildings could talk," Morgan cracked.

At that moment, Cyrus Caine was walking out of the main house and headed toward his car. He heard the plane before he saw it, stopped and looked up disapprovingly. Too damn low for his taste.

"You can almost feel him glaring at us," Kat said with a chuckle.

Morgan took the plane down even farther until it seemed like their wheels might touch the roof of Cy's house. Morgan circled around and made a second approach, and as he did he waggled the wings in greeting. Cyrus thrust his index finger at them.

Morgan eased back the stick and the plane climbed into the air again. They drifted back and forth over Croydon County, pointing out old familiar landmarks that looked completely new from up here.

"How long did it take you to learn to fly this thing?" Kat called to him.

"About ten minutes," Morgan said. "Flying's the easy part. It's getting up and getting down that takes a lot of practice. Here, I'll show you." Morgan took his hand off the stick and folded his arms over his chest.

"Morgan! What are you doing?"

"You're in charge now. Start flying."

"I don't know how to…"

Morgan didn't budge. "You better do something."

"No."

"Okay then." He pushed the stick forward and the nose of the plane dropped. They were pointed at the ground. Kat gasped, then she grasped the stick in front of her and pulled it back – a little too sharply at first, but the plane steadied itself. Morgan put his hand on top of hers.

"Just slow and steady, that's what you need to do with a plane like this. Like riding a horse, feel where she wants to go and guide her."

Kat settled in, and within minutes she felt more comfortable. She climbed to a higher altitude to give herself more room in case Morgan decided to get cute again. She banked a few times, making lazy circles in the pristine sky. Morgan showed her how to check her airspeed and her altimeter, and before long she was doing it unconsciously, like she was driving a car.

"Look at that," he said admiringly. "You're a natural."

"What's that little cork out on the hood?" she asked him.

"That's the gas gauge. See how the little cork bobbles out there? Speaking of which, we're getting a little low. We better head back to the airport." He took the controls again, and in a short time they were sliding smoothly down the landing strip. Morgan had not lost his touch.

But he did lose his airplane. From that day forward, Kat was the primary pilot. She took lessons from the one-legged aviator who took care of the hangars and came to hear all about his adventures flying P-51 Mustangs in the Pacific.

"Better to be taught by a stranger than a husband," she said when Morgan asked why she was paying for lessons when he could tutor her for free.

Kat became so proficient that the little Piper soon was not enough plane for her. She put in her flying hours and had her pilot's license within two years. She quickly outgrew the Piper, yearning for something faster, sleeker that could take her farther. She saved her money from equestrian lessons and bought a twin-engine Beechcraft Bonanza.

Kat never did anything by half measures. A born competitor, she eventually began to take part in speed and distance flying races across the country.

"I've created a monster," Morgan sighed, but he was incredibly proud of her abilities as a pilot. Naturally, she flew to win. After she won a few national championships, the media started to take notice, first the local newspapers and radio stations, then larger papers, eventually a four-page spread in *Look* magazine.

"'She's just your typical midwestern housewife," the article began. "If your typical housewife has the movie star looks of Rhonda Fleming…'"

"'Rhonda Fleming?'" Kat protested as Morgan read the article out loud, to her mortification. "I might have said Katharine Hepburn, a little."

"'…is one of the foremost *equestriennes* in the U.S. and can fly a Beechcraft Bonanza across the country at record speed.'" He looked up at her. "That's all true."

"Oh please. They just want to sell magazines."

The glossy pages were filled with pictures of Kat pursuing her various interests: riding in a dressage competition in Lake Forest, looking prim and confident in her tailored riding habit and top hat. Climbing out of the cockpit of her Bonanza after a cross-country race, red hair flying behind her. And because it was the 1950s, gathered around the hearth (literally) with her handsome husband and two adorable children.

There was one particular photograph that galled Cyrus Caine when he saw the article, although he would never confess to having read it. It was the picture in the lower left-hand corner of Morgan and Kat, gazing adoringly into each other's eyes, leaning against one of the railings at Harmony Stables with the sun setting gloriously behind them.

"Now they're the Golden Couple," he muttered. He studied the picture a long time, then crumpled the magazine and stuffed it in his wastebasket.

Chapter 17

Crossed Swords

I HATE THIS GOD-DAMN GAME, Cyrus Caine muttered to himself as he sat on his polo pony, waiting for the match to start. Lousy riding. So-so horses. Not much of a second career for a polo pony, so they made a lousy investment. To Cyrus, polo was like playing hockey, only with no goalies and no ice.

Polo had become a big thing in the Chicago horse world ever since millionaire Paul Butler set up a field and started putting together teams out in Oak Brook – "The Town That Polo Built." Maybe Butler did it for the love of the game, Cyrus reflected, but it was also a hell of a way to grow his business. That's what brought Cyrus out to play on a humid summer afternoon at the Oak Brook polo grounds.

Two things motivated Cyrus to spend his free time playing matches with the local yokels. He looked up in the stands and the first reason was obvious. Pasty-faced men in loud jackets wiping their brows and slurping Pimm's Cups. Expensive-looking women, inevitably blonde, wearing preposterous hats and trying not to sweat. They were the prime livestock at an event like this, Cyrus mused. This was a very monied crowd, whether they knew anything about the sport or not. They were there to be seen as much as to see, and many of them owned horses, or wanted to. Some of them sponsored the local teams, and that meant big money. A typical polo player would go through a minimum of three or four ponies in the course of a match. Most of the horses came from the racetrack, a world Cyrus knew intimately. He was more than happy to sell these marks as many ponies as they desired. Business was good.

Then there was the second reason. He looked up as the captain of the opposing team that afternoon trotted onto the field to polite cheering and applause. He looked like a movie star portraying a polo player: Strong-jawed and firm muscled in his polo shirt and whites, knee-high boots polished to a bright shine. He exercised his chestnut pony in a little stick-and-ball, riding gently up and down the field to get the horse warmed up, smacking the ball with his mallet in elegant and economical strokes, then turning and trotting back the other way. This was a man he knew too well, a man he had grown to deeply resent.

This was his brother, Morgan Caine.

Morgan had taken up polo for the same commercial reasons as Cyrus, combined with the fact that he was a natural athlete and a born leader. He was a four-goal player, and the fool actually seemed to enjoy the game. Cyrus would have much rather been back in the tack room, playing poker with his cronies than sitting astride a sweating pony. But here they were, doing a match for charity on a sweltering Sunday.

Cyrus decided to warm up his first pony of the afternoon, a sleek little bay he had bought in St Louis. As he cantered past Morgan they nodded to each other but gave no other sign of greeting.

"Ladies and gentlemen," came the announcer's voice from the reviewing stand, "if you'll all take your seats please, we're about to commence our feature match of the afternoon."

The spectators were seated on either side of the polo field, with tables and folding chairs under large umbrellas to protect them from the sun. Cyrus thought it ridiculous for the audience to be sitting so close. Horses charged up and down the field at speeds up to 35 miles per hour. The ball could travel at 100 miles per hour and could kill you in an instant if you were in the wrong place at the wrong time. But the wealthy spectators weren't accustomed to being told what to do and were content to let their preschoolers play along the boards while the match was going on. Madness.

The two teams rode to the center of the field, four players on a side. Cyrus's team wore black polo shirts, Morgan's wore white. The horsemen turned and faced the flag fluttering above the scoreboard as a stout woman in a gaudy floral dress sang the National Anthem in a quavering soprano over the PA speaker. Then the players reined their horses around, milling about the field until the two sides were aligned opposite each other, each man facing his opposite number: 1 facing 1, 2 facing 2, etc. Players 1 and 2 were the attackers, 3 and 4 were the defense. Cyrus and his brother were each number 1. They sat on their mounts facing each other without making eye contact.

The umpires trotted out, and one of them threw a wooden ball into the center of the field. The riders scrambled for it, clacking and whacking their mallets until someone made a decent contact and sent the ball down the field. Morgan's team had the first possession, and the game commenced.

Morgan took the first ball down the field, brought it around and passed it to one of his teammates, who took the first shot of the afternoon and missed the goal by ten yards.

Most polo players in this league were amateurs and so-so horsemen at best, except for the Caine brothers.

The black team took possession and Cyrus took control of the ball, pushing his pony down the field with Morgan charging after him. Cyrus had the field to himself, Morgan couldn't get there in time, and he took a powerful swing.

"Goal!" shouted the announcer, and the crowd applauded. The score was 1 to 0.

By the end of the first chukker, the score was tied 3 to 3. Cyrus had made two goals, Morgan had made two, and ponies had made the rest. In a match like this it wasn't unusual for the horses to be more adept at driving the ball in than their amateur riders.

UNBRIDLED

At the end of the first chukker Morgan took advantage of the pause in play to canter to the end of the field, where one of his grooms had his next pony warmed up, saddled and ready. Morgan swung effortlessly from one saddle to the other and cantered back to the center of the field. Cyrus saw that Morgan was switching horses early and decided to do the same.

As Cyrus trotted back onto the field on his fresh mount, he nodded to the Number 2 player on his team. The rider nodded back, signaling his understanding. Morgan happened to see the exchange between the two. Very soon, he understood what the signal meant.

One of the referees whistled the riders to the center of the field for the next throw in. The riders scrambled, and the Number 2 on the black team knocked the ball out and rode after it. He charged down the field, one of the white players fighting to keep up but losing. The Number 2 thwacked the ball with easy powerful strokes, his riding far more assured than it had seemed in the first chukker. He ran away with the ball and easily scored the goal.

The white team reformed the line and drove the ball halfway down the field, when the black rider suddenly dashed up and knocked the ball away with a backhand shot. Cyrus was there to pick it up and rode away with it. Score! Now it was 5-3.

Morgan took possession of the ball and then signaled the referees for a time out. A couple of the players took advantage of the pause to switch to new horses. Morgan rode up to one of the referees, close enough to speak to him without having to shout.

"That Number Two for the Blacks," he said. "Have you ever seen him before?"

The referee glanced over at the rider and shrugged. "No, looks new to me. Maybe Cyrus recruited him."

"Can you call him over here?" The referee signaled the man over. As he trotted toward the ref the player glanced uneasily at Cyrus, who followed.

"I don't believe we've had a chance to meet," Morgan said to the rider. "Can you tell me your name?"

The man stared back at him, perplexed. Cyrus jumped in.

"This is George Smith. He just moved here from out of town. Plays pretty good, doesn't he?"

"Moved here from where? Buenos Aires?" Morgan looked at Number Two. "*Como se llama?*"

The rider grinned at him and said, "George," but it sounded more like "Jorge." Cyrus hissed at him to keep quiet and turned on his brother.

"There's no rule says you have to be a U.S. citizen to play in this match."

"No, but there are rules about bringing in ringers," Morgan shot back.

The referee looked at Morgan. "If you want to file a complaint, I suggest you do it after the match. Otherwise, let's resume play."

Morgan shot his brother a stormy look, turned his horse around and rode off. Cyrus smirked after him, then tapped 'George' on the arm.

"*Vamonos.*"

Morgan rode close to George for the rest of the chukker and managed to keep him in check. By the end of the third chukker the Whites had scored another goal after Cyrus fouled one of the White players and he took the free shot. Now it was 5-4.

At half time the players withdrew to the end of the field, dismounted, drank some water while their fresh ponies were led out. The men were soaked in sweat, even though their actual playing time was only 22 minutes. While the players took a short rest, the spectators were invited to come out on the field and tamp down the divots the horses' cleated shoes had torn up on the field. Most of the audience had been drinking champagne or Pimm's Cups since noon, and they were a little wobbly on their feet but seemed to think this was great fun. The bell rang to announce the resumption of play, and eventually the spectators cleared the field and the riders cantered out to the center.

For the next two periods the Whites and the Blacks managed to play fairly evenly, charging up and down the field, switching directions after every goal so no one team had an unfair advantage because of the sun or conditions of the field. The score stayed within a one-goal difference.

Morgan took possession of the ball, tapped in, slowed it down and brought it around. He spurred his horse and started charging toward the goal. As he drew back his mallet to spike the ball home, Cyrus rode up beside him and hooked his mallet. He missed the shot, and the Blacks were there to take possession. No foul was called; hooking the other player's mallet was legal. Cyrus smiled at him as he rode off.

At the last chukker the score was Blacks 9, Whites 8. Both Morgan and Cyrus switched to their fastest ponies, the ones they held in reserve for the final moments of play. Morgan rode a handsome gray gelding – Cyrus remembered this particular horse from Arlington Race Track the year before – while Cyrus picked a large chestnut gelding. The horse was a brute, fast and powerful.

At the throw-in Morgan emerged from the melee and rode down the field with the ball, making hard contact and keeping it out ahead of him. Cyrus's horse caught up to him and kept pushing him toward the boards. Morgan managed to take a shot from under his horse's neck.

"Goal!" the announcer shouted. Now it was tied up, 9-9.

The Black team took possession and George threatened to break away, but two White riders were stepping up their game and kept him hemmed in. He managed to shake them loose and galloped toward the goal posts but came in at a sharp angle. A powerful shot, but the ball struck one of the goal posts and bounced back. One of the Black riders kicked it out of the line and the Whites took possession. The score was still tied.

With 30 seconds left in the last chukker, Morgan tapped the ball in, brought it around and made a break for the opposite side of the field. Cyrus on his mount charged along beside him, the horses galloping for all they were worth, as if they were back on the track. At midfield Cyrus lined his pony up shoulder to shoulder with Morgan's horse and kept pushing into him to try to move him off the line of the ball and take the line for himself. Cyrus used his horse's size to force the gray horse over, and when he was right next to his brother he tried to position his knee in front of Morgan's to try to control him. Morgan knew that trick and managed to push his brother away. Cyrus kept ramming into him, trying to throw him from his saddle, but Morgan managed to hang on and keep control of the ball. At 30 yards out he was able to find some room and drew his mallet back, but Cyrus used the opening to cut his horse in front of him before he could shoot.

The whistle pierced the air.

"Impingement on the play," the referee called. Cyrus and Morgan separated, and Morgan circled back and brought the ball around.

"What the hell do you mean?" Cyrus shouted at the ref, his face reddening.

"I mean it's a foul," the ref replied. "White gets a penalty shot."

Still cursing under his breath, Cyrus rode back to his own line. The Black team gathered around him. There was nothing they could do but watch Morgan take his shot, free and clear, unimpeded. Morgan brought the ball around again, cantered up and struck it with one smooth decisive stroke.

"Goal!" the announcer cried. "And that is the end of play, ladies and gentlemen. Final score, White team 10, Black team 9. What a magnificent game that was. All for a good cause."

The White team bunched in a circle, laughing and slapping each other on the back, all of them applauding their captain. They handed their ponies off to their grooms and assembled in front of the reviewing stand to receive their trophy and to have their pictures taken. The Black team limped off to the other side of the field. The man known as "George" quietly disappeared into the stables before questions could be raised. Cyrus dismounted and shoved his reins into the groom's hands, the cheers for his brother ringing in his ears.

One more insult added to the pile.

Chapter 18

Mister Ten Percent
1961-1964

CYRUS CAINE LEANED BACK in his leather chair, drew a Cuban cigar from the humidor on his desk, and trimmed the end with a gold cutter. He struck a match and toasted the end of the cigar, taking his time, enjoying the ritual but also the sight of the man seated across from him, squirming in the silence.

They were seated in Cyrus's office at Cold Creek Stables, now one of the most prominent horse facilities in the greater Chicagoland area. Two hundred acres of farmland, corn during the summer, winter wheat in the alternate season, with stables and paddocks clustered around the limestone castle, which had added a number of turrets in the years since Cyrus first built it. Cyrus owned a half dozen stables throughout the Midwest now, either outright or in partnership, but this was his home base.

Although barely in his forties, Cyrus's hair had already turned steel gray. He still had the perpetual suntan from all the hours outdoors, then Florida in the winter months. The lines around his unsmiling mouth had deepened, and the black eyes shone as hard and impenetrable as opals in his leathery face.

The man in front of him was a steady customer, a big LaSalle Street commodities broker named Roger Lamb. Slim, sleek, usually oozing confidence as only people with too much money can. Cyrus had never liked the man, but he was a steady customer, always ready to do a deal on a new horse whether he needed it or not. His checks always cleared. Today, sitting across from Cyrus like a truant schoolboy, perspiration streaming down the side of his face, he looked like a lamb about to be shorn.

"So, Roger," Cyrus began slowly as he ignited his cigar. "Things not going so well, is that what I'm hearing?"

"I've had some setbacks, Cy," the man replied, mopping his brow. "Got a little overextended, if you know what I mean."

"Uh huh. Cash flow problems, in other words."

"You could say that. My new wife – well, let's just say she has expensive tastes."

"So do you."

"That's true. The fact is …" another mop of the brow, "…I did a little unauthorized transfer to one of my accounts. I meant to pay it back, but, well…"

"Is that legal?" Cyrus asked, raising his eyebrows innocently. He was having fun.

"Well, if I got caught…." He leaned forward. "I need some help getting out of this one."

"You've got a lot of fine horses," Cyrus suggested. "Maybe you can sell one of them?"

"One horse wouldn't do it." The man looked levelly at Cyrus. "I need to liquidate some assets. Fast."

Cyrus nodded slowly, taking the man's meaning. He considered the glowing tip of his cigar.

"How many are you thinking?" he asked at last.

"All of them. And the stable besides." He reached into his pocket and pulled out what looked like an insurance policy. "The insurance is all paid up. That's one thing I do keep an eye on. I figure that would be enough to tide me over." He placed the policy on Cyrus's desk. Cyrus glanced at it but didn't touch it. Instead he stood up, took a couple of paces behind the big oak desk, then turned to the cornered man.

"I can help you, Roger."

The relief on the man's face was palpable. He sprang from his chair.

"That's great, Cy. I knew if anyone could help me it would be you. After that one horse…"

Cyrus cut him off with a sharp wave of his hand. He didn't need to be reminded of the last job he'd done to help Roger Lamb out of a jam. It was a simple matter: a car battery touched to the horse's testicles, the animal dropped dead, the insurance company paid up.

"Here's what we do," he said at last. "Three nights from now – Don't be home."

"I got it. No sir, I won't. Maybe the wife and I will spend the night downtown at the Drake."

"Whatever. Just don't be home. Now there's the question of the fee."

"Of course, Cy, whatever you think…"

"It'll cost you ten percent of the payout."

Roger's face collapsed.

"Ten percent? Don't you think that's pretty steep? I mean, I work on commission and I don't charge…"

"This is specialized work. And I have overhead."

Roger continued to balk. "I don't know, Cy. That's a lot of money. I don't know that I can go that high…."

Cyrus came around the desk and placed his hand on Roger's shoulder.

"Let me put it this way, Rog. If you don't pay, the next time it won't just be the stable going up. It'll be the house too. With you and the wife in it."

Roger's jaw dropped. He looked into the black eyes and knew that Cyrus Caine wasn't joking.

Three nights later, while Mr. and Mrs. Roger Lamb were in the city enjoying dinner and a show, a fire mysteriously broke out at the stable on their Barrington estate, burning the building to the ground and killing six show horses trapped inside. Firemen called to the scene were said to have gagged at the smell of roasting horse flesh, the sight of six horses charred black, but there was nothing to be done. The local sheriff's department investigated but found no signs of foul play. The insurance company spent weeks on the matter, and there were rumors that Mr. Lamb might have been behind the fire himself, but nothing could be proven. The estimated payout was in excess of two hundred thousand dollars.

Roger Lamb paid the ten percent.

No one ever knew – or at least was able to prove – that the Horse Mafia was behind the fire at Roger Lamb's. One fact even poor Roger didn't know was that before setting fire to the stable, Cyrus's henchmen had swapped the prime horses in Roger Lamb's stable for a half dozen broken-down gluepots that had been on their way to the abattoir before Cy sent them on a detour. Cyrus not only got his commission on the insurance money, but had six sleek horses he could resell besides, out of state.

Cyrus was known to have his hand in virtually every insurance scam that involved horses. If a client needed money, like the hapless Roger Lamb, Cyrus could arrange for the horse to be stolen or killed. A couple of wires from a car battery could be attached to the horse's rectum with alligator clips, electrocuting it. Horses were susceptible to all manner of intestinal distress, and Cyrus had a range of chemicals in the "doctor's bag" he had inherited from Old Cyrus before his untimely demise. But his signature move was arson. Cyrus and his men preferred a nice clean burn that left no traces of who had been in the neighborhood. The scam was so rampant that in Illinois, Cyrus's home state, it was getting difficult to take out insurance on a horse.

By the early 1960s Cyrus Caine was recognized as the undisputed king of the "A" Circuit in the Midwest – the horse world with the big money clientele. Cy had his hand in virtually every transaction – and often commanded a commission even when he wasn't officially involved. Few people in the horse community had the balls to refuse to pay, for fear their own horses might take a sudden turn for the worse or their stable might mysteriously catch fire. In addition to 'Horse Mafia Don,' Cyrus was also known as Mister Ten Percent.

Cyrus and his gang had made their peace with the Chicago Outfit nearly two decades before, and the organizations generally gave each other a wide berth, sometimes collaborating if the occasion demanded. The Horse Mafia didn't get involved in the Mob's businesses like drugs, gambling or prostitution. They specialized in the horse business. Their clientele tended to be white-collar professionals with (relatively) clean hands. Every gangster in Chicago knew that if a crime included sudden death of horses, extortion of owners or stables burning to the ground, odds were good the Horse Mafia was behind it. The Mob shrugged and looked the other way.

One area where The Mob and the Caine Gang were able to cooperate was in their control of law enforcement. Everyone knew the Chicago police force was riddled with people on The Mob's payroll and had been since Al Capone wore short pants. But Cyrus's influence was in the growing suburbs. When Rob Ward finally retired as sheriff of Croydon County in the 1950s, Cyrus put up his own candidate, First Deputy Ned Paulson. Ned won election with Cyrus's support, and had won every election since. Ned was firmly in Cyrus's pocket, as were his deputies and a lot of other police throughout the western suburbs. A policeman's salary wasn't lavish, and most cops were only too happy to do favors for Mr. Caine in exchange for cash and a case of Scotch at Christmastime.

Cyrus appeared to have it all: wealth, power, women when he was in the mood. Most important, he had the respect of his friends and he terrified his enemies. But for all his success, one person continued to grate on him: his brother Morgan.

"That bastard is a burr under my saddle," Cyrus would growl.

Mister Ten Percent 1961-1964

As Cyrus's notoriety grew, Morgan's reputation flourished in equal and opposite proportion. The younger brother was still active as a competitive rider and had dozens of trophies to show for his skill in the jumper ring. Now approaching 40, with just a touch of gray at the temples, Morgan still cast a dashing figure at all the leading horse competitions. People liked him, admired him. Usually he was in the company of his beautiful red-haired wife Kat and their two adorable children, who had taken up horseback riding and competitive showing from the time they could sit in a saddle.

Cyrus hated losing to anyone, be it a business deal or a jumping event – but he especially loathed losing to his younger brother. One crowning incident in the early 1960s sent Cyrus into an apoplectic fit. Morgan Caine was licensed as an A circuit judge, a prestigious position that vaulted him into the upper echelon of the competitive horse world. Cyrus was furious. He knew that he would never be licensed as a judge given his criminal record and shady reputation, no matter who he bribed. It wasn't fair. With each new slight to Cyrus's vanity–real or imagined–the rift between the brothers grew deeper. Cyrus began to think hard about how to fix the situation. Permanently.

This was more than a competition. This was personal.

Chapter 19

Catch Riders

WHEN CYRUS CAINE STOOD TRIAL for murder years later, witnesses from the horseshow community pointed to two occasions when the feud between the Caine brothers started to boil over into public view.

The American Royal had been one of the premiere horse shows in the country for more than half a century. Once held on the grounds of the old Kansas City Stockyards, the Royal now had its own complex, and the national competition attracted the best riders and stables in the country to this midwestern location. Anyone with an interest in saddle horses was attracted to the Royal. Families came every year and enjoyed the spectacle as well as the barbecue. That year, Kat flew the children down in her own plane while Morgan and his hands drove the long trailer through Iowa and on into Kansas City.

On opening day for the junior competition, Morgan and Kat were in the warm-up area getting their jumpers ready. It was a warm fall day, and Morgan wiped his brow as he checked the equipment and talked to the hands to make sure all the Harmony Stables competitors were ready for their rounds. Kat worked with the junior riders, offering them last-minute tips and reassurance. Morgan looked over at her and smiled. Kat was able to give these girls so much confidence, sooth jittery nerves with a joke and a laugh and a kind word. She had a gift.

"I have to run upstairs for a minute," Morgan said to Kat, and she nodded.

"Go on ahead, we'll be fine," she said, and turned her attention back to one of their junior competitors.

Morgan bounded up the stairs to the show office. He wanted to make sure that all his competitors had received their numbers and paid their class fees. As he rounded the corner and started down the hallway he heard a gale of laughter erupt from one of the meeting rooms and glanced through the open door. There was Cyrus at a table full of men, poker chips and dollar bills spilled across the green felt. Most of them were smoking Cuban cigars, crystal glasses of bourbon at the ready. Cyrus was holding court, and the men were laughing appreciatively at some story. Cyrus still came to all the major horse shows, but these days he preferred to spend his time playing poker during the events rather than watching "kids on their ponies," as he once remarked. Most of the serious horse trading got done before or after the competition, not during.

Cyrus turned his head at that moment and gazed out into the hallway, but his eyes seemed to look beyond his brother. Morgan thought about making a detour and saying hello, then thought better of it and continued on to the business office.

When he came out, carrying a handful of newly printed programs, Morgan stopped at the top of the stairs.

Cyrus stood on one of the lower steps, blocking the way of a young female rider. Morgan looked more closely at the woman, and when she turned her head slightly he realized it was Shelly Reid, a rider from his own stable. Dressed in her navy coat and fawn-colored riding breeches, she looked like any number of young riders at the event. Cyrus had blocked off her path so she couldn't get up the stairs.

"Hello, little lady," Cyrus said to her in a soft voice, maybe the same one the serpent had used on Eve in the Garden of Eden. "You in a hurry?"

"No, sir," Shelly replied. "But I do need to get upstairs." She stepped to the right, but Cyrus cut left and blocked her path.

"I don't believe I know you," Cyrus continued. The smell of bourbon wafted from him in waves. "Why don't you come upstairs and join me and my friends for a drink?"

"No thank you. I have to exercise the horses this afternoon."

"Really? Well, I admire your work ethic," Cyrus said.

"You should," Shelly replied evenly. "I used to work for you."

Cyrus looked genuinely surprised. "You did? Well, I think I'd remember somebody as pretty as you. When was that?"

"Last year. I was only there a month."

"A month? Well, no wonder I don't remember you. Did you get a better offer?"

Shelly looked at him pointedly. "I got a lot of offers. That's why I quit."

Cyrus gave her a crooked smile and leaned in close to her until their faces were almost touching.

"That's the way it is in the horse world, little lady. You got to play the game."

He stroked her arm with his open palm and seemed to draw even closer to her when he felt himself being shoved hard on the shoulder. He spun around and saw the angry face of Kat Caine. She pushed him back and stood between him and Shelly.

"Not this one you don't, Cyrus," Kat said to him, her blue eyes flashing. She pressed the flat of her hand against Cyrus's chest, her arm locked. "Go downstairs, Shelly," she said evenly. With a last nervous glance at Cyrus, the girl nodded and hurried away.

Cyrus and Kat locked eyes for a moment. Then she turned and followed Shelly to the stalls.

Morgan walked down the staircase as Cyrus spun on his heel and started back up. As they passed each other Cyrus muttered, "That is one bad-tempered woman you got there."

"Goes with the red hair," Morgan replied.

Later, he found Kat at the stalls, currying one of the horses with such force that he felt sorry for the horse.

"What was that all about?"

"Never mind," Kat said, continuing to brush the horse's coat in tight little swirls.

That evening, after two martinis at a dark-paneled steak house on Country Club Plaza, Morgan tried to broach the subject again. Shelly was back at the hotel with Meghan and Morgan Junior, and the two adults could have a little time to themselves.

"So what was that little dance on the staircase with you and Cyrus?" he asked, trying to keep his tone light.

"It wasn't about me," she said, taking a sip of her cocktail. "It was about Shelly."

"What about her?"

Kat gave him a long look, the one all women give when they can't believe how obtuse their men can be. She took another sip, drew in a breath, then put her glass down slowly on the table.

"Do you remember when we hired Shelly?"

"Sort of. She just showed up one day. Seemed to be good with horses, wanted to ride but didn't have any money, so you hired her."

"That's true. Well, partly true. You know what a 'catch rider' is, right?"

"Of course I do. We've got a lot of girls out at the stables who don't have the money for a horse of their own, so they do a little work and get to ride horses for the other clients, and for us."

"That's what *we* think it means. It means something very different over at Cyrus's place." She picked up the plastic spear holding the olive in her glass, twirled it thoughtfully. "Shelly worked at Cyrus's stable for a while before we met her."

"Yeah, you told me."

"What I didn't tell you is that there are certain …requirements for catch riders when you work for Cyrus Caine."

"Like?"

"Like, you're expected to party with the clients after hours. Make sure they're happy. And to service them."

Morgan's eyebrows raised slightly.

"'Service them.' You mean like…"

"Like fuck them. Yes, that's what I mean. Shelly found herself in some pretty nasty business over at old Cy's. She came to me crying, begging me to give her a job so she could get out of there."

A lot of those girls are no more than…"

"Fifteen or sixteen. Yes, I know. They even have a slogan."

"A slogan. And what would that be?"

"'You can ride anything you want at Cold Creek Stables.'" Kat picked up her drink and drained it, then set the glass down on the table again, a little too hard. "Your brother never changes."

Morgan rolled over and looked at the alarm clock on the bedside table. One thirty-two a.m. He sat up, and it took him a minute to realize where he was. Kansas City. The American Royal. A hotel room. With a 4:30 a.m. wakeup call.

The music from down the hall seemed to shake the walls of the hotel room. Kat turned over and put a pillow over her head to block out the noise. Their two children were sleeping, or trying to, in the adjacent room.

Morgan got up, slipped his trousers over his pajama bottoms and went down the hall.

The music was coming from the suite at the end of the corridor. Just my luck to get stuck on the party floor, Morgan thought to himself. The music grew even louder as he approached the suite. He gave a heavy knock on the door. No one answered. He knocked again, harder this time. Finally the door swung open.

His brother Cyrus stood in the half-opened doorway. His face was half-shaded but looked gray to Morgan, and sweat was dripping down the sides of his face. He was wearing a white dress shirt, unbuttoned all the way, and no pants, just boxer shorts.

There was a smudge of white powder at the cleft below his nose, which Morgan thought might have been shaving talc – or might not. Standing behind him, staring blankly over his shoulder, was a young girl, blond, pretty, maybe 16, not older. She was mostly naked from what Morgan could see of her. She hid herself behind Cyrus, one hand draped on his shoulder, looking glassy-eyed at the stranger in the hallway.

Cyrus stood uncertainly in the doorway, swaying slightly, his eyes unfocused. Then a glimmer of recognition appeared, and he smiled.

"Hey, little brother. Come on in. I didn't know you were the party type."

"Didn't come to party, Cyrus."

Cyrus stumbled a bit, and the door opened wider. Morgan gazed past him. The room smelled of cigars and whisky and sex. A blue cloud hovered over the hotel suite. It was mostly dark, but there was enough light from a pole lamp that rested on its side on the floor. One of the drapes was partially torn from the rod, and the lights of the Plaza shone in on the scene. Amid the haze, Morgan recognized several of the men he had seen playing cards with Cyrus earlier in the day. He knew a couple of them: a banker from St Louis, a doctor from Des Moines. Most of them were in their 40s or beyond.

One man sat in an armchair, shorts around his ankles, puffing a Havana while a topless girl performed oral sex on him. Two other young girls, maybe 16 or 17, naked except for panties, sat on a sofa and were kissing and touching each other while another man, fully dressed, watched them and jerked off. A third man lay at their feet, passed out on the floor. One of the girls happened to glance toward the door, and Morgan recognized her as a student from his Pony Club just a few years ago. She seemed to recognize Morgan too, because she broke off the kiss and tried to slide her bra up her arm and partially cover her breasts.

In the master bedroom, a white-haired man, naked except for a pair of cowboy boots, lay across the king-sized bed while a teenaged girl straddled him, doing the reverse cowgirl. Morgan could see the girl's face clearly; her movements were rhythmic, mechanical, as though she were riding a not very talented horse; her eyes were flat, dead looking, joyless. Every now and then the white-haired man would slap her on the haunch, usually missing, then fall back on the bed giggling hysterically. Morgan recognized the girl from his last visit to Cyrus's stable.

"Turn down the music," Morgan spat, and turned away in disgust.

As Morgan walked back to his room, shaken, he saw a door down the hallway open. A hairy arm appeared, then a disheveled young man lurched into the hallway, tucking his shirt in and zipping up his pants. The man in the doorway murmured something, and the younger man nodded. Morgan recognized him as one of Cy's associates, the good-looking one, Cary something-or-other. The two men didn't make eye contact.

Morgan returned to his room, realizing that his wife was right: he didn't know his brother at all anymore.

"Ladies and gentlemen, welcome to the final round of the American Royal Jumping Competition!"

It was the third day of the Royal. Morgan had managed to avoid Cyrus for most of the show, not knowing what he would say to his brother after seeing the private rodeo he was throwing in his suite. For the most part Cyrus secreted himself in the card room upstairs, content to play poker and swap stories with his cronies rather than be down at the ring. But for this final Cyrus decided to put in an appearance. One of his new jumpers had made a particularly impressive showing in the preliminaries, and Cyrus was confident his horse would win the afternoon's competition.

Cyrus took a seat in the VIP section of the stadium. He was wearing a tan suede jacket over white shirt and black gabardine slacks with a pair of hand-tooled black riding boots. He nodded to friends and acquaintances as he edged his way down the front row and took his seat.

Across the arena, Kat and Morgan were standing with Shelly Reid, about to ride in her last class of the afternoon. Morgan held the horse by its reins, stroking its neck gently, and looked at the young girl standing with his wife. Shelly was pretty and wholesome in the style of the day, with sandy blonde hair tucked under her riding derby and a splay of freckles across her upturned nose. She reminded Morgan of the young actresses in those Beach Party movies. She was just as shapely, and Morgan was embarrassed to have noticed after what he'd seen in his brother's hotel room. Shelly looked smart and professional in her form-fitting navy-blue tunic, fawn-colored breeches and black riding boots – a hand-me-down outfit Kat had found for her, since she couldn't afford fancy clothes herself.

Looking at the two women – one young and just starting her riding career, the other mature and still beautiful – Morgan felt himself getting upset all over again at the degrading spectacle he had seen in his brother's suite, and that he knew was all part of Cyrus's business model. He grimaced, realizing that his brother wasn't just a gangster; he was a pimp as well.

While Morgan settled the horse, a sleek gray mare and an excellent jumper, his wife settled Shelly.

"Take a deep breath," Kat was saying. "Leave yourself a little turning room as you approach that last fence. You'll do fine."

"Do you think so?" Shelly asked nervously.

"I know so. You're a champion."

The young rider smiled, and Morgan gave her a leg up and she swung into the saddle.

"And now, entering the arena, Number 234, Surfer Girl, owned by Harmony Stables and ridden by Miss Shelly Reid."

Shelly smiled at the Caines and whispered, "Here goes nothing" as she entered the arena.

Amid polite applause Shelly and her mount made their courtesy circle. When horse and rider were ready Shelly nodded to the judges and the clock started. She took the first two jumps with ease, the single fences no challenge for Surfer Girl's long legs. They picked up the pace as they approached the triple bar, and the horse's hind hooves cleared it cleanly. A rollback, and Shelly headed for a hedge with a water hazard in front and breathed a sigh of relief when Surfer Girl sailed over it dry.

"Coming up on two minutes," the announcer said. "Best time of the day so far. Miss Reid is on pace to overtake the current lead, Cyrus Caine's Black Hornet."

At the mention of Cyrus's name, Morgan and Kat took their eyes off Shelly and looked across the arena at Cyrus. He had heard the announcement too and turned from his conversation to stare intently down into the ring, his black eyes flashing with irritation. Kat saw him mutter something to his companion. She was pretty sure it wasn't a compliment about Shelly's riding ability.

A final turn, and Shelly and Surfer Girl took the last hurdles, a one-stride combination leading to an oxer consisting of a white gate with rails. The execution was flawless, and the audience burst into applause as the announcer said, "There it is, ladies and gentlemen! A clean ride, and a winning time of two point three six from Miss Shelly Reid of Harmony Stables."

Shelly, red faced but beaming, took Surfer Girl around the ring, patting the horse's long neck with pride and affection, then she rode to the open gate where Kat awaited her.

"That was perfect, honey," Kat said as she took the horse's reins and helped bring it to a full stop. Shelly nodded her thanks and slipped out of the saddle. She looked around for Morgan, but he was gone. He was on the move to the judge's box. He had seen Cyrus jump up at the end of the ride when the announcement was made and charge toward the judge's table.

As Morgan walked up he could hear Cyrus berating the officials.

"What the hell do you think you're doing? Did you not see the same ride I saw? That horse touched the last rail. She should be penalized."

"She did no such thing, Cyrus," Morgan said behind him. "She rode the course and she did it perfectly."

"Not the way I saw it."

One of the judges spoke up. "We were watching too, Mr. Caine . . .er, Cyrus. There was no rub and no penalty."

Cyrus looked from the official to his brother. "This how we do it now? You're a judge, so you all stick together, is that it?"

"I know what I saw, Cyrus. And the judges agree."

More people were starting to lean in, listening to the argument between the two Caine brothers. Cyrus's face was red with anger.

"You sonuvabitch. I ought to kill you."

The words hung in the air as the two brothers locked eyes. One of the judges was standing on their side of the table now and placed an arm between the two men to separate them.

"That kind of talk doesn't help," he said. "We're declaring Surfer Girl the winner."

For a minute it looked like Cyrus might hurl the man into the arena. Instead he froze, collected his temper, and became deadly quiet until he said to Morgan:

"This isn't over."

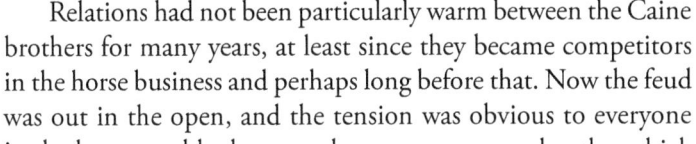

Relations had not been particularly warm between the Caine brothers for many years, at least since they became competitors in the horse business and perhaps long before that. Now the feud was out in the open, and the tension was obvious to everyone in the horse world whenever the two men crossed paths, which was often.

The Lake Forest Horse Show, held every year in the leafy, moneyed provinces of Lake Forest, Illinois, wasn't a big money event. But Morgan Caine and his family loved it. They enjoyed the Onwentsia Hunt Club, the environment of broad lawns and old money, in part for the proximity to their home but also for the warmth and friendliness of reuniting with good friends and neighbors each year.

Meghan Caine was 14 years old now. Like her mother, she was growing into a beautiful young woman and an accomplished athlete. Like all Caines, she lived and breathed horses. The Onwentsia was to be her first major show as a Junior. She had been working for two years with her horse, a roan mare she had named Concertina — Tina for short. All the horses in her distinguished line were named for musical instruments. Besides, in Meghan's view, Tina seemed to fit her. Meghan adored her horse, the way only 14-year-old girls can.

Meghan was in the barn at the Onwentsia Hunt Club stables, using a curry brush on her horse with long loving strokes, making sure the horse would look her best for their classes the next morning. She was so intent on her work that she didn't hear the man step up behind her.

"How you doing, little lady?"

Meghan whipped around at the sound of the man's voice. She let out a small gasp of surprise but kept her composure. When she didn't answer the man spoke again.

"What's the matter? Don't you know who I am?"

Meghan kept her eyes pointed down.

"I know who you are. You're my Uncle Cyrus."

The man smiled, but there was no warmth in his dark eyes.

"That's right. Your Uncle Cyrus." He took a step toward her. Meghan involuntarily took a step back. Cyrus studied her for a moment.

"Anybody ever tell you you look a lot like your mother?"

"Yes, sir. All the time."

It was true. The red hair, the clear blue eyes, the trim athletic physique. Cyrus remembered that girl well, the one he grew up with, before they cast him out of the family.

Cyrus moved closer and extended his hand. Meghan circled away from him. Cyrus's hand rested on Tina's long neck, patted it. He examined the horse's legs, then stroked its back and its muscular haunches, nodding appreciatively.

"You're riding tomorrow," Cyrus said. It was a statement, not a question.

"Yes, sir."

Cyrus nodded, his eyes still exploring the animal. "I got a horse in the competition too. A real beauty. Paid a fortune for her." He patted Tina again and let out a grunt of approval.

"Beautiful horse you got here, little lady. Be a damn shame if something happened to her."

Cyrus felt a firm hand on his shoulder, and when he whipped around he felt a sharp smack across the face. Kat was standing there, hand raised, eyes blazing.

The mother placed herself between her daughter and her brother-in-law. Her right hand was cocked and loaded, to point or to strike again, whatever suited the moment.

"Let me tell you something, Cyrus," she hissed at him, eyes flashing like blue diamonds.

"You ever threaten a child of mine, and I will bury you so deep they'll never find you."

Cyrus shrugged. "I was just talking to the girl. I didn't mean ..."

"I know just what you meant. You think you can intimidate anyone, anybody weaker than you." She took a step toward him, her hand still poised to strike. "I learned a lot from you, Cyrus. And I'm not afraid to use it against you."

Cyrus rubbed his hand across his jaw, where a red mark was blooming from Kat's blow.

"I'm sure you're not. He tipped his hat gallantly. "I believe I'll just wish you two ladies a good evening then."

He turned and walked out of the barn.

That night, Morgan hired a guard to watch over Concertina.

The afternoon of the Junior Riders Classes was a perfect Lake Forest day: sunny, cool, a light wind blowing in off Lake Michigan. The spectator stands were filled with horse aficionados come to see some of the area's most beautiful (and expensive) horses being ridden by talented young equestrians. But the buzz in the spectator stands was all about the growing competition between Cyrus Caine and his brother Morgan, who both had horses entered in the Junior divisions.

Cyrus had a handsome bay mare, Sandy Creek, ridden very capably by one of his newest proteges, a young woman of 16 named Laurie Green. Morgan saw the girl saddling her mount and recognized her: she was one of the catch riders he had seen hanging around Cyrus's stable. The nearest competitor in her class was Morgan Caine's 14-year-old daughter Meghan, riding her mare Concertina.

Cyrus leaned against the railing in the front row, chain smoking Pall Malls, his expression a stone mask. All his concentration was focused on the two young riders in the ring. Morgan and Kat stayed on the other side of the arena by the ring gate, leaving Cyrus a wide berth.

"Ladies and gentlemen," the announcer said after consulting with the judges, "we have two contestants tied for the championship in the junior jumper division: Sandy Creek, owned by Cold Creek Stables and ridden by Miss Laurie Green, and Concertina, owned by Harmony Stables and ridden by Miss Meghan Caine."

Encouraging applause rippled through the gallery.

"We are going to have a jump-off to determine today's winner."

Laurie Green went first. The bay mare, which Cyrus had taken a personal hand in training, performed expertly, making her round clean.

Meghan Caine was next. Morgan watched her with pride and whispered to his wife, "She reminds me of you."

Kat shook her head. "She's her own woman."

"Well, she sure knows how to ride."

Meghan looked mature and totally in command as Tina responded beautifully. A single, a double, then a rollback. Tina cleared the next hurdle, an oxer, and the final single with room to spare.

"At the end of the first round, we still have a tie!" the announcer said. The young riders put their horses through another course, waiting for one of them to make an error.

As they entered the third round, Cyrus paced back and forth. His explosive temper made this long wait unbearable.

"Let's get this over with," he was heard to mutter. Everyone assumed he meant the contest.

In the third round, Laurie was urging her mount into a canter and headed toward a double when she realized she had misjudged her distance. Her horse's rear hooves rubbed the second rail and it tumbled to the ground. The crowd groaned.

It was Meghan's turn next. All eyes were on her, especially her uncle's. She blocked him out of her vision and concentrated on putting Tina through her paces. When she came to the double Meghan knew she had judged the distance just right, and the crowd cheered as Tina cleared the second rail with ease.

"A beautiful ride," came the announcement. A few minutes passed while the judges compared notes and passed up their selection. "Our winner in the junior jumper division is Concertina of Harmony Stables, ridden by Miss Meghan Caine."

When her name was announced Meghan dropped her professional demeanor and beamed like the teenage girl she was. She gave a broad smile (her braces had only recently come off) and started her courtesy lap around the arena, her face flushed, patting and stroking Tina's neck. As she trotted past her uncle she kept her eyes locked straight ahead, avoiding the angry gaze he threw at her.

Meghan stopped her horse when she reached her parents at the show gate and handed the reins to her father. Her mother helped her down from the saddle.

"Honey, that was wonderful," Kat told her, and her dad gave her a tight hug.

They heard Cyrus before they saw him. He was yelling up at the judges as he stormed out of the visitors box.

"Rigged! This whole damn thing is rigged."

He pushed through the crowd of well-wishers around the Caines, his face black with fury. Morgan saw his brother coming and placed his body between Cyrus and his family, but Cyrus bulled past him.

"Aren't you even going to congratulate your niece, Cyrus?" Morgan called to him, taunting him. It was a mistake. He knew it from the way Kat squeezed his arm.

Cyrus spun on them.

"To hell with her. To hell with all of you." He waved a finger in his brother's face. "We're not done here, brother. Someday I'll kill you, you son of a bitch."

The crowd seemed to rear back. It was one thing to hear about a family feud, quite another to hear one brother threaten to murder the other. No one who heard Cyrus Caine that afternoon assumed that he was joking. He was deadly serious.

That was the beginning of the War.

Part 3
WAR
Bygones are not bygones

Chapter 20

Warning Shots
1965-1968

IT TOOK A LONG TIME for Morgan Caine to realize that his brother truly wanted him dead.

Shortly after the blow-up over Meghan's victory at the Lake Forest show, Morgan became aware of a strange series of incidents that potentially put his life in peril. Morgan was an optimist by nature and tended to look for the best in people. ("A sucker, in other words," his brother would say.) At first he wrote these incidents off to bad luck or coincidence, but as the list grew longer he came to understand that these were not accidents. Someone was sending him a warning or outright trying to kill him.

Morgan's new role as a horse show judge kept him busy and traveling much of the time. He was judging the Ohio State Fair Junior Horse Show at the exposition center outside of Columbus. Two of Kat's students had horses entered in the competition, and Morgan volunteered to haul the animals down to the show while the girls traveled separately.

After a long day of watching competitive riding, Morgan loaded the horses into the two-horse trailer towed by the Chevy pickup truck Alberto had driven down for him. Morgan threw the lock on the trailer, patted the Chevy's bumper and waved good-bye to Alberto.

An hour or so later, Morgan climbed behind the wheel of his own car, a gold Cadillac Sedan de Ville, and drove up to the exit.

He nodded to the security guard and rolled up his window. He switched on the radio and heard Patsy Cline singing "Crazy." He smiled. The song always made him think of his beautiful and sometimes unpredictable bride Kat. He cranked up the volume as he pulled out of the parking lot.

He didn't hear the guard calling after him and trying to wave him down. A second guard stepped up to the gate.

"What's the matter?" he asked his coworker.

"Looks like that fella's leaking some fluid," the first guard replied. He shrugged. "Oh well. Guess he won't get too far."

It was late. Morgan had a good 10-hour drive ahead of him, but he didn't mind. He liked to drive at night, liked the solitude, no traffic on the road and nothing but highway ahead of him, with the radio for company. With luck he'd be home in time for breakfast with Kat and the kids. As he pulled onto the interstate, he rolled down the window, lit a cigarette and enjoyed the sensation of the wind blowing on his cheek.

As the big Cadillac merged onto the highway, Morgan felt a shimmy in the steering wheel. That was a surprise. The Caddy was a well-mannered car to drive, and the handling was superb. He shrugged. Maybe it was time for a wheel alignment when he got home. Long road trips had a way of taking a toll on the rear wheels.

The lights of Columbus shimmered in his rearview mirror, and there was little traffic on the road. Morgan felt comfortable pushing the Cadillac over the speed limit, enjoying the smooth growl of the big V8 engine.

Ahead of him, a Peterbilt truck with a refrigerator car on the back was rolling down an entrance ramp and had started to merge ahead of him. Morgan decided he was going a little fast and tapped the brakes to give the big truck plenty of room.

Nothing happened.

He pumped the brakes, harder this time. Still nothing. He smashed his foot all the way to the floor and felt no response. The truck was coming on fast and swinging part way into the passing lane. Morgan had no choice: He hit the gas and flew around the truck, his left wheels cutting the lefthand shoulder, spewing gravel. Wrestling to keep the car under control, he swerved back into the righthand lane, cutting off the truck and getting a rude blast of the horn from the driver. Morgan lifted his foot from the gas again, clicking on his turn signal to indicate he was pulling over. The truck shot past him, issuing another long bleat of the horn, and powered on into the night. When the truck was safely past Morgan eased the Cadillac over to the shoulder of the road, slipped the gearshift into 'Low.' Eventually the weight of the car dragged him to a stop.

Morgan rested his forehead on the steering wheel, his breathing shallow, and waited for his heart rate to slow down. That was close. His memories flashed back to his days piloting B-17s, when sometimes the only thing that got you to a stop without crashing into the hay bales at the end of the runway was a little finesse and a whole lot of luck. He put the Cadillac in park and reached into the glove compartment, took out a flashlight. He opened the car door carefully and got out.

Crouching on the ground away from the road, Morgan ran the flashlight's bright beam along the undercarriage of the car. It didn't take him long to find the problem. He could see the damp red spot and the last few drops of brake fluid clinging to the line. The line had a puncture in it.

Morgan stood up, switched off the flashlight, looked up and down the deserted highway and cursed to himself. There was no sense trying to hoof it to the next exit. If he was lucky, a police car or a friendly trucker might stop and give him a lift. He walked to the back of the car, popped open the trunk and took out a couple of flares.

It was after 1 a.m. when Morgan finally had his car towed to a service station in the next town. Exhausted, he checked into a nearby motel and slept fitfully. He returned to the station the next day to pick up his car and settle up with the mechanic. He was a grisled man in a greasy set of overalls. The nametag on his chest said 'Gus.'

"Brake line's fixed," Gus said, wiping his hands with a rag. "Looks like it was cut clean through. Any idea how that mighta happened?"

"Not a clue," Morgan replied. "Maybe I drove over something on the fairgrounds?" Gus looked skeptical.

"Another funny thing . . . Some of your lug nuts on the tires was loose."

Morgan nodded. That accounted for the shimmy in the steering wheel.

"I'd say you was pretty lucky to be able to stop when you did," the mechanic observed, bending at a small metal desk to tally up the bill.

"Yep. Lucky's the word."

From that day on, Morgan was more vigilant about people loitering near his car. His caution should have extended to airplanes too.

Two weeks after the Columbus show, when he was out at the Croydon County Airport, Morgan spotted a stranger in coveralls tinkering with his wife's Piper Cherokee. Morgan stopped his car, got out and shouted to the man, who looked up quickly, turned and ran before Morgan could get a good look at him. He never mentioned the incident to Kat, knowing what she would say.

Weeks after the business at the airport, Morgan, Kat and the kids were home on a Saturday evening, one of the rare weekends one of them didn't have a horse show to attend. They were playing Monopoly in the family room. Morgan got up and went into the kitchen to fetch a beer from the fridge. As he walked into the kitchen he thought he saw a shadow moving outside the kitchen window.

He flung the door open and looked out, but there was no one on the back porch. He heard some rustling in the bushes in the back yard and thought he saw some movement.

Kat walked up behind him.

"What is it, Morgan?" she asked, peering over his shoulder. Morgan was still staring out into the darkness.

"Nothing. Thought I saw a shadow out on the porch. Might've been a deer."

Kat started to close the kitchen door when her eyes wandered downward and she froze.

"Morgan..." she started to say and pointed to an object on the doormat. It was a bundle of dynamite.

Morgan grabbed Kat around the waist and whirled her around, shielding her from the dynamite, tensing for an explosion. But there wasn't any. He noticed a piece of paper Scotch-taped to the bundle. He reached down cautiously, tore the paper away and read it. He handed it to Kat so she could read it too. All it said was

BOOM

"Somebody's idea of a joke," Morgan muttered.

"This is no joke, Morgan. And that was no deer," Kat protested. "You need to call the police."

"I'm not calling the police. What would I tell them? It's obviously a prank."

"It's a warning. Maybe next time they'll light the fuse. With the kids in the house."

Morgan was silent a moment. "I'm not calling the police," he repeated. But he did pick up the sticks of dynamite and moved them to the edge of the yard, far from the house and the other outbuildings. When he had done that he stood on the porch for a few moments, staring out into the woods where he had seen the motion just before. Then he switched off the porch light and went inside, making sure the double lock was set.

The next time left no room for doubt.

Morgan was working late in his office, going over some feed bills. He was absorbed in the numbers in front of him and didn't hear the car pulling up in front of the building. The headlights on the car had been extinguished.

The passenger door on the car outside needed to be oiled, and it squeaked when the rider opened it. Morgan looked up with a start, glanced out the window over the parking lot, saw no one. But the hair on his neck was standing up; he was sure someone was outside. He rose cautiously, turned out the desk lamp, and eased along the wall toward the back door.

The gunfire erupted and Morgan dove for the floor. He knew the rat-tat-tat of a machinegun when he heard it. Shards of glass and splintered wood spit across the room and he could see the strafing pattern in the wall as the bullets slammed into it. He heard a voice outside give a harsh whisper: "Come on, let's get out of here!" Then running footsteps, a car engine starting and tires spinning against the gravel.

Morgan lay still for a minute, making sure the gunmen were truly gone. He could hear people stirring in the house, and within a minute Kat was standing in the doorway, a look of horror on her face as she surveyed the scene. Morgan climbed to his feet, brushing broken glass from his shirt and his hair. Relief flooded through Kat, but when she spoke her tone was scornful.

"I suppose you're going to tell me this was a deer too?"

Morgan shot her a sour look and picked up the telephone receiver, still intact on his desk.

"Not this time," he answered as he dialed '0' and said, "Get me the sheriff's office."

It took nearly 30 minutes for the sheriff's car to reach them. A big man in the tan uniform and campaign hat of the Croydon County Sheriff's Department stood in the doorway. Morgan and Kat recognized him right away, even though he had gained at least 30 pounds since rising to Sheriff.

"Ned Paulson," Kat said, more as a statement than a greeting. "You came out here yourself?"

"Heard about it on the squawkbox," Ned said, stepping over shattered glass as he entered the room. He looked around like he was house hunting, his eyes landing on the bullet holes in the wall, the broken window, the overturned desk chair. He drawled, "They said you folks had some trouble out here."

"You think?" Morgan snapped at him, put off by the man's languid demeanor. Ned didn't rise to the bait.

"Any ideas who might of done this? Maybe kids in the neighborhood?"

"Kids," Kat exclaimed. "Kids? How many kids do you know with a machine gun?"

"There are 28 bullet holes in that wall, Ned," Morgan said. "This wasn't some schoolboy prank. Somebody was shooting for real."

"You know perfectly well who's behind this, Ned," Kat said, getting up into the sheriff's face. "This has your buddy Cyrus's fingerprints all over it."

Ned's eyes narrowed. "Can you prove that?"

"No," she admitted. "That's why we called the police. It's your job to prove it."

Ned drew a black imitation leather notebook from his breast pocket and took out a pen.

"Morgan, you do a lot of horse trading. I'm sure you've made a lot of enemies. Maybe you could give me some names and I'll be happy to have my deputies talk to them, check on their whereabouts."

"Why don't you start with his brother?" Kat challenged him. Her face was flushed with anger.

"Sounds to me like you're making some pretty wild charges without any proof, Mrs. Caine," the sheriff said, tucking the notebook back in his pocket. "If you come up with any actual evidence, you can call my office."

"How about the evidence that you've been in Cyrus's pocket for 20 years?" Kat spat at him. Morgan put his arm up and guided his wife away from the police officer, afraid her temper was getting the best of her. Ned tipped his hat and turned toward the door.

"You folks have a nice evening," he said, and he was gone.

The Flame was a popular steakhouse about a 20-minute drive from Harmony Stables. Dark wood, dim lighting, leather banquettes and red flocked wallpaper. Ned stepped into the dining room, nodded to the hostess on duty, Trudy – Ned was well known here – and looked around the darkened room until he spotted the person he was looking for, sitting alone in his usual booth at the back.

Cyrus didn't look up when the sheriff slid in across from him. A half-finished Manhattan sat in front of him. The unfiltered cigarette butts in the ashtray said he had been there for some time. Cyrus didn't offer the sheriff a drink. He didn't have to. The waitress automatically knew that Ned was having what Cyrus was having. She placed a Manhattan in front of him, and a fresh one for Cyrus.

Finally Ned spoke.

"I just came from your brother's place."

"And?"

"And there's been some shooting. Tore up the office pretty bad."

Cyrus sipped his drink. "Anybody hurt?" He sounded more hopeful than worried.

"Naw. Morgan's fine. That wife of his though…. She's pretty suspicious."

Cyrus shook his head. "Goddamned amateurs," he muttered, as if Ned weren't even there. "Time to bring in some professionals."

Ned made no comment. If he had a reaction to Cyrus's idea that it was time to hire professional killers he didn't show it. He quietly drained his drink, said "I better get going," and slid out of the booth.

Cyrus sat staring into his drink, contemplating his next move. It wouldn't be long.

Chapter 21

The Professionals

THE TWO MEN WALKED INTO McGonnagle's Hardware Store in the middle of a Tuesday afternoon, when the store wasn't very busy. One of the men was on the tall side, just under six feet, with a husky build, dark hair in a brush cut, heavy black brows dominating his face. He was wearing a faded denim jacket over a black tee shirt, blue jeans and black Frye boots. His companion was smaller and wiry, with greasy blond hair hanging limply across his forehead and a sparse goatee disguising a weak chin. He wore a fatigue jacket and jeans. No one in the store looked up when they walked in. They headed for the counter at the back of the store.

The clerk, an older woman wearing an efficient-looking apron over plaid shirt and mannish tan trousers, had a pencil over one ear, her wiry gray hair woven into a braid at the back of her head.

"Help you?" she asked with Midwestern pleasantness. Her name was Essie according to the name tag on her apron. The man in the blue jean jacket spoke.

"We need to buy some dynamite," he said.

"OK, how much you need?"

"Twenty-four sticks." His skinny companion muttered something, then he added, "Blasting caps too."

Essie took the pencil from behind her ear and wrote the order down. "You fellas doing some blasting, are you?" Just making conversation. The bigger man nodded.

"We've got a demolition company."

"What's the name?"

"Name?"

"The name of the company. Do you have a charge account with us?"

"Oh. Acme Demolition. It's in Lemont. But we'll be paying cash."

Essie nodded, not showing much interest. "Let me get that order ready for you then."

Morgan Caine was in his office on Friday afternoon, scrambling to get his affairs in order so he could get on the road to the Cincinnati Horse Show. He had a long drive ahead of him and he was running late.

Shelly Reid was in the office too, chasing behind him, sorting through the papers Morgan had scattered on his desk. Shelly had been with the Caines for a few years now, and both Morgan and Kat looked on her almost as a daughter. She seemed to get prettier every year – reddish blond hair, lively blue eyes, a sunny smile to match her disposition. She was wearing an angora sweater and a pair of buff riding britches that showed off her curvaceous figure. A black grosgrain ribbon bound the ponytail that danced behind her as she organized the desk.

"Have you seen the entry forms for the Cincinnati show?" Morgan asked, rifling through the stacks on his desk. With an exasperated sigh, Shelly picked up the buff folder that sat on top of the stack and handed it to him.

"Oh. Thanks. What about the hotel reservation?"

"In your hand."

"Right. Got it." Morgan crammed the papers in his worn leather briefcase and fastened the clasp.

"Don't forget you need to write a check for the feed bill before you go," Shelly reminded him.

"Can't it wait?"

"I promised Hanson's we'd be putting it in the mail at the end of the week."

Morgan sat down with a sigh and pulled open the desk drawer. "Now where's the checkbook?"

"Where it always is."

"Sorry," Morgan said with a weak smile. "I'm running way behind today."

"I can see that."

"Let me just get this done and…" he patted his shirt pocket. "Do you have a pen?"

Shelly smiled at him and handed him the ballpoint clipped to his shirt pocket. He started to write the check without looking up at her. "Then I have to go get the trailer hitched up."

"Why don't I take care of that?" Shelly offered. She held out her hand. "Car keys?"

Morgan dug into his pocket and tossed the Cadillac keys to her.

"You're a doll, Shelly. Don't know what we'd do without you around here."

"I don't either," she chirped. With a swirl of the ponytail she headed out the door.

The gold Cadillac was parked out front. Morgan smiled. Shelly loved to drive that car any chance she got, even if it was just down to the barn to hitch up a trailer.

Morgan stopped, pen poised in his hand. A sudden, horrible flash of intuition seized him. He started to call after the girl.

The explosion threw him across the desk and onto the floor. Fragments of glass and wood sprayed across the room. Morgan clawed his way up from the floor, the sound of the blast reverberating in his ears. His face and clothing were covered with dust and debris. He checked his arms and legs quickly, seemed to be all right. Slowly, he climbed to his feet, coughing, waving away the smoke and dust, and made his way to the front door. He threw it open, glad for the blast of air that hit him. Then his heart sank.

The Cadillac was a fiery, twisted metal ruin. The long metal hood had been thrown halfway across the yard, and what was left of the chassis was a blackened flaming hulk.

"Shelly!" he screamed and ran to the driver's side, knowing he was a minute too late. There was nothing left of her but bits of bone and hair and smoldering fabric. Morgan tried to grab the door handle but it was too hot to touch, and besides the door was welded shut. He sank to his knees and wept.

The police came quickly this time. The explosion had been heard halfway across Croydon County, and black smoke could be seen curling from Harmony Stables from a mile or two away. The yard was jammed with police cars and ambulances with their lights flashing. Sheriff's deputies swarmed the scene, taking measurements, making notes, gathering fragments from the shattered automobile.

Morgan sat on a chair that Kat had salvaged from the office, oblivious to the commotion around him. Kat stood next to him, one hand resting on his shoulder, the other shielding her eyes from the horrible sight in front of them.

Ned Paulson arrived on the scene with red lights flashing. Exiting his squad car, he shouted instructions to the deputies, took in the scene – the still smoldering chassis of the car, the shattered façade of the office, the handsome couple sitting outside looking like they had stumbled into a war zone. Paulson crossed the yard and joined them.

"Hell of a mess," was all he said, and he turned to Morgan. "Can you tell me what happened?"

"Shelly went outside to pull the car around to the barn," Morgan said. "I handed her the keys. A minute later I heard an explosion." He nodded to the smoking car. "You can see what happened."

The Professionals

"Damn shame," Ned offered. "She was a helluva good-looking girl. Who would want to do something like this to her?"

Kat flared at him. "You think this was meant for Shelly? How dumb are you, Ned? Shelly didn't drive a Cadillac. That's Morgan's car burning over there."

"I can't come to any conclusions until we've made a thorough investigation," Ned said stiffly. He turned to Morgan again. "What about you, Morgan? How did you and girl get along?"

Morgan looked up slowly. "What are you asking me, Ned?"

"Did you have a fight? Any bad blood between you?"

Morgan rose to his feet. He looked like he was about to take a swing.

"Ned, I'm afraid my wife makes a good point. Exactly how dumb are you? Somebody just tried to kill me. Not Shelly. Not some sweet innocent girl. Me."

"I don't know that until all the facts are in. I have to talk to everyone."

"Well I'm through talking to you."

"Then I'm going to have to take you in."

"Take *me* in. What for, exactly?"

"Obstruction, unless you want to answer my questions. You're a logical suspect."

Morgan's fist drew back. It took all of Kat's strength to keep him from swinging at the sheriff.

"Not now, Morg," she said. "Not now." She looked at the policeman scornfully. "Ned, go investigate something."

The plane from Miami was 45 minutes late getting into O'Hare. Among the passengers were two men in Madras plaid sportscoats with blond crewcuts and deep tans. Both wore dark glasses even inside the terminal.

One of the men scanned the crowded aisle until he spotted a bank of pay phones across from the gate. The men in sportscoats weaved through the terminal traffic, and one of them picked up a receiver, put a dime in the slot and dialed the number he had written on the back of a business card. The operator asked for 35 cents more, and he inserted the coins. A moment later he could hear the phone ringing.

Cyrus Caine answered. "Yeah?"

"It's Morris," said the man from Miami. "We just got in."

"Just got in?" Cyrus sounded confused. "Where the hell are you?"

"At O'Hare. Me and Gale just landed."

"What the fuck?" Cyrus sputtered. "You mean you didn't…."

"Didn't what? We just got here. Look, you hired us to do a job…."

"Looks like somebody else is trying to cut you out," Cyrus replied gruffly. He told the man about the bombing at the stable. Morris grunted in exasperation.

"What do you want us to do, turn around and fly back to Miami? We've got expenses."

"No, don't leave. The idiots who tried to do the job botched it. I'll still pay you the ten grand if you do it right." Morris heard the receiver slam down and stared at the dead phone in his hand. He looked at his partner, Gale, and slid the sunglasses down to the end of his nose.

"Something wrong?" Gale asked him.

Morris's face was troubled. "Something's way off."

Morgan Caine was sitting at his desk, which he had moved around so that he could see the front door at all times and have his back to the wall. The Hickok seat, he thought grimly. The shattered windows were boarded over with plywood, waiting for the repairmen to come and replace the glass, but he could still see out through the one remaining window.

Shelly Reid's death had shaken the entire stable. She was like family, and she had been brutally murdered for one reason only: she had started Morgan's car. The wreckage had been towed away, the debris was swept up after the investigators had sifted through every inch of it. Since then, they had heard nothing from the police. Morgan didn't expect to. They were too deep in Cyrus's pocket to be concerned about the death of a teenage girl.

Morgan heard a car pull into the yard and looked up. It was a late-model Ford Falcon; Morgan didn't recognize it. His hand slid into his desk drawer and gripped the handle of a Smith & Wesson .38 he now kept loaded and ready and within reach at all times.

Two men got out of the car, looked around the yard, taking in the boarded-up office, the scorch marks in the parking space in front of the building. They moved in for a closer look. As he heard a hand grasp the doorknob, Morgan withdrew the pistol and let it rest in his lap under the desk.

Two men entered the office and stood in front of him. Both were blonde and suntanned, wearing Madras plaid jackets. One man was a little bigger than the other, but they could have been brothers.

"Help you with something?" Morgan said warily. The larger man spoke.

"We came here to kill you," he said.

Morgan lifted the pistol from his lap and pointed it at the strangers. "You're a little late. Somebody already tried that today." The two men raised their hands.

"Hey hey," the larger man said. "Calm down. We're not armed." They opened their sportcoats. Neither seemed to be carrying.

"Then what are you doing here?" Morgan demanded, keeping the gun level.

"We were hired by an individual to kill a Mister Morgan Caine. I take it that's you."

"It is." Morgan waved the gun between the two men, trying to decide which to shoot first. "So you're the ones who blew up my car? Killed a young girl?"

"No, we're not," the bigger man, Morris, insisted. "If we had done the job we'd have done it right. That girl would be alive and you'd be dead."

"Why are you telling me this?"

"Because something is seriously screwed up around here. We don't know who the idiots are who killed that girl, but it never should have happened. We're not about to let somebody pin that job on us. Besides, we don't like it when some amateur cuts in on our contract."

Morgan considered this a moment. He laid the gun down gently, with his hand still resting on it, and said, "Have a seat, gentlemen."

Morris and Gale lowered themselves into the two leather chairs opposite Morgan, after brushing off the plaster dust.

"So what are you proposing?" Morgan asked.

"We know who ordered the hit."

"I do too."

"Maybe you do. But can you prove it?"

Morgan paused a moment, then shook his head.

"We know how to contact him," Morris said, "Maybe we call him up to renegotiate our fee since the first idiot screwed it up. Only this time the cops would be listening."

Morgan regarded the men closely, still unsure of what he was hearing, wondering if this was some sort of trap.

"The police around here won't be any help," Morgan said.

"Then find some other cops," Morris replied.

Detective Don Krause picked his large frame out of the wooden desk chair and heard a crack. Whether it was the chair or his knees Krause couldn't tell. Though he was only 42 he felt much older most days. His knees had bothered him since he was injured trying to land a bomber on a carrier deck in a roiling storm more than 20 years earlier. Now they mostly bothered him when the weather started to turn. He was a big man, carried a lot of weight – six feet four and 250 pounds on a good day — and that didn't help his knees very much.

Krause had joined the Illinois State Police after he mustered out of the service, trading one uniform for another. In 1950, when the Illinois governor approved a Criminal Investigation Division focused on gambling and slot machines, Krause signed up. Eventually he was promoted to plain clothes and spent a few years chasing auto theft rings. Then came a chance to join the Illinois Bureau of Investigation, working on everything from robbery to homicides and lending support to local law enforcement around the state.

Now, 50 pounds heavier and with hair that was totally white, he looked like a man in his 50s. He was grateful they didn't make the detectives pass a physical every year. Despite his bulk, he gave the impression of a strong and solid man who could more than hold his own, except perhaps in a foot race.

Krause glanced at the office door as it swung open and three men entered. The first one was a man about his own age – early 40s but looked younger. Tanned, very fit, with a full head of hair turning gray at the temples. He was wearing a navy blazer, an open-collared shirt, gray slacks and jodhpur boots – the only detail that didn't seem to fit his preppie look.

The two men with him fairly screamed "not from around here": loud plaid jackets, pants too thin for the midwestern climate, deeply tanned faces although it was only June. They wore sunglasses in the building, which Krause found odd. He stepped forward to meet them at the railing separating the detectives bullpen from the entryway.

"Something I can do for you gentlemen?" Krause asked, addressing the well-dressed man.

"I want to report a murder."

Krause's black eyebrows rose slightly. "Really. Whose?"

"Mine," the man replied.

Krause nodded. "Interesting. And who is responsible for this crime?"

"They are," the man answered, nodding to his companions.

Krause regarded the three men for a moment. The well-dressed man looked too respectable to be a crank. On the other hand, the two characters with him could very well be killers. Krause walked over and opened the gate.

"Maybe you gentlemen should come on in and tell me what this is about."

Burnt coffee was passed out in Styrofoam cups as the four men gathered around a conference table. The well-dressed man introduced himself as Morgan Caine. Krause recognized the name immediately – everyone in law enforcement knew the name Caine. He remembered that this Caine had been a pilot during the war as he had, and the two men bonded a bit with Air Corps stories before Caine launched into the reason for his visit.

Krause sat quietly at the conference table, a pen in hand, jotting the occasional note on a legal pad while Morgan talked. When he paused, apparently done, Krause looked at him levelly.

"So you think your brother Cyrus is behind these attempts on your life?"

"I know he is." Morgan nodded to Morris and Gale. "These two confirmed it."

"What about the car bomb that killed the girl?"

"That was meant for me."

Krause looked at the two men from Florida. "Did you have anything to do with planting the bomb?"

"We did not," said Gale. It was the first time Morgan had heard him speak. "But it was Cyrus Caine's idea. Some other fool got there before we did and bungled the job."

"You're saying you'd have done a more professional job of it," Krause suggested, his sarcasm barely concealed.

"Look, Detective," Morris said. "We felt bad about the girl. There was no reason for that to happen. We'd like to see you get the guy who did this."

Morgan nodded agreement. "This isn't going to stop until a lot more people get hurt. Not just me, my family, the people who work for me. My brother isn't the kind of man to quit before the job's done."

Krause stared down at the legal pad in front of him.

"And you want me to do what, exactly? It's not like the Croydon County sheriff has asked the IBI for help."

"And they never will," Morgan countered. "Ned Paulson has been in Cyrus's hip pocket since they were teenagers." Morgan walked to the window and looked down on State Street, nine stories below. "There are other things that could make this your jurisdiction," he said quietly.

"Such as?"

"What's the IBI interested in? Tax fraud? Race fixing? Arson? Extortion? You name it, Cyrus is in the middle of it."

The detective regarded him a minute, considering something. He stood and walked to a nearby filing cabinet, opened it and removed a file nearly two inches thick. He dropped it on the table with a soft thud.

"This is the IBI's file on the Horse Mafia. Arson. Extortion. Insurance fraud. And my particular favorite, 'equine fatalities.' Dozens of animals killed under suspicious circumstances. We haven't been able to make any of it stick."

Morgan flipped through the file, recognizing names and places, noting dates, connecting dots. He closed the folder decisively. "I can give you enough for probable cause. Then these two can get him talking and planning the murder. My murder."

Krause looked at the two hit men.

"Would you be willing to wear a wire? Get this on tape? Then we might be able to make a case for conspiracy."

Morris and Gale exchanged a glance, then they nodded.

Cyrus barely gave it a second thought when he got a call from the hitmen suggesting a meeting.

"We want to make sure this doesn't get screwed up again," Morris said to him on the phone. Cyrus agreed, and he told them to meet him at the Round House, a tavern on the Illinois-Wisconsin border – a place where none of them was likely to be recognized.

When the hitmen arrived Cyrus was at the bar nursing a bourbon and water. He knew who they were when they walked in – the only men in the dark room wearing sunglasses – and nodded to an open booth.

"So why did you gentlemen think it was so important to meet in person?" Cyrus asked, dispensing with the preliminaries.

"Too easy to screw things up when you're getting instructions by phone."

"I can see that," Cyrus agreed.

"Did you ever figure out who tried to cut us out of this deal?" Morris asked. Cyrus shook his head. Then he went silent. Morris continued, "Well, if you ever do, let us know and we'll take care of it. I resent somebody else jumping on my contract."

"Speaking of which," Gale added, "This business with the car bomb has put a lot more heat on us. We're going to have to renegotiate the terms of the deal."

"That so? What did you have in mind exactly?"

"The price is $15,000 to kill your brother."

"That's quite a little jump."

"We're worth it. At least working with us, he'll get dead and stay dead."

Cyrus considered a moment. "All right. We're agreed. Just get it done." He started to rise from the booth.

"Mind if we ask a question?" Morris said. "Why do you want him dead?"

Cyrus gave him a hard look. "The why is my business. The how is yours." With that he stood up and walked out of the bar. He got into his white Cadillac Eldorado, never noticing the nondescript van parked at the far side of the lot. In the back of the van, Don Krause looked at the officer handling the recording equipment. He took off his headphones.

"We got him."

"Your brother's been arrested. Conspiracy to commit murder."

The call came from Don Krause to Morgan Caine a few days later. Kat was standing next to him as the detective laid out the progress in the case:

After getting Cyrus Caine on tape hiring Morris and Gale to carry out the murder of his brother, Krause was able to get the state's attorney to seek charges against him. Agents from the IBI appeared at Cyrus's home, cuffed him and took him off to jail.

"Cussed up a storm all the way to the station," Krause related. "Words I never even heard in the Army."

"Sounds like Cyrus."

"There's more," said Krause. "We got a lead on two men who bought some dynamite at a hardware store about five miles from your house. Not so bright, these guys. We brought one of them in, and he flipped on his friend before he could get his coat off. The Chicago police picked him up. When they searched his apartment they found materials for building bombs. So, looks like our guy."

"Did they say anything about Cyrus? Do they know him?"

"The one guy claims he was out at one of Cyrus's stables visiting a friend. He overheard Cyrus on the phone hiring the job out – most likely to your friends Morris and Gale. Ten thousand dollars to – quote – 'kill some guy in a gold Cadillac.' They decided to cut themselves in on the action. Again, not so bright."

"What happens now?"

"We wait for the grand jury to indict, then the trial. One of the guys, Bobby Boudreau, has a long rap sheet. He was wanted on a prior offense, so we'll be holding him indefinitely. The other guy…" Krause checked his notes "…Kenny McKay, dishonorable discharge from the Army – munitions, by the way – but no priors."

"And Cyrus?" Kat leaned into the phone at that point, willing herself to hear the answer.

"Bailed himself out the same day. Had the cash on him. The State's Attorney might delay his case until they've tried the other two. Easier to prove conspiracy once they've been convicted of murder. Or he could try them all together. We'll have to wait and see."

"Thanks for letting us know, Detective," Morgan said. "And thanks for your help."

They hung up. Morgan put his arm around Kat's shoulder.

"Could this really be over?" she asked.

But she knew better.

Morris and Gale were having dinner in a steakhouse beneath the 'L' tracks on Wabash Avenue. It was a low-key place with decent steaks and a pretty good salad bar. The two gunmen-turned-state's-witnesses were determined to keep a low profile until after they had delivered their testimony in the Caine trial and could be on a flight back to Miami in a couple of days.

The two men settled up their check, left a respectable tip and headed for the exit. Just as they reached it Gale patted his pockets and turned back toward their table.

"Forgot my glasses," he told his partner. Morris nodded.

"See you outside," he said as he entered the revolving door.

The Professionals

As he stepped out on the other side Morris felt a cloth of some kind – maybe a blanket or a sack – being thrown over his head. Powerful hands grabbed his shoulders and pinned his arms. He struggled, but he was outnumbered at least two to one. He felt a hand snake under the blanket and caught a whiff of ether. Before he sank into unconsciousness he heard voices in hurried conversation.

"Where's the other guy?"

"Went back inside. Come on, we'll get him later."

Morris awoke to find himself in blackness. He was seated on a stool, hands bound tightly behind his back. Powerful smells wafted up into his nose, hay and sawdust and horseshit.

The bag was torn off his head, and Morris blinked in the light. The shapes of three men came into focus, two in shadow off to the side, and one directly in front of him, standing next to a spotlight that shone in his eyes. Though partially blinded, he recognized the man in front of him. It was Cyrus Caine.

"Welcome back," Cyrus said. "Thanks for joining us."

"Where the hell am I?" Morris growled, his voice still slurred from the anesthetic.

"Where's not important," Cyrus answered. "One of my stables."

"What do you want?"

"I got some questions for you." Cyrus stepped forward, and Morris was able to see him a little better. "You and your partner are on the witness list for the trial coming up. That true?"

Morris didn't answer. One of the men behind him grabbed his neck and pulled his head up. Cyrus asked again, "That true?"

Morris struggled to break the man's grip but couldn't. He nodded curtly.

"We're making progress. Now tell me, who'd you work with to roll over on me? Was it my brother?"

Morris didn't answer. Caine gave a jerk of the head, and one of the men smashed Morris across the face. The pain shot through his skull, but still he kept his mouth shut.

"We don't seem to be making a lot of progress here," Cyrus sighed. "Maybe you need a little more encouragement." He took another step forward. Morris now saw a stainless steel implement that looked like a long-handled pair of pliers gleaming in Cyrus's hands. The horseman tapped one end of the instrument against his open palm and held it close to Morris's face.

"Ever spend any time around horses, Mister Morris?" Cyrus asked absently. He spread the handles of the instrument, and the pincher-like jaws gaped open. He held the instrument under Morris's nose, and it flashed in the light. "This thing here. This is how a stallion gets turned into a gelding."

Morris's eyes grew wide with terror. He struggled as he felt two sets of iron hands grasp his arms. Cyrus smiled at him coldly as he said, "Hold him tight, boys…."

Gale checked his watch for the umpteenth time as he mounted the courthouse steps. He lowered his sunglasses and gave a worried look for Morris. His partner hadn't turned up after disappearing from the restaurant the night before. That wasn't like Morris. He hadn't returned to the hotel, hadn't called, left no message. Gale's last hope was that his partner would meet him at the courthouse before they testified, but that wasn't looking good either.

When Gale turned around he bumped into a tough-looking man leaning against one of the courthouse pillars reading a newspaper. Gale didn't recognize him, but it was Cole Harmon, Cyrus Caine's right-hand man.

"Hey friend," Cole greeted him, holding up the newspaper. "Did you see this story?"

The Professionals

"What story? I don't know you," Gale replied, trying to push past him. The big man blocked his way.

"A story about a guy who testified against the wrong people. He should have kept his mouth shut." The big man folded the paper under his arm. Then he pushed a paper sack into Gale's hands. "Don't forget your lunch," he said, then vanished around the pillar.

Gale went to call after him, but the man was gone. Gale looked down at the paper sack in his hands, opened the top cautiously and peered inside. Then he started to gag.

Staring back at him from the sack was a pair of testicles.

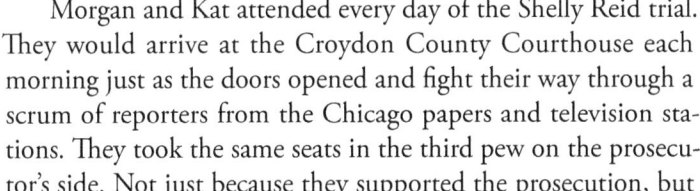

Morgan and Kat attended every day of the Shelly Reid trial. They would arrive at the Croydon County Courthouse each morning just as the doors opened and fight their way through a scrum of reporters from the Chicago papers and television stations. They took the same seats in the third pew on the prosecutor's side. Not just because they supported the prosecution, but so that they could have an unobstructed view of Cyrus Caine.

The state's attorney had decided that all three defendants – Bobby Boudreau, Kenny McKay and Cyrus Caine – should be tried together. Boudreau and McKay were facing first-degree murder as well as a raft of other charges including conspiracy. Cyrus was charged with conspiracy. Two of the defendants were being held without bail in the county jail. Cyrus arrived on his own recognizance each morning, freshly shaved, wearing a neatly pressed suit and a pair of boots so brightly polished he could see his own reflection in them. He sat quietly next to his attorney, never acknowledging the other defendants or turning to look over his shoulder at Morgan or Kat.

"Call Steven Gale to the stand," the bailiff announced later that morning. Gale, absent the sunglasses, looked paler than Morgan remembered him. Gale took the stand and was sworn in. His eyes shifted nervously to the defense table, where Cyrus Caine fixed his black stare upon him.

"Now, Mr. Gale," the prosecuting attorney began, "in your interview with the IBI you stated that you had been contracted by Cyrus Caine to kill his brother in exchange for fifteen thousand dollars. Is that correct?"

Gale didn't answer. The prosecutor prompted him again.

"Mr. Gale, is that correct?"

Gale's eyes were still locked with Cyrus's. He swallowed. Little beads of perspiration formed along his hairline.

"I don't know. Is it?"

"Mr. Gale, please keep in mind that you are under oath. Did you or did you not meet with Mr. Caine at the Round House Tavern, where he offered you fifteen thousand dollars to kill his brother?"

Gale hesitated again. A murmur went through the courtroom as everyone saw that something was very wrong with the witness. Kat leaned against Morgan and squeezed his arm, hard. The prosecuting attorney took out a handkerchief and dabbed at his forehead nervously. The testimony wasn't going as planned. The judge leaned down and addressed the witness.

"Mr. Gale, you are required to answer the prosecutor's question."

"I want to, Judge," Gale replied. "It's just that my memory isn't so good. It was a while ago. You know, I don't even remember what I had for breakfast." A nervous laugh.

After ten more minutes of evasion, it was clear Gale had lost his memory and wasn't giving up anything. The judge lost his patience and brought his gavel down.

"Mr. Gale, I am charging you with contempt of court. That will be a one thousand dollar fine and thirty days in jail. Bailiff, take this witness away."

As Gale was escorted out of the courtroom, he managed one last glance at Cyrus Caine, who threw him an icy smirk. At the rear of the courtroom Gale recognized the large man who had accosted him on the courthouse steps, who gave him a nod of approval as he was led past.

Cyrus's attorney was on his feet addressing the judge.

"Your honor, in light of the fact that the witness has failed to offer testimony, and the prosecution's other witness apparently cannot be located, I move to dismiss the charge of conspiracy against my client."

The judge looked at the prosecutor. "Mr. Higgins, any other witnesses who can corroborate the IBI's taped conversation?"

The prosecutor looked abashed. "No, your honor," he admitted. "We had another witness, but…well, he's disappeared."

"I'll bet," Kat whispered to Morgan.

"In that case," the judge announced, "you leave me no choice but to dismiss the charge of conspiracy against Mister Caine. Mister Caine, you are free to go."

Cyrus rose, shook hands with his attorney, and walked down the aisle of the courtroom. He paused when he got to Morgan and Kat's row, fixed them with a chilly smile, and left the courtroom, a free man.

That night there was a celebration at High Time Stables in Chicago. Cyrus was surrounded by his henchmen and cronies, and the bourbon flowed all night. Cole Harmon stood off to one side of the room, deep in his own thoughts. There was a warrant out for him, a little matter of arson at a competitor's stable. Now that the trial was done Harmon had decided it this might be a good time to take a vacation, maybe to Arizona.

When the crowd thinned a bit, Harmon crossed the room and joined his one-time cellmate and boss. He tipped his glass in congratulations, and the two men downed their drinks.

"I've got just one question," Harmon said in a voice too low for anyone else to hear. "What are you going to do about the rest of the evidence?"

Cyrus picked up a nearby bottle, topped up his glass and smiled. "You can buy a lot of justice for ten thousand dollars," he replied.

Chapter 22

Protection

IT WAS AFTER NINE O'CLOCK in the evening when the doorbell rang at the Morgan Caine home. The Caine children were upstairs in their rooms. Morgan and Kat were in the family room. Morgan flipped absently through the *Tribune*. Kat had the TV on, watching *I Spy* but not really watching. The doorbell made them jump. They exchanged looks and went to the door together.

Morgan looked through the peephole and recognized the man on their porch. He swung the door open.

"Detective, what brings you all the way out here?"

Don Krause took off his hat and gave it a shake. It was drizzling outside, and he had gotten a little wet on the short walk from his car to the front porch.

"Mind if I come in?"

The Caines showed him in. The three of them went into the livingroom. Kat snapped the television off.

"Can I get you something?" she said. "Some coffee? Something stronger?"

"Coffee would be great. Black."

Ten minutes later the three of them were sipping coffee, waiting for the detective to explain his presence. Finally he spoke.

"I wanted you to hear about this from me," he began. "It's about the evidence in the Shelly Reid case."

"What about it?"

"I got a call from the Chicago police. The evidence is missing."

Kat and Morgan exchanged puzzled looks.

"Missing? What do you mean, missing?" Morgan asked.

"Missing as in gone. Vanished. Misplaced, although I doubt that. The transcripts of Kenny McKay's testimony, the bomb-making equipment, the whole shebang. In short, the evidence against McKay and Boudreau has been 'disappeared.'"

"I don't get it," Morgan said. "How does something like that happen?"

"I can explain it in two words," Kat said. "Cyrus Caine. Cyrus doesn't just have his hooks in the sheriff's department here. He obviously has contacts in the Chicago police too."

"I'm afraid you're right, Mrs. Caine, although we can't prove it. Things go missing with the Chicago police all the time. Of course we can't prove anything."

"So," Morgan said slowly. "What does this mean for the trial?"

Krause studied his size 14 cordovans. "The case will be dismissed for lack of evidence."

The Caines looked at each other, and Morgan took Kat's hand as the import of the detective's statement sank in. Kat spoke first, making the detective meet her eye.

"It's bad enough that the judge let Cyrus walk. Now Shelly's killers get off as well?"

Krause nodded. "I wanted you to hear it from me. And know how sorry I am."

"We appreciate that, Detective," Kat said quietly. "So what do we do now?"

"How do you mean?"

"Detective, my family won't be safe while Cyrus Caine and his merry band of hitmen are walking the streets. There must be something you can do."

"Ma'am, I wish there was. But the IBI can't arrest him unless we have proof of a crime. I'm looking into some of the other leads you gave me," nodding to Morgan. "The arson, insurance fraud. But that all takes time."

Kat's blue eyes flashed. "And what do we do in the meantime? Wait for him to try to kill my husband again?"

Morgan tried to intercede. He said to Krause, "Maybe you could assign some men to watch the house?"

"I wish I could. But the IBI doesn't have those kinds of resources. Not without an imminent threat, something we could prove." Krause sighed and stood up, feeling the pain in his joints. "I promise you folks: Bring me something solid, something I can arrest him for, and I'll slap the cuffs on him myself. In the meantime," he added, picking up his hat, "you might want to look into getting yourself some protection."

A few days later, Morgan was in his office, looking across the desk at a lean young man with a military haircut and clean-cut looks. The young man wore a brown suit that looked like it might have been a hand-me-down, given that it was at least one size too large for him. His white shirt didn't seem to fit much better, and the absurdly wide floral tie didn't do much to pull the outfit together. Morgan thought to himself, *This is why police wear uniforms.*

He said to the young man, "Mr. Krause tells me you've been with the State Police for three years?"

"Yes, sir, that's right. I signed up right after I got back from the Army."

"Viet Nam?"

"Yes, sir. Two years. I was in the MPs, so police work kind of felt like a natural fit."

"Did Detective Krause tell you the nature of the services we need?"

"He said there had been some threats against you. That you were looking for someone to keep an eye on your family."

"That's about it. Any thoughts on the subject?"

The young man's brow furrowed. Morgan was starting to like that he took this seriously.

"To really protect your family takes a lot more than just one guy," he began. "You'd need a team, rotating around the clock. So far, all you have is me – assuming you hire me."

"Go on."

"Maybe the thing to do is, keep the other party under surveillance."

"And how do we do that?"

"They're doing some really interesting things with surveillance equipment," the young man replied, warming to his subject. "I'm kind of into gadgets. We could do motion sensors around the house. Maybe put a tracker on his car. That way you'd always know where he is."

Morgan thought for a moment, looked up at the young man again. "Martell, was it?"

"Yes, sir. John Martell."

"Mister Martell, you're on the case."

A couple of days later, Kat was in the kitchen putting away dishes from the night before. Sunlight was streaming through the kitchen window, although the radio said there was a chance of rain later in the afternoon. Kat loved this time of day, when Morgan was out of the house on his way down to his office. The children were home from school, and she thought they were still asleep upstairs. That gave her time to get some work done and have some time to herself.

Meghan Caine, still in her nightgown, rushed into the kitchen with an anxious look on her face.

"Mom," she said, "there's a man in a tree outside my window…."

Before she even finished the sentence, Kat rushed to the front door.

There was indeed a man outside, but he was on the front porch, standing at the top of a ladder. He was adjusting a small black box of some sort, screwing it into the boards at the corner of the porch roof. His short dark hair showed beads of perspiration as he worked even though the weather was cool.

He heard the CA-CLATCH of a pump-action Remington shotgun and froze. A woman's voice said steadily, "Move real slow, mister, and come down off that ladder."

John Martell put his hands up, the screwdriver still in one of them. He looked down at the determined-looking redhaired woman pointing the shotgun at his crotch.

"Take it easy, ma'am," he said slowly, lowering himself carefully one rung at a time. "I'm here to do some work."

"What kind of work?" Kat demanded.

"Security," the young man said. "Your husband hired me."

"It's all right, Kat. Let him be." It was Morgan's voice. He had seen the two of them from his office window, saw his wife with the shotgun, and knew this might not end well.

"This man says you hired him? Why didn't you tell me?"

"I thought he'd be more discreet. Come on down here, Mr. Martell. Meet Mrs. Caine."

Martell climbed down from the ladder, extended his hand to Kat, then thought better of it. "Pleased to meet you, ma'am."

"What were you doing up on that ladder?" Kat wanted to know. Martell looked a little more comfortable now that the shotgun was pointed away from him.

"That's a motion sensor," Martell explained, pointing with the screwdriver. "I'm putting them at different points around the house, covering the main doors and windows. When you turn it on, if someone steps into range…" he gestured with the screwdriver, taking in the area in front of the door "…they'll set off an alarm. Or we can do a silent alarm and alert the police."

Kat nodded, secretly pleased but trying not to look too impressed.

"What about that other thing you were working on?" Morgan asked Martell. "Is it functional yet?"

"What other thing?" Kat wanted to know, giving her husband a sharp look. "Mr. Martell, maybe you better come inside and have a cup of coffee. You can tell me everything – even if my husband won't."

The "other thing" was the tracking device Martell had planted in the bumper of Cyrus Caine's white Cadillac Eldorado.

So far the device was working brilliantly. For the first two weeks, John Martell knew where Cyrus was going, when he stopped, how long he stayed. When he was off duty, Martell followed the white Eldorado at a discreet distance, just to test the strength and accuracy of the signal and to make sure the equipment was working properly. Nothing he found from shadowing Cyrus surprised him. A lot of stops at horse farms in the area. An afternoon at Arlington Racetrack. Several evenings spent at The Flame, one of Cyrus's favorite haunts. A couple of evenings at what Martell learned – blushing as he gave his report to Morgan – was a local house of ill repute.

Then one day the signal stopped abruptly. Martell went to Morgan's office to report the bad news.

"I don't know why. Suddenly it just quit," the young police officer said, his face red with embarrassment. "Might be the battery. I'll have to find a time when he's not using the car so I can get close enough to change it."

Morgan nodded, and as he looked down at his cluttered desktop he happened to see his open Day Timer calendar sitting on top.

"Shit," he muttered.

"What is it?"

"It's the end of October," Morgan explained. "Cyrus trades his Cadillac in for a new one every year at this time, when the new models come out. That's why you can't get a signal."

Martell gulped. "Shit is right. These devices cost three grand – and I borrowed the equipment from a pal of mine in the State Police. I've got to find his old car."

"Yes. Then you have to plant the device on the new one."

Martell took a deep breath. "Wish me luck," he said as he headed for the door.

It was the last time Morgan and the young policeman spoke.

Two nights later, Martell held the recovered tracker in his hand. It was cold outside, and an early snow had covered the ground with about three inches earlier that afternoon. One of those freak midwestern snowstorms that had the kids out trick or treating with their winter coats over their costumes.

Martell was parked on the road outside Cyrus Caine's house at Cold Creek Stables. Cyrus was home, judging from the shiny new Cadillac Eldorado parked in the carport at the end of the driveway. The lights were off downstairs in the house, a single lamp burning in one of the upstairs bedrooms. Martell blew on his hands to keep them warm. When he felt confident the coast was clear he opened his car door carefully, turning off the dome light so it wouldn't reveal his presence. Quietly he made his way to the house, his wet cordovans crunching softly on the newly fallen snow.

The Cadillac was parked with its angular tail facing the house. The lantern lights on the garage didn't reach quite far enough to give away Martell's position, he noticed with relief. It also made it hard for the young police officer to see what he was doing. Stuffing his gloves in his coat pocket, Martell took out a pocket-sized flashlight and turned it on. He knelt down beside the rear bumper and held the flashlight in his mouth to illuminate his work area. He took the tracking device out of his other pocket and felt along the inside rim of the rear bumper, looking for the best spot to place the tracker.

Suddenly the area around him was flooded with light. Martell looked over his shoulder and was blinded by the hot white beam of a powerful flashlight. He could make out the dark outline of the figure holding it and recognized the man he'd been following for two weeks – Cyrus Caine. In one hand he held the torch. In the other he held a Smith & Wesson revolver.

"Stand up real slow," Cyrus growled at him, "and explain what the hell you're doing around my car."

"I was just…I was looking for…" the young man stammered once he took the penlight out of his mouth. He rose to his full height and held his hands above his head.

"What's that in your hand?"

The cop knew he'd been busted. "It's a tracking device."

Cyrus shook his head. He had to marvel at the innovation.

"Tracking device, huh? So who's so interested in tracking me? You with the IRS? I told those assholes if they want to audit me they'd have to talk to my lawyers."

"I'm not with the IRS," Martell replied. "I work for the State Police."

Cyrus bristled when he heard that. "Why would the State Police be interested in me?"

"Not the police, really," Martell answered. The cold was starting to get to him, and he as shivering. "This is kind of a freelance thing."

"So who's paying you?" When Martell didn't answer right away, Cyrus answered for him. "You working for my brother?" The young man still wouldn't answer. Cyrus waived the beam from his flashlight in the direction of the house. "Maybe you and me need to have a chat. Start moving. And keep your hands up."

Martell started to walk, and as he did the tracking device slipped out of his hand and landed in the snow. He hesitated, but Cyrus waved him forward with the muzzle of his gun. When he passed Cyrus the older man patted him down quickly and took his service revolver out of the holster on Martell's belt and stuck it in the waistband of his own trousers.

When they got to the landing by the front door Cyrus stepped in front of the young man.

"Do me a favor," Cyrus said. "Press the doorbell, would you? It's been sticking on me lately."

"The doorbell? Sure." Martell tried it, and they both heard the chimes inside. "Seems to work OK."

Cyrus was standing in the doorway now, Martell on the landing.

"OK then," Cyrus said as he wheeled around, the Smith & Wesson pointed at Martell's chest. Then he pulled the trigger. Once. Twice. He kept firing until all the chambers were empty.

Martell's hand went to his empty holster and his lips parted as if to shout, but everything happened so fast he was dead before he hit the ground. His body lay spreadeagled in the snow on the porch, like he was making a snow angel, blood streaming from the six wounds in his torso.

Cyrus heard the click on the empty chamber and reached into his trouser pocket. He took out a second gun, a Beretta 950 – his "mouse gun"–and fired three more shots into Martell just for good measure – the last one to the soft spot at the bridge of his nose. He stared down at the dead man, his blood running hot, his breathing heavy, the cold leaving streaming jets from his nostrils.

He tucked the Beretta back in his pants pocket and set his pistol on the parquet floor of his entry hall. He took Martell's weapon, a well-oiled snub nose .38 revolver, out of his waistband and stepped outside and around the body. He fired two shots from waist level, aiming a bit high and leaving two holes in the back wall of the foyer – careful not to hit the mirror in the center; that thing cost a lot of money.

He wiped the revolver down with his handkerchief, then he placed it in the dead man's right hand and squeezed the lifeless fingers around the grip and the trigger. He let Martell's hand go and it flopped onto the porch with the gun spilling from his grip.

Cyrus went inside the house, closed the front door and telephoned the sheriff's office.

"Ned? Cyrus. Better send your people out here. Somebody just tried to kill me."

Don Krause pulled his Oldsmobile up to the end of the lane leading to Cyrus Caine's house. He cursed under his breath. It stood to reason that Caine would have a long driveway, and at the moment it was clogged with police vehicles and an ambulance, all with their Mars lights flashing in the night. He would have to hike it up to the house. Walking on the snow wouldn't help his knees any.

Krause walked past an army of police and technicians, taping off the scene, snapping photographs and gathering evidence. No one paid him much attention until he reached the *porte cochere* attached to the driveway. He paused, looking at the Eldorado parked there, tracing the footprints in the snow, taking in the scene, memorizing it. He stepped up to the car, careful not to mar the trail of footprints leading to the front door of the house. He spotted something in the snow under the Eldorado's bumper, something shiny. He bent down, feeling his knees groaning, and with a gloved hand he picked up the small metal disk from the snow. He took a plastic evidence bag from his coat, slipped the disk into it and put it in his pocket, hoping the police on the scene were too busy to notice him. Then he walked on to the house, where a uniformed deputy blocked his path.

"This is a crime scene, sir. You can't be here."

Krause flashed his IBI badge, and the deputy let him pass reluctantly. He was a cop, but not one of theirs.

Krause reached the front steps and saw the body sprawled out on the top of the landing. Someone had thrown a tarp over it, and snowflakes were blowing onto it from the lawn. A coroner's assistant stood nearby.

"Let's have a look," Krause said, and the assistant complied. Krause took a sharp intake of breath. He stared down at Martell's lifeless body, the young face frozen as if in surprise, his body stippled with bullet wounds. Krause studied the body for what seemed like hours. Then he whispered a prayer to himself and made a quick sign of the Cross.

"That's enough. Cover him up." The attendant complied and beckoned the ambulance drivers to bring the gurney up.

The front door was open and Krause stepped inside. The sheriff's deputies were busy and didn't notice him at first. Krause looked around the foyer, took in the bullet holes on the back wall, saw the deputy pry a bullet out and place it in an evidence bag. Krause glanced back at the front door, calculating the angle of the shots. Another deputy walked past with a Smith & Wesson .38, bagged and tagged – the murder weapon, Krause assumed.

He heard voices murmuring in the living room and headed in that direction.

Cyrus Caine was standing with a tall, pot-bellied policeman wearing a shirling coat. He still had his Smokey the Bear hat on even though the room was warm. As Krause stepped forward the two men turned and looked at him and the conversation stopped.

"Who are you?" the big-bellied policeman asked. He looked over at one of the junior officers, his look clearly saying 'Who let this guy in?'

"Krause, Illinois Bureau of Investigation," he said, presenting his credentials. Ned Paulson glanced at the badge and the i.d., looked up at Krause, decided he may very well be who he said he was. His demeanor changed a bit.

"Oh, well. Hello, Detective." He offered a perfunctory handshake. "I'm Sheriff Paulson. Not sure what you're doing here. This is my jurisdiction."

"Of course it is," Krause replied. "It so happens I knew the victim."

Both Cyrus and Paulson stiffened a bit.

"Knew him how?" Ned wanted to know.

"He was a state trooper. A fine young man."

"Then what was that 'fine young man' doing on my doorstep taking shots at me?" Cyrus growled. Ned put a cautioning hand on his arm.

Krause replied evenly, "Is that your story?"

Ned interceded. "Mister Caine has already given his statement. It was a clear case of self defense."

"Oh?" Krause's black eyebrows lifted a bit, and he turned his gaze to Cyrus.

"Sure was," Cyrus affirmed. "Clear as can be. I heard someone at my door, ringing the doorbell. When I went downstairs and opened the door this fella was standing there and opens fire on me. Two shots. Lucky he missed. I was in fear of my life. So I shot him back."

"You just happened to have a gun on you when you answered the door?" Krause asked.

"Of course. You never know who might be on the other side."

"Mm-hm. May I ask you a question, Mister Caine?"

"Why not?"

"I counted nine bullet holes in the body outside."

Cyrus nodded. "Sounds about right."

"What gun were you carrying when you answered the door?"

"My .38. It's a good gun at close range."

"Uh huh. How many rounds does it hold?"

"Six, of course."

"Then why are there nine bullet holes?"

Cyrus smiled at such a childish question. "I had a second gun in my pocket, naturally. Wanted to make sure I finished the job. Like I said, I feared for my life."

"How much deader could you make him?" Krause said archly. Cyrus glared at him. Ned Paulson put up his hands.

"Let's keep it civil, if you don't mind, Detective. Mr. Caine answered your questions. All the evidence seems to back up his story. It is, like I said, a clearcut case of self defense."

Krause wasn't done. He turned to Ned. "Sheriff, did you happen to notice the tracks leading from the car?"

"Which car?" Paulson's eyes narrowed.

"That white Cadillac parked out front – Mister Caine's car, I assume?"

"It is," Cyrus said. "What about it?"

"There were two sets of tracks leading from the car to the front door. Either the victim didn't come here alone, or perhaps you didn't encounter him at the front door like you said."

Cyrus flushed. He was getting impatient. "I told you what happened. That's all there is to it."

"And you say that you came to the front door with two guns on your person."

"That's right."

"Do you own these guns?"

"Sure. What do you think?"

Krause paused, then placed a large hand on Cyrus's shoulder. "Mister Caine, could you turn around please?"

"Turn around? What for?" Cyrus started to pull away, but Krause spun him all the way around and grabbed one of his arms. Before the other men could react Krause produced a pair of handcuffs and slapped them on Cyrus's wrists behind his back.

"What the hell is this?" Cyrus bellowed at him when he realized what was happening. "Ned, stop standing there gaping like a fish and do something."

"What's the big idea, Detective?" Ned barked. "Mister Caine is an honest citizen."

"Mister Caine is a convicted felon. He just confessed to possession of firearms, which is a criminal violation. I'm taking him into custody."

With that Krause propelled Cyrus out of the room and out the front door. Ned Paulson chased after them, sputtering. "You can't do this. You have no jurisdiction. This is my crime scene."

Krause pulled Cyrus up short and looked back at Paulson.

"There's been a crime, all right. And I mean to find out what really happened here. Good night, Sheriff."

With that he marched Cyrus down to his car, reciting the new Miranda rights as they stumbled along the snow-covered drive. Once there Krause bent him into the back seat, got behind the wheel and started up the engine. The horseman cursed him the whole way as they drove off into the night.

"I'm going to sue your ass. You know that, don't you?"

Cyrus was handcuffed to his chair in a windowless interrogation room at IBI headquarters. He had put up a struggle as Krause led him into the headquarters, and it took two officers to subdue him and get him into his chair. An untouched cup of coffee sat in front of him. Krause sat in a chair on the other side of the table. If he was bothered by Cyrus's threats he didn't show it.

"I'm not the first cop you've gone after," the detective said wearily. "I'm not even the first one tonight."

"You've got a hell of a lot of nerve dragging me down here. I'm the victim here, you know."

Krause gave an ironic smile. "Mister Caine, I've seen a lot of victims in my career. You are surely not one of them." Krause took a pack of Chesterfields from his shirt pocket and tapped one out. He saw Cyrus eyeing it and produced a second one, which Cyrus accepted grudgingly. Krause lit Cyrus's cigarette with his battered Zippo, then his own. The two men smoked in silence for a moment.

"Let's approach this another way," Krause said. "Why do you think Officer Martell, a fairly junior state trooper, would suddenly show up at your doorstep and try to kill you?"

"How the hell should I know? Maybe someone hired him."

"Like who?"

"'Like who'?" Cyrus mimicked. "You know damn well who. My brother's trying to kill me, that's who."

"Your brother Morgan."

"That's the one. He's had it in for me for years. Makes all kinds of crazy accusations about me, like I'm out to get him. He ratted me out to the IRS, did you know that? Then somebody broke into my house, went through my safe. Oh, I wouldn't put anything past my brother."

"According to the two killers you hired, you're the one trying to kill him."

"That was a lie!" Cyrus roared. "The judge threw it out of court."

"What about Shelly Reid, the girl who died? Who was behind that?"

"No idea. I didn't even know the girl."

They went on like this for an hour, Krause probing, Cyrus snarling back, like a lion in a cage. They might have gone all night but there was a knock at the door. One of the detectives on night duty stuck his head in and beckoned Krause. He walked to the door, the two of them conferred. Krause gave a heavy sigh. Cyrus smirked at him.

"Don't tell me: My lawyer's here."

"Yes, he is. You're free to go."

"Took him long enough." Cyrus raised his manacled wrist and rattled it at Krause, taunting him. The detective dug into his pocket for the key, taking his sweet time. Cyrus raised himself from the chair and stretched. He rubbed his wrist as he headed for the door.

"This has been real fun, Detective. I hope we don't meet again."

Protection

It was after 2 a.m. when Krause sat down at his scarred state-issued desk, adjusted the gooseneck lamp with the green Bakelite shade and stared down at the moleskin journal in front of him. He had already written up his report on the Cyrus Caine arrest and put it in his captain's in-box. He was certain the gun charges would be tossed in the morning. Caine had a lot of friends in the judiciary. Krause had known it as he was cuffing the man that the charge likely wouldn't stick. He just wanted to let that arrogant SOB know that someone was paying attention, that not every cop in the state of Illinois was bought and paid for.

Krause dug into the pocket of his topcoat, slung over a nearby chair, and pulled out the evidence bag he had taken from the crime scene. He spilled the silver disk onto the desk blotter and stared at it awhile. He knew what it was: a tracking device of some kind. That's what had brought Martell to Cyrus's driveway, and what had gotten him killed. He scooped the device back into the plastic bag, careful not to touch it with his ungloved hand. He wrote out a tag showing the date and location of the find, added that to the bag and put it in his desk drawer. He would turn it over to the Croydon County Sheriff's Department in the morning, for all the good that would do. Probably that fat so-and-so sheriff would just use the evidence to bolster his case that Cyrus Caine was the victim, not the dead policeman on his doorstep.

Krause turned to the moleskin journal on his desk. He had kept journals for nearly 15 years, since his days as a young state trooper, working on that grisly case of the three murdered boys in Chicago. That crime still wasn't solved, and it still gnawed at him. Krause liked to record his impressions while they were fresh. He knew that, sooner or later, he or other police officers would cross paths with Cyrus Caine again. He rubbed his eyes, picked up a ball point pen and started to write:

'Interview with Cyrus Caine, horseman, on 29 October 1969. Same night he shot State Police Officer John Martell nine times, killing him. The man is a cold-blooded gangster, you can see it in his eyes. A narcissist and a sociopath. Given to long angry rants and going off on tangents that have nothing to do with the question at hand. Cursed and shouted and proclaimed his innocence to the skies while a police officer's blood is still splattered on his shirt. I understand now why his brother's family, particularly the wife, are so sure Cyrus wants to kill them. Now I believe it too…."

Chapter 23

The Hired Gun

NED PAULSON WAS SWEATING. Not because it was warm outside; the temperature had been well below freezing the last time Ned heard it on the radio. He was sitting in his squad car in a rest area off the highway, the engine off, wrapped in his down ski jacket with the hood up. The last thing he wanted to be doing was sitting in a cold car in the middle of nowhere. But Cyrus Caine wanted a meeting, somewhere outside of town, so Ned did what he always did: he obliged. The good thing about a police car is that nobody stopped to ask what you were doing.

The sun was starting to set, and Ned muttered under his breath, wishing Cyrus would show up. The temperature would drop even further once the sun went down. He looked in his rearview mirror, and sure enough, a white Cadillac Eldorado was pulling up behind him. He heard a car door slam and footsteps crunching in the snow. The passenger door on the squad car opened with a blast of cold air and Cyrus slid into the front seat. He shut the door forcefully and cursed.

"Colder than a witch's tit out there."

"Why'd we have to meet all the way out here then?" Ned whined. "We could've met in town."

"Nah. This is a private conversation," Cyrus replied, pulling out a pack of Pall Malls. He offered one to Ned, who declined. He fired up the cigarette and cracked the window to let the smoke out. The two men sat in silence for a moment, then he spoke again:

"I need someone to take care of my brother once and for all."

Ned looked shaken. "Cyrus, you know I can't be part of something like that. I shouldn't even be talking to you about something like that."

"I'm not looking to you to do anything, Ned," Cyrus hissed, like he was settling a horse. "I just need you to find me some talent. I tried going out of state, and what happened? Those two fellas flipped on me. I can't have anyone from my businesses, they'll link it right back to me. Plus I got that goddamned IBI detective sniffing around my shorts. I need to hire this job out."

"I don't know, Cyrus. This is an awfully big job."

"How about twenty thousand dollars? Think that would make it worthwhile to someone?"

Ned swallowed. You could buy a new house in northern Illinois for that kind of money.

"I want him dead," Cyrus went on. Ned could see he was getting amped up. "I want the whole family dead. They can shoot down that goddamn plane of theirs. Blast them out of the sky. Use a machine gun, or a bazooka, I don't care. This has gone on long enough. Just get rid of them."

"I'll ask around."

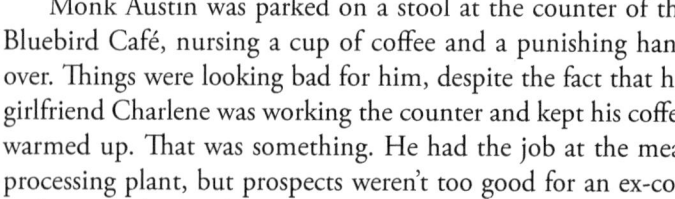

Monk Austin was parked on a stool at the counter of the Bluebird Café, nursing a cup of coffee and a punishing hangover. Things were looking bad for him, despite the fact that his girlfriend Charlene was working the counter and kept his coffee warmed up. That was something. He had the job at the meat processing plant, but prospects weren't too good for an ex-con without a high school diploma or even a GED. Warm coffee aside, Charlene was working mostly for tips at the Bluebird, and she was making a lot of noises about wanting the two of them to get married, maybe getting a house nearby. A house, thought Monk. They were barely scraping by as it was. Next thing you knew she'd be talking about having kids too. She wasn't getting any younger.

Charlene walked down to his end of the counter. Even when she was pissed at him, Monk still had to admire the long auburn hair, the wide hips and the impressive cleavage, which she wielded to great effect to generate bigger tips. The Bunn coffee pot was in her hand, but she set it down on the warmer before she got to him.

"Mind finishing up your coffee? You're scaring away the paying customers," she mocked him. Monk looked around.

"Doesn't look that busy to me." Only three or four booths were occupied: one by a couple of teenagers, an older couple counting out their change and getting ready to settle up. "Bet they're big tippers," Monk muttered to himself.

Then there was the cop in the nearby booth, who was staring at him right now. Monk was always unsettled at the sight of the police – one of the byproducts of having spent time in Joliet. This cop seemed to be studying Monk, and it made him nervous. They made eye contact, and the cop beckoned him over. Monk looked around, gave him a 'Who, me?' expression. The cop nodded. Monk slid off his stool and approached the cop's table.

He was a big guy, belly hanging over the edge, a uniform that Monk didn't recognize. The patch on his shoulder said 'Croydon County Sheriff's Department' – the next county over. The badge on his chest said 'Sheriff.'

"Hello, Monk," the big cop greeted him. Monk looked startled.

"How do you know my name?"

"I make it my business to know ex-cons in the area." He gestured to the empty vinyl bench across from him. "Have a seat."

Monk thought about saying no, but really, he had nothing better to do. He sat down.

"How're you and Charlene getting along?" the cop asked. Again, Monk looked startled.

"You know Charlene?"

"I know every waitress in every diner in a three-county area," the cop replied. "Seems like things are a little tight for you kids."

"We're getting by."

"Really? Living on what? The tips she makes here? Not great, I can tell you. What are you making over at the meat packing plant? Three fifty an hour? Three seventy-five?"

"Around that," Monk said defensively. "Why are you so interested in our finances?"

"I'm not, really. I'm looking for someone who might want to make some money and isn't too particular how he does it."

Monk's antennae were up. "I did my time. I'm not looking for trouble."

"What if we were talking about a lot of money?"

"Like what's a lot of money?"

"How about twenty thousand dollars? Would that get your attention?"

It did. Monk did some quick figuring in his head. It would take him years at the meat packing plant to make that kind of money.

"What exactly would I have to do for that kind of money?"

The big cop lit a Camel, picked a loose piece of tobacco off his tongue and looked steadily at Monk.

"How are you with a gun?"

Ned Paulson already knew the answer to that question. Flipping through the records of ex-cons in the vicinity, Ned had come across Monk's file. Monk Austin had a decent record as a marksman before the Army kicked him out for disorderly conduct. A series of armed robberies had landed him in Stateville, but his record was pretty clean there. A few fights in the yard, but he wasn't a hophead or a psycho. Just a run-of-the-mill career criminal who had the bad luck of getting caught, like most of them did eventually. Since his release Monk had kept his nose clean, checked in with his parole officer regularly, and started dating Charlene. But Ned recognized that lean hungry look some of them had coming out of the joint, still looking for the big score.

A few nights later, Monk found himself at a restaurant near Round Lake, Illinois. China Moon was not a big place, kind of run down, pretty quiet on a Tuesday night. There were only a few cars in the gravel driveway when Monk pulled up in an old truck he had borrowed from his brother-in-law. He looked around for Ned Paulson's police cruiser, but it wasn't there. The only vehicle of note was a white Cadillac Eldorado with red upholstery. Ned admired the car and stroked the fender as he approached the restaurant.

The lighting in the China Moon was poor, with cheap paper lanterns providing most of the illumination. Probably why they picked this place, Monk thought to himself. He had no trouble spotting Paulson, even though the sheriff was dressed in civilian clothes. There was another man sitting with him, leaning back out of the light like he didn't want to be seen. Monk approached the table and got a better look at him. He was a hard-looking man in his forties, with a full head of wavy gray hair, deep lines etched around his eyes and mouth. He looked like the Marlboro Man or some TV cowboy from the 1950s. When his black eyes locked on Monk, he knew that this was not someone to mess with. Monk had seen that look from a lot of men in prison and knew to stay clear of them.

Ned ushered Monk into the booth. Before he sat down, Ned quietly patted him down for weapons or listening devices.

"Have any trouble finding the place?" the sheriff asked.

"No, no problem."

"Good. What'll you have?"

Monk looked at the glasses in front of the two men. They were having what looked to be bourbon. "Beer's fine," he said. Ned beckoned the waitress and placed the order. The dark-eyed man still had not spoken. He was just looking Monk up and down, like he was thinking of buying him. Then they got down to business.

"Do you know who I am?" the dark-eyed man said at last. Monk shook his head. "Just as well. No need for names at this point. I'm looking for someone to do a job for me."

"What kind of job would that be?" Monk asked, although the fluttering in his stomach suggested he already had an idea.

The dark-eyed man flicked an eye at Ned Paulson. The sheriff reached under his suit coat, withdrew something wrapped in a cloth napkin and handed it to Monk under the table. Monk could feel the smooth steel of the gun barrel through the cloth. He took the gun, careful not to leave his fingerprints on it.

"I'm told you used to use one of these in your previous work," the dark-eyed man said. Monk nodded affirmatively. "This one is clean, no serial numbers on it."

"Let me explain how this plays out," the dark-eyed man continued. "I can get you anything you need. Weapons, lawyers, money – whatever it takes. I just need someone I can trust. Someone who's not shy about pulling the trigger."

"What do I get out of it?" Monk wanted to know, trying not to appear too eager.

"The job pays twenty thousand dollars. Plus expenses."

"Starting when?"

The dark-eyed man reached into his pocket and pulled out a gold horseshoe money clip. He peeled off five one-hundred-dollar bills, folded them between two fingers and held them out to Monk, like a tip.

"Right now." Monk hesitated less than a second before taking the money and tucking it into his pants pocket. The dark-eyed man nodded his satisfaction. "Good. Ned here is going to give you a photo, plus a name and a couple of addresses. I want you to find this man, stalk him for a bit, get a sense of his schedule. Then pick the right place and time."

He downed the last of his drink, threw a twenty on the table and stood up. He only had one more message for Monk:

"Don't leave any witnesses."

Monk was a little shocked when the sheriff handed him a piece of paper with the name 'Morgan Caine' on it, and an address at Harmony Farm in Croydon County. Monk had been around horses enough to recognize the Caine name. He vaguely remembered hearing something about a rivalry between two brothers by that name. That's when the penny dropped.

"Holy shit," Monk whispered to himself as he got into his brother-in-law's truck. "What have I gotten myself into?" He felt the heft of the Colt Python revolver in his jacket pocket, and the counterweight of five hundred dollars in his jeans.

When he got home Charlene was getting ready to go to work. She was pulling late shifts at the café to try to make some more money. Monk walked up behind her, threw his arms around her and twirled her around. She tried to wriggle away, but not too hard.

"What's got into you?" she said, laughing. She took a sniff. "Is that beer I smell?"

"Just one. Stopped off with some friends of mine after work." He reached into his pants pocket and pulled out one of the c-notes. He handed it to her and she squealed.

"Where did you get this?" she said, delighted at first. Then she looked worried. "Monk, you didn't do anything …."

"Don't worry about it. Just picked up some extra work from a guy. You can hang onto that. Maybe buy a new dress."

Charlene threw her arms around Monk's neck and kissed him. If she was that happy with a hundred-dollar bill, Monk thought to himself, what would she do for twenty thousand?

The next day, Monk started the hunt.

Turns out, Morgan Caine wasn't a hard guy to recognize. Handsome, tall, dark hair turning to gray, he looked like the picture Sheriff Paulson had given him, although it had been taken from a distance. Morgan was a hard guy to keep up with, however. Monk couldn't quit his job at the meat plant – employment was a condition of his parole – but he used his time off and called in sick often enough that he was able to stalk his quarry pretty regularly. When he was in the area, Morgan's life seemed to revolve around his home, his office and runs into town.

On the road was different. It seemed like Morgan traveled nearly every weekend in the spring – thank goodness, Monk didn't have to work weekends – going to horse shows or auctions or the racetrack. Sometimes Monk was able to borrow a car, and other times he rented one, with Ned reimbursing him (with the proper receipts). Monk especially enjoyed following Morgan at the track. The horseman seemed to know everyone, and he usually sat in a private box at some bigwig's invitation. Monk was uneasy about doing the shoot at the track: too many people, and Morgan was seldom alone. He decided to look for a better place.

Monk had a pang of conscience as he watched Morgan in action on the road. He seemed like a nice guy – popular, good-natured, quick to laugh. Nice-looking guy too, although he looked nothing like his older brother except for the full head of hair and the lean physique some of these horsemen seemed to have. Monk enjoyed watching him with his family too – the red-headed wife was a real stunner for an older gal, always in simple but expensive-looking clothes but sometimes just jeans and a flannel shirt. She was a real woman. One day, Monk followed the two of them out to the airport, at a discreet distance. He hung around the fence and watched as they crossed the tarmac and climbed into a twin-engine plane of some kind. He was amazed when he saw the woman settle in at the controls and take off down the runway.

He felt kind of bad, having to kill a man with so much going for him. But this was his chance to start his own life, with his own family, with the kind of money Cyrus Caine was paying. He put his qualms aside.

The weeks went by, until one day Ned Paulson showed up at the café and sat down next to him at the counter.

"Your employer is getting kind of impatient," Ned told him quietly. "He wants you to meet him tonight, same place as last time. Nine o'clock."

Monk swallowed hard. This wasn't a good sign.

He arrived at the China Moon at the appointed hour. He recognized the white Eldorado before Ned Paulson got out and waved him over to the car. Monk slid into the passenger seat. His employer sat at the wheel staring off into the night. Ned Paulson waited outside.

"What's the latest on the job?" the man said at last. "I'm seeing a lot of receipts for travel expenses, but no results."

"I know," Monk muttered. "This guy's kind of elusive." The man at the wheel snorted.

"You could say that. Hell, I've been trying to get him for ten years." The man reached into his inside coat pocket and Monk recoiled, thinking he was going to pull a gun. Instead the man pulled out an envelope with some fifty-dollar bills inside. "Take this. Do whatever you need to, just get the job done." He turned and looked Monk square in the eyes, and there was no mistaking the threat. "It's time to buy a horse."

"Yes, sir," Monk stammered. "I'll get it done. Don't you worry."

Monk understood the next meeting would end very differently if he didn't close the deal, and soon.

The first time Monk tried to murder Morgan Caine was at a horse show in Kankakee. Monk had tailed Morgan's car down to the fairgrounds at the Illinois river town, where Morgan was judging an event. (Monk was learning a lot about horses from shadowing Morgan.) After the show, when most of the audience and participants had departed, Morgan's car was still in the lot. Monk was waiting in his rental car, discreetly parked several rows away. He chain-smoked Marlboros, waiting for the horseman to appear. When he saw Morgan coming out of the arena and walking toward his car, Monk flicked his cigarette out the window, stepped over the pile of butts beneath his car door, and felt in his belt for the Colt Python Cyrus had given him. He started walking toward Morgan's car, hoping to catch him when he reached to open the door. That way he would be partially sheltered from the view of anyone looking out from the arena.

Monk's palms were sweaty. He wiped his forehead and tightened his grip on the pistol. He closed to within twenty yards of his prey and started to draw the gun when a voice cut across the parking lot.

"Hey Mister Caine! Call for you. Think it's your wife." Some kid came running out from the loading ramp. Morgan whirled around when he heard the voice and waved.

"Thanks, Jimmy. Tell her I'll be right there."

Morgan walked back toward the arena. Monk came to a stop like a cartoon figure, his heels skidding in the dirt of the open field. He hesitated, patted his pockets like he had forgotten his keys, then jumped back in his car and drove away, cursing his bad luck.

The second time, Monk decided there was just too much activity at these horse shows. He would try to get Morgan someplace more private. Like his home.

Monk pulled the white paneled van over to the shoulder of the road running in front of Harmony Farm. He had rented the truck for the day, so if anyone noticed him (who paid attention to white vans?) they would assume he was in the area making repairs. Monk already knew that the Caine boy was away at college. The daughter – a real looker, the spitting image of her red-haired mother – was newly married and lived two towns away. Mrs. Caine, the hot redhead, had driven off early that morning in her Jaguar sedan; probably headed out on one of her airplane race events. She seemed to be in a hurry. By Monk's count, that meant that Morgan was still in the house. And he was alone.

Monk took out the Colt revolver and checked that all the chambers were loaded. He tucked the gun back in his belt, put the van into Drive and glided up the long driveway to the main house.

He parked a good distance from the house, so the van was out of sight from the front entrance. Checking the gun again, he eased himself out of the truck and walked around the house to the kitchen door at the rear, keeping his head down like he was checking for cables or something.

Monk was wearing a black knit ski cap. When he reached the kitchen door he pulled it down, rolled it over his face so that only his eyes and mouth were showing through the holes. He tried the doorknob and found it unlocked. People in the country hardly ever locked their back doors. He glanced up and noticed a small camera in the corner of the porch roof. He cursed to himself, hoping that the thing wasn't working, but he had gone this far. He turned the knob, eased open the door and slipped inside.

Monk looked around the kitchen – no one there. He drew the pistol and crept toward the living room and the main staircase, thinking Morgan might be up there.

Suddenly he heard padded feet on the wooden floors, and an enormous black shape loomed in the doorway. At first Monk thought it was a bear and wondered how it got into the Caine house. He raised his pistol and braced himself for an attack. But staring into the wet black nose and pink tongue he realized it was the Caines' black Labrador, Max. The dog stared at the stranger for a moment, but his tail was wagging. Instead of lunging, the dog trotted toward Monk, maybe hoping for a treat or a romp outside. When Monk didn't move, Max tried to plead with him through a series of throaty grunts and rumbles.

"Shhh, doggie! Nice doggie. Go away," Monk hissed.

Max wouldn't budge. He dropped his oversized head and let out a half-hearted bark. Monk looked around in panic, afraid the dog would sound the alarm or maybe lick him to death. He stuck the gun back in his waistband, scrambled to the kitchen door and fled. The Labrador nuzzled the door and started to whine.

The third time, Monk was filled with resolve. Ned Paulson seemed to be showing up at the café where Charlene worked every couple of days, asking about him. Monk knew the sheriff wasn't just making chit-chat with his fiancée; this was a warning he'd better take action. Having failed at home invasion, he went back to tracking Morgan's activities and decided he'd look for the first reasonable opportunity to get Morgan while he was alone.

The moment presented itself two weeks later when Morgan made a trip to Arlington Park Racetrack.

Monk had a fondness for Arlington Park himself, and he was thrilled when he realized that Morgan's golden Cadillac was headed down route 53 toward Arlington Heights. Monk loved the ponies in his younger days, any time he had a few spare bucks to bet, and Arlington was one of the great racetracks in the country. He had changed his mind about the suitability of the track as a killing site. Arlington presented a perfect venue for Monk to move around unnoticed, keep an eye on his quarry and wait for a moment when Morgan would be alone and unguarded.

Morgan pulled his Cadillac around to the backstretch, where the stables were. Arlington had space for up to 2,000 horses. Monk realized he had a problem: Morgan was going in through the owner's entrance; undoubtedly he had a VIP pass of some kind. Monk didn't. He drove past Morgan's car and found a place around the other side of the building, in general parking. He would just have to buy a ticket and catch up with Morgan as best he could.

The crowd was still pretty light. Morgan always came to these events early, so he could take a look at the horses as they warmed up and shoot the breeze with the owners and jockeys. Monk paid his admission, got a copy of the day's program and moved toward the stable area.

It wasn't hard to spot Morgan. Standing in a circle of jockeys, swapping tips and gossip, the younger Caine brother was a full head taller. He looked like a movie star surrounded by Munchkins. The jockeys clearly liked him though, judging from the sound of laughter drifting across the paddock. Morgan gave the riders a casual wave and wished them luck then headed into the stables. Monk followed at a discreet distance.

Morgan cruised down the rows of stalls, greeting the trainers, occasionally pausing to take a closer look at the horses or to ask a question. Monk loitered in the wide archway to the stables where he could keep an eye on his quarry from a discreet distance. He pulled out a pack of Marlboros, turned his head away to block the wind as he lit it. He took a drag and looked back into the darkened stable.

Morgan was gone.

Panicked, Monk tossed his cigarette into the dirt and walked quickly through the cluttered alley, scooting around horses and groomsmen. At the other end of the stable was a ramp that led out to the track where the horses made their entrance. Morgan might have gone up there. Monk skirted around the corner to the long tunnel, deserted now until the races started.

Monk practically bumped into Morgan, coming the other way. Both men looked startled.

Monk reached for his pistol. This was the moment. They were alone, no one was near the empty hallway. His hand tightened around the pistol grip and he started to draw. Morgan stood still and the two of them locked eyes.

"Excuse me," Monk mumbled. He drew his hand away and brushed past Morgan.

That's when he knew he couldn't do it. As much as he wanted the big purse Cyrus Caine was offering, a badly as he needed the money, he was no killer. It was one thing to wave a gun at some people in a bank or a gas station, hoping you'd never have to pull the trigger. But to look a man eye to eye and shoot him dead? Monk just couldn't bring himself to do it.

He got back in his car and drove home, dejected. What was he going to do now? And what was he going to tell Ned Paulson?

That he'd failed? That he didn't have it in him? He had looked into the dead eyes of Cyrus Caine and figured he'd be the one looking down the barrel of a gun. The older Caine would have no qualms about snuffing him out. He was a loser, a failure.

By the time he got home, Monk knew what he had to do. He was going to need to enlist some help.

Chapter 24

The Hunter

BY THAT FALL, MONK thought he had found just the man. Charlene had dropped Monk off at the meat packing plant at 7:45 a.m. so he could start his shift at 8. A battered green pickup truck was pulling into the parking lot at the same moment, and a black man in his early 30s jumped down from the bed. He was wearing a green fatigue jacket and a pair of well-worn Army surplus boots. As the man reached into the truck bed to grab a canvas bag, Monk noticed the ten-point buck carcass laid out in the back. The man waived his thanks to the driver of the truck and headed into the plant.

Monk knew Jesse Barrett, but only well enough to nod a greeting to. They didn't always work the same shifts, and there weren't many opportunities to shoot the breeze at work; the plant was too noisy and too spread out. Monk made it his business to ask around about his coworker.

Clearly he liked to hunt, and he was good at it judging from the game Monk had seen in the truck bed. He was a Viet Nam veteran, back less than two years, had seen a lot of action, was said to have a Purple Heart. He lived on his own, didn't seem to have any family in the immediate area. Someone thought he had a sister on the South Side of Chicago. When he wasn't hunting he mostly kept to himself.

Monk waited for the right moment to approach him.

He was in the locker room changing into his coveralls when Jesse walked in. The two men nodded to each other, and Jesse proceeded to his locker at the other end of the room.

"Did you bag that big buck I saw the other day?" Monk asked him. The other man nodded.

"That was me."

"You must be one hell of a shot. You get out hunting much?"

"Every chance I get, in season. Not a lot of time though."

"I hear that." Monk finished snapping up his white coveralls and approached with his hand out. "Monk Austin."

"Jesse Barrett." They shook.

Monk made it a point to seek Jesse out after that: in the mornings before their shift, during smoking breaks outside the plant, at lunch. As the two men got more comfortable with each other, Monk asked Jesse if he'd like to go for a beer after work.

They ended up at the Olde Lantern Tavern, about 10 minutes from the plant. Monk had borrowed his brother-in-law's truck for the occasion.

"I keep trying to save up enough to get a car of my own," he explained to Jesse as they took their seats at an open booth. "Can't seem to get enough cash together to make it happen." The waitress set a couple of Hamms down in front of them. Monk took a sip and said, "That might be changing though."

"How so?" Jesse asked, more out of politeness than real curiosity.

"I have a job – an outside job – that could set me up for a long time." Another sip, and he wiped the foam from his upper lip. "Might be some that could come your way too, if you're interested."

"Doing what?" Now Monk had his attention.

"Doing what you're good at. Hunting."

"Hunting for what?"

"Not what. Who," Monk replied. The two men sat in silence, nursing their beers, while Jesse absorbed what Monk was suggesting.

"What makes you think I'd be interested in a job like that?" Jesse asked finally.

"I figure you might be open to it, if the money's right."

"Why? Because I'm black?"

Monk hurried to answer, "No no, that's not it at all. I mean, because you're a veteran. You saw a lot of action in Nam I hear."

"So that makes us all a bunch of killers?"

"Not exactly. But you know what it's like to shoot another man. That's all I'm saying. This would just be doing it for money."

"How much money we talking?"

"How does ten thousand dollars sound?"

Jesse stopped cold. The dollar amount hung in the air between them. Then Jesse's lip curled up into a sneer.

"Yeah, you're full of shit." The two men let the subject drop.

A week later, Jesse caught Monk before the start of their shift.

"Been thinking about that ten grand you were talking about. Is that for real?"

"It's for real," Monk affirmed. Just to emphasize the point, Monk opened his wallet and flashed some large bills. Jesse was surprised. What was a low-life cracker like Monk Austin doing walking around with that kind of cash? Maybe he was for real after all.

"I might be interested." Jesse said, looking around at the peeling walls, the blood stains in the cement floor. "Could get me out of here anyway. Start someplace else."

It was that simple. From that moment on, the two men were partners. Or a better word for it: accomplices. Monk took charge of the logistics of the hit – the how, when and where. One afternoon the two men drove out to Harmony Farm – in a rented van once again – and Monk described the layout of the place.

"We can't get too close to the house," Monk cautioned. "I'm told he had a bunch of cameras and motion sensors and shit installed around the doors a couple of years ago. We'll have to figure out a way to draw him out, do this long range."

Jesse grunted. "At this range, I'd need something high powered. A thirty-ought-six. With a scope."

"Do you have one?"

"Hell no. I'm not using my own weapon for something like this."

That afternoon Monk approached Ned Paulson about getting an advance so he could buy a rifle that met Jesse's specifications. But the law man balked at that.

"For a one-time job? That's a waste of money. Leave it to me. I'll find you a gun."

True to his word, one late night Ned Paulson left instructions for Monk and Jesse to meet him at a rest area off route 45. As they pulled up behind the squad car, Ned opened the trunk, took out something wrapped in a blanket and handed it to Jesse. The light wasn't very good, but Jesse could feel what he had in his hands.

"Remington 700, chambered for thirty-ought-six," Ned said. Jesse pulled the rifle up to his shoulder. The weapon was perfectly balanced, long and sleek and tight. The barrel was blued, so it wouldn't reflect at night. He tried the bolt action and heard the authoritative snap when he locked it into place. It also had a Tasco 3-9X scope attached, just as he had requested. Jesse nodded his approval.

"Deputy of mine knows a guy, big sportsman. Claims this is the most accurate hunting rifle on the market," the sheriff said.

"Yeah. If you've got the scope zeroed in," Jesse replied. Paulson thought a minute.

"I know just the place," the sheriff said. "I'll call you tomorrow with directions."

The next afternoon, Monk and Jesse drove out to the property in the borrowed truck. It was a farm over in Kane County that looked like dozens of others — fields of corn, some wire fences, a gray shingle farmhouse about a quarter mile up the lane. No one seemed to be around.

"Who owns this place?" Jesse asked.

The Hunter

"Our boss," Monk replied. "At least that's what the sheriff told me."

Monk pulled the truck over before they got to the house and the two men got out. Jesse surveyed the surroundings and found a spot behind the barn that would serve well for his purposes. He pulled a couple of cardboard targets out from behind his seat, spied an oak tree at the edge of the field, and with a hammer and nail he pulled from the pocket of his fatigue jacket he nailed one of the targets to the tree. He paced off to a spot about 35 yards away.

Monk was standing nearby and approached with the Remington rifle in its case. He handed it to Jesse, who removed the rifle, pausing to admire it before he went to work. It was a beautiful piece of equipment, especially considering how hard Remington had worked to keep the price down. It had a checkered walnut stock and a high-gloss finish that made it look like a much more expensive gun. More important though, the weapon was deadly accurate, whether hunting deer or some other sort of prey.

"What are you doing now?" Monk wanted to know.

"Making sure the scope is zeroed in just right."

Jesse raised the gun to his shoulder and sighted down the Tasco scope to the target he had just put up. He reached into his coat pocket and pulled out a 30-06 cartridge. He retracted the bolt action, inserted the round, slapped the chamber closed with a commanding click and aimed carefully at the target.

The first shot was high and off center. Jesse replaced the cartridge and fired again, taking the wind into account. A little closer, but still high. He adjusted the scope and fired another round, and repeated the process until he was satisfied that the scope was properly focused and he was hitting dead center every time.

Next, he spied a twisted black oak tree on a slight rise about a hundred yards out in the field. He waded through the sheafs until he came to the big tree, affixed a target to the trunk and marched back to his spot about a hundred yards away. After a few shots, he was hitting the target dead center every time.

Jesse ejected the last spent cartridge and turned to Monk.

"We're ready," he said. "Now help me pick up this brass."

Chapter 25

The Night of

THE RED FORD TORINO rolled to a stop on the shoulder of a quiet two-lane road that ran along the western edge of Harmony Farm. Monk Austin was driving as usual. He hadn't wanted to rent a car that could be traced back to him when he showed his driver's license. His girlfriend Charlene was able to borrow a car from one of her steady customers – "A really nice guy. Kind of cute too" – after she told him she needed a car to do some moving. It was a nice ride: two years old, black vinyl top over a red chassis. Monk loved the thrum of the 302 V8 engine. Maybe he'd get one of these once he got his money from Cyrus Caine.

Jesse Barrett sat next to him in silence. Monk was usually loquacious, but even he could tell that this was a time to just let Jesse be. The other man stared out the windshield, running through the plan in his mind, hoping everything would go right and he'd be able to get a clean shot off when the moment came.

Monk threw the car into park, and the two men sat for a moment, not speaking, listening to the engine idle. It was a little after 11 pm. There was a new moon, so the road was even darker than it would be normally. That's the way they had planned it. Jesse had cased the property before and would know how to find his way through the woods to the stables. Monk switched off the engine.

"You ready?" Monk asked finally.

"I'm ready."

"Remember," Monk continued, "they don't want any witnesses."

Jesse looked at him sharply. "Let's get one thing straight: I ain't shootin' no women or children. I got one job to do, and I'll do it. But that's as far as I go."

"All right all right," Monk said, motioning with his hand to quiet his companion. "Let's just get it done."

The two men opened their car doors as quietly as they could and walked around to the trunk. Monk opened it and Jesse took out the Remington rifle. He removed it from its case and slung his arm through the leather strap. He checked his pockets for extra cartridges, as he had a half dozen times on the ride over. He was ready.

"You go on ahead and get set up. I'll be right behind you," Monk whispered.

Jesse nodded and disappeared into the woods. Monk placed the gun case back in the trunk, reached in and pulled out the next key ingredient: a can of gasoline.

Just as Monk straightened up he found himself blinded by the glare of two oncoming headlights. A blue Camaro coming from the other direction was on him before he knew it was there. Monk held up one hand to shade his eyes from the twin beams. The car slowed down as it closed on him, the driver as surprised as he was to find another vehicle on the road at that time of night. Monk caught a glimpse of red hair – looked like some teenager at the wheel. Coming home from a Hallowe'en party? Late for curfew? Monk stood frozen in the lights. The kid only slowed down a little as he passed, didn't stop to ask if Monk needed help. Maybe he didn't notice the gas can in Monk's other hand.

"Shit," Monk muttered. His eyes followed the Camaro as it continued down the road. "Just my luck." He shut the trunk quietly. Then he lifted the hood of the Torino so that it looked like it was having motor trouble, in case some other good Samaritan came along. Gas can in hand, he ran into the woods following the same path Jesse had used.

The Night of

The shooter had already taken his prearranged position next to a maple tree across the yard from the stables. There was no light to speak of, and he was sure he would be virtually invisible to anyone who might chance to look outside from the main house or from the ranch hands' quarters on the far side of the barn. His own eyes had adjusted to the dark, and he heard more than saw Monk come thrashing out of the woods. He tucked the rifle stock against his shoulder and sighted down the scope.

Monk moved more quietly as he crossed the yard. With his free hand he scattered loose straw along the wide wooden doors of the stable. No one was about, and the only sound was the wind whistling through the trees and the occasional snort of the horses inside the stalls nearby. All that would change shortly.

Once he had the straw in place, Monk splashed the gasoline onto the piles until he had nearly emptied the can. He pulled a rag from his jacket pocket and stuffed it in the nozzle of the gas can. He looked over at Jesse, set in his position. The gunman gave him a nod.

Monk took a lighter from his pocket and set the rag on fire, then tossed the gas can on top of the straw. The dry grass started to smoke at once, then burst into flame and spread along the bottom of the stable doors as planned. Once the fire was going Monk retreated to the edge of the woods and waited.

Monk could hear the horses coming awake in the barn, first with nervous snorts and whinnies, then becoming panicked, kicking the wooden stalls and thrashing about. He felt bad for the horses. They were trapped, nowhere to run. The fire spread quickly, and the terror of the animals grew louder by the minute.

In a few minutes there was motion inside the big house. A light went on in a downstairs room, and a minute later the front door flew open. A man in a pajama top rushed out, squinting into the night toward the stables, spotting the fire and then running forward. He had a gun in his left hand, looked like an Army Colt.

UNBRIDLED

Jesse sighted in carefully and squeezed the trigger of the Remington. At the last second the man turned to yell something to a woman who had come charging out of the house and was framed in the doorway. The shot was off, and the bullet struck the man in his left shoulder. He fell to his knees, waving his pistol around but seemed to have lost control of his arm.

"Morgan!" the woman screamed and ran toward her husband.

Jesse ejected the spent cartridge, reloaded smoothly and sighted in again. He fired. This time he hit the man dead center in the chest and saw him hurtle backwards with the force of the bullet. Blood spurted from the hole in his chest, and he crumpled into the arms of the sobbing woman. The .45 slipped from the man's useless arm and fell to the ground next to his dying body.

Jesse ejected the second cartridge, considered a third shot. But the woman was too close, he stood too good a chance of hitting her by mistake, and he wasn't here to shoot a woman. Besides, he could tell: the kill was good. The man was done. Jesse knelt down quickly, picked up the two spent cartridges, tucked them in his pocket and fled into the woods.

Monk was waiting back at the car. The engine was running, the hood was down, the trunk was open and waiting. Jesse threw the rifle into its case and laid it out on the floor of the trunk, closed the lid and jumped into the passenger seat.

Jesse was breathing hard as he closed the door. Monk looked over at him.

"Did you get him?"

"Yeah, I got him," Jesse said quietly. "Let's get the hell out of here."

Chapter 26

The Investigator

DON KRAUSE PULLED HIS OLDSMOBILE into the yard at Morgan Caine's house. He remembered vividly the last time he had visited a crime scene at a home belonging to one of the Caine brothers. The first time, it was a young State Trooper who had been murdered by Cyrus Caine, although the DA had failed to prosecute. This time, according to Krause's police scanner, it was the brother who had been murdered.

What greeted him was a scene from hell. The fire department was busy extinguishing the last of a blaze that had destroyed half of the Caines' riding stables. A quick-thinking young Mexican couple who lived at the rear of the property had managed to lead some of the horses to safety and were hosing down the stable when the fire department arrived. The acrid smell of charred meat filled Krause's nostrils as he got out of his car, and he realized it must be the aroma of burnt horseflesh. Some of the rescued animals were being herded into an adjoining paddock, where the frightened horses shivered and whinnied and walked around in circles, homeless and bereft. Krause saw crime scene personnel at the edge of a forest adjacent to the smoldering barn, men pointing into the woods and flashlights scanning the other side. But the most distressing sight was right in front of him.

Katherine Caine was kneeling on the front lawn, cradling the head of the man Krause recognized as her late husband. Her pink peignoir was soaked in blood – her husband's, presumably – and the blood was congealing in the cold night air. Her face was a mask of grief, streaked with smoke and soot. Her shoulders heaved with the occasional sob as she stroked her husband's lifeless head. Two crime scene investigators huddled nearby, unable to proceed but unwilling to impose on the woman's desperate sorrow.

Krause saw one of his IBI detectives coming up the drive toward him. An ambulance waited in the driveway, lights flashing but silent. Krause summoned his detective over.

"What are we looking at?" Krause asked him.

"One dead, no one else injured, no one in the house. Shots fired from over there …" He pointed in the direction of a maple tree at the edge of the clearing. "Looks like a high-powered rifle. The deceased was struck twice as he ran out of the house. At least we think so. The wife won't let us get close enough to examine the body."

Krause grimaced. "Let me give it a try." He waved to one of the ambulance attendants, who was standing nearby holding a blanket while her partner wheeled out the gurney. Krause took the blanket from her and approached the grieving woman on the lawn. He gently draped the blanket over her shoulders and knelt down, placing a supportive arm around her.

"Mrs. Caine," the detective said softly, "come inside. You have to let these people do their job."

Kat didn't seem to hear him. Krause could feel his joints creaking, but he planted himself next to her. "Here, let me help you into the house…." He placed his free hand on her other arm and lifted her to her feet. She was a slender woman, but at the moment she was dead weight. Krause supported her by her elbows and wrapped the blanket around her more tightly. She offered less resistance as he pulled her away, but her eyes were still fixed on the sight of her martyred husband as her legs moved toward the house. The investigators nodded their thanks to the chief and began their examination of the body and its surroundings.

The Investigator

When Kat reached the front door she looked up suddenly, as if just recognizing Krause, and grabbed his sleeve. "You know what you have to do."

"What's that, Mrs. Caine?"

"You need to arrest him. You need to arrest Cyrus."

"Mrs. Caine," the detective replied gently, "let my officers do their job. We have to investigate the scene first."

"Investigate? What is there to investigate? Cyrus Caine murdered my husband. He murdered his own brother in cold blood."

"We have to be able to prove he did it," Krause replied. "That's why you need to let us do our job." He turned to the ambulance attendant and said, "Could you please take Mrs. Caine into the house and check her out? We want to be sure she wasn't injured too."

"I'm fine," Kat protested, shrugging off the blanket. "No thanks to Cyrus. Next time he'll kill me too, I'm sure of it. He's not done. He's never done." The paramedic placed an arm around her and steered her through the front door.

Krause stood on the front steps a moment and surveyed the lawn, the smoldering remains of the stable. She's probably right, Krause thought to himself. This looks like a Cyrus Caine production. And he isn't finished.

When the body had been bagged and taken away, the evidence gathered, all but one of the police cars driven off, Krause and his deputies reviewed the known facts:

"Looks like there were two of them," one of his detectives began, "at least there are two sets of tracks leading to and from the woods over there. Long strides leading into the woods, like they were running. Two slugs, one still in the body, the other tore through the left shoulder. A .45-caliber Colt Commander found near the body, doesn't seem to have been fired. We assume it was Caine's. They torched the barn after spreading some gasoline around. Found the remains of a gas can by the side of the barn. Well, what used to be the barn."

"Any prints?" The other detective shook his head. "Ejected cartridges?" Another head shake.

"They cleaned up pretty good after themselves. Seemed to know what they were doing."

"Where does that path lead?"

"Out to the access road. Our men are out right now checking with neighbors, see if anyone saw a car or people prowling around. Not too many folks around that time of night, but it's worth a try."

A few days later, they were no further along than they were that night.

None of the neighbors had heard anything, except for one older farmer who thought he had heard two gunshots sometime after 11 p.m. The old man suffered from indigestion and sometimes had trouble sleeping. He looked out the window, thinking there might be some hunters in his woods. Then he spotted flames shooting into the sky over by Harmony Stables and called the fire department.

That was it. The road alongside the Caine property had not yielded any useful clues with the exception of a single skid mark. The footprints through the woods were a dead end given the layers of decomposing leaves that carpeted the forest floor. They had no lead on the murder weapon except that it was a 30-06 hunting rifle judging from the slug the coroner had extracted from Morgan Caine's body. No strangers had been seen in the area, no unusual events, no nothing. Krause dreaded his next encounter with Mrs. Caine.

The next occasion was her husband's funeral. Krause arrived at the cemetery late, hoping to hang at the back of the crowd and not attract attention, but being six feet four it was hard to be inconspicuous. Morgan Caine had been a hero in the community, well liked, a business leader and a family man, and there was a crush of people at the graveside when Krause arrived.

It wasn't difficult to spot Katherine Caine. Unlike the last time he had seen her – blood soaked and sobbing – she looked preternaturally beautiful, trim in a black silk suit under a black cashmere topcoat, her red hair tucked up under a wide-brimmed hat with a veil that made her look vaguely like a Russian spy. She was thoroughly composed as the minister read verses and offered prayers for Morgan. Standing next to her was a young woman obviously her daughter, the same red hair and pale complexion. While Kat seemed to radiate composure, it was the daughter's turn to lose it. Krause remembered her name was Meghan, and she was newly married. A solicitous young man, no doubt the husband, stood with his arm around her and provided her with fresh tissues. Kat's son, Morgan Junior, a tall handsome lad who looked uncannily like his late father, stood on her other side, looking resolute and stunned as only a college boy who has lost his father can look.

At the roadside of the cemetery the media vultures from the local television stations had gathered, hoping to get some footage or maybe a quote. The murder of one of the country's most accomplished horsemen made for big news in the Chicago market, and the reporters, for the most part a lazy lot, tended to bring in some of the more salacious tales of the Caine family. Krause was pleased to see that for once the Croydon Sheriff's Department was making itself useful directing traffic and keeping the reporters cordoned off.

Krause waited until the service was over and most of the mourners had offered their regrets and melted away, back to their own lives. Then he approached her, his fedora in hand. She spoke before he did.

"Did you notice who wasn't here?" she asked the detective. She gave the answer before Krause could. "His one and only brother. I don't suppose it's because you've arrested him?"

"No, we haven't. We have no evidence, nothing to connect him," Krause replied. "I wish I had better news."

Kat stopped, raised the veil of her hat and regarded him a moment. "Maybe we should make some." She brushed past him and walked resolutely toward the scrum of reporters, her children trailing in her wake. The wolf pack came to life when they saw the elegant widow advancing on them. Cameras were pointed, microphones thrust in her face, questions shouted at her. Kat stood her ground and addressed the cameras.

"There are two people who know who killed my husband: One is the murderer. The other is me. My hope is that there are other people who have knowledge of this terrible crime. I am offering a substantial reward to anyone who comes forward with information leading to the arrest and conviction of the person or persons who killed my husband." She turned on her heel, ignoring their shouted questions, and marched toward the waiting limo.

"Are you sure that was a wise thing to do?" Krause said as she passed him. "You're going to hear from every kook between here and Kalamazoo."

Kat shrugged. "Doing the wise thing hasn't gotten us very far, has it, Detective?" she said, and walked away.

Monk Austin and Charlene watched the footage of the funeral on Channel 7 that night. Monk heard the Widow Caine say "…a substantial reward to anyone who comes forward with information…." He switched off the TV. Charlene, stretched out next to him on the sofa, punched his arm.

"Hey! I was watching that."

"Ah, it's just the same old shit night after night."

"I wanted to hear what she had to say. I feel sorry for that poor woman."

Monk said, "She's rich and good looking. She'll be OK."

"She lost her husband," Charlene said. She snuggled closer to Monk, placed her head on his shoulder. "Just think how I'd feel if I lost you."

Monk stared straight ahead at the blackened TV screen.

The Investigator

When he left the funeral, Detective Don Krause knew what he needed to do.

It was time to interview Cyrus Caine.

By this time Krause knew his way to Cyrus's farm by heart. It took him fifteen minutes to cruise the county roads until he pulled through the big black wrought-iron gates with the double-horseshoe insignia forged into them. He pulled up to the massive limestone house and approached the front door. He rang the bell, then took a step to his left and turned sideways out of instinct, the way he might have if he was rushing the doorway. With his size, thought Krause, it didn't matter if he turned sideways or not if Cyrus Caine came out shooting.

He didn't. The door opened and there was the master of the house, in slippers rather than his usual cowboy boots. Caine didn't seem at all surprised to see him.

"Detective Krause," he said with a small smile. "I wondered how long it would be before you showed up on my doorstep."

"Policemen have to be careful when they come to your doorstep," Krause replied. The memory of the young state trooper's body dead on the ground flashed through his mind. "I need to ask you a few questions."

"Sure, sure. Come on in. I have all the time in the world."

Cyrus led the detective inside and they went to Cyrus's study, all done in green tartan wallpaper and dark wood and horse prints. Instead of going behind his desk, which would have been the typical power play, Cyrus sat them down in adjoining leather club chairs by the fire.

"Get you something to drink?"

"I'm good." The two men sat in companionable silence for a moment, studying the fire. Finally the policeman spoke.

"You weren't at the funeral."

"No, no I wasn't. The family saw fit to leave my name out of the obituary. I figured maybe my presence wasn't welcome." A ration of Scotch sat in a cut crystal glass next to Cyrus's chair, suggesting he had been sitting there when the doorbell rang. He lifted the glass and took a sip. "You know, Detective, there's a lot of wild stories about me and my brother. Oh, we were competitive, no question about that. You have to be, in the horse business. But people forget I practically raised that young man from the time he was a colt. We'd fight, but then we'd shake hands and make up, like brothers do."

"That's not the story I've heard. I've heard you threatened his life in public, numerous times."

Cyrus waved his hand dismissively. "Just talk. Sometimes my blood runs kind of high."

"Your sister-in-law is sure you had people following her husband. They shot up his office. Sabotaged his brakes. Blew up his car and killed that girl by mistake."

Cyrus's face went red at this last part. "You know goddamned well they never proved any of that. My 'sister-in-law'" — he spat out the words, like a seed stuck between his teeth – "well, talk about someone whose blood runs high. She's had it in for me since she was a teenager. All I ever did was try to be nice to her. Ungrateful bitch." Cyrus realized his tongue was getting a little loose. He smiled at the detective and took another sip of Scotch.

"Mind telling me where you were on the night of October 30th?"

Cyrus smiled again. Now they were back on scripted ground.

"I was playing poker with five other fellas over to the Hunt Club. They'll all swear to it."

"I'm sure they will," Krause said evenly. "I'll need their names."

"Of course. Anything else you need to know before you go, Detective?"

"Just one thing: You don't happen to own a thirty-ought-six hunting rifle with a mounted scope, do you?"

Cyrus gave a chilly smile and shook his head. "Haven't hunted in years." He rose, signaling that the audience was over. Krause stood too, and he felt the black eyes burning into his own. "I hope you catch the people what killed my brother, Detective. I truly do wish you luck."

The Investigator

Walking back to his car, Krause was sure of two things, could feel them in his gut: Cyrus Caine had been behind the murder. And there was no evidence to prove it.

One other thing Don Krause knew for sure: Once you'd done the investigating, once every neighborhood had been canvassed, once every possible witness had been interviewed and interviewed again, once the shoe leather had been worn through and there were still no leads, you had to get lucky.

Two days after Mrs. Caine made her appeal on the local TV stations, Krause got lucky.

He assigned a couple of young troupers to man the "hot line" for all the calls and tips the police started to receive. In the first two days there must have been more than a hundred calls, most of them (as Krause had predicted) totally baseless, either crazies trying to get attention or grifters looking for a share of the reward money.

Late one afternoon one of the troopers, a square-cut blond guy named Havlecek, stuck his head in the detective bullpen. He looked excited.

"Detective," he said to Krause, "there's a kid outside claims he saw a car on the road next to Harmony Farm the night of the murder."

Krause sat up straight in his chair. "Don't just stand there. Bring him on in."

The young man, a red-haired teenager named Kevin O'Donnell, was given a seat in an interview room, offered a soda and began his story, addressing the big detective while the blond trooper took notes.

"My mom saw the lady on TV, that Mrs. Caine," he began. "She knows her from town. I think they went to school together. She told me I had to come down here."

"I'm glad you did, Kevin," Krause replied. "So you were out that night, the 30th?"

"Yeah, I was. I was at a party and it got late. It was after curfew. That's why I didn't tell anybody."

"So you were driving…where exactly?"

"On Harmony Road, runs along the edge of the Caine property. There was a red car parked on the side of the road." He took a swig of pop. "I didn't know what somebody would be doing out there in the middle of the night. I thought maybe the guy broke down. He had a can of gasoline in his hand."

"Gasoline," Krause repeated, trying to contain his excitement.

"Yeah. I figured he ran out of gas, but he looked like he had it under control, and like I said, I was late already."

"I understand. Can you describe the car?"

"Sure can. It was a red Torino, black vinyl top, custom wheels. Really nice ride."

Havlecek wrinkled his brow but kept writing.

"You didn't happen to get a license number, did you?"

"They were Illinois plates, I know that. Think they started with a T or an F. No, it was a T. T-C-4, then some other numbers. That's all I remember."

Havlecek paled and dropped his pencil. Krause looked at him in annoyance.

"T-C-4-6-2-4," the young trooper said.

"How do you know that?" Krause asked him.

"Because," the trooper said, "that's my car."

"You borrowed the car from a state trooper?"

Monk and Charlene were in their kitchen. Charlene was in tears, relating to Monk how a detective had come around to the diner asking questions about the red car.

"I didn't know he was a trooper," she said between sniffles. "He never wore his uniform at the diner. He was just a nice young guy who liked to flirt with me and brag about his car."

"What did you tell the cops?"

"What could I tell them? That yeah, I borrowed the car. I needed it to help a friend move, like you told me to say. But then it was in our driveway all night."

"And where was I?"

"You were with me." Charlene's expression changed to one of concern. "Monk, where did you go that night? Why are the cops asking about the car? What did you do, Monk?"

He decided he'd better tell her. Because now they were both in deep shit.

"We think we've found the vehicle the killers were driving that night," Krause told Mrs. Caine as they sat in her living room the next evening. After days of no news, Krause was pleased to be able to offer at least a little information to her. Kat listened carefully as Krause gave her the details.

"Forensics is going over the car now. The owner," — he didn't feel it necessary to add that the owner was a member of the Illinois State Police – "says he loaned it to a woman who works at the Bluebird Café, Charlene Devereaux. Do you know her by chance?"

Kat shook her head.

"She says she loaned it to her boyfriend, Monk Austin. He's an ex-con, dishonorable discharge from the Army. Hasn't been in trouble since he got out of Joliet, but you never know. I'm going to interview him tomorrow."

Kat's hands were folded primly in her lap.

"I want to come," she said. No was not an option.

"Remember, let me do the talking," Monk hissed at Charlene as the big detective entered the Bluebird Café. The bell above the door jingled, and the policeman took a step back to admit the woman accompanying him. Charlene and Monk were astonished to recognize Katherine Caine. The woman wasn't wearing the dark suit she'd worn at the funeral, but the red hair was unmistakable. She wore a loden green barn coat over a black cashmere sweater, a pair of form-fitting blue jeans tucked into an expensive pair of riding boots. She was carrying a satchel that looked too big to be a purse, but rich women could carry whatever they liked. Charlene, who read a lot of glamor magazines at the beauty parlor where her mom worked, recognized the bag as a Louis Vuitton. It cost more than she made in a month at the Bluebird.

Monk and Charlene were seated in a booth at the farthest end of the diner. Carl, the manager, was glaring at them, but screw him, she was on her break. The big detective spotted Charlene, and he and the widow approached the table.

"You're Monk Austin?" the detective said as he squeezed into the booth. The lady sat down next to him and tucked her bag under the table. "I'm Detective Krause of the IBI." A flash of badge. "This is Mrs. Katherine Caine."

"I know," said Charlene, gushing like she was meeting a movie star. "We saw you on TV. I'm sorry for your loss."

"Thank you," Kat said, managing a tight smile. "You're very kind."

"We need to talk to you about the business of the Ford Torino you were driving on the night of October 30th. You were driving that car, correct?"

Charlene started to answer but Monk cut her off. "Charlene borrowed the car, but I never drove it. It was at our place the whole night. With us. We were together."

Krause raised an eyebrow and looked over at Charlene. "You were together. That true, Charlene?"

She glanced over at Monk, stammered a little, "Sure, what he said. We were together."

"That's too bad. Because we've had a chance to look the car over. Carefully. The owner gave us permission." Krause flipped open the manila folder he had carried in with him, although he knew every pertinent detail about the car. "Know the first thing we noticed when we opened the trunk?"

"The trunk?" Monk said, his voice rising slightly. "What about the trunk?"

"First thing was, someone had wiped it down pretty thoroughly. There were no fingerprints on the trunk lid. Know what else?"

"No, what?" The corner of Monk's mouth twitched a bit.

"It smelled like gasoline." Monk's face fell. Krause looked him square in the eye. "You did a pretty good job of wiping down the car, Monk. No prints on the trunk, nothing on the steering wheel or the glove box, nothing inside. But you missed one spot." Krause pulled out a photograph, studied it a moment, then turned it around for Monk to see. "The underside of the hood. We found fingerprints. Guess whose prints they matched?"

Monk swallowed, tried to look confident. "That doesn't prove anything. Maybe I checked the oil when Charlene brought the car home."

"Maybe you did," Krause said evenly. He turned to Charlene again. "Charlene, do you know what 'accessory to murder' means? It's a very serious charge."

Charlene looked nervous. She had heard that term on *Perry Mason* growing up. "Monk just said, he never drove the car."

"I'm not talking about Monk, Charlene. I'm talking about you. Monk is lying – we both know that. If Monk lies to us, and you help him cover it up, you can be charged and sent to prison too."

Charlene looked shocked, like she might burst into tears. Kat held up a hand and spoke for the first time.

"Maybe we can approach this another way," she said. She reached under the table, lifted the Louis Vuitton bag and set in down in front of the young couple. "Charlene, take a look inside this bag."

Charlene dabbed at her eyes with a napkin, then wiped her hands before she reached out and unzipped the satchel. Her eyes grew wide.

"That's twenty-five thousand dollars," Kat said, as if she always carried that much cash in her purse. "You two" – taking in Monk – "know something about the man who murdered my husband. I'm not interested in sending you to jail, and I'm sure Detective Krause isn't either. What we need is for the two of you to cooperate with the police."

"Cooperate how?" Monk asked, his eyes fixed on the money peeking out of the bag.

"Tell the detective everything you know. Help him gather the evidence he needs. Do that, and the money is yours."

"The bag too?" Charlene asked. Kat smiled.

"If you like."

Jesse Barrett was laying on his bed in the rented room he called home, looking though the shoebox resting on his stomach. He counted out the money for the umpteenth time. After paying off some debts and making a down payment on a car, he still had more than three thousand dollars. Now he just needed for Monk to come through with the rest of the ten thousand he had been promised from the job. Someone pounded on his door. Jesse threw the money back in the box and stashed it under his bed.

"Barrett. Telephone for you," one of his neighbors called from the hallway. Jesse went down the hall to the pay phone. It was Monk.

"I've got the rest of your money," he said, just what Jesse had been thinking about. "I can meet you somewhere and bring it to you. One thing though."

"Yeah, what's that?"

"We have to return the guns. Mister Caine says he needs them back."

Jesse paused. Monk had never spoken the "boss's" name out loud before. But if he was ready to pay up, what did Jesse care? He gave Monk an address on the south side of Chicago – "My sister's place. I'll meet you there at eight o'clock tomorrow night."

Monk hung up and looked over at Detective Krause, who had taped the call.

"How was that?"

"So far, so good."

Monk arrived a little after 8:30. Jesse was waiting for him at a side gate that led to the rear of a green two-story clapboard house with black shutters. Somewhere in the neighborhood a dog barked.

"Sorry I'm late. I don't come down to the South Side much, took a wrong turn…."

Jesse shushed him. "My sister's got her kids asleep in there," he said with a nod to the house. "We got to be quiet."

He led Monk to a row of hydrangea bushes that ran along the fence. There was an open hole about four feet long and two feet deep. A shovel rested nearby. Monk peered into the hole and saw a piece of oilcloth lying at the bottom.

"I got a head start," Jesse explained. "You got the money?"

Monk nodded and held out the shoebox under his arm. Jesse took the lid off and tilted the box so he could see the cash inside using the streetlight above him.

"It's all there. Four thousand dollars. That makes ten thousand total."

Satisfied, Jesse set the box down, reached into the hole and removed the oilcloth parcel. He opened it reverently. There was the Remington as well as Monk's Colt Python, which Monk had given him to hide the night of the murder.

"It's a beautiful thing," Jesse said, admiring the rifle one last time. "Kind of hate to give it up."

Suddenly the streetlight got a lot brighter, although it wasn't the streetlight, it was a pair of spotlights coming from two police cars beyond the fence. Blue lights flashed in the night, and Jesse realized the place was surrounded by cops. He stood up and locked his hands behind his head. Monk looked at him sheepishly and did the same.

When they got to the police station Monk and Jesse were taken to separate rooms, per procedure. This was the moment Jesse had been dreading. It figured: as he's standing there with the rifle in one hand and a box of cash at his feet, the police show up. He had rehearsed his answers a hundred times. Now if that stupid cracker Monk just kept his head and stuck to the story they had worked out, maybe they would get through this.

The first few hours were brutal. The big cop with the white hair kept asking him the same questions: "Where'd you get the rifle?" "Borrowed it from a guy at work." "What's this guy's name?" "Dunno. Just see him around sometimes." "Why'd you bury it in the back yard?" "Didn't want it to get stolen."

They took a break. Jesse was moved to a bench out in the hallway and handcuffed to the railing. A few minutes later a uniformed policeman led Monk down the hallway, sat him down on the same bench and cuffed him.

"Wait here." The cop said. Thought he was funny.

Jesse and Monk sat in silence for a moment, to be sure no one else was around. Then Jesse whispered, "How much do they know?"

"They know everything," Monk answered. Jesse felt the blood draining from his face. "They're willing to make a deal. If we give up the boss, there's immunity on the table. But we need to tell them the whole story."

What Monk didn't explain is that the immunity deal only covered him. Jesse didn't know that. When the big cop took him back into the interrogation room, he started talking.

Cyrus Caine was losing his patience. First that big detective had insisted that he come down to IBI headquarters for a second interview. It wasn't good enough to talk in his den like civilized men. Then he was escorted to an airless interrogation room and told to sit and wait. Finally Krause showed up. The two men glared at each other across the table. Krause produced a manila folder, flipped through it absently, then laid a mug shot down in front of Cyrus. It was a photograph of Monk Austin.

"Do you know this man?" Krause asked. Cyrus barely glanced at the photo and grunted.

"Never seen him before."

Krause pursed his lips. He flipped down another photo, this one of Jesse Barrett.

"How about this man?"

"Detective, you can flip through the entire Sears catalog and my answer will be the same: I don't know them."

Krause spread the two photos out on the table in front of Cyrus and left them there.

"These two men claim that you're the one who hired them to kill your brother, Morgan Caine."

"Then they're a couple of damn liars."

"This one," Krause tapped his finger on the picture of Monk, "says that he met with you on multiple occasions and that you offered him twenty thousand dollars to kill your brother."

"Hell of a lot of money."

"When we searched each of their apartments, they were in possession of stacks of fifty-dollar bills."

"What does that prove?"

Krause's temper was flaring a bit. "Mister Caine, this isn't the Croydon County Comedy Cops you're dealing with. We are the IBI. We have examined each and every one of the bills in their possession. And guess what? Nearly a third of them have your fingerprints on them."

Cyrus flinched but controlled himself. "I do a lot of business in cash. There's a hundred ways they could have bills with my fingerprints."

"But we both know the truth, don't we, Mister Caine?"

Cyrus leveled his malignant black eyes across the table and smirked. "Detective, you can keep after me all night. Trot in these losers with their cash and their tall tales. You can't connect me to anything those fellas might of done."

Krause was silent. He stood, picked up the receiver of a phone in the corner of the room, murmured something into it, and hung up.

"You might be right, Mister Caine. Maybe I can't connect you to these men. But there are others who can."

Krause crossed the room and opened the door, as if the room were suddenly stifling and he needed some air. Cyrus turned and looked out in the hallway just in time to see a uniformed officer leading another man down the hallway in handcuffs. The two of them paused in the doorway, and the man in handcuffs looked up plaintively. It was Ned Paulson. He and Cyrus locked eyes. Ned started to speak, but the escort gave him a nudge and moved him down the hallway.

Krause closed the door quietly and leaned against it, arms folded. He watched Cyrus, looking for his reaction. The horseman didn't flinch. He reached into his shirt pocket, took out a cream-colored business card on heavy stock, and handed it to Krause.

"My lawyer," said Cyrus. "Talk to him."

Part 4
THE TRIAL

Chapter 27

The Litigator

J. BARR FINLEY WASN'T JUST A FAMOUS LAWYER. He was the most famous criminal defense attorney in the country, arguably the most famous since Clarence Darrow. ("Why bring Clarence Darrow into it?" he would retort.) On the day Cyrus Caine was interrogated by Detective Don Krause, he was on a retainer from Cyrus.

Born in Indiana, the son of a billboard salesman and a schoolteacher, Jerome Barr Finley Junior (he despised the name 'Jerome,' never used it; hated 'Jerry' even more) decided at a young age that he was going to be famous. He just didn't know how he was going to get there. His parents didn't offer him connections or any other kind of springboard to celebrity, and the schools he attended were undistinguished, although he did well there. Like so many men of his generation, his opportunity came through war. Too young to have been in World War II and lamenting it, he was quick to enlist when the Korean conflict broke out. He joined the Marines and saw action all over the peninsula, rising to the rank of captain and receiving multiple decorations including the Silver Star. Upon discharge he enrolled in a branch of Indiana University, which counted his three years of military service toward his degree. He was accepted at Northwestern University School of Law and received the highest marks in his class.

The first big trial to bring him to national attention was the famous case of a University of Chicago history professor who had been convicted of murdering his wife. The evidence seemed circumstantial, and Finley managed to win on appeal by showing that the professor had been denied due process and "was convicted primarily because the jury thought he was an asshole." Finley had learned that talking like a Marine sometimes worked to his advantage. The murder electrified the press and the public, and Finley's legal maneuvers made headlines.

The trial that really put him in the limelight was the sensational Case of the Northside Butcher. Rocco Valponi, a mild-mannered owner of a butcher shop on the Near North Side of Chicago, was charged with murdering five women, chopping them into pieces and disposing of them by running them through the meat grinder in the basement of his store. "The physical evidence was sparse," Finley noted drily when the case came to court. The national media was captivated by Finley's swashbuckling approach to the case and his flamboyant speeches in the courtroom. Valponi was eventually found guilty on two counts of assault, but he was never convicted of the murders and had the good sense to die in prison.

When Cyrus heard through his friends in the Chicago P.D. that the IBI had identified two suspects in the Morgan Caine shooting, Cyrus decided to circle the wagons just in case. He arranged to meet the famous attorney for dinner at Gene & Georgetti's, a popular Chicago steakhouse and a place for power dining. Cyrus was nursing his second Manhattan when the attorney breezed into the restaurant and was led to their table upstairs.

He looked just like he did on TV: powerfully built although shorter than Cyrus expected, with a thick neck emerging from the squared shoulders of a former Marine. His salt-and-pepper hair was longer than in his military days and had receded deeply from his forehead, leaving a prominent V-shaped point at the front. His suit was custom made, a gray worsted, and the shoes were Italian, not that that meant anything to Cyrus. The most important thing was, for all his polish and powdered jowls, he looked like a genuine hardass. Cyrus took to him immediately.

The Litigator

Of course Finley was familiar with the murder and surprisingly conversant on the particulars of the case, as if he had been expecting this call.

"My brother and his wife have been after me for years," Cyrus explained as he waved to the white-jacketed waiter for another drink. Finley needed to catch up and ordered another round as well. "Especially the wife. Now she's got this detective doing her dirty work, trying to wrap this thing around me."

"Don Krause," Finley said.

"That's the guy. He's got a hard-on for me, I can tell."

"Krause is a straight shooter. So's the IBI, for that matter. They're not like the Chicago cops or the county mounties out in your neighborhood. They go by the book." Finley took a sip of his martini. "So what can I do for you, Mister Caine?"

"I want you to represent me if they come after me. They say you're the best there is at this sort of case."

"I am. That means I don't come cheap. My retainer is ten thousand dollars. If we go to trial, my fee is two hundred fifty thousand."

Cyrus looked at him levelly. "Not a problem," he said. He pulled a money belt out from his waistband, zipped it open and pulled out a bundle of bills. He counted out ten thousand dollars and put it on the table in a neat stack. Finley reached for it and felt his wrist gripped in an iron vise. Caine locked eyes with the lawyer.

"Let's be clear," Cyrus said. "I'm not going back inside."

Finley cleared his throat. "Understood." Cyrus released his grip, and the money disappeared into the folds of the lawyer's silk-lined suit.

Two days later, when Finley's office got the call that Cyrus had been arrested and charged with murder and conspiracy, Finley was ready for action.

It was a foregone conclusion that the grand jury would return indictments against the three men: Cyrus Caine, Ned Paulson and Jesse Barrett.

"A good D.A. can get a grand jury to indict a ham sandwich," Finley told Cyrus, quoting the conventional wisdom. They were seated in Finley's plush wood-paneled offices overlooking Lake Michigan. "Don't worry about it. The real action starts when we get to trial. That's what you're paying me for."

"And paying a fortune," Cyrus grumbled.

Finley wasn't quite as sanguine when he learned that Ned Paulson had cut a plea deal with the State's Attorney. The ex-sheriff had agreed to plead guilty to the conspiracy charge in exchange for the murder charges being dropped. The likely sentence was 3 to 10 years in prison, but that looked a lot better than doing a minimum of 20 years on a murder conviction.

"Prison isn't a hospitable place to ex-lawmen," Finley opined. "The good news is, Paulson refused to roll on you. Now the conspiracy is down to you, Barrett and Monk Austin."

"Don't they have to prove there's a conspiracy before he can cop a plea?" Cyrus demanded.

"Paulson will have to assert that he took part in conversations about the murder. But that doesn't necessarily mean he's going to point to you. Most of his contact was with Austin. That's the guy we have to go after."

"What do you plan to do?" Cyrus pressed.

"I plan to destroy him in court," Finley answered, taking a large Havana from the humidor on his desk, snipping the end with a solid gold cutter tucked in his vest pocket. He lit the other end of the cigar and puffed contemplatively for a moment, then continued.

"We've got to take Jesse Barrett down too – which shouldn't be too hard. The idiot goes into a police interrogation thinking that Monk Austin has arranged immunity for the two of them. Of course he did no such thing: The immunity only covered Monk. But Jesse, the poor sap, didn't know that. So he sits down and gives the state's attorney an 18-page confession." Finley shook his head. Most criminals were idiots, in his experience, and Jesse Barrett was living proof. He would also be a useful idiot, if J. Barr Finley could hang the murder on him instead of on his client.

"They can't connect Barrett to me. I never met the guy."

"Correct. That's our defense. I'll keep an eye on Barrett's lawyer, make sure that confession stays in. Then we'll tear him apart at trial, hang that confession around his neck. But the real target here is Monk Austin. He's their case." Finley rose and showed Cyrus to the door. "Don't worry, Cyrus. You're in capable hands."

Kat Caine leaned forward and looked out the window from the back seat of her limousine. It had rained on the way into the city, and water ran like tears down the side of the glass. Kat held her hand up to the window and touched it. She could see a shard of sunlight trying to break through the clouds. Perfect weather for the first day of the trial, she thought.

It was a long drive into the city, and Kat was determined to make a dignified entrance. Ed McBroom, the state senator and owner of the Cadillac dealership in Kankakee where both Cyrus and Morgan had always bought their cars, had given her the use of a discreet black four-door Sedan de Ville for the duration of the trial, along with a driver from his shop. While Kat was not the star of the drama, she knew she was a featured player, The Widow Caine. The press would be fixated on her every movement throughout the trial, the attorneys had warned her. Kat was ready, or as ready as she would ever be to face her husband's killers.

She felt someone take her hand and squeeze it. She turned to her daughter Meghan, seated next to her. Kat looked at her blankly for a moment.

"Mom? Are you all right?""

"Fine, darling," she replied, and forced a smile. She looked over at Meghan then up at her son, Morgan Junior, seated next to the driver, Joe. She was so proud of both her children, knew that Morgan had been proud of them too. They would have their own roles to play in the drama to come.

"We're here, Mrs. Caine," she heard the driver say.

"Thanks, Joe. Get as close as you can to the main entrance."

That was easier said than done. The plaza in front of the courthouse was swarming with reporters and television cameras, waiting as the principals in the Cyrus Caine trial started to arrive. Kat and her children were among the ones the photographers were most interested in capturing that morning. Kat had made sure they would have plenty of time to get their photos ready for the next edition and for the evening news report. She observed with satisfaction that there were cameras from the national networks at the scene, not just the local stations. The murder of Morgan Caine had been a juicy story for months.

The limousine pulled over to the curb. Joe slipped the Cadillac into park and ran around to the back door on the street side to help his passengers out. Kat slipped on a pair of sunglasses, took a breath and went first through the door. She was immediately barraged with questions, light bulbs flashing, microphones thrust in her face.

"Mrs. Caine! Do you think your brother-in-law murdered your husband?"

"Mrs. Caine, over here! Do you have anything you want to say to the killers?"

"Mrs. Caine! What do you want to see come out of this trial?"

Kat was cool and composed as she waded through the sea of reporters, but at this last question she paused and spoke to the ensemble.

"What do I want? I want to see my husband's killers convicted and sent away for life." She joined arms with her children and marched up the steps and into the courthouse.

The Litigator

Courtroom Number One had been reserved for what many in the media were calling the biggest trial since Al Capone was charged with tax evasion. The room was packed. Kat and her children took their assigned places in the gallery behind the prosecution table, on the other side of the bar. As one of the key prosecution witnesses, she would have a front row seat to the goings-on, once she delivered her testimony.

The Assistant State's Attorney noticed that the Caine family had arrived and came over to greet them. Stephen Hanaway was a stork-like man in his late 40s with thinning blond hair and wirerimmed glasses that made him look like a minister or an undertaker. His suit was charcoal gray, and the white shirt and dark solid tie added to the funereal appearance. Kat had spoken to him a number of times while the case was being prepared and thought he seemed highly intelligent and methodical but not at all charismatic. How would he be able to stand up to the number one criminal defense attorney in the country?

As she was thinking this, J. Barr Finley exploded through a side door followed by a phalanx of junior partners. Finley's entrances always seemed to create a commotion even when he was alone. The junior lawyers fanned out in the row behind Finley. The Greatest Defense Attorney in the Country – 'The G-DAC' as Kat's family had nicknamed him — placed his expensive Italian leather briefcase on the defense table and started handing files to a nervous-looking young man whom most people in the room assumed to be Finley's law clerk. He was in his late 20s, an African-American, his hair cut very short, wire-rimmed glasses, a three-piece polyester suit (the vest was reversible) that he had purchased at JC Penney. Kat knew that this was the public defender who would be representing the man they were calling the "shooter," Jesse Barrett. The PD's name was Simpkins, or Simmons, or something like that.

Kat heard a commotion in the courtroom and looked at the defense table. The side door opened and the two defendants appeared. It was the first time Kat had seen Jesse Barrett in person.

UNBRIDLED

She had only seen pictures of him in the newspapers, and when Detective Krause had shown her a mug shot and asked if she recognized him. It had been too dark that night, and he was much too far away for her to have any sense of what he looked like. All she remembered was a shadow and a muzzle flash that an instant later ended her husband's life.

Barrett seemed nervous, and for good reason. He was a big man, over six feet, in a tight brown suit that had undoubtedly been provided for him for the trial. Barrett almost certainly knew – as most of the room already knew – how a legal procedure like this was likely to work out for a black man on trial for murder, the most sensational crime of the decade. The question was, would he be the only one to take the fall, or would his co-defendant go down too?

Cyrus Caine was standing behind Jesse, only a little taller but looming much larger. His suit was cut from a better cloth, and for the first time in many years that Kat could remember he was wearing a necktie. Usually if he wore a tie at all it was a bolo with a horse's head clasp. But this wasn't a horse show. Cyrus's hair was lighter than the last time Kat had seen him, more white than gray now, and the creases in his face were even deeper. His eyes had not changed though; they were still the cold black orbs of a killer. A shiver ran through Kat at the sight of him. After 40 years he still had that effect on her, as if someone had walked across her grave.

As he moved behind the defense table Cyrus spotted Kat on the other side of the aisle, but his gaze didn't linger on her. He sat down next to Finley and whispered something to him, and the lawyer nodded. Kat stared at the back of his head, wondering what he must be thinking. Was he worried about the outcome? Or did he think his money would buy him out of this predicament as it had so many times in the past?

"All rise."

There was a great shuffling in the courtroom as all eyes faced front and the judge took his place at the bench. Judge Thomas Kimball was a tall man in his deep 50s, thin brown hair that may have once been parted in the middle pasted to his skull. His eyes were a faded blue and the flesh around his jaw line had slackened over the years, but Kat knew he had a reputation among attorneys as a serious jurist. He was not likely to brook any nonsense from the GDAC.

The bailiff read out, "People of the State of Illinois versus Cyrus Caine and Jesse Barrett, Indictment Number 71-3021 on the charge of Murder. The Honorable Judge Thomas J. Kimball presiding."

The spectators settled into their seats and prepared for a long morning. The opposing attorneys waived a reading of the indictment, and eventually they launched into the business of jury selection. Kat noticed that every time a prospective juror began to answer the attorneys' questions, Cyrus fixed them with his menacing glare. Most of them seemed relieved when they were not selected and exited the box as quickly as they could. It was amazing to Kat that they could find 12 people who did not know enough about the Caine murder case to have a firm opinion, since it had been the subject of endless news reports for months. After two days of questioning the attorneys were satisfied, the jurors were sworn in, and the trial was ready to commence.

Stephen Hanaway, the assistant state's attorney, delivered his opening remarks first.

"Your Honor, distinguished counsel, ladies and gentlemen of the jury. In our society, there is no crime more serious, more shocking than murder. To take another person's life in a premeditated and cold-blooded manner carries the most serious penalties our judicial system allows.

"What you are going to hear over the coming days is evidence of a crime even more loathsome than murder between two parties. That is the premeditated murder of one's own brother. Fratricide is so antithetical to our norms of behavior that it is one of the first things revealed in the Bible, in the Book of Genesis. The story of Cain and Abel is about two brothers who develop a deep rivalry. One day Cain strikes his brother and slays him. And the Lord said to Cain, 'What hast thou done? The voice of thy brother's blood crieth unto me from the ground.' And Cain was cast out, cursed to wander the earth, a fugitive and a vagabond forever."

Hanaway took a sip of water, allowing his words to sink in with the jury. "Ladies and gentlemen, what you will hear in the coming days is a story as ghastly and as shocking as that Biblical tale. You will hear how this man," pointing to Cyrus, who looked away, "hired this man," pointing to Jesse Barrett, "to murder his own brother, in front of his brother's wife."

Kat felt the searing heat of those words pierce her heart as that fatal night flashed through her mind.

"The State intends to prove, beyond all reasonable doubt, that Cyrus Caine and Jesse Barrett entered into a conspiracy to murder Morgan Caine. You will hear from first-hand witnesses about the bitter rivalry between the brothers that precipitated the crime, the years of threats, and the conspiracy from people with first-hand knowledge. We will prove to you that the story of Cain and Abel does not live merely in the Scripture, but in the suburbs of Chicago as well." He sat down.

J. Barr Finley sat still at his table for a moment, hands in front of him, fingers forming a steeple while he gathered his thoughts. He rose, turned to the jury with a bemused smile.

"Ladies and gentlemen, I appreciate the assistant state's attorney turning to Scripture in his introductory remarks. I'm afraid he will need more than that to win his case. In fact, he will need a miracle."

A few of the jurors chuckled.

"As His Honor will go over with you in his instructions at the conclusion of this trial, the assistant state's attorney is required to convince you – all of you – that my client is guilty *beyond a reasonable doubt*. That Is a very high threshold. How, for example, will you believe my client entered into a conspiracy with a man he has never met, never heard of before? I'm sure the prosecution will introduce all manner of speculation, but speculation won't win the case. Only the facts. We are prepared to lay the facts out for you as clearly and succinctly as possible, and to refute any confusing or contradictory ideas the prosecution may try to introduce. But bear in mind as we go through these proceedings and you hear the evidence, ladies and gentlemen: You must be certain of my client's guilt beyond a reasonable doubt. Otherwise there is only one just verdict: Not guilty."

Finley sat down with a flourish. Kat half expected a round of applause. She had to admit, Cyrus seemed to be getting his money's worth so far.

Jesse Barrett's defense attorney was next to speak. The spectators didn't envy him; it was no small job to follow the Greatest Defense Attorney in the Country. This was a big case, and for this young PA, whose name was Howard Simmons, one of the first cases he'd ever tried. Usually he did plea bargains for dope dealers and other small-time offenders. Now he found himself on the biggest case in Chicago. He rose to his feet and shuffled the papers in his hands. He cleared his throat and started to talk, staring at his shoes until the judge urged him to speak a little louder.

"I represent Jesse Barrett in this case, ladies and gentlemen," with an awkward nod at the other defendant. "We intend to show that Mr. Barrett was tricked into making a confession to these alleged crimes, and that he has no connection to Cyrus Caine whatsoever, like Mr. Finley just said. My client is the victim of a gross miscarriage of justice. We ask that you find him not guilty."

As Simmons sat down, J. Barr Finley leaned over and put his recognizable visage right in the young lawyer's face.

"What do you mean he was 'tricked'?" Finley demanded. "Do you plan to challenge the confession?"

If so, that was bad news for Finley and his client. Having the murderer tied up with an 18-page confession took the pressure off Cyrus. Finley would then only have to worry about knocking out the conspiracy charge while Jesse Barrett bore the brunt of the murder.

Simmons swallowed hard but held his ground.

"I plan to move that the confession be thrown out," he replied.

Later that afternoon, young Simmons got his chance in front of the judge, and in his first at-bat he struck out.

"Your Honor," Simmons began, "my client underwent four hours of interrogation in which he proclaimed his innocence and denied any knowledge of this shooting. He was then locked to a bench out in a hallway, where he was seated next to a man named Monk Austin, who is on the prosecution's witness list. Somehow, after that hallway conversation, my client was given to believe that there was a deal in place for him and for Mister Austin – only that wasn't true. Only Mister Austin had an immunity deal with the prosecutor, not my client.

"Having been deliberately misled by the state's attorney's office, my client was then coerced into signing a confession admitting his part in the shooting. This confession was obtained under false pretenses, and I move that it be excluded."

Judge Kimball stroked his chin a bit, then looked at the Assistant State's Attorney.

"Mister Hanaway? Comments?"

"Your Honor, the confession of Mister Barrett was legally obtained after advising him of his rights. The document runs 18 pages – with far too much detail for any attorney to have embellished it. We will be calling as a witness the assistant state's attorney who took that confession, who will testify as to its accuracy."

The judge studied his hands for a moment, then announced, "I'll take the motion under advisement. I want to hear from the assistant state's attorney before I rule. Now, Mister Hanaway, if you're ready to present your case…."

Howard Simmons slumped into his seat, dejected. This had been his strongest card – in truth, his only card. He would have felt even worse if he had been able to read J. Barr Finley's mind, cheering the decision. There needed to be one villain of this piece, Finley was thinking, and that villain was Jesse Barrett. Now that his confession was in, at least for the time being, Finley's task was to keep him as far away from his client as he possibly could.

Chapter 28

The Witnesses

"STATE YOUR NAME FOR THE RECORD, please."

"Meghan Caine McGee."

The striking young woman, demure in a simple black dress and matching shoes, took her seat on the witness stand. Her long red hair was pulled back in a chignon, which made her look more mature than her 24 years. She sat with her ankles crossed, hands resting in her lap, a handkerchief held lightly in case she needed it. The most startling things about her – aside from her beauty and her poise – was her physical resemblance to her mother. She was a ringer for Kat, with the same trim athletic build, luxurious mane of hair, and faint spray of freckles across her nose. Her eyes were not the same piercing blue as her mother's, but a softer blue-gray. The audience in the courtroom looked from mother to daughter and back again, as if they were watching a tennis ball in a match, while the court artists painted madly on their sketchpads.

Once Meghan was sworn in, the Assistant State's Attorney stood up at his table, took a sip of water from a glass, and began the questioning.

"Mrs. McGee, would you please state your relationship to the victim in this case, Morgan Caine?"

Meghan took a slight breath. "He was my father."

"And what is your relationship to the defendant in this trial, Cyrus Caine?"

"He's my uncle. My father's older brother."

"Are you close to your uncle?"

"No."

"Spend much time with him growing up?"

"Very little. We'd mostly see Uncle Cy at horse shows. Once I started competing, we would see him fairly frequently, but other than that…."

"Now Mrs. McGee, I'd like to take you back to one particular horse show. I believe…"

Hanaway looked down at the notes in his hand, "…I believe it was the Lake Forest Horse Show in 1961. Do you remember that event?"

"I'll never forget it."

"How old were you at the time?"

"I was fourteen."

"And you were competing in this horse show?"

"Yes. I was one of two finalists in the Junior Event."

Hanaway looked at his notes again. "You won that event, didn't you?"

Meghan smiled faintly at the memory. "I did."

"Was your Uncle Cyrus there that day?"

Meghan's face clouded over. "He was there, yes."

"And what happened after you won the competition? Did your uncle come over and congratulate you? Tell you what a good job you'd done? What did he say exactly?"

Meghan's blue eyes turned like two lasers and focused on her uncle.

"He told my father he was going to kill him."

A murmur rippled through the courtroom. The judge let it make its way through the crowd, then lightly tapped his gavel for order. The state's attorney continued.

"You're sure that's what he said?"

"His exact words were, 'Someday I'll kill you, you son of a bitch.'"

The crowd reacted again, summoning two raps of the gavel from the judge.

"Mrs. McGee," Hanaway said, "why would Cyrus Caine threaten to kill your father, his own brother?"

"Uncle Cyrus had a horse of his own in that event. He was mad because his horse came in second. My family's very competitive."

"And you're sure you recollect his words correctly?"

"I'll never forget them as long as I live."

"Thank you, Mrs. McGee. No more questions."

The prosecutor sat down. Judge Kimball looked at J. Barr Finley, who was still seated at his table, writing notes on a yellow legal pad.

"Mister Finley, your witness."

Finley looked up slowly, as if just realizing there was a proceeding going on.

"No questions for this witness, Your Honor." He resumed making his notes.

Cyrus looked over at his lawyer, wondering if perhaps the man had suddenly gone insane. He started to say something, but Finley cut him off with a hand motion. The judge said, "You are excused, Mrs. McGee." Meghan rose, stepped down from the witness stand, and strode past her uncle without a second glance and left the courtroom. To nearly everyone present, it was clear the prosecution had drawn first blood.

For those in the courtroom who were hoping the State's Attorney would call the mother next, they were disappointed.

"Your Honor, we next call Mrs. Clarissa Raines to the stand."

The bailiff repeated the name, and an elegant woman *d'un certain age* approached the bench and was sworn in. Her posture was erect, her champagne silver hair coiffed just so, wearing a trim tailored suit that might have been of French design.

"State your name for the record, please," Mr. Hanaway began.

"Clarissa Raines. My friends call me CeCe."

"Mrs. Raines, you are very active in the world of horse shows, is that correct?"

"I am. I have been riding and showing horses for many years."

"You have won a number of championships along the way, is that not true?"

"Oh yes. I've won just about every exposition in this country, and quite a few in Europe as well."

"Would you consider yourself an authority when it comes to showing horses?"

"I believe that would be accurate, yes."

Hanaway paused to clear his throat. "And in the course of your horse competitions, did you have dealings with Morgan and Cyrus Caine?"

"Certainly. No one moves in the world of horses without knowing the Caine brothers. And Morgan's lovely family as well." The older woman smiled and nodded to Meghan.

"So you attended many events where both brothers were present?"

"Many, yes."

"Would you say there was bad blood between them?"

J. Barr Finley shot to his feet.

"Objection, Your Honor. Calls for a conclusion on the part of the witness."

"Sustained."

"Let me rephrase," Hanaway said. "Did you personally ever see any angry exchanges between Cyrus Caine and his brother?"

CeCe shot a brief look at Cyrus, who was glaring at her. She was unphased.

"Many times. At a show in Oak Brook one time, I saw them arguing. Cyrus threatened to kill Morgan."

Hanaway raised his eyebrows and let the statement sink in with the jury.

"Really? Do you know what the argument was about?"

"Horses, I assume. Cyrus hated to lose. But he especially hated losing to Morgan."

"Mrs. Raines, tell me a bit about the world of horse competition. Is there prize money involved?"

"Sometimes. It depends on the show. Sometimes the prize is just a blue ribbon. But other contests, there can be a significant purse."

"So if I were in the business of buying and selling horses, winning would have a financial impact on the value of my horse?"

"Yes, it certainly could. A horse that wins a major show or two could increase in value by thousands of dollars."

"And the Caine brothers were competitors in this business, is that correct?"

"Correct."

Hanaway looked down at his papers again. "Mrs. Raines, you say you heard Cyrus Caine threaten to kill his brother Morgan, correct?"

"Objection, Your Honor," Finley said without rising. "Asked and answered."

Hanaway nodded to his opponent, acknowledging the point. "Let me ask it another way: Mrs. Raines, did you ever beat Cyrus Caine in a competition?"

"Yes, a number of times."

"Did he threaten to kill you?"

Finley rose to his feet. Hanaway raised his hand before the judge could recognize him.

"In fact, did you ever hear Cyrus Caine threaten to kill anyone who beat him in a contest, other than his brother?"

"Your Honor," Finley protested, "counsel is being deliberately provocative."

"I'll let the witness answer. Mrs. Raines?"

CeCe's pale patrician features turned hard. She looked at Cyrus coldly.

"No, I did not. Only his brother Morgan."

"No further questions, Your Honor."

Hanaway took his seat, pleased with the testimony. J. Barr Finley stood slowly and stood with one hand resting on the defense table.

"Mrs. Raines, in your testimony you claim you heard my client threaten his brother."

"That's correct."

"When you were asked what the argument was about you said…" – Finley looked down at his yellow pad, "…and I quote: 'Horses.'"

"That was mostly what they fought about."

"'Mostly.' Hmm. Did you hear any of the actual conversation?"

"Not specifically. I just saw Cyrus waving his arms at Morgan. He was angry about something. Then I heard him say, 'I'll kill you.'"

"So without actually hearing the conversation, you assumed he was making a threat? He might have been joking."

Mrs. Raines's smile was icy. "He wasn't joking."

"Your Honor, I move that this witness's testimony be stricken. This is nothing but hearsay."

The judge tugged at his upper lip, then replied, "Overruled."

CeCe looked from the defense attorney to the judge. "Am I finished here?"

Finley answered, "I have no further questions for this witness, Your Honor."

The prosecution's next five witnesses all told a variation of the same story: They were horse owners or competitors who knew the Caines. All of them had heard Cyrus threaten to kill his brother at one time or another, causing J. Barr Finley to mutter to his client during a break, "Is there anyone who *didn't* hear you threaten your brother?" What Finley could not have known is that for every person who had come forward to testify against Cyrus Caine, there were ten who didn't, for one reason: they were terrified of him. As each of the witnesses took the stand, Cyrus fixed them with a murderous glare. A couple of them actually changed their story and said that No, maybe that *wasn't* what Cyrus had said. Only two witnesses remained unflappable: CeCe Raines, who was too old and too rich to be afraid of anything. And his niece.

The Witnesses

After setting the table with the parade of witnesses saying that Cyrus had threatened to kill Morgan on several occasions, it was time for the procedural witnesses. They were present to establish that a murder had indeed been committed. One by one, the assistant state's attorney called the police officers who had been part of the case, beginning with the first officer on the scene. Then Don Krause, the lead investigator, walked the jury through the painstaking process the crime scene personnel had performed collecting the evidence from the Caine property. Firearms experts described the weapon used and matched it to the bullet they had found in Morgan's body. (The first shot had passed through him and exited his body and was never found.) The coroner, who had declared Morgan dead at the scene, then showed the jury gruesome photos of the body and the damage wreaked by a 30-06 bullet.

As the coroner presented a series of blown-up photographs detailing the wounds to her dead husband's body, describing entrance and egress wounds and the fatal damage delivered to his heart, his lungs, and his other organs, Kat Caine sat by stoically, unflinching, staring at the photos, taking in the testimony. At one point she shut her eyes firmly and took a sharp breath, reliving the moment she took her husband's shattered body in her arms. Then she steeled herself and forced herself to train her eyes on the ghastly photos, then at her brother-in-law.

As the days wore on, the prosecution piled the facts slowly layer by layer, one upon the other until the jury understood what had likely taken place on the night of the 30th.

After building a tidy campfire and laying the wood and the kindling just so, it was time to light the fire with the star witness: the widow, Katherine Caine.

After expressing his condolences, Stephen Hanaway began to lead Kat through her testimony.

"Mrs. Caine, could you describe for us please, what happened on the night of October 30th, 1970?"

Kat drew a breath, tightened her grip on the handkerchief in her hand. She was perfectly composed.

"That evening, my husband and I had dinner with our daughter Meghan and her husband Mike at our house. After dinner we played euchre – that's a card game – until about 9 p.m. Then Mike and Meghan went home and Morgan and I went upstairs to bed.

"Sometime after 11 – I remember looking at the clock, thinking how late it was – my husband sat up in bed. At first I thought he was having a nightmare. He often had nightmares, ever since he was a little boy. He ran to the bedroom window, looked out and said, 'The barn is on fire.' He threw on some jeans and a pair of boots and ran down the stairs."

"What happened then?"

"I called the fire department from the phone in our bedroom, then I ran down the stairs after Morgan. The front door was open, so I assumed he was already on his way to the barn to get a closer look." Kat paused, her blue eyes drifting toward the floor for a moment.

"Mrs. Caine?" said the assistant DA. "Do you need a moment? A glass of water perhaps?"

Kat shook her head and continued.

"I ran out onto the front lawn and saw Morgan about halfway to the stable. I could make him out very clearly in the light of the fire – the front of the barn was ablaze. I heard a sound like a crack, but I assumed it came from the barn. I saw him stop and stagger backwards. He turned to me and waved for me to get back. Something was clearly wrong with him but I didn't know what. That's when I heard the second shot."

"You heard a second gunshot?"

"Yes. I didn't realize until I reached him that he had already been hit once. There was blood on his chest and running down his arm."

"Go on, please."

"The second shot knocked him off his feet and he fell to the ground. I screamed and ran to him, caught him just as he was falling backwards. We both sank to the ground. There was blood everywhere, he was… he was choking on it. He kept trying to speak to me, I kept telling him to lie still. Finally he managed to utter a single word."

"What was that word, Mrs. Caine? Can you tell us?"

Kat raised her head and looked squarely at her brother-in-law. "He said, 'Cyrus.'"

A deep murmur ran throughout the courtroom. The judge permitted it for a moment, then quietly tapped his gavel. "Order, please. We'll have order in the courtroom."

"Then what happened, Mrs. Caine?"

"Then he died in my arms. I started screaming, holding his head, rocking him. I don't remember anything after that until someone – I realized later it was Detective Krause – lifted me to my feet and helped me into the house."

"Thank you, Mrs. Caine," Hanaway said quietly. To the judge: "I have no further questions."

Judge Kimball called for a short recess. J. Barr Finley and Cyrus sat in stony silence, not regarding each other, while the assistant state's attorney helped Kat down from the witness stand, patting her arm and murmuring to her.

Twenty minutes later, it was Finley's turn to ask the questions. He rose slowly, a picture of dignity, placed one hand on his hip to show off his well-tailored vest to best effect.

"Mrs. Caine, first of all, please allow me to express my deepest condolences on your loss."

Kat's face was a mask. "Thank you."

"I have just a few questions. I want to clarify some of the points you made earlier. You said that you heard a gunshot, is that correct?"

"That's correct."

"Did you hear one shot, or two?"

"I only heard one for sure. I was coming out the front door, running, I wasn't paying attention. And there was a lot of commotion because of the fire in the stable."

"I understand." Finley looked down at his Italian loafers, pivoted one of his well-shod feet to the side and studied it. "Was your husband carrying a gun?"

"He had a Colt 1911 in his hand. When he was hit a second time the gun slid out of his hand."

"Is it possible that your husband was the one who fired the shot?"

Hanaway rose to his feet. "You Honor, we have already heard testimony from the IBI's forensics expert that Mister Caine's pistol was found at the scene and had not been fired."

The judge responded, "I'll let Mrs. Caine answer."

Kat looked hard at Finley and said, "I grew up on a farm, Mister Finley. I know the difference between a rifle shot and a pistol shot. This was the sound of a high-powered rifle."

Finley nodded, acknowledging the point. "Did you see who might have fired the shot?"

Kat admitted, "I saw some motion down at the edge of the trees, when the flames shot up. I thought I saw a figure turn and run into the woods." She paused. "I wasn't focused on that. I was looking at my husband dying in my arms."

Finley cleared his throat. He decided to change tack before the widow completely got the best of him.

"Let me explore another issue with you, Mrs. Caine. You accompanied Detective Donald Krause to a meeting with a Monk Austin and his then-girlfriend, Charlene Devereaux, at the Bluebird Café, is that correct?"

"Yes."

"And in that meeting, you offered Mr. Austin and said girlfriend twenty-five thousand dollars if they would implicate my client in the murder of your husband, is that correct?"

"No, it's not. I offered them twenty-five thousand dollars if they would tell the police everything they knew about the murder."

The Witnesses

"So, in effect, you paid them to testify against Cyrus Caine."

"Objection, Your Honor," Stephen Hanaway shouted, rising so fast he nearly knocked his glasses off his face. "The defense is trying to prejudice the jury against one of the prosecution's key witnesses before he's even had a chance to testify."

"Sustained."

"No further questions, Your Honor," Finley stated, satisfied, and sat down. At least he had drawn a little blood without appearing to bully a grieving woman. There was no point in making Kat Caine even more sympathetic than she was naturally.

The judge turned to Howard Simmons, sitting meekly at the defense table.

"Any questions for the witness, Mister Simmons?"

"Yes, Your Honor, just a couple." The young attorney stood up and shifted his feet, barely glancing at Kat. He looked like a shy suitor trying to work up the courage to ask the prettiest girl in school to the prom. "Mrs. Caine, you said that on the night of October 30th you heard a gunshot just as you ran out of your house, is that correct?"

"Yes."

"And you said you *thought* you saw some motion down by the trees?"

"Yes."

"And maybe someone running into the woods?"

"Yes."

Simmons stepped to one side, so that Kat could have an unobstructed view of Jesse Barrett, seated next to him.

"Mrs. Caine, is this the man you saw running into the woods?"

Kat's mouth opened slightly, and she hesitated. "I…I really can't say. It was very dark, except for the fire coming from the stable. He was pretty far away."

"In other words, you cannot identify my client, Jesse Barrett, as the man who fired the shot that killed your husband."

"No," Kat admitted. "I can't."

"So it could have been someone else."

"Yes, I suppose so."

"Thank you, Mrs. Caine. I have no more questions."

Simmons sat down. Finley turned and stared at him for a moment, thinking *Look who decided to be a defense attorney.* He had to admit, Simmons had dealt with the Widow Caine as well as – hell, maybe better than – he had.

"Nice work," he said under his breath. Simmons seemed not to hear.

"If there are no further questions, you are excused, Mrs. Caine," said the judge. Kat stepped down.

That was round one. There was much more to come. Kat was the featured attraction, there was no doubt. But the prosecution's key witness would take the stand the next day.

Chapter 29

Thirty Pieces

MONK AUSTIN WAS NERVOUS. As he sat on a hard bench outside the courtroom, waiting to hear his name called, he ran his fingers through his unkempt hair. His feet kept up a syncopated tapping on the tiled floor. Charlene sat next to him, trying to smooth his hair (hopeless), straightening his tie.

"Nothing to be worried about, baby," she purred. "You're going to be great."

Monk waived her off impatiently. "If I'm not, it could be me going to prison."

"Relax," Charlene replied. "You've got a plea deal. There's nothing they can do to you."

"It's not the cops I'm worried about," Monk moaned. "Do you know what happens to people who testify against Cyrus Caine? Why do you think they've had us tucked away out of town for so long?"

"It'll be all right. They said they'd protect us."

Monk sneered. His feet were tapping out a wild rhythm now. "I've seen that lawyer of his on TV, that Finley guy. He chews these witnesses up and spits them out." His head sank into his hands. "I'm next on the menu."

The courtroom door swung open at that moment as if on cue, and a uniformed guard waived Monk inside. "Call Monk Austin to the stand," the bailiff's voice boomed.

Monk squeezed Charlene's hand one last time. "This is it," he said, and marched up to the witness stand as if it were a guillotine.

As he turned to face the courtroom, Monk could see every eye in the place focused on him. He imagined what they were thinking. *They're looking at me like I'm the killer.* And in fact, he was. He just didn't pull the trigger. He reminded himself that he was not the one on trial. Today, he was there as a witness for the prosecution.

"Do you solemnly swear that the testimony you are about to give will be the truth, the whole truth, and nothing but the truth?"

"I do." Monk lowered his hand and sank into the witness chair.

The Assistant State's Attorney rose slowly, giving Monk a moment to settle in. He knew this scruffy young man wasn't the most compelling witness, but he was the key to the trial, and the best they had. Hanaway's job was to make Monk Austin look good, or if not good, then at least credible to the jury. He just needed to guide him to get the testimony into the record.

"Could you state your name for the record?"

"John Monk Austin. People call me Monk."

"Mister Austin, let me ask you to look over at the defense table." Monk complied. Jesse Barrett stared straight ahead and didn't meet his eye. Cyrus Caine gave him a black look that burned right through his skull. Monk gripped the arm of his chair.

"Mister Austin, can you tell the jury, do you recognize any of the men seated at the defense table?"

"I do. I know two of them."

"Could you point them out, please?"

Monk pointed to the defense table. "That fella there, the black guy." He added quickly, "Not the guy with the glasses, the other one. That's Jesse Barrett."

"Anyone else?"

Monk fought hard to keep his hand from shaking. "That's Mister Cyrus Caine."

"How do you know Mister Caine?"

"He hired me to kill his brother, Morgan Caine."

Hanaway nodded. "When you say he 'hired' you, can you tell us about that? Take your time."

Monk went through the sequence of events that brought him into the business of assassination, how Ned Paulson, then the sheriff of Croydon County, had sought him out and solicited his interest. Then the meeting at the China Moon, where Cyrus gave him a 'retainer' and some pictures and told him to shadow a man who turned out to be Morgan Caine.

"Did Mister Caine give you anything else when he commissioned you for this job?"

"Yeah. He gave me a gun. Or really, the sheriff give it to me. Really nice one, a Colt Python. Said the serial numbers had been filed down so it couldn't be traced."

The Assistant State's Attorney picked up a plastic evidence bag from the table and carefully removed a Colt revolver. "Your Honor, this is People's exhibit number 3. May I show it to the witness?"

"You may."

Hanaway approached the witness stand and held the weapon out for Austin to see. "Is this the gun Mister Caine – or his accomplice, Sheriff Paulson – gave you that night at the China Moon?"

"Looks like it."

Hanaway handed the gun to the witness. "Take a closer look. We want you to be sure."

Monk held the gun in his hand and studied it. "Yeah, this is the one. See here, how the numbers have been sawed down so you can't make them out?"

"I see," Hanaway replied, taking the weapon back from Monk. "You may be interested to know, Mister Austin, that the technicians at the Illinois Crime Laboratory has some pretty sophisticated equipment. They were able to raise the serial numbers on that gun and trace it to the owner. Would you like to know who first purchased that weapon?"

"Sure."

Hanaway looked over at the defense table. "Mister Cyrus Caine."

Finley was on his feet, exasperated. "Your Honor, it appears the Assistant State's Attorney has now decided he is also giving testimony in this case."

"Mister Hanaway?"

"Your Honor, I would refer my learned colleague to the written report from Miss Roxanne Young at the Illinois Crime Laboratory that has already been submitted into evidence. I am merely informing the witness of facts already in evidence."

Before the judge could rule against him, Finley waved his hand and sat down.

The point made, the prosecutor next walked Monk through the weeks of stalking Morgan Caine, at horse fairs and racetracks and even at his home. He described how he had lost his nerve after a couple of tries at shooting Morgan himself and brought in some help.

"What made you think to approach Jesse Barrett to help you in this murder?"

"I knew he liked to hunt, and he was a good shot. Plus he was a vet, you know…spent time in Viet Nam. So I thought he wouldn't be squeamish about pulling the trigger. And he needed the money, just like me."

"How much money are we talking about?"

"Caine promised me twenty thousand dollars if I killed his brother. I offered to split it with Jesse, fifty-fifty."

"And he agreed to help you?"

"Yeah."

Next, Hanaway produced the 30-06 hunting rifle and entered it into evidence. Monk went through the provenance of the weapon, described how Ned Paulson had given it to them.

"Isn't it true that you and Mister Barrett took this rifle out for target practice one afternoon?"

"Not target practice exactly," Monk replied. "Jesse said that we needed to 'zero in' the scope."

"'Zero in.' What does that term mean?"

"I wasn't exactly sure either. Jesse set up some targets. Then he'd take a shot, check where it hit, adjust the scope a little and kept doing that until it was all lined up the way he wanted it."

"I see. Where did this exercise take place?"

"Out on some farm. I found out later the place belonged to Mister Caine."

"So you and Jesse Barrett went to Cyrus Caine's farm to do some target shooting and to zero in the telescopic sight?"

"That's right."

Stephen Hanaway paused, hand behind his back, as he contemplated his next question.

"Mister Austin, were you present at Harmony Farm the night Morgan Caine was killed?"

"Yes I was." Kevin O'Donnell, the red-haired teenager who had spotted Monk Austin on Harmony Road the night of the murder, had already established Monk's presence there.

"Did you fire the shots that killed Morgan Caine?"

"No, I did not."

"Who fired the shots?"

Monk looked a little miserable as he answered. "Jesse Barrett."

"And who hired you to do the killing?"

"Cyrus Caine."

"No further questions, Your Honor."

J. Barr Finley stood at the defense table, studying Monk Austin like a headmaster appraising a delinquent student. He took a long pause, then began his cross-examination.

"Mister Austin, you are here today because of a plea agreement with the district attorney that grants you immunity in exchange for your testimony. That about right?"

"That's right."

"Can you tell us, who planned the murder of Morgan Caine?"

"I did."

"Who followed Morgan Caine around for months, trying to understand his movements and his patterns?"

"I did."

"Who had possession of the murder weapon prior to the shooting?"

"I did, but then I…"

"That's enough. Finally, who was present at the Caine home the night of the murder?"

"I was."

"Mister Austin," Finley said, one arched eyebrow pointed at the jury, "doesn't it seem pretty clear that the real killer here is you? And that if it were not for this immunity deal, it would be you standing trial, not my client?"

"Objection," Hanaway thundered. "The witness is not on trial."

"No, but he should be. He is the architect of this crime."

"Your Honor…."

"Withdrawn." Finley picked up his yellow note pad, referred to it, took a new line.

"You testified that you met my client twice at the China Moon restaurant, is that correct?"

"Yes sir."

"This second meeting – when was that, exactly?"

"Um, sometime in August maybe? Or September? I'm not exactly sure of the date."

"August or September. Interesting. Considering that the China Moon Restaurant was closed for renovations all that summer."

One of Finley's junior associates handed him a document, which he walked up and presented to the judge with a flourish.

"Your Honor, I would like to enter this document into the record. This is a sworn affidavit from Mister Kenny Lin, the owner of the China Moon, in which he states under oath that his restaurant was closed for renovations at the time of this alleged meeting." Finley handed a copy to Hanaway on his way back to his table. The judge studied it and handed it to his clerk.

"I'll allow it. Continue."

"So, Mister Austin, how is it that you met with my client at a restaurant that had been closed for months?"

"I never said we went inside."

Finley's jaws flexed, like he was chewing a particularly tough piece of steak.

"You didn't."

"Nah. The second time we met in his car. In the parking lot."

"In his car." Finley recovered quickly. "And were there lights in the parking lot, even though the building was closed?"

"It was pretty dark. But I recognized his car, so I knew it was Mister Caine."

"How did you know it was his car?"

"I recognized it from the first time. Kinda hard to miss a white Cadillac Eldorado."

Finley chortled. "Come now, Mister Austin. There must be lots of white Cadillac Eldorados."

"This one had a silver horse's head on the hood."

A few people in the courtroom chuckled. Monk Austin smiled, not realizing he had said anything witty but going along. Finley lowered his eyes to the floor but pressed on. "So you had a conversation with a man in a parking lot whom you allege was my client. What did he say to you?"

"Well, he was pretty mad. He told me I needed to get on with the job or else. Then he handed me some money and said, 'It's time to buy a horse.'"

Finley paced a few steps, turned, looked hard at Monk for a long moment.

"Let's review the facts, Mister Austin. By your own admission, *you* are the one who planned the murder of Morgan Caine. *You* are the one who followed him around for months, waiting for a chance to kill him. *You* are the one who went to the Caine house in the middle of the night and lured him out by setting fire to their stable. My client had nothing to do with any of this. But you've decided to try to hang this on him."

Monk looked confused. "Why would I do that?"

"Money, Mister Austin. Money. One of the oldest reasons there is – for thirty pieces of silver. Isn't it true that Katherine Caine offered you twenty-five thousand dollars to tell this story to the police?"

"She offered us money, it's true." His voice dropped. "But I didn't take it."

Finley stopped pacing. This was new information. "You say you didn't take it?"

"I couldn't. I've done too much…. What I mean is, I'm not proud of what I did, of my part in all this. She seems like a nice lady, and now her husband is gone. I can't take her money."

The courtroom was still. Finley walked to his table and set his notes down heavily.

"No further questions, Your Honor."

It was dark by the time Finley and his client assembled again in the visitors room of the county jail. Cyrus was being held without bail pending the outcome of the trial. Finley took off his suitcoat, folded it in half and draped it over the arm of a metal chair. Cyrus sat across from him, hands folded, studying the tiles in the ceiling.

"Rough day," Cyrus observed. The lawyer shrugged.

"Not too bad. That punk got in a couple of shots, but nothing we can't clean up when we start our defense." He flipped through his notes, looking for what he wasn't sure. "I wish I'd known he hadn't accepted the money. My associates screwed up. 'Never ask a question you don't know the answer to,' as the old saying goes."

"What happens now?"

"We stick to the strategy. Every drama has to have a villain. And in this case, that villain in Jesse Barrett. He's the shooter. He's the one connected to Monk Austin. There's no connection to you."

"What if the judge throws out his confession?"

"He won't. I know the attorney who took that confession. He's an Eagle Scout, a straight shooter, everything by the book. There's nothing irregular about the confession. All eighteen pages of it. Barrett is done. Stick a fork in him." Finley taped his fingers restlessly on the Formica tabletop. "What we have to do now is muddy up Monk Austin's story and make sure none of it sticks to you. That means I'll have to put you on the witness stand."

"Thought you said you didn't want me testifying."

"Normally I wouldn't. But you have to refute some of the things in young Austin's testimony. And make the jury believe you, not him."

"Who else are you calling to testify?"

Finley gave him a long look and replied, "Nobody." Cyrus looked surprised. "Do you know how many character witnesses I was able to line up to testify on your behalf? Not one. Nada. Oh, I talked to a lot of people who are afraid of you. But there aren't a lot of people willing to speak to your fine upright character."

"I don't give a shit if people like me or not."

"Well, that's really paying off for you now." Finley stood up and reached for his coat. "Don't worry about it, Cyrus. I'll guide you through your testimony. By the time we're done, the jury will be convinced you've never met Monk Austin. And Jesse Barrett will be on his way to prison for a long long time."

Chapter 30

The Defense

HOWARD SIMMONS PACED THE FLOOR of his office, eyes focused downward at the worn floorboards in front of his desk. In less than an hour he would begin his defense of Jesse Barrett, and he still wasn't completely sure what he would say.

Howard had been pleased when J. Barr Finley, the greatest defense attorney in the country, had told him that their clients would be tried together rather than separating the cases. Illinois law required that all the defendants be tried together, although Howard suspected that wasn't the only motive Finley had in mind. Howard Simmons had never handled such a high-profile case in his brief career as a public defender, and he believed it would be in his client's best interest to draft along on the work of a superb litigator like J. Barr Finley. He imagined himself taking briefings with his co-counsel, debating points of law, analyzing the evidence, learning at the elbow of the Great Man. It had not worked out that way. In fact, they had barely spoken prior to court.

Now that they were deep into the trial, Simmons was pretty sure that Finley's plan was to screw him and let Jesse Barrett take the fall. In that, he was succeeding brilliantly. Maybe he does deserve his reputation, Howard thought ruefully.

The cross-examination of Monk Austin had not gone brilliantly, in Howard's estimation. There had been a couple of unexpected fumbles, like that business about the China Moon restaurant being closed. Rather than undermining Austin's credibility, it allowed the witness to add other details that seemed to support his story. If Monk Austin's testimony was the deciding factor for the jury, then Jesse Barrett would almost certainly be headed to prison. As for Cyrus Caine, that was still a wild card. Howard was certain that J. Barr Finley would try to put as much daylight between his deep-pocketed client and Jesse Barrett as possible. He very well might succeed.

Howard's biggest obstacle was the confession his client had dictated the night he was arrested. The young lawyer was dismayed when Judge Kimball denied his motion to have the confession thrown out. This morning he would take another run at it, but he wasn't optimistic. Jesse had already described, in painful candor and excruciating detail, all the particulars of the murder, thinking that he had been granted immunity. Monk Austin had verified that story on the stand. If the confession stayed in, Jesse was as good as gone.

Howard straightened his polyester tie, picked up his briefcase and headed for the door. If he lost today, he still had one desperate card to play.

"State your name, please."

"Jesse James Barrett."

A couple of people in the audience giggled. Howard winced. He had asked his client not to use his middle name. It didn't help his image with the jury being named Jesse James.

"Mister Barrett," Howard Simmons moved on quickly, "can you tell us what happened the night you were arrested by the Chicago police?"

"They took us downtown and booked us."

"'Us' referring to you and Monk Austin, is that correct?"

"Yes, sir. Only they separated us right away. I got taken to an interview room by myself. The detectives must o' ast me questions for four-five hours."

"So after several hours of interrogation, what happened next?"

"They took me out in the hallway, handcuffed me to a bench, told me to wait there."

"Then what?"

"A little while later, Monk come walking through with two policemen. They cuff him to the bench too, leave the two of us there together."

"Did you talk to each other?"

"Sure. I ast him, 'What are we here for? What do they know?'"

"What did Monk Austin say?"

"He said, 'They know everything. But don't worry. There's an immunity deal on the table if we tell them everything.'"

"'An immunity deal.' Did Monk Austin tell you the state's attorney was giving you immunity?"

"That's what it sounded like to me."

"So what did you do?"

"I told them everything."

"Could you be more specific?"

"This attorney comes in, clean-cut white guy, has a lot of questions, seems to know a lot about what me 'n Monk been up to. He took a lot of notes. Then he ast me to write it all down and sign it."

"Did he offer you the chance to have an attorney present?"

"I didn't think I needed one. I was gonna get immunity."

"Thank you, Mister Barrett. That's all."

Judge Kimball peered over his half-glasses and looked over at the jury box. "Ladies and gentlemen, I'm going to ask the bailiff to escort you back to the jury room while I confer with counsel. We'll call you back in a little while."

Once the jury had left, the state's attorneys and the defense attorneys lined up before the bench.

"Gentlemen, having heard the testimony of Mr. Barrett, and the earlier testimony of Assistant State's Attorney Mark Sheridan, who took Mr. Barrett's confession, I am satisfied that the defendant was made aware of his right to counsel and that the confession was done by the book. The motion to suppress is denied."

Howard's head drooped. J. Barr Finley placed a hand on the young man's shoulder as they walked back to their table. "Tough break, kid."

Howard was sure he didn't mean a word of it.

When court resumed after lunch, the judge looked at Howard Simmons and asked, "Do you have any further witnesses you want to call, Mister Simmons?"

"Yes, Your Honor. I call Clyde E. Poole to the stand."

Finley and his legal team exchanged quizzical glances. The junior associates shuffled through papers, looking for the name on the witness lists. The lawyers at the prosecution's table were doing the same thing.

A tall, barrel-chested man with snow white hair and dressed in clean but worn bib overalls walked down the aisle. He was well north of seventy but seemed hale and hearty. He looked more like he was on his way to a state fair than appearing in a court of law. When prompted, he placed his hand on the Bible with great solemnity and swore to tell the truth.

"State your name, please, sir."

The man placed his mouth close to the microphone. "Clyde E. Poole."

"Mister Poole, can you tell us your occupation?"

"I farm a little."

"Where is your farm?"

"Out on Route 47, about two miles outside of Elburn."

"I see. Do you own the farm?"

"No, I lease it."

"Oh? Can you tell us, please, who owns the farm?"

The witness raised a large ruddy hand and pointed to the defense table. "That fella there. Mister Cyrus Caine."

Finley looked over at his client, who did not seem perturbed.

"Now Mister Poole," Howard continued. "We have heard testimony from Monk Austin that he and my client," Howard indicated the other defendant "…came out to your farm on an afternoon in October 1970 and did some target practice. I think the phrase Mister Austin used was that they needed to 'zero in' a sight on their rifle. Do you recall seeing these two men on your farm?"

"Can't say that I do."

"Oh? But they were out there taking target practice in your corn field?"

"It couldn't have happened," Poole declared definitively.

"It couldn't have happened. Why is that?"

"Because. That time of the year, corn would have been eight to ten feet tall. No way they could ha' seen any targets to shoot at."

"Thank you, Mister Poole. Your Honor, I wish to call the court's attention to the prosecution's own Exhibit 21." An easel had been set up next to the defense table. Howard placed a blow-up of a sketch on the easel and pointed to it. "This is a drawing depicting where Monk Austin and Jesse Barrett were standing when they took their target practice, with targets set up on these trees here…"–he pointed–"…and here. Now Mister Poole, looking at this sketch, and knowing the location of these trees, will you tell the jury again, could these defendants have been taking target practice at this time of year?"

Poole squinted at the sketch. "Not possible. They couldn't see through the stalks of corn."

"Thank you, Mister Poole."

Howard Simmons sat down, looking satisfied. Finley looked over at him with something close to astonishment. Score one for the public defender.

The Defense

Simmons' victory was short lived. The judge adjourned court for the day, whereupon the prosecutor's table became a hive of activity as lawyers rustled through papers and photos and sketches related to the farm. By the time court reconvened the next morning, the prosecution looked less rattled. And they had photos of their own.

A new easel, larger than the first, had been set up in the courtroom. There was a large blow-up photograph resting on it. The Assistant DA reminded Mr. Poole that he was still under oath.

"Mister Poole," Hanaway began. "This is an aerial photograph of your farm. Do you recognize it?"

Clyde Poole squinted at the photo for a moment, then drawled, "Yep, that looks like it."

"Good. Now Mister Poole, do you see this large area here…" He used a pointer. "…where the ground seems to be indented? There's no corn growing in this part of the field. Would you agree?"

"Yep. There's a drainage problem in that section of the field. Hard to grow anything there."

"So then it would be possible to have a clear view of the trees, and to shoot some targets from there, would it not?"

The old farmer studied the photo for a moment, then looked over at the police sketch showing where Austin and Barrett had taken their target practice.

"Mind if I take a closer look at that drawing?" Hanaway obliged him. Poole squinted at it for some time, then announced with satisfaction, "Here's your problem. You got these fellas standing in the wrong place."

"Would you explain?"

"Sure. These Xs ought to be over here, facing west. If they stood here…" he tapped his index finger on the sketch, "…they'd be able to see the trees just fine."

"Then it was entirely possible that Mr. Austin and Mr. Barrett were at your farm and would have been able to shoot at the targets."

"Guess so."

"Thank you, Mister Poole. No further questions."

Howard Simmons sat at the table with his mouth slightly agape. He realized the judge was talking to him.

"Mister Simmons? Any redirect?"

"Oh, well…Mister Poole, just to confirm, you did not actually see these two men taking target practice in your field?"

"Can't say I did because I didn't."

"Thank you. No more questions."

As Clyde Poole stepped down, the judge asked, "Any other witnesses you'd like to call, Mister Simmons?"

"No, Your Honor."

With that, Howard Simmons had played every card in his hand and come up short. Now it was J. Barr Finley's turn, and the feature show was just about to start.

"Mister Finley?" the Judge said. "Call your next witness."

"I call to the stand Mister Cyrus Caine."

Chapter 31

Lies and Damn Lies

THE COURTROOM WAS PACKED the morning Cyrus Caine was scheduled to testify. Extra security had been posted at the entrance to Courtroom Number One, and the flow of people coming in and out was strictly monitored. The press had bumped and bullied their way inside, naturally. Most of the other spectators were there just to gawk at the man they said was King of the Horse Mafia.

Kat Caine and her daughter Meghan were ushered in through the side door by one of Stephen Hanaway's attorneys and took their usual seats behind the bar. Sketch artists went to work drawing the two beautiful women for later airing on the local news shows.

Cyrus had gone to special pains in his appearance for his day in court. He had not followed Finley's advice to have a suit made by Finley's custom tailor (*"Pay two grand for a suit? I could buy a damn horse for that much money. Hell, I could buy ten horses."*) But he had sprung for a nicely cut ready-made from Capper & Capper, a gray wool herringbone, paired with a crisp white shirt with French cuffs and silver dollar cufflinks. Instead of his usual bolo tie, Cyrus added a red and green repp stripe with gold mallets from one of his polo clubs. He wore a pair of black jodhpur boots, a concession to his role as a horseman of note.

The room stood as Judge Kimball made his entrance and took his position on the bench.

"Mister Finley, call your witness."

"I call Mister Cyrus Caine."

Cyrus mounted the step to the witness box. When he placed his hand on the Bible, Kat leaned over to her daughter and whispered, "Let's see if he bursts into flames."

J. Barr Finley, sporting a new custom-tailored suit of his own, rose and stood with one hand on the defense table.

"Could you state your name for the record, please?"

"Cyrus Caine Junior."

Kat cocked an eyebrow. She had never in forty years heard Cyrus refer to himself as a 'junior.' This would be an interesting exhibition, she could tell already.

"What is your occupation, Mister Caine?"

"I'm in the horse business."

"How long have you been in the horse business?"

"Since I was a boy."

"When you say 'horse business,' is there a particular aspect of the business you concentrate on?"

"I'm in the business of show horses mainly."

"Is that a big business? A lot of money in it?"

"Yes. At least there can be."

"Competitive?"

"Very. It's all about competition."

"Mister Caine, you have heard the testimony of the prosecution's witnesses throughout this trial. Including a number of people who are also in the horse business."

"I heard them all right. What I heard was a bunch of lies and damn lies."

The judge rapped his gavel and scowled at Cyrus. "Mister Caine, I will remind you that you are in a courtroom, not a barnyard. Be careful of your language."

"Yes, Your Honor. Sorry."

"Mister Caine," Finley continued smoothly, "I want to call particular attention to the series of witnesses my distinguished opponent called to testify about your relationship with your brother Morgan. Several witnesses claim that you did not have a very good relationship with your brother, that there was bad blood between you. Is that true?"

"I'd say those people don't know what the f… They don't know what they're talking about." Cyrus adjusted his position, leaned in the direction of the jury as he had been coached to do. "Sure, my brother and I would argue sometimes. We were brothers. We were also competitors. Sometimes the competition could get a little heated. But then we'd forget about it and move on to the next town, the next show."

"Would you describe your relationship as close?"

"Not close, exactly. But we were blood. Now that he's gone, I kind of wish we'd been closer."

Kat rolled her eyes before reminding herself to keep her face impassive, no matter how outrageous Cyrus became.

Finley pressed on. "These witnesses stated that in the last few years the relationship between you and Morgan seemed to become colder, more hostile. Is that true?"

"There might be a little truth to that, I'll admit," Cyrus replied. His face dropped, and his tone became more confidential. "What those people didn't know was, my brother was up to some bad stuff."

Kat felt like an electric charge had passed through her chair. She sat bolt upright.

"Can you elaborate?"

"He was doping horses."

"'Doping' horses. What does that mean exactly?"

"There's this substance you can give them called acepromazine – ACE for short. It's a tranquilizer. It can make the horse settle down, seem easier to handle than it naturally would be. Then you get it home and you've got a completely different animal on your hands. It's a way of cheating. You can take a five-cent horse and sell him for five thousand dollars with a couple dollars' worth of juice."

Kat wanted to leap from her seat and strangle him. Lies and damn lies indeed.

"And your brother Morgan was involved in this activity?"

"Yes, he was. Big time."

"Isn't doping horses illegal?"

"It is if they find out. You'd be committing fraud."

"So you and your brother would fight about this."

"You bet. I called him out on it all the time, said he better cut that stuff out. It's bad for the sport. And bad for the family name. It was my reputation on the line too, you see." Cyrus turned and faced the jury full on, as if they were at his dining room table. "That's what a lot of those people heard us arguing about."

Finley held up his yellow legal pad, made a show of studying it.

"Mister Caine, I'd like to take you back to October 1969. The American Royal in Kansas City. Do you remember that particular horse show?"

Caine nodded. "Remember it well. That was the year Arthur Godfrey was there with his horse Goldie. Beautiful Palomino. Arthur was a big fan of dressage, and he and this horse would come to some of the big events and do tricks. Damn fine horse. I tried to buy him once."

Stephen Hanaway rose and gave an exaggerated sigh. "Your Honor, while I'm sure we are all admirers of Arthur Godfrey and his … horse, what does this have to do with the case at hand?"

"I'm establishing a timeline, Your Honor," Finley retorted. The judge nodded his assent.

"Continue, Mister Caine."

"I remember that show in particular because it was Arthur himself who told me I should patch things up with Morgan."

"Arthur Godfrey told you this?"

"He did. Guess he saw that Morg and I was kinda prickly around each other. Arthur knew us both from the horse show circuit. He puts his arm around me one afternoon and says, 'Ya know, pally, you and Morgan ought to bury the hatchet. You're brothers, after all.'"

Kat stared at Cyrus in stupefaction. This was the first time she had ever heard this story and knew it was just that: a story. But Cyrus had the crowd spellbound, dropping the name of a famous TV personality into the narrative. Finley was coaxing him to go on.

"What did you do?"

"You know, I thought about it, and Arthur was right. So I took Morgan aside after the next event and had a little heart to heart."

"Go on."

"I said, 'You're my only brother, it's not right that we should have hard feelings. It's gone on too long. But I can't have you doping horses – that's not good for any of us. I want you to cut that sh… stop doing that stuff. If you straighten out and fly right, we can forget the whole thing and be like brothers again."

"What did Morgan say?"

"Well, he was kind of reluctant to get out of that business –he was making a lot of money. But he saw I was serious. He said all right, he'd do it." Cyrus appeared to mist up a little. "I grabbed him in a bearhug, and we made up, then and there."

Kat and her daughter sat with their mouths slightly open while Cyrus spun this tale. Meghan heard her mother whisper one word, which she had never heard her use before:

"Horseshit."

"So, Mister Caine, you are saying that you and your brother had reconciled."

"Yes we did. For the good of the family."

If Kat could have wretched she'd have done so on the spot.

"Let me turn to another piece of so-called evidence the Prosecution introduced." Finley held up the evidence bag containing the Colt Python recovered from Jesse Barrett's backyard. "You heard the testimony from Miss Roxanne Young at the Illinois Crime Laboratory who claimed that they had raised the serial numbers on this weapon even though they appeared to have been filed off."

"I remember."

"And that the gun had originally been purchased by you. Is that true?"

"It is. I bought that gun a few years ago. But then I traded it."

"You traded it."

"Yes. I traded with Ned Paulson, the Sheriff of Croydon County, soon after. Can't say what happened to it after that."

Stephen Hanaway leaned over to one of his associates and whispered, "Convenient, since Paulson is sitting in jail on a plea bargain right now."

"Now I'd like to address another issue, if I may." Finley turned to the defense table, and with an elegant sweep of the arm indicated Jesse Barrett. "Do you know this man, the defendant Jesse Barrett?"

"Never seen him in my life until I walked into this courtroom."

"Experts from the Illinois Crime Laboratory testified that when he was arrested, Mister Barrett was in possession of more than three thousand dollars in fifty-dollar bills, and that some of those bills had your fingerprints on them. Do you recall that?"

"I do."

"Does that surprise you?"

"Not at all. I do most of my business in cash. Probably a lot of people walking around with my fingerprints. It would make total sense if he was partners with that other fella, that Monk Austin."

"Oh? And why is that?"

"Because Monk Austin worked for me."

Finley looked at his client in mock surprise. "You're saying Monk Austin worked for you?"

"That's right, sometimes. I'd hire him to do security for my horses, keep an eye on them at shows and such. That's why he was turning up at all those horse shows. I always paid him in cash." Cyrus turned conspiratorially to the jury. "You know – under the table like. The IRS…."

"So you're saying Monk Austin was a sometime-hired hand, and that's why you gave him money."

"Correct."

"Mister Caine, did you hire Monk Austin to kill your brother?"

"I did not," Cyrus said with vehemence. "That's nothing but a lie."

"Why would Mister Austin lie about your involvement?"

"I don't know. Maybe you should ask the woman who offered him a sack of money to tell those lies in the first place."

Hanaway was on his feet with objections, the judge pounded his gavel to settle the noisy courtroom down. Cyrus sat stone-faced on the witness stand, secretly enjoying the clamor he had created. The judge ordered the remark stricken. Finley went on.

"Just one more question, Mister Caine. Monk Austin testified that you met him in the parking lot at the China Moon restaurant. You gave him an envelope with money in it. You said, and I quote, 'It's time to buy a horse.' What did you mean by that?"

"Just what I said. I wanted him to buy a horse for me. He was on his way to a horse show, and I gave him his instructions. No big mystery to it."

"So you weren't saying, 'I want you to kill my brother.'"

Cyrus snorted. "Hell no. I told you, we made up. Besides," he added, looking hard at the jury, "if I was to hire a man to do a job big as that, I'd sure as hell hire someone smarter than Monk Austin."

"Your Honor, I wish to recall Mrs. Clarissa Raines to the stand."

Finley waited, whistling softly under his breath while the imperious Mrs. Raines took the stand. Today the "doyenne of the horse world" (as the *Chicago Tribune* described her) was wearing a red riding coat with a black velvet collar and cuffs and a long black skirt. 'Wonder if the old bitch is going fox hunting after court?' Finley thought to himself. He smiled at the woman as she was reminded she was still under oath.

"Mrs. Raines, just some follow-up questions for you if you don't mind. Did you attend the American Royal in October 1969?"

"I did. I go every year. I have family in Kansas City."

"How nice. Do you recall seeing Morgan and Cyrus Caine at that event?"

"I did. I recall thinking at the time, it had been a few years since I'd seen the two of them at the same event."

"Did you witness an exchange between the two brothers?"

"I did. I remember seeing them off to one side of the arena after a jumping event. I kept watching them because, well, there had been fireworks between them several times before, as I testified."

"What about this time?"

"Well, I wasn't close enough to hear what they were actually saying. But it looked like a very intense conversation. Cyrus was waving his arms, as he's prone to do. Morgan was more restrained, but he looked very serious."

"I see. What happened then?"

"Well, I remember it seemed rather odd to me. They stopped talking. Then suddenly Cyrus threw his arms around Morgan and held him in a big hug. Then they went their separate ways."

"Would you say that they looked like two men who were feuding, or two men who were making up?"

"Objection, Your Honor," Hanaway interrupted. "Calls for conjecture on the part of the witness."

"Sustained."

"No further questions, Your Honor." With a courtly bow to the witness Finley added, "Thank you, Mrs. Raines."

What CeCe Raines did not know, could not have known, was that a year after that scene at the Royal, Morgan Caine would be murdered.

Chapter 32

The Royal
1969

*C*YRUS CAINE STOOD WITH ONE BOOT RESTING *against a railing that had been used in the jumping competition just ended. His money belt was open, and he was counting out bills, hundreds and fifties, and handing them to the owner of the jumper he had just purchased. The owner counted the money, smiled, tucked the bills in his own pocket, then shook Cyrus's hand and walked off.*

Cyrus turned and saw his brother Morgan standing a few feet away behind him. He was surprised.

"By God, they'll let anybody into this event these days," he murmured.

"We need to talk, Cyrus."

"What's to talk about? We've done all our talking."

"This has gone on too long, this ...thing between us. It's one thing when you tamper with my car. Shoot up my office. Try to run me off the road. But people are dying here, Cyrus. That poor girl..." *Meaning Shelly Reid, the girl who'd been blown up when she started Morgan's car.*

"Ah, you're crazy. I had nothing to do with that."

"You and I know better. I'm here to warn you, you need to stop this madness now, before more people get hurt."

"Or you'll do what?"

Morgan's face was turning red, and his eyes flashed with a seriousness that gave even Cyrus pause. He lowered his voice.

"You forget, I know everything about you, <u>brother.</u> Every dirty deal you've done. The fires you've set, the horses you've doped. I know where all the bodies are–literally. And I'm not afraid to talk."

Cyrus's temper was hot but his voice rumbled with a low threat. "You do, and it's the end of you too, you know. The end of the Caines in this business."

"I know other things too. I've put them all in a letter, to be opened in the event something happens to me."

"You got me quaking in my boots. What's in this big letter of yours?"

Morgan hesitated. Then he looked Cyrus square in the eye and said, "I know what you did to Pa."

Cyrus's jaw dropped. He was, for once, speechless, whether from shock or anger or both. Morgan pressed on.

"There's no statute of limitations on murder, Cyrus. Not in Kentucky, not anywhere. If you don't end this, I'll tell the world what you did. And I'll show them this."

Morgan held his coat open. There, strapped to his side, was Cyrus's dagger, the one he had carried throughout his youth, the one he had in his hand when he walked out of the burning stable where his father's body lay.

"Where the hell did you get that?" Cyrus choked. "It was stolen out of my office."

"You're not the only one who knows how to break into places, brother," Morgan answered. "I suspect they'll be able to match this knife to the cuts they found in Pa's body when they dug him out of that stable."

Cyrus stared at his younger brother, the hate and anger and jealousy of a generation pulsing through his veins. There was only one person who knew his deepest secret, and that person was threatening to reveal him now. Cyrus raised his powerful hands, and for a moment Morgan thought Cyrus was going for his throat. Instead his older brother grabbed him by the arms and pulled him close to his body in a bone-crushing embrace, so hard Morgan found it impossible to move, or even to breathe. Cyrus held him like that a long awkward moment, then whispered in his ear.

"*You're a dead man.*"

Chapter 33

'I Do Love Thee So'

THE ASSISTANT STATE'S ATTORNEY rested his elbows on the prosecution table, lifted his glasses and rubbed his eyes. It had been a long trial, with more theatrics than he cared for or was used to. Stephen Hanaway was reasonably confident that he had built a strong case for the indictments of Cyrus Caine and Jesse Barrett, but juries could be fickle creatures, and his opponent was almost as good a litigator as his own publicity proclaimed him to be. Now it was time for the State to make its closing argument and leave the verdict in the hands of twelve men and women.

Hanaway adjusted his glasses, smoothed his suitcoat as the judge called his name, and began to speak:

"Your Honor, Judge Kimball; counsel for the defense; ladies and gentlemen of the jury: It has been a long four weeks. We appreciate the patience and attention you have shown in this case. It will soon be time for you to consider your verdict, based not on the words or speeches of the lawyers in this case, but strictly on the evidence presented to you.

"The defendants you see sitting here before you…" A nod in the direction of Cyrus and Jesse. "…are charged on an indictment which has three counts: that they knowingly and intentionally killed Morgan Caine; that they engaged in activities that created the strong likelihood of his death; and that they conspired with one another to commit the murder of Morgan Caine.

"We began this case with the testimony of Mrs. Meghan Caine McGee, the daughter of the deceased, soon, we are told, to become a mother herself..." A small smile at Meghan, seated in the gallery behind him. "...now most cruelly separated from her loving father. The child she is carrying will never know a grandfather's love, never play games with him or go to the park, because his life was snuffed out long before his time.

"Mrs. McGee testified that Cyrus Caine, her uncle, was known to have a bad temper and to argue publicly with his brother, who was a competitor in the horse business. She told you that in 1961 a feud began between the two brothers – a feud which led, tragically, to one brother conspiring to murder the other. She testified that in 1961, at the Lake Forest Horse Show, she heard her uncle, Cyrus Caine – her own uncle – say to her father, 'I'll kill you, you son of a bitch.'

"Later, you heard the heartbreaking testimony of Mrs. Katherine Caine..." Another nod to the front pew; Kat lowered her eyes demurely. "You heard how she and her husband were in bed after an evening spent with family when Morgan heard a commotion coming from the stable. He rushed outside to find that the stable was on fire. But before he could get halfway across the yard, an assassin's bullet cut him down. Then another, until he lay dying in his wife's arms. What was the last word he spoke on this earth? He identified his killer with a single word, one name only: 'Cyrus.'"

The jury sat in rapt silence, hanging on Hanaway's description. He paused, letting his words soak in, before he began again.

"You heard the testimony of Officer Cassidy, the first policeman who arrived on the scene the night of the murder. Detective Krause led you through the work done at the crime scene by the investigators, and described what he found when he arrived on the scene: the burned-out stable at Harmony Farm, with fire fighters still battling the blaze. The discarded gasoline can that undoubtedly had been used to start the fire that lured Morgan Caine to his death. The crime scene investigators described the footprints of two people they found leading to and from the Caine property, through the path in the woods to the western edge of Harmony Road. One of the sets of tracks suggested a taller man – about the same height as the defendant, Jesse Barrett – that were spaced farther apart, suggesting someone who had run from the scene.

"You heard the testimony of the young man, Kevin O'Donnell, who was driving on Harmony Road late that night and saw a man whom he identified as Monk Austin standing by a parked car near that path, holding what looked like a gas can.

"Doctor Ryan, the pathologist, was next. In any murder trial, it is necessary to prove the *corpus delecti,* as well as the cause of death. Doctor Ryan testified that the cause of death was a bullet wound to the chest area and lodging in the left back, after a first bullet had entered the left shoulder and continued on through the body. The bullet fragments that were removed from the body matched the high-powered hunting rifle that was recovered from the backyard of Jesse Barrett's sister. The fingerprints on that rifle and on the telescopic sight were a match to those of Jesse Barrett.

"You heard Roxanne Young from the Illinois Crime Laboratory describe a second gun found in Jesse Barrett's possession, a .357 Colt Python revolver. Although someone had tried to file down the serial numbers on that weapon, Miss Young and her clever colleagues at the Laboratory were able to 'raise' the numbers again. And what did they find? That the weapon's original owner was none other than Cyrus Caine, the other defendant in this trial. Mister Caine testified that he had 'traded' that gun to the Croydon County Sheriff, Ned Paulson – as though this somehow exonerated him. But Sheriff Paulson – former sheriff, I should say – has already pled guilty to conspiracy in this case, for acting as Monk Austin's go-between.

"Miss Young also testified as to the fingerprints found on the fifty-dollar bills in both Jesse Barrett's and Monk Austin's possession. Nearly one third of those bills – one third, ladies and gentlemen – bore the 'mark of Caine.'" Hanaway smiled at his own Biblical reference, and saw that a couple of the jurors did too.

"You heard from several respected members of the horse show community, beginning with Mrs. Clarissa Raines. People who knew both of the Caine brothers, spent time with them at countless horse shows, did business with them, socialized with them. Each of these individuals swore that in this high-stakes world of horse competition, Cyrus and Morgan were bitter rivals, and that on multiple occasions they heard Cyrus Caine threaten to kill him brother, or to have him killed.

"The defendant tried to tell you that he and his brother had patched things up, that the feud was about Morgan doping horses and bringing dishonor on the family name. Where were the witnesses with any proof that Morgan Caine was doping horses? Multiple witnesses described Morgan Caine as gentleman, an honest businessman, a respected judge on the horse show circuit. Who has a greater motivation to lie: these witnesses? Or the man on trial for murder, Cyrus Caine?

"Finally, we come to the testimony of Monk Austin. What can I tell you about Monk Austin? I'm sure that after seeing him here in this courtroom you may have formed your own impression of the man. He is, I suggest, the most important witness the State presented.

"Let us be clear: Monk Austin is a murderer. He is an admitted murderer, and has other crimes in his background as well. He is a man who accepted twenty thousand dollars from Cyrus Caine to commit an act of cold-blooded murder, and who enlisted Jesse Barrett, an expert marksman, to help him do it.

"Remember this, ladies and gentlemen: it wasn't the Defense that brought Monk Austin's crimes to light. It wasn't the Defense that exposed that he was granted immunity in exchange for his testimony in this trial. It was the State. Monk Austin brought out the secrets of the confessional. He told all. And I believe you will conclude, correctly, that Monk Austin told you the truth.

"Monk Austin is not a nice guy. Nice guys don't enter into conspiracies to commit murder. They don't hang around with other murderers. You wouldn't want to know Monk Austin or have him over for dinner. The only question you need concern yourself with is this: did he tell the truth? I submit to you, he did. He told you the truth.

"Let me also submit to you, ladies and gentlemen of the jury, that we are not talking about a criminal mastermind here. That somehow Monk Austin took it into his head to murder Morgan Caine, a man he had never heard of until Ned Paulson handed him a photograph and said 'Go find him.' This isn't a criminal genius who ensnared the poor unwitting dupe, Jesse Barrett – as his lawyer would have you believe – and had him carry out the actual murder, then walked away with a plea deal himself.

"No, ladies and gentlemen, there was a mastermind behind this crime, but it wasn't Monk Austin. It was a man who for many years nursed a murderous grudge against his younger brother. Who despised him because he was everything he was not: a respected member of the community, a man of high integrity, a recognized judge in the American Horse Show Association, an honest man with a beautiful family. Over the years, the two men were competitors in the big-money world of show horses, and the bitterness between them festered. The unbridled hatred for his brother became so intense over the years that Cyrus Caine threatened repeatedly, in front of many witnesses, in front of his own niece, to kill his brother.

"Mister Caine testified that the so-called feud had ended thanks, preposterously enough, to Arthur Godfrey's intervention. Mrs. Raines was interviewed again to testify about this meeting at the American Royal. And while she did admit to seeing the brothers in an exchange ending in an embrace, she didn't hear what was actually said. No one heard them. No one heard the actual words that passed between the brothers. We have only Cyrus Caine's word for what was said. And he has every motive to lie to you about it.

'I Do Love Thee So'

"Cyrus Caine tried to tell you he had made peace with his brother, even though he was a bad man who doped horses and cheated his customers. Having heard all the testimony for all these weeks, which Caine brother do you think this describes – the victim Morgan Caine, or the man on trial?"

Hanaway paused as he approached his last remarks. He dropped his head a moment, then lifted it and looked straight at Cyrus Caine, who stared stonily ahead, avoiding his gaze. The Assistant State's Attorney continued:

"Shakespeare would have loved to have the Caine brothers to write about. For this was a rivalry of truly Shakespearean proportions, full of sound and fury, ending, inevitably, in murder. Shakespeare did write about two other brothers, in *Richard III,* when Richard, speaking about his brother Clarence, said, 'I do love thee so that I will shortly send thy soul to heaven and thee to the grave, I do love thee so.'

"On behalf of the State of Illinois, I urge you to find these two murderers guilty of the crimes they have committed and render a true verdict based on the evidence."

Chapter 34

'That Venomous Woman'

IT WAS NEARLY FOUR O'CLOCK in the afternoon when the prosecuting attorney finished his closing statement, but J. Barr Finley asked the judge to press on with a promise to be brief. He wanted his voice to be the last one the jury heard before they adjourned for the night. No one in the courtroom moved to leave. The featured performer of the day, the Greatest Defense Attorney in the Country, was about to make his closing argument.

Finley was ready to deliver. The navy suit he wore that day had cost a thousand dollars and looked it. The white shirt, from the Custom Shop on Michigan Avenue, looked fresh – Finley had taken the opportunity to make a change during a brief recess. When the judge nodded to him, Finley rose solemnly, shot his cuffs and stepped toward the jury.

"If it please the Court, Counsel, ladies and gentlemen of the jury. It's late in the day, and you have been very patient. After weeks of listening to the evidence, hearing lawyers squabbling with each other over points of law – which must get tedious – the moment is approaching for you to perform that most critical part of every trial: determining who is telling the truth and who is not. For that is the crux of the matter.

"My distinguished opponent is fond of quoting the Bible and Shakespeare when he describes the events leading to this trial. I will try to spare you all that. Instead, I am going to focus on the facts of the case, for that is where the innocence of the defendants will be found.

'That Venomous Woman'

"Let's start with some simple facts," Finley continued. "The slender thread that binds my client, Cyrus Caine, to any conspiracy or any murder is Monk Austin.

"Mister Caine testified – and no one has suggested otherwise – that before this trial Mister Caine had never met the other defendant, Jesse Barrett. Never saw him. Never spoke to him. Never asked him for a match. They are total strangers. So ask yourselves, who is it who *does* know Jesse Barrett? Who worked with him at the meat packing plant? Who befriended him, then induced him to take part in a murder for hire? One man: Monk Austin.

"By the prosecution's own admission, and I quote, 'Monk Austin is not a nice guy.' More than that: he is a murderer. It was Monk Austin who followed Morgan Caine around from horse show to horse show, had his picture in his wallet, seemed to become obsessed with him, tried to kill him on a number of occasions, but finding himself too timid or too inept, tried to persuade Jesse Barrett to do the killing for him. This is the man, this convicted felon, this professional liar, that the prosecution wants you to believe. This is the man who points his finger at my client, and you are expected to accept his word as gospel.

"It reminds me of the guy who is seen hunting around in the gutter under a lamp post. Another man comes up to him and says, 'What are you looking for?'

"'I dropped a ten-dollar bill,' the first man says.

"'I'll help you look for it. Where did you drop it?'

"'Across the street.'

"'Then what in the world are you looking over here for?'

"'The light's better over here.'"

Finley paused while the jurors and some of the spectators chuckled. Then he continued, "The prosecution's case is based on misdirection. They don't want you to look too hard at Monk Austin, their star witness. Instead they want to look over here…" he pointed to the defense table "…to direct your attention to these two men, not to the killer sitting on the witness stand.

"Let's take a look at some of Monk Austin's statements and see how well they hold up in the light. First he claims that Cyrus Caine hired him, sight unseen, to carry out a murder. They met not once, but twice, at the China Moon restaurant. Really now. Is it customary for someone hiring a hit man to meet with him, not once but twice? Doesn't that rather defeat the point? Wouldn't you instead try to keep your distance?

"Monk Austin didn't remember the exact date of the second meeting, so he said it was sometime in a two-week period in August, or maybe September. All well and good – except that the restaurant was closed for remodeling during that time. Then he scrambles for an answer and decides no, they met in Mister Caine's car.

"He testified that Mister Caine gave him a handgun to commit this murder. That it was a 'clean' gun, no serial numbers on it. All well and good – except that Mister Caine had traded away this gun years before, to a man – a former sheriff — who now sits in the state penitentiary on a charge of conspiracy.

"He talked about the money that Mister Caine was supposed to have given him to carry out the crime, a stack of fifty-dollar bills which the State asserts had Mister Caine's fingerprints on them. Ladies and gentlemen, fifty-dollar bills are not used that commonly. Look in your own wallets. If you have a fifty-dollar bill – and fortunate for you if you have – chances are it has Cyrus Caine's thumb print on it. Mister Caine is known to do most of his transactions in cash.

"Next, Monk Austin tried to tell you that he and Jesse Barrett went to a farm owned by Cyrus Caine to do some target shooting. That was news to Mister Caine, and to the farmer who actually lives on the property. We also learned from Mister Poole's testimony that at that time of year the corn is eight to ten feet high — not exactly ideal for setting up targets. So the prosecution shows you a photograph taken from two miles high and starts talking about drainage. Once again, ladies and gentlemen, I ask you, who are you going to believe?

'That Venomous Woman'

"All of these inconsistencies, this mountain of lies Monk Austin presented to you. You have to ask yourself, why? Why is he telling this tall tale? I can think of the best reason of all, one of the greatest motives known to man: Greed.

"We know that Monk Austin is a bad man, a terrible human being. Ask yourself this question: Would a man who agrees to kill someone for ten thousand dollars be willing to lie for twenty-five thousand?"

Finley paused to let his point soak in, rested his fingertips on the edge of the table. He continued:

"Monk Austin was hired to do one thing during this trial, one job for which he was paid handsomely. Monk Austin was brought here to tell you lies about Cyrus Caine, to convince you that Mister Caine plotted the murder of his brother.

"Who would want you to believe that Cyrus Caine is a murderer? The same woman who offered to pay him twenty-five thousand dollars to tell this story. Maybe I do have to tip my hat to the Assistant State's Attorney and refer to Shakespeare. Because there is one major character the prosecution overlooked in this drama — Lady Macbeth."

Members of the audience who understood the reference were turning to look at Kat Caine. Finley didn't even have to turn to know where the attention was directed. Some of the jurors looked in her direction too, Finley noted with satisfaction. Kat remained motionless.

"The unbridled hatred Mrs. Caine feels toward my client following years of rivalry between the families is so deep, so all consuming, that she offered Monk Austin a fortune to come here and testify. To convince you that Mister Caine was somehow part of a 'conspiracy'…" the word fairly dripped with sarcasm "…to murder her husband, when Monk Austin himself was the real perpetrator. That venomous woman hates my client so much that she would pay anything, tell any lie, to get her revenge on him."

Finley's voice was rising and falling. He paused to catch his breath a moment.

"Ladies and gentlemen, look hard at the testimony of Monk Austin. It is the fruit of a poisonous tree, from a thoroughly discredited source, full of inconsistencies and outright falsehoods. If you take Monk Austin's testimony out of this case – testimony that was bought and paid for by a venomous woman – this case is nothing but a cruel joke.

"What you have been watching is a vicious vendetta against Cyrus Caine, with this poor man," pointing to Barrett, "as the fall guy. I ask you to examine the facts, eliminate the falsehoods, and come to the only reasonable verdict available to you: not guilty."

Don Krause rested his back against one of the granite pillars in front of the courthouse, smoking a Chesterfield and waiting for the verdict like everyone else. After days of sitting in the courtroom listening to testimony, then to the attorneys make their closing arguments, then waiting while the jury deliberated, his back was sore and his knees weren't much better. Now and then an eager reporter would wander past and ask, "Any word yet?" Krause would shake his head and they would move on. There was nothing to do now but wait.

Krause took a last draw, flicked the cigarette away and decided to go inside. He knew the bailiff from back in the day. Maybe he could see if there was any gossip floating around about the jury deliberations.

The bailiff didn't have much to offer. "They asked to see the diagrams of the Poole farm, and the aerial photos," he said. Krause snorted.

"The fate of the verdict hangs on how high the corn was? Doesn't sound very encouraging."

Krause thanked the bailiff and headed into the corridor to find an empty bench. At the end of the hall he spied a trim red-haired woman with her back to him, talking to one of the state's attorneys. He decided to approach her.

'That Venomous Woman'

"How you holding up, Mrs. Caine?" he said, but when the woman turned around he realized it wasn't Kat but her daughter. "Oh, I'm sorry, I thought…"

"Don't worry about it, Detective," Meghan said with a smile. "Happens all the time."

"How is your mother?" he asked, trying to recover.

"Like always: stronger than anybody. She'll be back in a moment."

Just then Kat rounded the corner, coming from the direction of the ladies room. As usual, she looked cool and put together despite the stress of a long trial and the interminable wait for the verdict to be delivered. She saw Krause from a distance, smiled and gave him a small wave, but before they could speak there was a sudden commotion in the hallway, people running back and forth. One of the state's attorneys appeared and said, "Jury's in," and the mob streamed into the courtroom. The Caine women reclaimed their accustomed seats just behind the bar. Krause hung back and took a seat close to the doors where he had a better view of the entire room, spectators included.

The lawyers for the two opposing sides were already taking their places at their respective tables. J. Barr Finley looked fresh and relaxed. The young PD, Simmons, was nervously playing with a paper clip in front of him, whispering meaningless words to his client Jesse Barrett, who sat frozen like a statue. Cyrus Caine sat next to Finley, his black eyes hooded, revealing no emotion.

The jurors filed in, and Krause studied their expressions. A trial attorney had told him once that if the jurors look at the defendant when they file in, it's a sign they voted for acquittal. The jurors seemed to be keeping their eyes straight ahead and avoiding the defense table. Krause didn't know if that was good or not.

"All rise." Judge Kimball made his way to the bench, took his seat, cleared his throat.

"Ladies and gentlemen of the jury, have you reached a verdict?"

The jury foreman, a middle-aged man with a comb-over who was a hardware salesman in real life, stood up.

"We have, Your Honor." He handed a folded piece of paper to the clerk, who delivered it to the judge. Kimball unfolded the paper and studied it a moment, giving not a clue to what was written on it. He passed the paper back to the clerk.

"Mister Foreman, would you please read the verdicts?"

"Yes, Your Honor."

At the defense table, Jesse Barrett and Cyrus Caine stood up, and their lawyers rose with them. The courtroom held its breath.

"In the matter of the State of Illinois versus Jesse Barrett, on the first count, murder in the first degree, we find the defendant Jesse Barrett guilty. On the second count, conspiracy to commit murder, we find the defendant Jesse Barrett guilty."

There was a hum from the spectators in the room, but no surprise. Jesse Barrett stood immobile, the least surprised person in the room. Howard Simmons was the only one at the table showing emotion. His lower lip trembled, and he took off his wire-rimmed glasses and wiped his eyes.

The judge said to the foreman, "Proceed."

"In the matter of the State of Illinois versus Cyrus Caine, on the first count, murder in the first degree, we find the defendant Cyrus Caine not guilty." The hum in the courtroom was louder now. Cyrus turned to his lawyer with a satisfied smirk. Finley turned his head and so nearly missed what the foreman said next.

"On the second count, conspiracy to commit murder, we find the defendant Cyrus Caine guilty."

The rumble in the courtroom grew louder, whether from pleasure or surprise it was hard to tell. Cyrus and his lawyer looked at each other first in astonishment, as if not sure they had heard correctly. Then Cyrus's face clouded over with anger, and he spat a few words at Finley. Finley's mouth twitched, before he could find something to say.

"Your Honor, I ask that you poll the jury."

'That Venomous Woman'

Judge Kimball, who had been about to gavel the courtroom into order again, looked over his glasses at the defense attorney. Then his gaze turned to the jury. The twelve men and women in the jury box were staring up at him, their expressions ranging from surprise to apprehension to horror. Cyrus Caine was glaring at them, fixing them with a murderous gaze. The judge sighed.

"Very well." One by one, he asked each juror if this was their verdict. One by one, each juror had to look at Cyrus Caine and say they found him guilty. One woman looked like she might faint. One of the men looked like he might swallow his Adam's apple before he could get the words out. Finally, the last juror agreed, this was their unanimous verdict.

The judge looked to the bailiff and said, "Sentencing will be in three weeks. Bailiff, take the defendants into custody."

Four deputies stepped forward, turned Cyrus Caine and Jesse Barrett around and placed handcuffs on their wrists. J. Barr Finley was talking to his client a mile a minute, but Cyrus wasn't listening. His eyes were locked on Kat Caine, who returned his gaze without wavering. As the deputies dragged him out of the courtroom to jail, Cyrus thought he detected a smile on her lips.

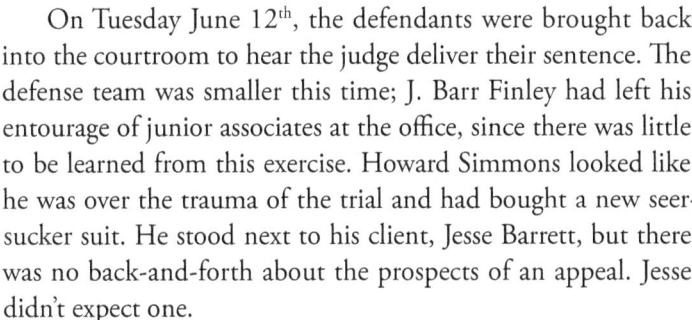

On Tuesday June 12th, the defendants were brought back into the courtroom to hear the judge deliver their sentence. The defense team was smaller this time; J. Barr Finley had left his entourage of junior associates at the office, since there was little to be learned from this exercise. Howard Simmons looked like he was over the trauma of the trial and had bought a new seersucker suit. He stood next to his client, Jesse Barrett, but there was no back-and-forth about the prospects of an appeal. Jesse didn't expect one.

Cyrus looked a little grayer than the last time he had appeared in court. He hadn't bothered with a tie, but had his shirt buttoned at the throat. Finley was assuring him he'd be out in no time, whatever sentence this judge imposed.

Kat and her daughter were in their usual seats behind the prosecution. Kat looked calm, but this moment was as important to her as the verdict itself. She and Cyrus did not look at each other.

"All rise."

Once the judge was seated at the bench, he asked the defendants to stand. The two men and their attorneys rose to their feet.

"Jesse Barrett, having been found guilty on the charges of murder in the first degree and conspiracy to commit murder, I hereby sentence you to 35 years in the Illinois correctional facility, sentence to commence immediately."

Jesse blinked once but had no other visible reaction. The judge turned to the other defendant.

"Cyrus Caine, you have been found guilty of conspiracy to commit murder. I will admit, this is one of the most confounding verdicts I have encountered in my years on the bench. It is unusual, to say the least, to have one party found guilty of murder and the other guilty of conspiracy. Nonetheless, that was the jury's verdict.

"I have read your attorney's motion for a mistrial. The motion is denied. Having heard the evidence, I can only say that this is one of the most cold-blooded crimes it has ever been my misfortune to rule upon. Therefore I sentence you to the maximum penalty I am allowed to render under Illinois law – twenty years, sentence to begin immediately. Bailiff, take the prisoners away."

Outside the courtroom, the press was waiting to gather their photos and quotes. J. Barr Finley exited first, never unhappy in the spotlight whatever the verdict.

"Mister Finley, how do you feel now that you've lost the case?" one reporter shouted through the commotion. Finley smirked.

'That Venomous Woman'

"Lost? We haven't lost. Anyone who understands the judicial system knows that this is just Round One. We have a very strong case for appeal and will be filing immediately."

He took a few more questions, then waved the reporters off and climbed into the rear of a waiting stretch limo, on to the next big headline-grabbing case.

Kat Caine descended the steps, her arm linked with her daughter Meghan's. Flashbulbs fired from every angle. Kat stepped forward to take questions.

"Mrs. Caine, are you satisfied with the sentence?"

Kat offered a rueful smile. "Am I satisfied? Cyrus Caine is going to prison. That's a positive step. But let me make one thing clear, ladies and gentlemen: My family and I will not be safe while Cyrus Caine is still living."

She was right.

Part 5
RECKONINGS

Chapter 35

The List

CYRUS CAINE STRETCHED OUT on his bunk and picked up a black and white composition book and a pencil. The notebook and the pencil were both contraband, but Cyrus had found ways to see to his own needs and comforts in prison. Every evening just before lights out he had developed this ritual which seemed to settle his mind. He had been doing this for two years now. Turning to a fresh sheet of lined paper, he began to make a list of people he would kill once he was released from prison. Some names came and went, but the top of the list always remained the same, and in the same order:

1. Kat Caine
2. Meghan Caine McGee
3. Morgan Caine Jr.
4. Monk Austin
5. Stephen Hanaway, Assistant State's Attorney

To his Top Five List he added two more names:
6. Judge Thomas Kimball
7. Donald Krause (fat IBI detective)
8. CeCe Raines (snooty bitch)

The rest of the list ebbed and flowed, depending on business affairs and rivalries inside and outside the prison, or sometimes based on some slight Cyrus had experienced in the food line or the exercise yard that day. Tonight's list had twelve names, including the cook who had slopped chili on his plate at dinner that night. That man had a bad attitude, Cyrus thought to himself. He studied the list one more time, gave a satisfied sigh, then crumpled it up and threw it in the toilet. A final flush, and he was ready for bed.

The years in prison had not been bad up to this point. He wouldn't call it easy, but it wasn't hard time. A lot of former associates were incarcerated with him, and they passed the time in the yard or at meals talking about horses they'd owned and races they'd seen and marks they had played. Cyrus had a couple of his former hands from High Time Stables with him, and they served as protection and as gofers, securing whatever Cyrus might need in terms of provisions or services.

J. Barr Finley had submitted a lengthy appeal after the trial, citing as grounds everything from the denial of the motion of severance for Caine and Barrett to the admissibility of expert testimony to the drainage report on the Kane County farm to the judge's jury instructions. "The kitchen sink approach," Finley called it. The appeal was denied. Finley claimed there was a second one in the works, but Cyrus heard from him less and less and doubted the second appeal would be any more successful than the first.

Cyrus had no difficulty managing his business interests from the relative comfort of his prison cell. He still had his business associates on the outside (Cole Harmon had returned from Arizona once the outstanding warrants against him were dropped, and he kept the stables running and the money flowing). Cyrus's rivals and customers in the horse world knew that, locked up or not, Cyrus still had a long reach if they crossed him.

Jesse Barrett, his codefendant, had been assigned to another prison farther downstate, and it was a good thing. If he and Cyrus had been incarcerated together, it would not have been long before Barrett's name ended up on The List. Damn fool, Cyrus thought, making that confession, then denying it, then having the judge decide not to throw it out. Instead of giving Cyrus a scapegoat, Barrett's obvious guilt had managed to sink both of them, in Cyrus's view. Still, the man would be in prison the rest of his life, so Cyrus was inclined to be charitable (sometimes).

Cyrus was taking his hour in the exercise yard, walking in a slow clockwise circle attended by his stable hands, when one of the guards, a useful man named Chick who did a lot of favors for Cyrus and his friends, hailed him over.

"Warden wants to see you, Cyrus," the guard announced, and led him inside.

The warden's office was a grim institutional square with metal furniture and walls painted the same pea-green color as every other interior of the prison. Cyrus entered and stood in the middle of the room. The warden stood at his desk and looked up as Cyrus entered.

"Got something for you, Cyrus," he said, and held out a set of papers in a blue wrapper that Cyrus recognized instantly as a subpoena. Maybe the new appeal was going through after all? The warden turned to the guard and said, "Chick, why don't you take Mister Caine back to his cell so he can study this in private?" The guard nodded, and he escorted Cyrus back to his cell and slid the iron bars shut with a loud clang.

Cyrus sat on the edge of his bunk and looked around for his cheaters, the cheap glasses the prison provided. He hated to be seen with them, hated even more that he was becoming more dependent on them. He unfolded the papers slowly and studied them a moment, realizing that they were not from J. Barr Finley, but from some other law office in Chicago. He read on, and as he did, his face began to cloud over with anger and his breathing became more labored until he leaped up from his bed and screamed.

"That goddamn bitch!" he yelled to no one in particular. He hurled the papers to the floor and stomped his heavy shoe on them. Thrashing about with rage, he grabbed whatever possessions he had on hand and hurled them against the wall. He snatched the girly calendar he had taped over his bed and threw that across the room too. He was like a caged beast.

Chick the guard came running back and rattled his metal club against the bars of the cell.

"Cyrus, what the hell? What are you screaming about?"

Cyrus turned on him, his features contorted with fury.

"That goddamn bitch! That she-demon! She can't do this to me!"

"Can't do what? What are you talking about?"

"My sister-in-law. She's suing me for seven million dollars."

Chick gave a low whistle. "Hell of a lot of money. What's she suing you for?"

"Wrongful death or some horseshit like that."

Cyrus grabbed a tin cup from the table next to his bed and threw that in the direction of the window while Chick discreetly withdrew to let him vent in private.

Cyrus's heart was pounding and his eyes were filled with blood. Prison hadn't seemed so bad until this moment. Now every minute would be torture until he could get out and wrap his hands around Kat Caine's throat, or have someone do it for him. He couldn't wait until he made his list that night. And to make a few phone calls to the outside.

Kat eased the nose of the Piper Twin Comanche up as she made her final approach to the runway. As she felt the wheels touch down she allowed herself a quick peek at the stopwatch she had hanging from the dash and smiled in silent satisfaction. She had broken the record for this air race – a record she had set herself just the year before.

The red and white Piper rolled smoothly toward the hanger. A reviewing stand had been set up out in front, replete with red-white-and-blue bunting. As she slowed to a stop she could hear the applause coming from the reviewing stand.

The List

Since Morgan's death, flying had become Kat's driving passion. She spent countless hours each week putting the Twin Comanche through its paces, working on aerial maneuvers, trying to figure out ways to get just a little more speed out of her. She had won several air races against some very accomplished women pilots, including a cross-country race that broke the previous record. Kat adored flying. Maybe it brought her closer to Morgan, she thought, helped her to hold on to those heady early days when he had first introduced her to flying, his thorough delight when she quickly became, as he used to boast, "not just the best pilot in the family. Maybe the best in the country." She still felt a twinge of sorrow and longing every time she took the controls, but once she was in the air she knew, without a moment's doubt, that he was in the cockpit with her, murmuring to her, urging her on.

Kat had become so proficient that she was making plans to achieve her ultimate goal: setting a new speed record in a flight around the world.

As the plane rolled to a halt, Kat switched off the engines and watched the propellers slow to a stop. She swung the door open and waved to her daughter Meghan, who was beaming from the reviewing stand. Kat had been so proud when Meghan announced that she too wanted to be a pilot. "And there's no one better in the world to teach me," she told her mother. Now the two of them were inseparable at various airshows and events. Meghan was also very active in establishing a women's aviation museum, and had set up a mail order catalog business targeted to outdoor women. All of this while rearing three beautiful children. Kat could not have been prouder of her.

As Kat approached the reviewing stand she saw the president of the Flying Association getting ready to present the trophy to her. Meghan stepped forward, still waving, ready to greet her mother and help her up onto the makeshift reviewing stand. The wind was flapping the pennants, a small band was playing some sprightly music, and a decent crowd of aviation aficionados had gathered at the spot to congratulate her.

As her eyes swept the stand Kat felt a sudden terror grip her throat.

"Meghan, look out!"

Meghan froze at the top of the stairs and whipped around. Kat was pointing to a spot behind her, where a man in dark glasses wearing a nylon jacket and a cloth cap had been standing just seconds before.

"He has a gun!" Kat yelled. There were screams from some of the audience as they all looked around to see the gunman. Kat ran to her daughter, and the two of them grasped each other in a half crouch. But no gunshot came. The president and some of the other men scurried around the reviewing stand.

"There he is!" someone shouted, pointing to a figure – maybe it was the gunman, maybe not — just turning the corner into the hangar. A couple of men ran toward the figure, but he was gone.

Kat held her daughter for a moment, then slowly the two of them stood up.

"Mom, are you all right? Are you sure you saw someone?"

"I wasn't imagining things," Kat insisted, but she wasn't so sure. She had been certain she had seen a gunman, and not for the first time. It was always like this, even though Cyrus was in prison. The wrongful death suit had only made him angrier, and while Kat had been happy at first to torment him, she wondered now if perhaps she had not kicked a rattlesnake. Cyrus or one of his henchmen would always be there, always lurking around a corner with a gun in hand, just as they had stalked and killed Morgan.

Kat knew that this was another race she would have to win, once and for all, if she were to keep her family safe.

Chapter 36

Settling Up

THE FIRST THING CYRUS CAINE DID when he was released from prison in 1980 was get arrested again.

Cyrus had served nearly seven years of his sentence and was eligible for parole – "supervised release," as they were calling it now. The prison system had not been sorry to see him go. While he wasn't a violent offender, he was a lot of trouble. Whatever schemes were going on inside or outside the walls often had Cyrus's fingerprints on them. Other prisoners who made the mistake of crossing Cyrus or his associates would find their way to the infirmary soon afterward.

Cyrus had been home less than two weeks when his doorbell rang, and there stood a familiar figure: Don Krause, now a lieutenant, poised in the doorway dangling a pair of handcuffs.

"Welcome home, Cyrus. You're under arrest."

"What the hell kind of harassment is this?" Cyrus sputtered as Krause turned him around and clasped the cuffs on him. "I hain't been home long enough to sort my socks, let alone commit a crime."

"I'll explain it all downtown."

Cyrus was escorted to the familiar interrogation room at IBI headquarters and was soon joined by his latest attorney. (J. Barr Finley had moved on to other sensational cases – not that Cyrus would have kept him on at his exorbitant rates. "Man's a bigger thief than I am.")

"Now, Lieutenant," Cyrus began, "what is all this horseshit? You do know I've been in prison the last seven years?"

Krause ignored him and focused on sorting through the photos in the folder he was holding. He laid a few out on the table, and Cyrus and his attorney peered at them out of curiosity and boredom. The attorney, whose name was Marc Rachlin, furrowed his brow as he recognized some of the photos from the newspaper coverage. Krause explained.

"These are pictures of a stable in Hampshire, Illinois that burned down a few months ago. Thirty-three horses were burned to death in the fire, and damage was estimated at more than four hundred thousand dollars. The police are certain it was arson."

"The Noble Farms fire? That's what you think my client was involved in?" Rachlin protested. Cyrus smirked.

"And just how the hell would I have anything to do with that? Did I suddenly turn invisible and just walk out of prison? Did I dematerialize and walk through the bars?"

Krause didn't reply. Instead he laid down two more photos, both prison headshots.

"Do you know these men?"

Cyrus gave the photos a scant look and passed them back to Krause. "I may've seen them around."

"They served time with you."

"Did they? Lots of fellas in that place. So what?"

"So they were released a few months ago. The state police are pretty confident these were the boys who set fire to the stables. And that you hired them to do it."

Cyrus let out a snort of contempt. "Good luck proving that."

The grand jury seemed to think there was a case to be made for that argument, and a few months later Cyrus found himself in a courtroom again charged with conspiracy to commit arson.

When the case came to trial, the US Attorney theorized that Cyrus Caine had paid two recently released inmates from the correctional facility to set the fire as revenge for a feud with the owner of Noble Farms. Cyrus's attorney maintained that the

Settling Up

charges were a setup by the state to keep him in prison the rest of his life.

It took the jury less than four hours to return a verdict of not guilty.

Cyrus and his attorney met the press on the steps of the courthouse.

"I just want you boys to know that I am suing the governor of the State of Illinois and the Department of Corrections for ten million dollars for interrupting my furlough and throwing me back in prison."

Although Cyrus Caine still had some of his old snap and bark and made good copy, a couple of the newspaper reports noted that he seemed rather gaunt. His suit jacket seemed to drape him loosely. His silver head of hair was still thick but had turned snow white during the time behind bars, and he had the prison pallor common to men who had spent years inside. They speculated that perhaps the stress of the arson trial had taken more of a toll on the old criminal than he let on.

They didn't realize that there was another pending legal matter that gave him more heartburn than anything the State of Illinois could throw at him.

Kat Caine's wrongful death lawsuit against Cyrus had been dragging on for years. Finally, while Cyrus was still in prison, Kat was awarded a one-million-dollar judgment against Cyrus. It was a lot less than the seven million dollars she had originally been seeking, but Kat saw it as vindication and was all over the local news crowing about it.

From jail, Cyrus suddenly proclaimed that he had no money so he could not pay the judgment.

Then came one of the most bizarre business deals of Cyrus's colorful career.

Cyrus decided that he was going to buy an interest in Valhalla Stables, a sprawling horse complex near Northbrook, Illinois. He issued a press release to that effect and wrote a check to one of the current owners of Valhalla, a Colonel T. Ron Heck, for $160,000.

Heck was partners with Stuart Ransom, who had worked for Cyrus many years before. A horseman and polo player of some renown, Stuart was also being questioned in the disappearance of millionaire heiress Clarissa "CeCe" Raines, with whom he had been romantically involved despite a considerable age difference. Now Heck and Ransom needed money, and Cyrus was willing to buy them out at fire-sale prices. The horse complex was valued at over a million and a half dollars.

The biggest problem was, no one had consulted the other co-owner of the complex, a successful mortgage broker named Robert Arbogast, who was the majority partner. Arbogast protested the sale and said it was illegal under the Illinois Uniform Partnership Act. He filed an emergency order in Cook County Circuit Court to bar Cyrus Caine from the premises.

Arbogast's attorney told the court that "Mister Caine burst onto the premises, waiving a press release and backed up by two or three unsavory-looking characters announced that he was taking over the place." The police were called and asked to evict the trespassers. The deputies took one look at Cyrus's companions and decided this was a civil matter, and Cyrus could stay.

The morning Cyrus arrived in Circuit Court for the hearing, he was served with papers seeking to attach his assets for the one-million-dollar judgment awarded to Katherine Caine.

"So what's the story, Mister Caine?" Judge Williams asked when it was Cyrus's turn to testify. "You claimed you were no longer wealthy when the judgment was filed against you. Then you write a check for a hundred and sixty thousand dollars to buy a stable, even though the owners don't want to sell. Do you or do you not have the money?"

"I have access to money, Your Honor. I've got enough in my checking account to cover that check and then some. I have associates who will advance me the money I need to make the Valhalla purchase. Hell, I could buy the whole thing today if I wanted to."

Judge Williams didn't pursue who these "associates" might be. Instead he turned to Robert Arbogast.

Settling Up

"Mister Arbogast, can you tell me why you object to Mister Caine buying an interest in this property?"

"It comes down to one word: reputation, Your Honor," Arbogast answered. "Mister Caine is on supervised release after spending seven years in prison."

Cyrus jumped to his feet. "I served my time," he shouted, until the judge gaveled him down. Arbogast continued.

"Cyrus Caine will come in with his gang and tear the place down. He has a reputation for intimidating people. I'll never recover my investment."

Arbogast's attorney jumped in. "If I may, Your Honor, Mister Arbogast makes a valid point. As soon as word got around that Cyrus Caine was buying an interest in Valhalla, fourteen boarders removed their horses from the stables. What's more, the fire insurance on the property has been cancelled because of Mister Caine's potential involvement in the business." He noted that Cyrus had been acquitted on charges of conspiracy to commit arson recently in the Noble Farms fire, where thirty-three horses had burned to death. The judge grimaced.

The court issued a preliminary injunction barring Cyrus from Valhalla and continued the case to the following February.

Cyrus, worn down and thwarted at every attempt to get back into the horse business, decided there was only one thing that would put his life in order and bring him peace.

He would settle things with Kat Caine.

Chapter 37

The Arena

KAT CAINE STOOD AT HER DESK, a pencil poised between her lips, studying the building plans in front of her for the thousandth time. Work on the new indoor riding arena was progressing well, and Kat had worked closely with the architect and the engineer for many months to make sure she got just what she wanted. She reminded herself that, just like flying a plane, the precheck procedure was the most important part of the takeoff, so she was very particular about every last detail.

When the phone on her desk rang she didn't hear it at first, she was so immersed in the plans. She looked up suddenly and picked up the receiver. When she heard the voice on the other end she froze.

"Hello, Barn Cat."

She opened her mouth to speak, but no words came out. She thought she heard a raspy chuckle on the other end – Cyrus laughing at her, certain he had caught her off guard.

"You still there? Cat got your tongue?"

"I'm here," Kat replied, finding her voice again. "This is a surprise."

"I'll bet."

"Is there something you want, Cyrus?"

"Yeah, there is," the man replied. "I think it's time for you and me to settle up. Close the account, as it were."

"Oh? And what exactly does that mean to you? A car bomb? More gunmen shooting up my property?"

The Arena

"Nothing like that." His voice, she thought, sounded weary and far away. "We've had this lawsuit of yours hanging over us for years. I'm calling to tell you I'm ready to pay what I owe."

Kat was startled. Cyrus was always one to fight to the bitter end, especially where money was concerned.

"Did you hear me? I'm ready to pay. In cash, if you like."

"I'm just a little surprised, that's all. It's not like you to give up a fight."

There was a pause at the end of the line. Then he said, "Feels like I've been fighting my whole life. A lot of that time, the fight's been with you. I never wanted that. There was a time I hoped …" He broke off. Kat heard silence on the other end.

"Hoped what? Cyrus, are you there?"

Finally he spoke, the mood broken, whatever ghosts were visiting him dispersed.

"Never mind. That was a hundred years ago. All done now."

Kat was having trouble taking all this in. She suspected a trap. Finally she replied,

"All right, Cyrus. Let's do this then. You come out to my office tomorrow night around seven. Bring the cash with you. Will that give you enough time?"

"That'll do it. See you then." He hung up.

Kat stared at the receiver in her hand, then slowly returned it to the cradle. Part of her wanted to feel relief that the fight with Cyrus may indeed be over. The other part of her knew that Cyrus was an evil and devious man, and this was most likely a setup to get her to drop her defenses so that he could damage her or even kill her. She reminded herself of the overriding fact that had consumed both their lives: Cyrus had killed his own brother, her husband. There was no making amends.

When he came by the next evening, she would be ready.

She saw the headlights flicker across the wall before she heard the wheels on the gravel outside. Kat's stomach tightened but she remained calm. It would all be over soon – one way or another.

Cyrus cut the engine to the white Eldorado and sat in the car in silence a moment. He rested his hand on the leather Gladstone bag on the seat next to him. There was a rueful smile on his lined face as he gazed fondly at the bag, as he once might have peered at a good-looking catch rider while his hand caressed her knee. But that was long ago too. He took the keys out of the ignition, grabbed the bag by the handle and got out of the car.

It didn't take Cyrus long to find Kat. He knew when she referred to her "office" that could only mean one place: Harmony Stables. Sure enough, there was a light coming from the building. The structure had changed a lot since the last time Cyrus had seen it. That was in the photos shown at his trial, when part of the building had burned down. At Cyrus's order, he recalled without remorse. Kat had rebuilt the stable, as everyone knew she would, and Morgan's old office was now hers.

What Cyrus had not been ready for was the looming structure adjacent to the original stable. Two hundred feet long and maybe half as wide, it was a steel-framed cathedral of equestrian art. Cyrus could see earth-moving equipment outside the arena; probably still working on the inside too, he imagined. He gave a whistle of grudging admiration as he made his way to the office.

"Knock knock."

Cyrus nudged the office door open and stepped inside. Kat was standing behind the desk. Damn, Cyrus had to admit, she was still a fine-looking woman. She had not changed much since the last time he saw her on television, cursing his name, filing her charges. Her hair was still red and hung down to her shoulders, and her skin had the same pale sheen with just the fine spattering of freckles across her nose, just like when they were kids. She held herself tall and erect, a long Australian riding coat draped around her. It was chilly in the office. The windows to the arena next door had not all been installed yet, and the night breeze rolled throughout the stable complex.

Kat met his eye directly, and the two regarded each other for a moment.

"Come in, Cyrus," Kat said at last. There was a pause. Not a lot of chitchat to make with a murderer. "It's been a long time."

"It has that," Cyrus agreed. "A lot of miles been ridden."

"Did you bring the money?" She indicated the Gladstone bag in his hand. Cyrus chuckled.

"Same old Barn Cat. Straight to the point."

"That's the best way to do business."

"Can't say I disagree." Cyrus approached the desk, and he could see Kat take an involuntary step away from him. He raised the bag carefully and set it down on top of the desk. "Here it is. Take a look."

Kat waited for Cyrus to move back a bit, then she approached the bag warily. She opened the clasp, keeping one eye fixed on Cyrus. She opened the top wide and saw the neat bundles of hundred-dollar bills inside.

"It's all there," Cyrus assured her. "One million dollars cash."

"Where'd you get it?" Kat asked, curious despite herself. "I thought you were broke. That's what you kept telling the court anyway."

"Well, you know…. There's broke, and then there's dead broke. I'm down to my last couple o' million."

"So you decided you needed to share it with me?"

"I decided there was no point fighting with you anymore. I'm tired of it. Just plain tired."

Kat looked at him more closely now, appraising him, and she could see he might be telling the truth. He did look tired, or worse. His face was gray and deeply lined, and his dark eyes looked rheumy. He was thinner than she had ever seen him, and his tweed riding jacket hung loosely on him. He was only in his early 60s but looked much older, like one who had seen a lot and lived hard. Kat found herself almost feeling sorry for him. Then she remembered who he was and steeled herself.

Cyrus's eyes wandered around the office and gazed out the glass partition to the riding arena. "You've done a hell of a job with the place, Kat. The old man would be proud of you."

The allusion to her grandfather – the man who had rescued the two fugitive boys so long ago, who had given them a life as horsemen — did nothing to warm Kat to him. She said, "Care to have a look around? I'll show you the new riding ring." A forced smile. "After all, you're paying for most of it."

She reached out for the bag, but Cyrus was quicker, like a snake. Kat gave a start. Cyrus smiled reassuringly, knowing he had frightened her. He said in a soothing tone, "I'll keep it for now, if you don't mind. Don't want to leave this much money lying around."

"Whatever you say." She headed for the door that led out to the new arena and beckoned him to follow. Cyrus closed the bag, hefted his keys and followed her.

As they walked into the arena, Cyrus looked up at the cathedral ceiling, admired the crossed wooden planks that gave the place a classic but contemporary feel. Kat served as the tour guide.

"I've been working on this project for years, after...." She paused. "It's been a labor of love. Stainless steel frame, roof and the walls are insulated – Chicago winters and all that. The windows along the two walls let in a lot of light whatever the season. Fortunately we were able to work off the electrical system of the current stables, so we didn't have to run new power out here."

"How big is this place?"

"Two hundred feet by one hundred feet. Big enough that we'll be able to do jumping events as well as dressage." She stopped suddenly and held out her arm. "Watch your step here."

Cyrus looked down and noticed in the half-darkness that the flooring wasn't complete. Most of the arena floor had been filled in with dirt, but just at his feet there was still a gaping hole, eight feet deep and twice again as far across. Two wooden sawhorses marked the space on either side. A small bulldozer and a backhoe were parked nearby.

Kat continued, "Once we fill this in, I'll be laying four inches of limestone on top. Then several inches of sand."

"Impressive."

"Glad you approve. I wanted you to see it." Cyrus was still busy looking around, didn't notice that she was quietly angling away from him. When he turned back to her she was about ten feet away, well out of arm's reach.

"Like I said…" He looked down at the .45 Colt Commander in Kat's hand. "Oh now. What's this?"

"Morgan's gun. The one he had in his hand when your goons killed him." She was holding the weapon in a two-handed grip, as Cyrus had taught her so many years before. "Our business is finished I think. Set the bag down, Cyrus. Slowly, please."

Cyrus shook his head and gave a harsh laugh. "I thought we'd agreed to bury the hatchet."

"We're going to bury something, that's for sure."

Cyrus regarded the gun again. "I thought I taught you a long time ago, never put your finger on the trigger unless you intend to shoot."

"Yes, you did." Her finger stayed exactly where it was, resting on the trigger. "Put down the bag."

Cyrus lowered the Gladstone to the ground.

"Kick it toward me. Gently. No tricks."

Cyrus slid the bag over with his foot.

"Keys too, please." Cyrus tossed his car keys next to the bag.

"So what do we do now, Barn Cat?"

"Now I'm going to kill you."

Cyrus smiled again. "Goddamn redheads. You always did have a temper on you."

"Do you blame me?"

"Here I come to make peace, I give you a fortune in cash, and you point a gun at me. The thing is, Barn Cat," he continued, "I know you're angry. Hell, I'll even say you've got a right to be. But I don't think you have it in you to be a killer."

"You've always underestimated me, Cyrus. That was your mistake."

"I don't think so. You're not a killer. Neither was Morgan. That was his weakness. He wasn't prepared to do what needed doing."

"But I am. Raise your hands. Say your prayers, if you know any."

"No, don't think I will. It's a little late for praying."

Cyrus took a step toward her. Kat raised the Colt to eye level and cocked the hammer. Cyrus held her eyes as he lowered his hands, and Kat could see one of them moving toward the right-hand pocket of his coat.

"I wouldn't do that," she warned him.

"Or what? You'll shoot me?"

Cyrus plunged his hand into his suitcoat pocket and his jacket flew up, something pointed at Kat as he raised it. Kat fired first, one shot that struck Cyrus in the chest.

He stayed on his feet and rocked a little as the bullet entered him. He smiled at her, almost in approval, then he raised his jacket and pointed at her again. She fired a second shot and hit him within a nickel's distance of the first. Cyrus staggered this time and fell to one knee. He held his free hand out in front of him, like a greeting or perhaps farewell, as she fired a third time.

As the fatal shot struck him, Cyrus drew the gun from his pocket. Except there was no gun, just his finger, pointing at her like a gun, as he had when they were kids. He pointed his finger at her head, cocked his thumb, and whispered, "Bang." Then he collapsed.

Kat stared at the body a moment to see if he would move, whether this was a trick to get her to come closer. A minute passed, and she walked toward his motionless form, her gun trained on him. She nudged his shoulder with the tip of her boot; he didn't respond. She checked the pulse in his neck, found none, still suspecting a trick. With the gun still pointed at the body, Kat edged backward, picked up the bag with one hand and moved it away. Then she picked up Cyrus's car keys and tucked them into the pocket of her driver's coat.

She walked back to the body and stared down at the man who had haunted her life for so long. Without a second's hesitancy or remorse she pushed the body with the sole of her boot, hard, and rolled him into the open dirt chasm that would be his eternal home. The body landed at the bottom of the hole face up, arms sprawled out in each direction.

Kat reached into one of the deep pockets of her coat and withdrew an object. A *sgian dubh*. Cyrus's Scottish dagger. The one that had belonged to his father. The one Morgan had left in his safe along with a letter detailing Cyrus's crimes. Evidence of another murder, another Caine, another time. She tossed the knife into the grave where it landed next to Cyrus's body.

Now their business was done. Kat walked toward the earth-movers parked at the edge of the arena. There was still a lot of work to do tonight.

Chapter 38

Morgan's Lady

KAT HELD THE REINS LIGHTLY, maintaining a steady contact with the bit in the horse's mouth. Her riding posture was erect, her weight centered in the middle of the saddle in the classical dressage seat. The horse beneath her, a sleek and glorious gray mare, was a champion in her breeding and in her bones. Kat could feel it by the instinctive way the horse responded to the cues Kat delivered with her legs and her weight. The horse had Olympics potential. That was why Kat had agreed to train her in the advanced levels of dressage.

There was another reason too, a sentimental one. Kat and Morgan had owned the horse's dam and had been training her just before Morgan was killed. When the brood mare delivered a filly the owners paid a kind tribute to the Caines by naming her Morgan's Lady. Kat felt a little closer to Morgan every time she put the horse through her paces.

Kat had given up riding jumpers as she grew older and taken up dressage. She loved the elegance and precision of the horse's movements and had begun working with a local trainer who was a Grand Prix rider. She had become so accomplished that she became an instructor herself, though not quite at that level.

She had been working Morgan's Lady for two years. The young mare had a talent for dressage, and Kat had taken her through the various levels fairly rapidly without skipping any steps. At First Level the horse learned to perform at the trot and to make transitions and changes. At Second Level the horse could perform two-track movements, traveling simultaneously forward and to the side. Now they were at Third Level, and Morgan's Lady had a true gift for shifting her weight to her hind legs, resulting in a gait that was springy, light and graceful. It wouldn't be too much longer before she was ready for pirouettes.

Kat was so focused on the horse's movements that at first she didn't hear the car pulling up in front of the stables. She saw the headlights flash across the far wall of the arena and drew the horse to a stop. Horse and rider both listened, detected the sound of footsteps on the gravel outside. Kat patted the horse's smooth neck and resumed her lesson, taking her into a light canter. She had been expecting this visitor for some time.

One of the big side doors rolled open and Lieutenant Don Krause stood there a moment, bathed in the moonlight from outside. He stepped in and closed the door behind him as quietly as he could. He moved toward the arena, his movements as light as he could make them given his bulk. He stood along the railing for a few minutes, watching the lady and her horse going through their paces. Kat cantered up close to him and stopped.

"Good evening, Lieutenant. What brings you all the way out here?"

"Evening, Mrs. Caine. I was in the area…."

"And thought you'd drop by?"

Krause smiled. "Something like that. I have some questions for you if you have the time."

"I have time but my horse doesn't. Mind if I keep riding while we talk? She gets a little out of sorts if I throw her rhythm off."

"Sure, fine with me." Krause held his fedora in both hands, kept running it around his hands by the rim. How many men still wore hats, Kat wondered? But then, Krause was old school.

"You heard about your brother-in-law," Krause began.

"Cyrus? Can't say that I have."

"It seems he's disappeared."

"Disappeared, really? You never know with Cyrus. He was always one to keep his business to himself."

"That's true. About three weeks ago, he withdrew a large sum of money from his various banks, took it out in cash – we figure close to a million dollars. Never told anyone what he intended to do with it. No one's seen him since."

"There's your answer then," Kat replied. She and Morgan's Lady were doing tight little circles in the center of the arena. "Maybe he took a trip, or went on a buying spree. He's been known to do that."

"We thought of that possibility. Especially after they found his car parked at O'Hare in the long-term lot."

"Makes sense," she replied, barely showing interest. She was focused on the horse.

"May I ask you, Mrs. Caine…I hate to ask you this. May I ask where you were on the night of the 27th of last month?"

"The 27th?"

"Yes. The night Mister Caine took the money out."

"That's easy, Lieutenant. I flew downstate, checking out my plane and doing some time trials for the race I have coming up. I flew my own plane down to Decatur and back. I think I got home…I'm not sure, but it was late. Around midnight maybe? I'm sure I have it in my flight log."

"You fly at night?"

"All the time. I'm an instrument-rated pilot, after all."

Krause nodded. His notes showed that the Twin Comanche registered to Kat had landed at Croydon County Airport at around midnight. There was sparse staff on duty that time of night, but one of the attendants did see a woman who looked like Mrs. Caine making a last inspection of the plane before she walked to the parking lot, got in her British green Jaguar sedan and drove off in the direction of Harmony Stables.

"Mm-hm, that checks," Krause said, more to himself than to Kat. Another thought occurred to him.

"What about your daughter? Where was she that night, do you know?"

"I'm sure I don't. Home, probably. She has three young children, after all."

"She's a pilot too, right?"

"She is. A very good one." Kat was sure Meghan's landing was impeccable that night, as was the Hermes scarf she kept wrapped around her head and the tinted glasses that obscured her face in case anyone ventured too close. Kat's instructions had been specific: *Fly down to Decatur, let yourself be seen, fly back to Croydon. Be sure to wear your scarf.* From a distance, no one could tell mother from daughter. Sometimes it came in handy.

Morgan's Lady was doing two-track movements now, up and forward and side to side. Krause shook his head in admiration.

"Incredible how you can teach a horse to do that."

"She's very talented. You can teach a smart horse to do a lot of things."

Krause looked around the vast arena. The inside was larger than the church where he attended Mass every Sunday, with the high cathedral ceiling and the elegant wooden cross beams. It was peaceful here. He looked down at the flooring and nudged a bit of the top layer with the toe of his shoe. Like brown sugar, immaculately combed and dragged every night he was sure.

"Wonderful place you've built here. Is this flooring new?"

"The whole arena is new. We just finished it off a few weeks ago."

Kat did not plan to go into the details with the detective: Filling in the dirt with the earthmover herself that night. Smoothing and grading it until two in the morning. She was raised on a farm, after all, and knew how to use big equipment. Then the drive in Cyrus's car to O'Hare, where Meghan picked her up in the Jaguar. The crew arrived at 6:30 the next morning as usual and did the final grading, then poured the four-inch layer of limestone that covered the base. Finally, the sand, a little looser and fluffier than the usual medium-coarse grade you found in the area but perfect for dressage. Then the flooring was done, taking all its secrets with it.

Krause was still fiddling with his hat. Kat continued with her exercises, wondering if there was something else on the big detective's mind. Finally he spoke.

"Had you talked to Mister Caine before he disappeared? I mean, did he reach out to you in any way?"

"Why would Cyrus reach out to me?"

"Well, I'm not sure. Maybe because he was so ill."

Morgan's Lady took a small misstep. Kat knew it was her fault, not the horse's, an involuntary twitch of her leg.

"Was he ill?"

Krause nodded. "He'd gotten the diagnosis a few days before he withdrew the money. Pancreatic cancer, stage IV. He was a goner."

Kat thought to herself, 'You bastard. You set me up – one last time.' That explained the pantomime with the gun in his pocket. Trying to threaten her, to goad her, to make her react. To make her kill him.

Out loud she said, "Sounds to me like you have your explanation, Lieutenant. A man gets a fatal diagnosis, takes a lot of money out of the bank, drives to the airport and catches a plane to Tahiti or wherever to spend his final days in peace and comfort. I'd say the chances of seeing Cyrus Caine again are pretty slim."

Krause stared up at the elegant horsewoman, admired her cool composure. He studied his hat for a moment, then placed it back on his head.

"I suppose you're right, ma'am. But then, I'm not keen on looking too hard. I'll say good night then."

"Good night, Lieutenant. And thank you."

Krause left the way he had come. As the big doors slid shut, Kat reined to a stop and stroked the horse's velvety neck. It had been a good ride. Morgan's Lady let out a soft snort and bobbed her head once or twice. Then, knowing the exercise was done for the evening, she lifted her luxurious tail and unloaded a magnificent steaming pile, which landed with a satisfying 'plop' on Cyrus Caine's final resting place.

THE END

NEXT IN THE 'UNBRIDLED' TRILOGY
THROWAWAY BOYS

In the 1950s, three young boys leave their homes on a Sunday afternoon to go to the movies in downtown Chicago. They are never seen alive again. The last place they may have been seen: High Time Stables, owned by Cyrus Caine. It will be more than 40 years before the real story of one of the most shocking murders in Chicago history is revealed and the killers brought to justice.

www.ingramcontent.com/pod-product-compliance
Lightning Source LLC
Chambersburg PA
CBHW072057201224
19272CB00031B/777

9 781662 897023